BONDS OF HERCULES

Also by Jasmine Mas

Cruel Shifterverse

Psycho Shifters
Psycho Fae
Psycho Beasts
Psycho Academy
Psycho Devils
Psycho Gods

Villains of Lore

Blood of Hercules

Bonds of Hercules

Jasmine Mas

HARPER
Voyager

Harper *Voyager*
An imprint of
HarperCollins*Publishers* Ltd
1 London Bridge Street
London SE1 9GF

www.harpercollins.co.uk

HarperCollins*Publishers*
Macken House,
39/40 Mayor Street Upper,
Dublin 1, D01 C9W8
Ireland

First published by HarperCollins*Publishers* Ltd 2025

1

Copyright © Jasmine Mas 2025

Internal chapter heading images by Shutterstock.com
Family tree by Steamy Designs LLC
Other internal images © Palau83/Depositphotos.com

Jasmine Mas asserts the moral right to
be identified as the author of this work.

A catalogue record for this book is available from the British Library.

ISBN: 978-0-00-874447-2 (HB)
ISBN: 978-0-00-874448-9 (TPB)

This novel is entirely a work of fiction.
The names, characters and incidents portrayed in it are
the work of the author's imagination. Any resemblance to
actual persons, living or dead, events or localities is
entirely coincidental.

Printed and bound in the UK using 100% renewable electricity by CPI Group (UK) Ltd

All rights reserved. No part of this publication may be
reproduced, stored in a retrieval system, or transmitted,
in any form or by any means, electronic, mechanical,
photocopying, recording or otherwise, without the prior
written permission of the publishers.

Without limiting the exclusive rights of any author, contributor or the publisher
of this publication, any unauthorized use of this publication to train generative
artificial intelligence (AI) technologies is expressly prohibited. HarperCollins also
exercise their rights under Article 4(3) of the Digital Single Market Directive 2019/790
and expressly reserve this publication from the text and data mining exception.

This book contains FSC™ certified paper and other controlled sources
to ensure responsible forest management.

For more information visit: www.harpercollins.co.uk/green

This book is dedicated to all the people who spend their nights reading fan fiction about relationships that make them wonder "Am I okay?"

This one's for you.

CONTENT WARNING

This book contains excessive violence, language, and a brief allusion to sexual violence. Please take care of yourself while reading.

THE 12 HOUSES OF SPARTA

OLYMPIAN HOUSES

THE HOUSE OF ZEUS.

THE HOUSE OF HERA.

THE HOUSE OF ATHENA.

THE HOUSE OF HERMES.

THE HOUSE OF POSEIDON.

THE HOUSE OF DEMETER.

THE HOUSE OF APOLLO.

THE HOUSE OF DIONYSUS.

CHTHONIC HOUSES

THE HOUSE OF ARES.

THE HOUSE OF HADES.

THE HOUSE OF ARTEMIS.

THE HOUSE OF APHRODITE.

CHTHONIC HOUSE LINEAGES

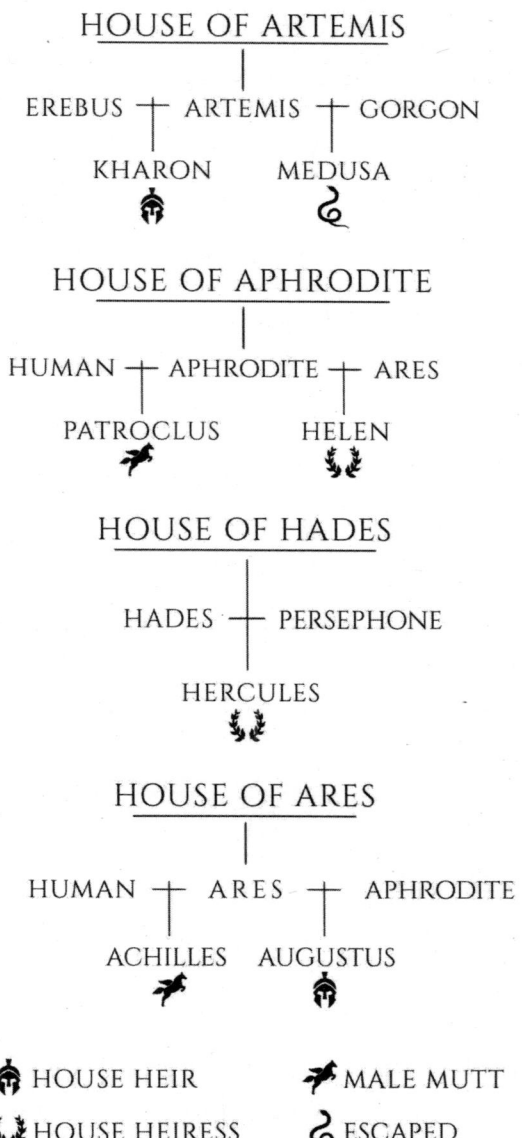

CHTHONIC MALES: STATS

AUGUSTUS

NAME: Augustus, heir to the House of Ares.

NICKNAMES: The eldest Chthonic heir. Heir to the House of War. The Diplomat.

LINEAGE: Father—Ares, leader of the House of Ares. Mother—Aphrodite, leader of the House of Aphrodite.

SPARTAN HOUSE AFFILIATION: Chthonic.

HEIGHT: 6 feet, 6 inches.

WEIGHT: 255 pounds.

BIRTHDAY: August 1, 2067.

POWER: Mental compulsion, breaks minds.

ANIMAL PROTECTOR: Raccoon (rabid).

POWER RANKING: 85 out of 100.

OCCUPATIONS: Assembly of Death member. Founded WSDL weapons manufacturing with Patro, Achilles, and Kharon. Majority shareholder of WSDL weapons manufacturing.

NET WORTH: $6 billion.

KHARON

NAME: Kharon, heir to the House of Artemis.

NICKNAMES: The Hunter. Killer. Sociopath. Hades's favorite soldier. The ferryman.

LINEAGE: Father—Erebus, ancient dark creature. Mother—Artemis, leader of the House of Artemis.

SPARTAN HOUSE AFFILIATION: Chthonic.

HEIGHT: 6 feet, 5 inches.

WEIGHT: 265 pounds.

BIRTHDAY: February 1, 2073.

POWER: Touch, emotional manipulation.

ANIMAL PROTECTOR: Hellhounds.

POWER RANKING: 70 out of 100.

OCCUPATIONS: Assembly of Death member. Founded WSDL weapons manufacturing with Patro, Augustus, and Achilles.

NET WORTH: $4 billion.

Patro

NAME: Patroclus.

NICKNAMES: Patro. The Son of Sex. The Leader of the Crimson Duo. The Ideal Man. Achilles's Handler.

LINEAGE: Mother—Aphrodite, leader of the House of Aphrodite. Father—human.

SPARTAN HOUSE AFFILIATION: Chthonic.

HEIGHT: 6 feet, 4 inches.

WEIGHT: 240 pounds.

BIRTHDAY: August 23, 2078.

POWER: Touch, detects lies.

POWER RANKING: 70 out of 100.

ANIMAL PROTECTOR: Nemean jaguar.

OCCUPATIONS: Assembly of Death member. Founded WSDL weapons manufacturing with Achilles, Augustus, and Kharon.

NET WORTH: $3.5 billion.

ACHILLES

NAME: Achilles.

NICKNAMES: The Son of War. The Killer. The Beast of the Crimson Duo.

LINEAGE: Father—Ares, leader of the House of Ares. Mother—human.

SPARTAN HOUSE AFFILIATION: Chthonic.

HEIGHT: 6 feet, 7 inches.

WEIGHT: 290 pounds.

BIRTHDAY: March 23, 2077.

POWER: Voice torture ability, details unknown.

ANIMAL PROTECTOR: Wolf.

POWER RANKING: 95 out of 100.

OCCUPATIONS: Assembly of Death member. Founded WSDL weapons manufacturing with Patro, Augustus, and Kharon.

NET WORTH: $3 billion.

Agathokakological (adj., Greek origin)
Composed of both good and evil

According to Greek mythology, humans were originally created with four arms, four legs, and a head with two faces. Fearing their power, Zeus split them into two separate parts, condemning them to spend their lives in search of their other halves.
—Plato, *The Symposium*

Fate's Partial Unseen Prophecy

Fate: One Day in the Future

I tipped my head back, sucking on the smoking pipe as I inhaled the herbs deep into my ancient lungs.

Symbols, numbers, and letters swirled in nonsensical patterns—each a drop of water in a churning ocean.

Eyes rolling back, I engaged my powers fully.

I focused on the current.

Individual glistening droplets rose up, out above the stormy sea, separating themselves, speaking their words to me:

"The lost one shall change what is before
Chained to death's soldiers, becoming evermore
Her lgingihlthae shall—the—four
—,—, hrakno, and the Serpent of Lore

The chained one shall reveal the evil underscore
Derguda by mneonsircm men,—afore
Their—shall—the tides of war

The monstrous one shall mend and restore
For the otls eon hears his—roar."

My eyes widened.

Water splattered across my face as the sky opened up with rain.

For the first time in years, the cryptic words revealed to me were *still* tangled and obscured. The incompleteness of the path was abrasive in its wrongness, deeply unsettling.

The pipe fell from my parted lips as I gripped my toga.

It could mean only one thing—someone else could also read the words of premonition.

There was another Spartan alive, not just with the power of Fate, but with the rare ability to *wield* it.

A once-in-a-millennium event had occurred, *again*.

This changed everything.

1
The Survivor

Alexis: May, Crete. 2100

"Were the human casualties avoidable?" Persephone asked softly as Hades stepped through the front door, his boots drenched in crimson blood.

Hades laughed and kissed her forehead. "The mission was a success."

Weeks later, their interaction still haunted me.

Titan blood was black.

He'd never answered her question.

Now I slowly backed away from the sprawling House of Hades palace.

The ancient marble structure was perched atop a hill on the island of Crete, and the Aegean Sea spread out in every direction. On the western horizon, the sun set with burnt-orange rays.

Insects droned.

"Please, sweetheart, you *don't* have to do this," Persephone whispered. Charlie stood solemnly beside her. Hydra, the dragon protector perched on her shoulder, let out a mournful cry mixed with fire.

The flames were bright in the dusk.

Persephone's frown deepened.

A sharp ringing sound echoed, and I tilted my head to see her better.

Only Charlie knew my secret—my left eye was blind, and my left ear was permanently damaged. A violent childhood had bestowed its marks on me.

It forged me into this.

A symphony of dying voices screamed inside my head—I'd slain them all.

Alexis, you're not an evil person.

My real name was Hercules.

Yes, you are.

I gritted my teeth.

It wasn't real.

Yes, it is.

It had only taken twenty years for me to lose my mind.

Persephone's fingers whitened where she clung to Charlie's arm, their togas whipping in the spring sea breeze.

Shadowy waves crept along the shoreline as the sun disappeared.

Night had arrived.

I pushed back the sleeve of my cloak. Lips pulling up in a false smile, I gently pressed my fingers to the "C+A" tattooed messily across my forearm. Persephone's recent gift to me, two dainty golden cuffs, covered my scarred wrists. My wedding bracelet clinked against one of them.

Charlie nodded at me solemnly from his lanky height, his yellow eyes soft as he mimicked the gesture.

Nyx shifted beneath the loose folds of my exercise toga, her grip tighter than usual around my torso. Fluffy Jr. let out a low whine as he crouched at my feet, our protector bond trembling.

Trepidation prickled the back of my neck.

Every instinct screamed at me to wrap myself around Charlie.

In a perfect world I'd never leave his side. In a perfect world I'd be human.

I wasn't.

This was Sparta.

God, please save my soul.

The flame from the torches lining the palace entrance cast warped shadows across our faces: mother, daughter, and newly adopted son.

It was *far* too late for my salvation.

"I know exactly what you're feeling." Persephone's voice echoed, her bare toes curling into the short grasses that competed with rocks to decorate the landscape. "Your fear and rage leave a bitter residue in the earth. I can taste your . . . *impulses*."

She was being kind. Holding back from airing the depth of my shame in front of Charlie. But I saw it in the panicked expression on her face.

She could taste my delirium. She knew my murderous blood was boiling me alive and my thoughts were slowly melting with it.

In my mind, Father John was throwing holy water at my face. "You're possessed," he whispered, eyes wide with terror. "You're one of *them*. An abomination."

I nodded solemnly in agreement.

"Alexis, snap out of it." Persephone's voice vibrated with power.

I startled back into reality.

Father John was somewhere in Montana.

I was hyperventilating on Crete.

The blessed and the cursed, existing beneath the same stars.

"Alexis, *please*," Persephone urged, blond curls rising beneath her gold laurel crown as she used her powers to commune with the land.

Her mother was Demeter, but her father was Iasion, a terrifying dark creature who was rumored to have power over plants—she took after him.

Persephone was gentle and caring, but her powers were *petrifying*.

Case in point: I was losing my mind, and she could literally feel it happening.

In the last few months living on Crete—avoiding Satan and Evil Incarnate (my husbands) and trying to find a single smidgen of mental health (still searching)—I'd learned that it was a common misconception that the House of Hades owned the island.

Hades didn't own Crete.

Persephone did.

Their marriage bond had twisted her creature powers into something insidious.

She'd sunk them deep into the rocky soil and claimed the land. She could literally *feel* every person, animal, and plant that roamed across it. The longer anyone stayed, the more attuned she was to them.

You could never deceive her.

It was why, except for my parents, the island was abandoned.

No one from Sparta visited. *Ever.*

"You're so troubled with ugly emotions, daughter . . . Please don't let them guide you," Persephone said slowly, carefully choosing her words. "You can live here safely—your time fighting can be over."

Her curls rose higher, defying gravity.

"The federation can*not* force you to participate in the Assembly of Death," she said, as Hydra let out another roar of orange flame. "They can't take you from this land."

Dragon fire illuminated the love in her eyes.

"Live in safety—be *better* than those who hurt you."

All I'd ever wanted was a quiet, simple life for Charlie and me. Food, bed, and a roof above our heads. The freedom to spend my days learning and studying.

What she offered was heaven.

But after twenty agonizing years in this world, I'd finally accepted the truth. I wasn't made for a life of ease—I was destined to make those who hurt me suffer.

Sparta would learn.

I would wield my powers, or I'd die trying. *Most likely the latter.*

Penance and revenge were separated by a razor-sharp edge, and I was already inching across it.

Persephone's voice echoed with power. "If you walk this path, Alexis, it will not be easy. The cost to your soul will be great—but I *believe* in you. You can pay it. You just won't emerge the same. Remember . . . our world is not a kind one."

I pulled the hood of my new cloak over my spiked ruby crown. "Neither was mine."

I'd already lost everything: my freedom, morality, and *humanity.*

Suffocating on existential dread, I turned away from Persephone and Charlie, hurrying down the hill before I lost my courage. Fluffy Jr. ran beside me, a blur of misshapen fur.

At the edge of the lawn, Hades was waiting for me. Cerberus sat beside him and all three heads turned to me, tongues flopping, tails wagging with excitement.

Fluffy Jr. jumped on him and they rolled together in the grass, both about the same size.

Hades shook his head at their antics.

Inky fog wrapped around his pale skin and long black toga in insidious coils; new voices from his power joined the chorus.

"She doesn't understand what it's like," Hades said softly, breaking the silence. "Her power isn't . . . *restless* like ours. We were born for battle."

He reached for me—I stumbled away. He'd never hurt me, but lessons from years of abuse were hard to unlearn. When someone moved quickly toward you, you ducked. *Always.*

Hades dropped his hand, dark eyes lighting with fury—fog thickened around us and the world plunged into coldness—screams intensified.

He breathed out and his shrieking fog retreated.

Water lapped against rocks as the island sounds returned.

Hades's lips thinned. "Remember what I've taught you these past months—survival in Sparta is all about power and fear. You must learn to embrace and harness your more . . . complicated feelings. No one fears the sane."

I nodded, but my head felt like it belonged on someone else's shoulders.

"There are only two paths forward in life for Spartans like us," Hades continued softly. "Either we run from what we really are, or we hone it and become . . . legends."

His black eyes burned with intensity.

"*We* are the ones who shape Sparta," he said. "Your power is poison—you will excel in the Gladiator Competition."

I wanted to cry.

Hades spoke vehemently. "You have nothing to fear from the Assembly of Death. You are *my* daughter. They will come to fear you."

Hades smiled wistfully. "Both our blood runs in your veins." He looked back up the hill fondly to where Persephone stood. "You're our miracle child."

I tried to smile, but my lips wouldn't comply.

I don't want to do this.

Hades straightened the long robe of his toga. "Do you have all your weapons?"

With shaking fingers, I patted the new leather holster that rested on my hips and nodded.

"And do you remember everything I told you about the Assembly of Death's hunt?" he asked. "It's just hazing."

"I think s-so."

"Perfect." Hades cracked his neck. "I can't wait to watch you fight this summer in the coliseum, daughter."

I have to do this.

I would make my husbands pay for trapping me.

Hades stepped closer. "You and I are two of the most dangerous Spartans on earth. But danger is nothing without power—and power doesn't exist without fear . . . *Make* them fear you, daughter." His voice dropped an octave, like he was letting me in on a treacherous secret. "What have I taught you? Repeat it to me. One last time before we leap."

He stared down at me expectantly.

"No one fears the sane," I said on numb lips.

You're already there, and no one is afraid except you.

"Don't forget it," Hades said as he extended his hand and pointedly looked down at his outstretched arm.

I laid my trembling hand atop his, and tendrils of his vicious power wrapped around my forearm, embracing me.

The House of Hades was synonymous with evil, and I was its favorite daughter.

"Domus." Hades's voice faded as darkness exploded around us.

Crack.

The landscape changed.

For the second time in my life, I stepped into Hell.

This time, I went willingly.

Smoke rose around my feet as pale moonlight filtered through an ice-covered forest and a frozen breeze whipped our togas. Hades dropped my arm and stepped to the side.

A long jet-black geometric building sat inconspicuously in the shadows of snow-covered trees—the Assembly of Death's unofficial outpost.

Six Chthonic assassins stood in front of it.

Location: *Siberia.*

Every hair on my body stood on end.

Two men looked *particularly* murderous. Their gazes scoured the side of my face with knifelike sharpness.

Three months ago, they'd placed me on an altar. They'd kneeled before me, worshipping my flesh with soft lips and reverent touches.

Now vitriol wafted off them in punishing waves, its intensity more biting than the icy wind. They were wrathful gods pretending to be men.

Run for your life, my inner voice screamed.

But I was done fleeing.

Straightening my spine, I matched their unnaturally stiff postures and pretended I wasn't intimidated by the Chthonics.

Loaded armpit and thigh holsters stretched across their black T-shirts and cargo pants.

Spartan helmets sat atop their heads.

Ancient warriors dressed as modern killers, ready to induct a new cultist.

I was ready.

No, you're not.

I ignored the voice of reason; there was no place for it here.

Rural Montana had prepared me for two things: selling my organs on the black market, and cult life. For some reason, dark times were a breeding ground for uncomfortable group participation in dangerous activities.

Nyx slithered under my toga. "It's so cold, I want to die," she hissed in an inspirational display of mental toughness.

Hades shifted beside me. Cerberus, stoic and calm, stood at his feet.

In contrast, Fluffy Jr. dug in the snow. Ears perking up, he bit the end of a stick, then gulped it down his throat.

Not now.

Everyone watched as my protector hacked.

Finally, just when I was about to intervene, he regurgitated the half-eaten piece of bark, and looked back at me with his tail wagging.

God gives his toughest battles to his strongest soldiers.

I prayed for death.

A familiar scoff echoed.

I looked over, before I could remember why I shouldn't.

Dear God.

The Devil had answered my prayer.

Ice-blue eyes met mine, and the temperature in the forest plummeted. Frostbite dug its frozen claws into my sternum.

Kharon's lips curved up with a predatory promise.

"Furia" flashed, the tattoo stark across the front of his pale throat.

Dried blood was also smeared across his mouth; his nails were painted black; holsters stretched obscenely across powerful thighs and the chiseled lines of a cut torso; ink covered his right arm, shading his skin in an illusion of skeletal bones that mirrored what lay beneath the skin.

Time slowed.

"Honey," he mouthed slowly, not a sound falling from his crimson stained lips. "I'm *home.*"

My heart stopped beating.

Complete cardiovascular meltdown.

I'd forgotten what it felt like to meet his gaze; I'd forgotten how my cells froze with abject terror as a deep animalistic instinct screamed at me to *get away from him*; I'd forgotten how he'd mockingly called out the greeting each time he'd leapt to Corfu.

Now I remembered.

"Hello, carissima," Kharon mouthed silently. His posture was hostile, his expression downright disrespectful.

Carnivores like to play with their prey.

The Hunter stood before me, a creature capable of unholy depravity, and he wanted one thing.

Me.

I looked down, turning slightly so he was in my blind spot, faint with panic.

He was searching for a weakness, desperate to exploit me. This was nothing but a power trip for him.

He can never know about my eye and ear.

Two hellhounds crouched at Kharon's feet, their bones flickering in and out of existence as if they were glitching. Blue flames danced in their eye sockets.

They shouldn't have been visible.

"Alexis," a baritone voice said, smooth as silk. "*Look* at me."

I obeyed.

Augustus's black eyes trailed down my body from head to toe, *caressing*, checking for injuries.

My name lingered between us in the icy air—three short syllables—yet he'd managed to make it sound like the most depraved of curses. He always did.

Midnight eyes locked on mine—I gasped.

Augustus's expression was *ravenous*.

Black and white hair hung loose down his back, the strands blowing around his wide shoulders. The scarlet edge of his scar peeked out beneath his helmet.

Tendons strained in his neck.

Danger, a subconscious voice screamed as my pulse pounded in my ears.

Crimson pooled in the whites of Augustus's eyes as he activated his Chthonic powers.

He looked *enraptured*.

Beside him, Kharon slowly licked his lips.

The world faded and there was just the three of us meeting in the snowy woods, the dangerous villains and their reluctant wife. A trifecta of lethal abilities.

Absolute power corrupts absolutely. Even Lord Acton couldn't have imagined the depraved power of Chthonics.

A droplet of blood spilled from Augustus's lashes, streaking down his cheek like a tear and disappearing beneath his Spartan helmet. *I've never seen a Chthonic do that before.*

He's going to invade my mind and smash it to pieces.

Terror crawled down my spine. He'd torn into my head during the crucible and forced his will upon me. He could do it again.

RUN.

Augustus was a monster.

So are you.

Poco screeched, black hands wrapping around Augustus's neck as he climbed up onto his shoulder. Raccoon whiskers quivered, black eyes flashing.

Augustus didn't move. He just stared at me with leaking, bloody eyes.

With tingling fingers, I rubbed at my chest where the new marriage bond strummed, the one that was supposed to make our powers stronger. The same bond that forged Persephone's terrifying powers.

Augustus and Kharon were two indomitable forces. There was nowhere to run from them, nowhere I could hide where they wouldn't eventually find me, and even Crete wasn't safe. I knew it in my bones.

Looking around, I focused on *anything* but the two dark gods bonded to my soul.

Branches clattered in the wind.

My neck prickled because my husbands weren't the only ones staring.

Achilles and Patro stood beside them, watching me with an intensity that bordered on deranged.

My mentors.

Achilles glared, a cigarette hanging between the grates of his muzzle. Smoke rose around his face, red eyes bright through the hazy tendrils. Hair pulled back tightly with *DEATH* tattooed across his knuckles, he was a blazing presence in the frigid forest.

Nero, his mammoth shaggy black wolf, sat obediently next to him with a matching scarlet gaze.

Patro smirked haughtily, leaning casually against his lover. Poppae, his sleek jaguar, flicked her tail back and forth, emerald eyes bright.

A strangling pressure squeezed my neck. I touched my throat protectively.

Predators everywhere.

I looked away.

Hermos and Agatha were at the end of the line—two dark creatures with Chthonic blood somewhere in their lineage.

Hermos was an infamous Gorgon. Agatha was an Empusa, a rare type of shape-shifting creature that *ate* men.

She inspired me.

Crack.

I screamed as something huge leapt into the clearing.

A woman astride a monstrous black horse scoffed at me, crimson droplets sparkling in the air around her.

Artemis.

Ice-blue eyes peered down an aristocratic nose, the air around her full of fear, *literally*. Her power surrounded her in a mist of glittering red—it was terror incarnate.

The immense horse pranced in place.

A familiar stocky figure in a black exercise toga stood between the trees.

No.

This can't be.

Drex shrugged sheepishly as his golden toucan flapped its wings with agitation.

"But y-you're an Olympian," I sputtered.

The entire *point* of the Assembly of Death was to oppress and punish Chthonics after they lost the Great War.

Drex stepped closer. "The Olympians exiled me because Theros was my mentor." His voice cracked. "I had no choice—at least here I can fight Titans . . . with you."

Sparta was still reeling over Theros's betrayal and subsequent disappearance. *The Falcon Chronicles* reported that Ceres, a muse from the crucible's library, had helped Theros kidnap me and other House of Zeus heirs. She'd planted the warning notes in my textbooks.

After the article dropped, Ceres had also disappeared without a trace.

"I'll be fine," Drex whispered. "Maybe." He narrowed his eyes. "Hopefully?"

We're both dead.

"We're here," Artemis announced, "because we have two new recruits to welcome—a fellow Chthonic daughter, and the first . . . *idiot* . . . to ever volunteer for induction."

She bared her teeth, eyes manic, as she cocked a bloodstained bow and raised it to the full moon.

Yep, that's definitely Kharon's (Karen's) mother.

"At the Spartan Gladiator Competition this August, we will showcase our powers and strike fear into the hearts of the Olympians."

She shot an arrow into the sky.

Please let it hit me.

A squirrel fell from the top branch with a loud thud.

Okay, Arthritis (Artemis) needs to be stopped.

Artemis turned her horse to face us. "Per tradition, in honor of Pheidippides of the House of Ares—you will be hunted by our youngest members, twenty-five miles through the woods."

Was that blood on her teeth?

"They will give you an *entire* hour's head start before they come after you." Artemis scoffed, like she thought that was too much time. "While you're in the forest, leaping and fighting back is *forbidden*. It doesn't matter how many bullets you take."

She smiled.

"If you fail to make it out of the woods and are captured, you *will* be killed."

Drex whimpered.

Oh nice, Arthritis looks genuinely excited.

Hades shot me a reassuring smile.

He'd explained all this before and said everyone always survived, but Artemis made it sound like our demise was a *very* real possibility, and she was personally going to make it happen.

"After the woods, you can leap," Artemis said flippantly, like she didn't need to explain it because we'd already be dead by then.

"If you're uncaptured by the first morning light, you'll be in the Assembly of Death, and can choose who you want to partner with for your first mission. If you're caught, the two Spartans who capture you will fill that role."

Kharon bared his teeth and Augustus smirked, his eyes still dripping crimson.

Achilles cracked his neck back and forth, muzzle concealing his expression. Patro winked, looking smug.

Artemis raised her bloody bow.

"RUN FOR YOUR LIVES!"

Drex and I didn't need to be told twice. We turned and sprinted into the icy woods.

2

The Hunter

Kharon

Hell and Hound led the way through the dark woods, bones flashing as they sprinted between the snow-covered trees.

Augustus ran beside me.

The sky opened up and freezing rain fell sharply, covering everything in a layer of treacherous ice.

It was a perilous night for a hunt.

Old scar tissue and misshapen joints ached in my ruined right knee.

I'd been steadily spiraling out of control since Alexis left us. We'd rushed down the aisle to avoid violating the marriage law, since I'd turned twenty-seven on the first of February.

We'd hunted Alexis and yet she'd still gotten away.

You're nothing but a failure.

Dark memories strangled.

Artemis and Erebus had enrolled me in the SGC when I was eighteen, to show off the strength of their prodigy.

But I'd done the unforgivable.

I lost.

Defeated and broken, gasping on the hot sand with a mangled ruined right leg—bones protruding, bloody brands across my chest—I'd dragged myself out of the Dolomites Coliseum by my arms, and collapsed in the wings.

I'd whimpered with pain, fading in and out of consciousness, waiting for my parents.

No one had come.

When I finally woke up, Artemis was standing over me with a disgusted expression. "You're no son of mine."

It was the last thing we'd ever said to each other.

Officially, to save face in front of Olympians, I was a member of the House of Artemis. Unofficially, I was dishonored.

If it wasn't for Augustus taking me in and helping me prepare for the crucible, I don't know what I would have done.

Don't think about it.

I focused on the present.

Lowering my head, I activated my powers—protector bond strumming in my chest, I shoved my consciousness into my hellhounds while maintaining a full-out sprint—my senses strengthened.

The forest illuminated with the neon green of night vision.

Vanilla smoke filled my lungs.

I'd inhaled that scent when I'd dragged my tongue across Alexis's delicate golden skin ninety-nine days, twelve hours, thirty minutes, and ten seconds ago.

"They're not going to make it to the clearing in time," Augustus said stoically as he scanned the forest.

He was my hunting partner.

It wasn't romantic between us—we hovered on the narrow border between friendship and unequivocal devotion—Alexis was the new glue that bridged the gap.

"You won't win," Patro taunted in a singsong voice at our heels. "Alex hates you."

Fuck him.

I'd once considered him my brother.

Patro chuckled darkly.

Not anymore.

Augustus glared back at the approaching Chthonics, murder in his gaze—blood dripped from his eyes like tears—it was a new development.

Ever since the marriage bond settled into place, our powers had been more volatile. Stronger, but more painful.

We got everything we ever wanted, and it was torment.

Up ahead, a few hundred feet away, two fluttering dark cloaks ran through the woods.

Are they even trying?

Alexis and Drex were moving like snails. It was only a marathon, for fuck's sake; it wasn't even that long.

Messy golden curls flashed.

Alexis looked back over her right shoulder, eyes widening with fear—one dark, one white—locked on me.

Electricity exploded through my chest as our bond lit up.

Alexis's face twisted with pain. She stumbled, turned forward, and barely avoided colliding with a tree.

"Be fucking careful!" I shouted. "Watch where you're going."

"Don't worry about him, my *darling mentee*," Patro called out mockingly. "Achilles and I are here for you!"

Hermos shouted something to Agatha, and a safety clicked off.

Augustus turned back in slow motion, his black eyes widening with sheer horror.

Pop. Pop. Pop. Pop. Pop.

Muzzle flashes lit the night as bark exploded.

Drex staggered.

Two bullets lodged in his arm.

Alexis grabbed him by the front of his toga and dragged him forward as they zigzagged wildly through the trees.

Their lead was disappearing.

Forty feet.

Patro screamed something and Agatha yelled back; both sounds were swallowed by the wind.

Alexis jerkily yanked Drex closer, draping one of his arms over her shoulders. She half ran, half dragged him through the dark woods. His arm was bleeding all over her.

"LEAVE HIM!" I shouted.

Alexis tightened her grip around the injured boy as she dragged him through the woods.

A muzzle flashed.

Pop.

Alexis's body rocked. She grunted and stumbled.

She wiped at her leg—her gloves were coated in crimson.

Copper stained the air.

She grabbed Drex's wounded arm, he cried out in pain, and she resumed pulling him through the remaining trees.

A bullet was lodged in Alexis's right calf.

They.

Shot.

My.

Wife.

Augustus bellowed.

Patro shouted.

A strange pain burned my leg.

I looked back—Hermos, the vile Gorgon, had a gun in his outstretched hand, the barrel smoking with fresh gunpowder.

He'd shot my wife using one of the Spartan guns *I'd* designed.

I knew all about his kind.

The trainers at the House of Aphrodite were all Gorgons—they'd tortured Patro as a child, for fun. He was fucked up because of their sadistic culture.

"Get to her first!" Patro shouted, and Achilles sped up, his muzzle coated with ice.

Augustus matched him stride for stride.

The two behemoths of the House of Ares moved in a blur, faster than the rest of the Chthonics. They were built for power.

"Handle Hermos—or I'll destroy him . . . permanently," Augustus ordered, blood dripping profusely from his eyes as he weaved through the branches.

Spinning around, I came to a stop—raising both weapons—and fired at point-blank range.

Pop. Pop. Pop.

Hermos didn't have time to blink.

Bullets ripped through his skull—eyes, mouth, and forehead—his brain exploded. Momentum threw him onto the ice as he bounced off a tree.

I stomped over to Hermos's fallen body, kicking off his Spartan helmet.

"What the fuck was that for?" Agatha screeched as she stumbled to a stop and kneeled beside her downed partner.

My chest heaved with rage.

"He *shot* my wife."

Agatha cradled Hermos's bloody snake head, her face shifting rapidly between a woman and a demon. "It's the rules!"

"It's my wife."

I turned and ran, resuming the hunt.

An eerie hum filled the air as sleet poured harder and slammed against ice.

Shadows moved up ahead.

When I finally broke out of the forest, Drex was lying in a heap cradling his arm, but his bullet wounds were somehow already healing over.

That's strange.

I stepped over him.

In the middle of the clearing, Alexis was limping backward. Her strange protector crouched in front of her.

Lightning lit up the inky sky, illuminating wet golden curls. Augustus and Patro were slowly approaching her.

"Just come with us!" Patro shouted over the wind. "You hate your husbands. *We* never betrayed you. Not like they did."

Poppae and Nero crept forward with him.

Augustus shook his head. "Don't listen to him—let *me* help you, my carus." Poco was a lump on his back, hiding from the elements under his cloak.

Achilles stood with his arms crossed, smoking in the sleet, as he watched the two men approach Alexis.

I stalked along the shadows of the tree line.

"Let us help you!" Patro held out his hand. "It's different with us . . . We're not like them."

Thunder cracked.

"Careful." Augustus turned his head to the other man. "That's my wife you're talking to."

Patro's laugh was cold and humorless. "Tell me, does the marriage truly count . . . if the bride is trapped, deceived, and forced into it?"

Augustus raised his fist.

Achilles moved in a flash, shoving Patro back as he stood in front of him.

"*Don't* test me," Augustus said as he pointed at Patro. "I won't hold back. Not when it comes to her."

Lightning flashed.

Achilles's ice-covered muzzle glinted as he pulled out a serrated hunting knife. He held it up to Augustus's throat.

Blood dripped from Augustus's lashes, freezing as it spilled over.

I crept closer, ignoring the pain in my leg.

Alexis held her hands to her chest and closed her eyes like she was concentrating.

She disappeared from the clearing.

Crack.

Lightning flashed.

Alexis rematerialized on the tree line in a cloud of smoke, a foot away from me, looking shocked.

Not only had she leapt a short distance—highly dangerous because of the increased odds of slamming into objects—but she'd leapt directly *to* me.

"You could have decapitated yourself on a tree!" I lunged for her, snow crunching.

Alexis threw herself backward, grimacing when she backed into a tree. Leaping while injured was *also* extremely dangerous. She'd exacerbated the hemorrhaging.

"Let me help you."

Alexis moved away.

I stalked after her.

"Alexis, you shouldn't leap when you're injured. You could have hurt yourself!" Augustus shouted from the clearing.

He sprinted toward us with Patro and Achilles on his heels.

Alexis looked back and forth between the approaching men and the deeper woods with wild eyes, like she was debating her options.

She wouldn't.

When injured, Spartans didn't leap multiple times in a row because the odds of blood loss, permanent damage, and severe dismemberment were high. We were born with an innate sense of self-preservation.

Alexis took a deep breath.

Yes, she fucking would.

On instinct, I threw myself at her, my hand grabbing her bicep.

Crack.

The two of us were alone.

We were standing in a field of green grass.

The May temperature was mild. Shining softly, the sun was setting in a pink haze.

A hundred feet away, barbed wire fenced in a forest. A sign proclaimed in red letters, "Spartan Federation Militarized Protected Zone, Titans Beware."

She'd taken us back to Montana, where we'd found her living under a fucking tarp.

"Do you have no sense of self-preservation?" I yelled in horror.

Alexis yanked out of my grip.

Stumbling, she ripped off her blood-soaked gloves and stared down at her trembling fingers. "Drex," she mouthed silently.

Is there a faint glow coming from her hands?

She wiped it off and it looked normal.

"Leaping twice in a row? What were you thinking? Are you *trying* to kill yourself?" I snarled.

Her gaze shuttered.

Eyelashes coated in ice, wild curls frozen to her flushed face, she swayed on her feet like she was going to pass out as blood poured from her leg.

Rage and fear mixed inside my chest in a toxic combination.

"Look at me," I demanded.

She turned away.

Dark thoughts mixed with helpless emotions. My aggression was chasing her away. I was known as the hunter of my generation for a reason—I knew when it was time to switch tactics.

I need to pretend to be a nice man.

With a deep breath, I lowered my voice and relaxed my posture. "Please . . . let me help you."

The setting sun cast streaks of pink across her stubborn expression.

I pulled off my helmet and dropped it to show her I wasn't a threat (I was). "We need to create a tourniquet around your leg and tie off your wound. You're losing a lot of blood."

Slowly, I unbuckled my armpit holsters and dropped my weapons onto the grass. I tugged off my black hunting shirt and handed the fabric over to her.

"Tie this around your leg."

Alexis stared at it.

"Here—let me help." I dropped to my knees.

The pads of my fingers grazed across her calf—awareness tingled up my arm, and I swallowed a guttural groan. Shifting to hide the inappropriate bulge in my pants, I wrapped the shirt around the top of her calf.

Keep it together. She's fucking injured, you animal. As gently as possible, I tied it off in a knot.

"Thanks," Alexis whispered hoarsely.

Water melted off her eyelashes and dripped onto my cheek—she was looking down at me with a strange expression.

Badump-Badump-Badump. My heart was in my throat.

It was the first word she'd said to me in months.

Moisture blurred my vision—I blinked it away.

Tie her up. Grab her quickly; she's not expecting it. Throw her over your shoulder and leap away. Chain her to your side.

I swallowed thickly.

No. Give her a choice.

I forced my shoulders to relax.

"Let's . . . get you back to the base so we can bandage you up properly." I stood up to my full height and offered her my hand. "I'll leap us back."

Be the good guy.

Her expression became guarded.

Fuck, I should have grabbed her.

"Why—not?" My neck tensed and I tried not to bare my teeth like a predator.

I expected silence.

Alexis's head whipped around, her two-colored eyes boring through me with intensity.

Blood dripped down her cheeks from where she'd cut herself on tree branches—curls stuck out in every direction—her face twisted with dark emotions.

"You betrayed me."

Shaking my head, I held out my arm for her to take. "No—I *married* you."

Alexis's voice was cold as ice. "Was it worth hurting me . . . just for your p-powers? Did you get everything you wanted?"

"You *don't* understand," I said through gritted teeth. "It wasn't like that. The Olympians . . . the oppression."

She rolled her eyes and waved her hand dismissively. The ten-carat diamond we'd gifted her danced on her finger.

Don't attack your wife.

I held my hand out for her patiently. "Just come with me."

Don't kidnap her.

"You trapped me," Alexis said hoarsely. "Stalked me like an *animal*. Tortured me with your messed-up powers—"

"YOUR POWERS ARE STRONGER NOW TOO," I shouted, losing all control. "Wake up. The marriage law would have applied to you too, princess. You also benefited from this arrangement—I'm trying to be a better man *for you*."

"I NEVER ASKED YOU TO BE ANYTHING!" she screamed.

I shoved my knuckles into my mouth to stop myself from saying something I'd regret.

When I finally regained control of myself, I choked out, "I'm *sorry* for trapping you . . . the stalking . . . marriage . . . kidnapping. I'm going to be better."

"And the body p-parts in the boxes?" she whispered.

I narrowed my eyes. "What about them? Those *disgraces* of men touched you against your will. What the fuck did you expect me to do?"

"Literally *anything* else," she said. "Except butchering them!"

I scoffed. "Don't be ridiculous, Alexis."

She gasped like she was struggling to breathe.

I continued. "I still don't understand why you rejected the jewels. Were they not up to your standards? Augustus said humans once revered the Hope Diamond. He thought you'd appreciate the history. Did you want something nicer?"

Alexis covered her mouth and made a choking sound as her face turned purple.

I softened my features. "We'll be better men for—"

"This is j-just physical," she blurted.

I blinked.

Icy fury doused me.

"What . . . the fuck did you just say to me?"

Alexis tipped her head back, jaw set.

Blood continued to streak down her cheeks as she set her chin stubbornly, refusing to cower before my rage. I would have been impressed if I wasn't so fucking furious.

"Say it again," I said quietly. "I fucking dare you."

She bared her teeth, eyes flashing. "It's just physical."

I lunged.

3

THE HUNTED

ALEXIS

Kharon gripped my arms.

Sun streaks from the Montana dusk accentuated the sharp cut of his disturbingly handsome features.

The skeleton ink on top of his right hand extended to his shoulder in a sleeve. It ended where layers of painful scar tissue began. His chest was a mess of circular welts.

What happened to him? Whatever could leave so many lasting scars on an immortal was truly heinous.

Blood was splattered across his striated naked torso and the deep V of muscle on his lower stomach disappeared into the top of his cargo pants, framing a thin dark trail.

Humans called Chthonics dark gods for a reason.

This was the reason.

Face flaming with heat, I struggled to breathe. Apparently, I wasn't asexual; I was just into tattooed, violent, Machiavellian men. *A fate worse than death.*

Gathering my courage, I searched for my voice.

"Release m-me," I whispered.

Icy eyes flashed with danger. "Or . . . what?" Kharon asked mockingly.

I took a deep cleansing breath.

Pop. Pop.

Kharon inhaled with shock.

He slowly lowered his gaze to my hands—the Spartan gun Hades had gifted me was smoking.

Kharon's lips thinned.

I'd missed.

Seconds bled into minutes as we sized each other up, me (shooter) and Satan (sadly, not shot).

The field was eerily quiet.

"Use both hands, carissima," Kharon finally said, his voice husky. "You want to hold the gun out in front of you and aim for my torso."

He widened his stance and mimed pointing an imaginary gun at my heart.

"Pow," Kharon whispered, his fingers flexing like he pulled a trigger.

Blood was streaked across his parted lips.

He smiled cockily. "In emergencies, try to lock your elbows so the recoil doesn't throw you off—"

I pulled out the Taser Persephone had gifted me and slammed down on the black button.

It was an emergency; my husband was an ass.

Kharon dropped like a rock.

Every vein on his body protruded as he writhed on the grass and his body lit up with bright blue streaks of electricity.

"Good." He choked out. "Job." *Gasp.* "That." He made a horrible, strangled sound. "Also works."

I slapped at the black button, trying to turn it off.

Kharon grunted as the voltage increased.

I hit the Taser, trying to stop the current.

Kharon grinned, convulsing helplessly on the ground.

"Wahoooo!" Nyx shouted, as she woke up and slithered around my waist. "Yes. *Electrocute* him to death. We have no mercy on our enemies."

A lot was happening (none of it was good).

Kharon made another awful, pained sound and rolled around, tensing as the blue streaks of electricity flashed across his skin.

"This is so fun—why didn't we do this earlier?" Nyx slithered around my neck with excitement.

"This is not fun," I whispered frantically. "How do I turn this stupid freaking thing off?"

I banged at the box again, and the agonized grunts increased.

"Why would you turn it off?" Nyx sounded genuinely confused.

Kharon rolled over.

Ohmygod.

He ripped one of the Taser prongs out of his chest with spasming fingers—blood and chunks of skin sprayed.

"Wait . . . he's not getting up . . ." Nyx hissed with shock. "Right?"

Kharon sat up and turned toward me.

I shrieked.

He was no longer bothering to hide the depths of his madness—eyes promising unspeakable corruption, bright blue currents danced across his pale, nearly translucent skin.

The most skilled hunter on the planet got to his feet before me.

"Holy shit . . . he's standing," Nyx whispered. "How is he standing? Are you seeing this?"

I dropped the Taser and backed away. The excruciating pain in my leg was not the imminent danger; it was the man calmly standing there as a live current was electrocuting him.

Kharon wiped his sparking lips—fresh blood sizzled as he smeared it across his face.

"Carissima," he purred darkly as he took a step toward me. "If you wanted to play . . . you just had to say something."

Streaks of neon blue jumped across pale skin as a burning metallic scent filled the air.

His jaw clenched.

That was my only warning.

He lunged.

Long fingers grasped my chin and tipped my face up—my skin sparked as the current ran between us—I was rooted to the spot.

Something sizzled.

Kharon lowered his head until our lips brushed.

Zap. A spark leapt between us—our breaths mingled.

His tongue darted out to lick the blood off my lower lip. Tingles danced across the edge of my mouth where his tongue had lightly brushed.

It was the faintest touch.

My skin smoldered in his wake.

"Carissima," he groaned, full of anguish.

Crack. "What in *Kronos's kingdom* is going on here?" Augustus's deep voice rang out, breaking the spell.

Both our heads snapped toward him like we'd been caught doing something depraved (we had).

Augustus looked around with a furrowed brow like he was surprised where he was, then he focused on us. He stared for a long second, and his surprise morphed into something . . . dangerous.

"Don't stop on my behalf. Kiss her," Augustus ordered, his voice velvety smooth. "Now."

Wait. What did he just say—

Kharon grabbed my jaw and slammed our mouths together.

Electricity exploded.

His tongue plunged into my mouth. I whimpered as he bit down on my lower lip—hard. He groaned, our breaths mixing.

Kharon kissed harder, like he was trying to devour me. His

lips were bruising, and I pressed against him, onto my tiptoes, needing more.

Sparks sizzled. A current pulsed between us.

"Enough," Augustus ordered, and Kharon yanked his mouth away, panting heavily, but he kept his fingers wrapped around my chin. I leaned into his touch.

A single spark pulled taut between us; it buzzed through the air, connected to our lips. It snapped.

I licked away the sting.

Augustus adjusted his pants.

He enjoys watching us.

Poco stuck his head up over Augustus's shoulder, tipped his furry head back, and screamed at me accusingly.

Yes, I am a pervert.

Next question.

Calluses dug into my chin—Kharon turned my face so I was staring up at him. He still hadn't released me.

"You taste . . . exquisite." His voice was hoarse and gravelly.

My teeth ached as electricity traveled through my jaw.

A long second passed.

Heart pounding, face flaming, I gathered my courage.

"Just . . . physical," I whispered.

Kharon dropped his hand from my jaw like I'd scalded him.

I smiled, victorious as I stumbled back.

"Wait—why is there a Taser in your stomach? Why are there scorch marks on her chin?" Augustus looked between us like we'd both lost our ever-loving minds (we had).

"I'm seducing her."

"He's trying to k-kill me."

Kharon had the audacity to look offended.

I shook my head, trying to find words that wouldn't come.

How did I explain Karen was secondhand Tasering me . . . and I liked it?

Do the Olympian health clinics offer lobotomies?

Kharon's abs flexed and contracted in rhythm to the electric shock. My mouth went dry.

Mental note, need to get one. Immediately.

Augustus sighed heavily. "Kharon, you're clearly scaring her. Tone it down. We talked about this." He pointed at me. "She's bleeding out from a fucking bullet wound and looks like shit. We need to get her back to the outpost. Patro and Achilles are leaping all over trying to find her first."

Why do my mentors care so much?

"Look at her!" Augustus yelled.

Okay, now he was just being rude.

"You're the one who told us to kiss," I mumbled under my breath.

Blood pooled in the corners of Augustus's eyes. "What was that, my carus?" he asked softly. "Speak up, darling—do you have a . . . complaint?"

I opened my mouth to argue, but no sound came out. He wasn't like Kharon; arguing with Augustus felt different.

There was a dangerous energy around him. An authority.

I wanted his approval.

Dear God, I'm ready to die.

Kharon blanched as he stared at my leg, like he'd forgotten all about the bullet lodged in my calf. Grabbing the second Taser wire still in his skin with both hands, he ripped it out of his flesh like it was nothing.

The sputtering wires dropped to the ground.

"Yep, I'm into that," Nyx said.

Me too.

"I'll leap all three of us back," Augustus ordered. "Since I'm the only one of us not actively *fucking* bleeding."

Both men looked at me expectantly.

Oh god.

I wanted to take him up on his offer and leap back to safety.

You're a strong, independent woman.

A couple of months ago, I would have done it. It was the logical choice. But that was before their betrayal.

Girding my lady loins, I took a deep steadying breath and shot up a quick prayer to God to not mangle my corpse so badly . . . Carl Gauss was waiting.

No cost is too high for vengeance.

"Uh, kid," Nyx said. "I really don't think you should—"

Augustus and Kharon's eyes widened.

"Domus," I whispered as I concentrated on the feeling of home. *Warmth. Acceptance.* Hades and Persephone flashed through my mind.

I screamed as I plunged into darkness.

Unlike the other times I leapt, the agony was unimaginable. Something had gone wrong. I was being torn apart in every direction, limbs stretched and contorted.

I was lying on my back, ruined limbs spread wide.

Smoke rose around me.

Everything was dark.

A woman was screaming. *Is it me?*

Nyx hissed and slithered off my neck. "Are . . . you . . . kid." Her tongue dragged across my cheek, but her voice sounded far away.

I coughed as the world spun.

Nausea cramping my stomach, I rolled onto my side and retched up everything I'd eaten the day before.

"Need . . . move . . . help." Nyx sounded worried. That made two of us.

My eyes rolled to the back of my head, and I barely found the will to pull them forward.

Steel beams spaced out across the low rock ceiling. The air was humid and thick. Shadows flickered from torchlight on the walls.

"Kid, you gotta get up," Nyx said as my ears cleared.

A woman wailed heinously.

Is that me, or just in my head?

The wail steadily increased, confirming it wasn't me.

I rolled onto my hands, vision blurry. Groaning, I pushed up to my feet.

You can do this, Alexis—you're a Spartan.

Hunched over, with my hands on my knees, muffled male voices shouted expletives as a woman screamed.

Throbbing pain pierced my skull as I swiveled my head, taking in the opposite ends of the narrow rock tunnel.

A light shone at the end of one. *An exit.*

A scream echoed from the other one; it was dark. *A dead end.*

The hairs on the back of my neck stood on end as I looked between the two options.

"We need to get out of here—run, Alexis. Now," Nyx hissed as she slithered down my legs onto the floor.

With a deep breath, I staggered forward in agony.

I made my choice.

Unlike Icarus, I didn't fall to my demise trying to escape—I walked into it willingly.

4

The Eldest Heir

*Augustus: Twenty-Four Hours Later,
Assembly of Death Unofficial Outpost, Siberia*

Silently, I slipped around the corner and crept forward.

Poco was asleep, his chubby raccoon arms wrapped tightly around my calf.

"I found her unconscious in an alcove in the dungeon beneath our palace at Crete," Hades said as he paced outside the medic room. "She jumped from Montana to Greece while injured . . . She's lucky she's not in a coma."

He was speaking to Ares—my father.

The jagged scar across Ares's mouth pulled tight as he listened to Hades, red rings flaring around his eyes.

Memories of torture played.

Every member of the House of War had a facial scar—he demanded it.

Lights flickered and there was a loud sputtering as the generator struggled to sustain power.

As I crept through the shadows, all three of Cerberus's heads turned to me.

Animals could sense the Chthonic power in my eyes, and their instincts warned them I was a predator not to be messed with.

Unaware of his protector's stand-off, Hades leaned closer to Ares. "Thank Kronos I found Alexis when I did."

"Yes," Ares said like he was carefully choosing each word. "It's a good thing . . . *you* were the one to find her."

Pain pierced my skull.

Migraines from the strength of my Chthonic abilities had plagued me all my life, but they were sharper now. Ever since the marriage bond, blood dripped from my eyes whenever I used my abilities or felt strong emotions.

My power had increased, in the most awful of ways—Kronos himself was punishing me for trapping my wife.

Hades made a strange face.

Does he have a secret?

The door slammed open and a doctor rushed out, bright light flooding the hall.

On the doctor's Olympian white coat was the ancient symbol of Spartan healing—the Rod of Asclepius—it was a glowing staff with a snake wrapped around it, framed with wings.

The wings represented creatures. A snake for Chthonics. Olympians were the rod.

The ancient symbol of life and death was splattered with unnaturally vibrant blood, which meant a Spartan was hemorrhaging, excessively.

My stomach sank.

The doctor bowed shakily to Hades. "I'm going to contact my colleagues and get her the newest Olympian paste," she said in a rush. "For the damage."

Hades nodded, and she leapt away.

Olympian research laboratories produced lifesaving medical products.

I stared down at the WSDL engraving on my gun.

Ares started the weapons company, formerly called Death Tools. He specialized in spiky spears nicknamed *lizard killers*; the slain flopped around on them before they died.

Ares refused to manufacture anything else, even though they didn't perform well in modern times, so the other Chthonic leaders gave the business to me.

He'd never forgiven me for taking it over and renaming it WSDL, even though the inheritance laws were written in the company's bylaws.

I rubbed at my facial scar, the one he gave me.

There was a loud creaking as the door to the sterile white medical room swung back and forth. Inside, two figures were hooked up to beeping machines.

Fuck.

Hermos had a thick cast wrapped around his head (Kharon's handiwork).

Alexis was across from him lying on a gurney, covered head to toe in bandages—half of her face was swollen and bruised, a sickly shade of purple under the neon lights. Her strange protector lay with its head on its paws on the floor beside her bed.

She was shot and leapt three times. It's all your fault.

I should have acted sooner. I should have stopped her, but I'd wanted to respect her autonomy.

No woman should ever be so heavily bandaged, and certainly not *my* woman.

She should be always guarded. Coddled. Pampered.

Your wife is injured under your fucking watch. You're a Kronos damned disgrace of a man.

The pounding in my skull escalated as the door swung.

"What are you doing?" Hades's voice echoed like a gunshot and Cerberus growled. "Only leaders are allowed here. You were told to wait in the rec room."

Ares looked at me with disgust, then turned and left, leaving me alone with the other leader.

Fuck you, Father.

Hades stepped in front of the door, blocking me from entering the medical room.

I didn't remember moving forward.

"Why does she look like . . . *that?*" My voice shook as I tried to look over his shoulder through the small glass window.

There was a loud sputtering. Everything went dark as the lights all went out at once.

The hall was pitch-black except for Cerberus's six yellow eyes.

Hades took a step closer.

The generator groaned noisily and there was a whirring—sickly green lights flickered back on weakly, dimmer than before.

"She leapt *multiple* times with a bullet wound," Hades spat. "She staggered around our cellar disoriented and collapsed face-first against rocks. Her body was so weak from leaping that she bruised easily."

There was an unnatural tenor to his voice. He looked almost . . . guilty.

"I need to see her." I stepped to the side to see past him.

Hades moved with me. "She *doesn't* want to see you."

Inky tendrils of fog poured off him in an insidious stream.

Hundreds of voices screamed—"*You're a killer. A monster. No one could ever care for someone like you.*"

Every mind that I'd tortured—tortured me back.

Alexis's soft voice was the loudest of them all. "*I hate you. You violated me. I will never love you. You will never be my husband.*"

The pounding in my skull reached a fever pitch and my right knee almost gave out.

The voices shrieked louder.

"You've done enough damage to my daughter already." Hades spoke my fears aloud.

His power wrapped around my neck in a noose—all warmth disappeared from the world—my breath came out in an icy cloud.

Frozen lips cracked as I parted them. "I *need* to be with her."

It was getting harder to see.

"No—you need to leave her the fuck alone," Hades said icily. "You're a disgrace of a Spartan, and if it wasn't for the bond between you and my precious daughter . . . I'd gut you right here."

He shoved me across the hall.

CRACK. My head slammed against the wall—the pain added to my delirium.

Cerberus barked.

"Leave," Hades ordered. "Now."

You need to get to her.

I opened my mouth to argue, but all that came out was a pained grunt. Soon the migraine would progress, and I wouldn't be able to see anything.

"I didn't mean to hurt her," I whispered. "I do care for her and—"

"*Leave!*" Hades roared.

High heels clicked across marble. "Hades?" Aphrodite called out from down the hall. "Unusual Titan presence has been sighted near Rome—Artemis has assigned you and Ares to investigate. Wait, Augustus—why the fuck aren't you in the rec room with the others?"

"I'm heading there now," I said hoarsely.

I waited for Hades to walk away first.

He didn't.

"Leave," Hades ordered, reading my intentions. "Now."

I turned and staggered down the hall.

Ice nipped at my ankles as his power chased after me.

Usually, my migraines came with waves of numbness, but every bone in my body ached. Moaning with pain, disoriented and woozy, I bounced off walls.

A chattering noise broke through the anguish.

Something tugged at my pant leg.

I staggered to a stop and squinted down.

In the green haze, Poco tilted his black-and-gray face up like he was trying to tell me something.

He held up a little black hand, paw open expectantly.

"I don't have any treats," I croaked.

Poco bared his sharp teeth and shook his head. Then he held his black paw up higher, like he was waiting for something.

"No treats." I grabbed my head.

He chittered louder, our bond heating with anxiety. Poco clasped his tiny hands together, then held one up to me.

"Oh," I whispered.

Tentatively, I bent over and gave him my pointer finger.

Poco clutched it, his miniature hand unable to wrap fully around it.

Gently Poco tugged me forward, balancing against me as he led the way on two fluffy legs.

Moisture blurred my vision.

"Thank you."

He chittered back.

Warmth flooded the bond between us.

No one understood why I bonded with a raccoon and not one of the class six beasts that lived in the back of the menagerie.

There were hundreds of different species in Sparta, but only a handful fell on the beast scale: class one to seven, with seven being the highest and most dangerous.

Class seven beasts were virtually extinct. Spartans were mandated to kill them on sight.

Titans and Typhons were the two most recent creatures to be labeled as class seven.

Most Chthonics bonded with class five or six creatures in the menagerie: Nemean land mammals, the violent winged Pegasuses, the three-headed dog cousins of Cerberus, or the invisible dragons that nested in the secret caves.

None of those animals were of any interest to me.

It was the little guy hanging from a tree, who held out his arms for a hug with a bashful smile on his face, that did it for me.

Poco wasn't ranked, but I didn't care.

He was perfect how he was.

Now Poco looked up at me with worry as he slowly guided me down the halls. His little black fingers squeezed mine tightly, as if he was worried he'd lose me.

Raccoons were fierce, intelligent, loyal creatures.

After a lifetime of Ares coldly lecturing me on power and honor, animals growling and running away, and Chthonics reminding me of my responsibilities, it was wonderful to have a true companion.

Poco didn't care that I was the eldest Chthonic heir.

Strangely, he was one of the few animals I'd ever met that wasn't afraid of me.

He just wanted to cuddle and play with my hair.

Years ago, when it all got burned off from Colchian dragon fire, Poco had cried and refused to leave my bed for a week as he scratched at my skull, in what I'm pretty sure was Earth's first case of raccoon depression.

I'd grown my hair out ever since; I kept it long for him.

He was everything to me.

I'd slaughter *anyone* who dared try to hurt him.

Poco chirped and tugged at my hand.

I staggered to a stop in front of a familiar metal door with a dagger carved into it. Before I could reach for the handle, the hall once again plunged into darkness.

Silence descended.

The hair on the back of my neck prickled.

When the generator surged it usually made noises, but there were none.

Poco let out a nervous screech.

Sirens erupted. "Emergency . . . Emergency . . . Emergency."

A monotone voice crackled over the hall speakers as it repeated the warning.

Piercing pain stabbed my skull. I doubled over at the onslaught.

Poco climbed up my body, his fur pressed against the back of my head as he hugged me from behind—I blinked with confusion.

It took me a second.

Poco was covering both of my ears with his little hands and trying to protect me from the piercing sounds.

The generator whirred and the overhead lights turned back on, but they weren't green.

They were neon red.

Vibrant crimson lights flashed as the sirens continued to blare.

With Poco still covering my ears, I shoved my shoulder into the heavy metal door and staggered straight into a body.

"Did you see her?" Kharon asked frantically as he steadied me. "Is she okay? What happened? Did the leaders catch you? Why's the emergency system going off?"

"No," I whispered as I pushed him away.

Kharon followed me. "No—to what?" he asked. His hellhounds watched us from the corner, their bony bodies flickering into existence, then disappearing.

Kharon's powers were also getting stronger because of our marriage bond.

"You're bad for Alexis," Patro taunted. He was leaning against the wall with his arms crossed. "All you two do is hurt her."

Kharon turned to him with a growl; Patro met his anger with a smirk.

I threw myself headfirst onto the worn couch and groaned with misery.

In my peripheral vision, Drex sat on the other side with wide eyes. An ugly bird flew above his head in small circles.

Poco repositioned himself into a fuzzy lump on my chest.

"Did you see Hermos?" Agatha asked as she stood up from where she was sitting on the floor. She stalked across the room and got in my face.

Poco hissed and tried to bite her.

She jumped back out of his reach.

"Hermos is in a . . . coma," I croaked, fighting through nausea. "Head all wrapped."

"Screw you," Agatha said as she whirled around and pointed a finger accusingly at Kharon. "You just had to fucking *shoot* him."

"He's lucky he's still alive," he said dismissively.

Agatha snarled.

Kharon pushed past her. "How is Alexis? Is she . . . okay?" he asked me softly.

I shook my head no.

"Of course she's not okay," Patro sneered from where he was still leaning against the far wall. "She's married to *you*."

Grunts echoed as Kharon threw himself at Patro and they wrestled.

Tiny black fingers covered my ears.

At the end of the couch, Drex muttered what sounded like a prayer to Jesus? *He's not going to help you here. This is Sparta.*

Poco forgot what he was doing and started playing with my earlobe. He stuck a tiny finger deep into my ear.

Crack.

I peeked open my eyes.

Achilles materialized in the middle of the room in a cloud of smoke, with Poppae and Nero crouched at his feet.

Kharon and Patro had pulled apart, both looking guilty, like they were trying to hide the fact that they were fighting from Achilles.

Achilles signed something rapidly to Patro and handed him a scroll.

As Patro read it, Achilles threw himself down on the couch beside me, rubbing at his temples like he was exhausted.

An unlit cigarette hung between the grates of his muzzle.

Drex whimpered with fear on the other side of the couch, and we rolled our eyes, sharing a long-suffering look—*this new Olympian boy isn't going to last a week in the Assembly of Death.*

I stiffened.

"Stay away from Alexis," I whispered. As my half brother who also grew up in the House of Ares, I'd always considered him my closest family next to Helen.

Red eyes flashed as Achilles arched a brow mockingly.

I reached for my gun holster.

He mimicked the gesture.

He's not family anymore.

Poco hissed at Achilles, then he pointed his tiny finger and mimed shooting at him. Kharon had spent the last months teaching him the gesture.

Nero prowled over to the couch with a low growl.

I glanced at the wolf.

It tucked its tail and slunk away.

"EVERYONE!" Patro shouted as he waved a yellow scroll through the neon-red air. "Medusa . . . escaped from the Underworld." His voice shook like he'd seen a ghost. "She murdered two Olympians—two *immortals*."

The sirens seemed to wail louder.

Patro flipped it around for all to see.

The entire page was a picture of Medusa. Pale and small-boned, her eyes looked much too large for her head. Covered in blood and dirt, she stared blankly from behind prison bars.

Patro read the headline, "Manhunt mobilized because monstrous Medusa is rampaging again, two Olympians dead: Is she now coming for the Chthonics who locked her up?"

I rolled my eyes.

Agatha laughed.

"Why aren't you panicking? What the fuck is wrong with you people?" Patro pointed the scroll at me accusingly. "Now the disgusting Gorgon is going to come after all of us . . . She should have just fucking died. Snake scum."

Agatha stepped forward. "Do you have a problem with Gorgons, Patro?" she asked. "Because that sounded like a slur."

Patro sneered. "Yeah, maybe I do . . . They're violent dark creatures who can't figure out how to fucking act right. They're more like animals than—"

"I wouldn't finish that sentence if I were you." Agatha cut him off, razor-sharp teeth glinting in her mouth as the skin on her face started to peel away, revealing a monstrous visage.

She opened her maw wider.

In a blur, Achilles moved across the room and stood in front of Patro protectively.

He leaned forward like he was also baring his teeth behind his muzzle; the smoking end of his cigarette matched his eyes.

Flashing crimson lights bathed all of them in shadows as the emergency warning continued blaring.

"They don't fear her because she's part Gorgon," I said.

Everyone turned toward me.

I spoke slowly, "Recessive traits . . . can be expressed when Spartans breed with creatures . . . That's why it doesn't often happen."

"What are you talking about?" Patro asked with narrowed eyes.

"There are *strange* ancestors in the Artemis line," I said quietly, not looking at Kharon across the room. "Medusa wasn't born with Chthonic powers—she's a Gorgon, born with the power of Fate."

Patro gasped, and the scroll clattered as it dropped from his fingers. "*That's* why everyone fears Medusa?" he asked with disbelief.

Drex whimpered.

Patro's face contorted with disgust. "She's a fucking monster." He shivered dramatically. "Snake scum with the power of Fate. She shouldn't exist."

Agatha rolled her eyes and sat down primly on the couch. "You're such a bigot."

"Oh please," Patro said. "We're all thinking it."

Kharon stared blankly at the wall.

Medusa was his sister.

Poco clambered up my chest, whiskers prickling my cheek as he licked at my eyebrows.

"Thanks, buddy," I whispered, not really sure if he was helping or making it worse.

He purred and pulled out a chunk of my eyebrow.

Definitely worse.

Kharon picked up *The Falcon Chronicles* and sat down next to me on the couch. He unrolled to the next story.

"Interesting," Kharon said as he read. "An Olympian doctor has successfully stitched human body parts onto a Spartan."

I grunted, not really that surprised.

Spartan physiology was adept at transmutation.

We could regenerate soft tissues like brains, eyes, and organs. But we couldn't regrow missing hard tissues—bones and cartilage. If a bone was badly fractured, it would heal with time because most of the pieces were still intact.

As a result, we couldn't regrow missing appendages, but our bodies could accept other people's.

Immortal biology was nothing if not fucked up.

Thousands of years ago, it was even a tradition for lower-ranked Spartan soldiers to slice off their fingers, hands, feet, and sometimes entire legs. They'd stitch them onto higher-ranked Spartans who'd lost appendages in battle.

It used to be the ultimate sign of respect and honor, but the practice was now considered barbaric.

For good reason.

Poco chittered, clapping his hands to get Kharon's attention.

Kharon put the scroll down, then pivoted. "Pow," he said as he pretended to shoot Poco with a finger gun.

There was a long pause as they stared at each other.

Poco slumped over like he was dead.

Three seconds later, he popped up and screamed, gray fur sticking out in all directions, as he aimed two finger guns back.

Kharon slumped back with his eyes closed, tongue out.

Poco chittered with excitement.

They high-fived each other, then proceeded to play the "shooting" game no less than a dozen times.

I closed my eyes.

Sleep came quickly.

Bang.

I jolted awake when the door swung open. It felt like I'd been asleep for seconds, but the clock on the wall said it had been hours.

Artemis walked into the room.

The lights above hummed their usual green hue. It was quiet. Poco was draped over my head like a hat, snoring.

Achilles jolted awake where he was asleep next to me on the couch. Patro sat between his knees, still reading the scroll with a frown.

Kharon and Agatha were playing a game of chess on the floor. Drex was cowering in the corner.

I rubbed at my bleary eyes.

Poco chittered on my shoulder and clapped his hands with excitement.

It took my tired brain a moment to process that Alexis was standing next to Artemis.

My heart skipped a beat.

Her bandages had been removed, but dark bruises covered her face. She looked tired and worn out.

We did this to her.

"Who do you choose for your first mission?" Artemis asked with clear impatience as she gestured to the members in the room. "Drex is with Agatha and Hermos, so choose either Augustus and his partner, or Achilles and Patro."

Kharon stared at Alexis like he was trying to read her mind.

Patro perked up.

"I'll choose—" Alexis's voice was hoarse, and she scrunched up her face like she was making a major decision. "Achilles and Patro."

The pain that zapped through our bond was nothing compared to the twisting in my stomach.

Poco shoved a wad of my hair into his mouth.

"Fine," Artemis said as she addressed the room with boredom. "The leaders have conferred—everyone will stay at Augustus's villa until Medusa is captured." She glanced over at me. "Engage the defenses. You have one week before your next Titan assignments," Artemis said coldly.

Crack. She leapt away.

Patro smirked over at both of us, his arm draped over Achilles.

"Fuck," Kharon swore.

Poco wailed at the top of his lungs, then bit down on my bicep, as hard as he could.

After he detached his dagger-sharp fangs, Poco licked at the wound, mewling with regret.

"Don't worry about it," I whispered as I patted his fluffy head, blood dripping down my arm. He suffered from anxious biting syndrome.

Poco whined, and I handed him a cookie from my pocket. He carefully took it with two hands.

"It's not even bad," I reassured Poco, looking anywhere but at Alexis. My heart shattered.

Poco chittered with relief as he licked at his treat.

I staunched the gushing wound and made a mental note—*get stitches and a tetanus shot.*

Today was not my day.

5

Prisoners of War

Alexis

Smoke rose as we leapt into a gilded high-ceilinged atrium.
Location: *Lake Como.*
Goose bumps exploded across my arms.
We were back in the villa where I'd gotten married. *Where they devoured me sexually, and I liked it.* Perversion really crept up on a person.
The altar was gone, but the grand staircase, dramatic windows, and ceiling fresco were the same.
Kharon stalked toward me across the waxed marble floor, hellhounds prowling at his feet. He was stopped by a servant, a tall man in a dark cloak who looked more like a warrior than a housekeeper.
Where's Augustus?
I looked around in confusion.
Patro and Achilles were both staring at me—one with haughty smugness, the other danger.
I'd chosen them because they were the lesser of two evils,

but from the way Achilles's eyes were narrowed, I wasn't so sure that was true.

Chest tightening with dread, I shuffled closer to Drex.

Crack.

Augustus appeared a few feet away, smoke rising around him.

I gasped.

A boy stood beside him.

They were of similar height, but where Augustus was powerfully built, the boy was skinny and lean, his shoulders hunched inward like he was trying to hide.

Charlie.

"For you, my carus," Augustus said as he held my gaze. "Persephone has agreed that he can join Helen in tutoring—she said he's turning eighteen on April 1st, barely a year's difference—it will be good for both of them to have a classmate until they're nineteen."

Charlie shook his head at me. The movement was barely a twitch and no one else saw. Persephone had lied; he would turn nineteen in a few weeks.

I opened my mouth to respond, but no sound came out.

Augustus's expression softened. "Get a good night's sleep—your training begins tomorrow. We only have a week to prepare for Titans."

Augustus addressed a servant with a fierce scowl. "*Raise* the perimeter defenses."

There was a whirling groan—the atrium vibrated, amphoras and bronze statues rattled—outside the grand windows an electric fence slowly rose from the earth.

"It's to keep the enemy out," Augustus said coldly.

The Titans or Medusa?

"The Olympians."

Drex choked.

Augustus turned and walked away, back ramrod straight,

shoulders tensed. He snapped at Achilles and Patro, something about weapons and a board meeting.

A bad feeling settled into my gut.

Screw Sparta and its convoluted politics.

Blond hair blurred in my blind spot—Charlie slammed against me—he smelled like clean soap and the forest at dawn. *Home.* My still-aching bones creaked under his strength, but I squeezed him back fiercely.

Long moments passed as we held each other.

Someone tapped my shoulder.

I turned, arm still wrapped around Charlie.

Helen looked up at me, shy and uncertain. "Would you two mind . . . sleeping in my room with me?" she whispered as she twisted her hands. "Just for safety."

This was not the sixteen-year-old girl who'd talked a mile a minute.

Heart breaking for what she'd been through, what we'd survived, I nodded.

When we got up to her bedroom, we all turned.

"What?" Drex asked sheepishly. "I'm not sleeping in a room with any of those psychopaths. I'm also not sleeping alone in this place—it's probably haunted." He paused. "Is that okay?"

Thus commenced my first official sleepover.

Moonlight filtered through ancient stained glass windows, a wire fence between us and the shimmering Lake Como.

The landscape was silvery and cold.

Inside was a different story.

Pink silk sheets were draped across a four-poster bed covered in crystal-encrusted chiffon. Wigs, dresses, and pearls were strewn across the floor. Makeup was also scattered over every surface.

Amongst the frills, a life-sized poster covered the wall—Erebus wore his signature mask and held a smoking gun.

"Kill or be killed" was written across the top in gothic letters, dripping blood.

I like Helen's style.

A dangerous-looking servant pushed inside a rolling table covered in a dozen silver plates.

He pulled off the lids.

Ten minutes later, Charlie and I had finished half of the food. We clutched our stomachs, still eating. In contrast, Helen and Drex picked at their plates, gaping at us with wide eyes.

They didn't understand.

A lifetime of starvation left claw marks on your soul.

That night, stomach sickly full, thoughts racing, body bruised, I fell into a fitful sleep.

Nightmares devoured.

Gasping, I sat up in bed—the room was quiet—everyone else was still resting.

I need to go back to Crete and check on her. My thoughts were jumbled.

Wiping sweat away with trembling fingers, I sighed.

I was wearing one of Helen's purple nightgowns, body aching like I'd been hit by a Spartan car. The bruises were fading thanks to the Olympians' healing paste, but my bones were still brittle and stiff.

Helen snored softly in the bed beside me, wearing a pink sparkly bonnet, and a loaded Spartan gun peeked out from beneath her pillow.

An arsenal of weapons was also mounted on the bow-covered headboard, every gun bedazzled with pink gems.

A loud snore echoed up from the pile of cushions on the floor.

Charlie was sprawled next to Fluffy Jr., whose four long legs were sticking straight in the air. Every few seconds, he paddled his paws like he was swimming.

On the other end of the floor, closer to the door and opposite of the bed to Charlie, Drex was asleep on purple cushions with his golden toucan protector—that he'd ingeniously named Toucey—tucked under his arm.

Tingles skittered across my fingers, and claustrophobia crushed my lungs.

Picking up a snoring Nyx, I wrapped her around my neck like a scarf and quietly slipped out of the luxurious bed.

As I stood up, everything *throbbed*, and my knee buckled painfully. It took a few moments of trial and error to figure out how to move.

With a gasp of relief, I finally stumbled into the cooler air of the corridor.

I paused, listening.

What was that sound?

Marble gleamed and columns lined the walls with bronze sculptures displayed between them—naked warriors in various battle poses.

Crystals clattered, refracting candlelight, as chandeliers swayed.

It was eerie.

Helen had said the entire villa was off the electric grid, something about tinted windows and limiting light exposure for privacy. The new fence with neon-green searchlights seemed to moot that point.

A shriek echoed.

The calm shattered.

"Did you hear that?" I whispered down to Nyx.

Scales tightened around my neck. "Shut up and go to sleep," she mumbled tiredly.

This can't be happening again. It's probably all in your imagination and not rea—

Marble vibrated beneath my bare toes as a woman screamed.

Thirst forgotten, I followed the sound.

Countless turns later, a heavy unmarked metal door sat in the shadows of a hall.

A dead end.

Footsteps echoed behind me—I whirled around, heart pounding.

No one was there.

Holding my breath, I crept forward and pressed my ear against the metal door.

Chains rattled. A woman screamed in pain.

Déjà vu hit me.

Grabbing the handle, I pulled with all my might—the hinges groaned—I huffed as I wedged the door open and slipped inside.

It slammed shut behind me.

Old copper and mildew filled my nose as I crept down dark, narrow stairs into a dungeon. A sliver of moonlight crawled through a narrow window and illuminated the dank space.

I stopped.

A tall woman lifted her head from the wall and stopped screaming—dark eyes filled with emotions as she glared at me.

My lips parted on a silent gasp.

Fresh blood dripped from her eyes, ears, and mouth—Augustus was torturing her.

Her dirt-encrusted hair was pink, the color unmistakable. I'd seen the same shade at the top of *The Falcon Chronicles*.

Ceres.

I was standing in front of the muse who'd betrayed me to Theros. The one who'd recently disappeared. The report said there was little concrete evidence, but the circumstantial proof was damning. She was a longtime spy for the House of Zeus.

My *husbands* had been the ones who'd kidnapped her.

Chains clattered in the far corner as another prisoner groaned in agony.

"Uh—kid," Nyx hissed. "*What* are you doing?"

I took a shaky step back.

"Help me," Ceres demanded with a growl. She grunted, chains clanking as she pulled at them frantically. "Help!"

Hades's advice drifted through my mind.

Ceres tipped her head back and screamed with frustration, the sound of a broken woman.

"Did you . . . help Theros kill all those children?" I asked softly.

Ceres went still, eyes widening.

"Did you assist Theros?" I repeated. "Yes or no?"

I stood outside the entrance to the dungeon, in the villa's ornate hall, blocking Ceres from Augustus and Kharon's view.

We'd barely made it out of the dungeon.

Helen stood beside me in her nightgown with her hands on her hips.

The gilded hall was dark with shadowy candlelight. Decorative marble statues glared down at me.

I was covered in sweat, heart pounding painfully.

I'd decided to free Ceres from the dungeon without anyone knowing.

The releasing part went smoothly, the secrecy part *not* so much.

Helen had heard me slip out of bed and had followed me. She'd confronted me in the dungeon.

When I'd *finally* convinced Helen not to tell anyone—just when we'd crept out of the darkness into the hall—Kharon and Augustus had appeared.

Apparently, I'd set off one of the villa's alarm systems.

Now Augustus scowled down at a pager device for the tenth time. "It *says* the security perimeter was breached and that two Spartans leapt into the villa."

I opened my mouth—my voice cracked, throat closing over with fear. No words emerged.

"It's wrong," Helen stated calmly beside me. "I told you, no one left. I followed Alexis out of bed, and then she freed Ceres. That's *all* that happened."

Kharon made a choking sound, eyes narrowed with fury like he didn't know what the truth was. His hellhounds stood at his feet.

Poco was perched on Augustus's shoulder, his fluffy arms crossed indignantly.

Make them believe you.

I gathered every ounce of courage I possessed.

"There's no concrete evidence against Ceres and she s-swears she wasn't involved," I said. "I'm v-vouching for her. She's innocent."

Augustus slashed his hand through the air. "I was finding evidence *by* interrogating her . . . That's the entire Kronos damned point! It's not safe for you and Helen to be around her."

I held myself still.

"I agree with Alexis." Helen raised both her hands in a placating gesture at the men. "No evidence has been found, and you both already interrogated her . . . You didn't find anything, right?"

Kharon covered his mouth like he was stopping himself from saying something he'd regret. He'd been doing that a lot lately.

Long, tense seconds stretched.

Augustus bared his teeth. "Then *why* . . . is there blood on your face?" His eyes narrowed as he stared at me.

I touched my cheek, heart racing with fear that I'd been caught.

Ceres whimpered behind me.

Think, Alexis.

Shaking my head, I yanked up the sleeve of my nightgown.

Augustus and Kharon stilled as I revealed the deep marks I'd itched into myself in my sleep.

"Nightmares," I blurted.

Augustus closed his eyes and tensed like he was struggling to regain control.

"*Why* are you having nightmares?" Kharon asked accusingly.

I arched my brow at him.

He had the decency to blush.

Augustus cleared his throat. "Where . . . would Ceres even stay?"

"Next to me," Helen answered immediately, just as we'd hastily planned. "She can stay in the room that's connected to mine. There's plenty of space."

"That's *not* safe," Augustus said through gritted teeth, veins protruding from his forehead.

Poco climbed up to the top of his head and carefully separated three strands of his hair.

Wait, can the raccoon braid?

Helen tipped her chin back and leveled her brother with a glare, emerald eyes on fire. In the shadowy night, she looked like a mini Aphrodite.

"You can have your soldiers watch her," Helen snapped. "You know, the ones that pretend to be servants . . . but *follow* me around."

Augustus didn't bother to deny it.

Well, that explained why they stalked around the villa looking like they'd rather snap a neck than do housework (relatable).

Kharon took a deep, steadying breath.

"The girls can look after themselves," he said through gritted teeth. "We should . . . let them decide what to do."

All of us gaped at him.

Wow, he really is trying.

A blush stained the top of Kharon's cheeks as he looked over at Augustus.

Long minutes stretched.

We all waited as Augustus worked his jaw back and forth.

"*Don't* make me regret this," he finally said, raking his hands through his hair in agitation. "Alexis, your training begins at eight o'clock sharp. Be ready."

Wait—our plan actually worked?

This was completely unexpected.

Helen ran over to Augustus and threw her arms around his neck. "Thank you so much for being so understanding—I promise you *won't* regret it."

Augustus hugged her back tightly. "You better stay safe," he whispered, looking over his shoulder at me. "You *both* better. Don't make me regret this."

Poco joined the hug.

Then he chittered and proudly held up a section of Augustus's hair so everyone could see his work.

Never mind, he can't braid.

It was a giant knot.

Augustus shook his head with exasperation as he felt the rat's nest on the top of his head.

"What's going on here?" Patro's cruel voice echoed from around the corner.

My blood froze.

We were so close.

Helen pulled away from Augustus.

Achilles stalked behind Patro with another smoking cigarette hanging from his muzzle.

"Nothing." Kharon glared at them, his eyes sharpening. "Leave—you're not welcome."

Poco hissed.

Patro didn't react to him, instead he focused on me. "Alexis, why do you have blood on your face?"

Achilles's gaze snapped to me.

I opened my mouth to speak, and once again, no words came out.

"She's fine," Augustus said sharply.

"*Bullshit*, what the fuck is going on here?" Patro looked at Kharon and Augustus with distrust. "Why are you two cornering her? Alexis—do you need our help? Are they hurting you?"

Kharon unholstered a gun. "I would *never* hurt my wife."

Patro's expression turned cruel. "But . . . you already have?"

Kharon clicked off the safety.

"*Stop it!*" Augustus bit out.

"What the fuck is on the side of your head?" Patro asked Augustus.

Poco hissed and grabbed his creation protectively (knotted wad of hair).

"Poco is *none* of your concern." Kharon's voice was icy. "Stay away from him."

Patro scoffed at them. "What are you two going to do to me? *Please* share."

Kharon raised his gun.

Achilles yanked Patro back behind him, smoke billowing around his face.

The scent of violence filled the hall.

"P-please," I said.

Kharon lowered his gun with a heavy sigh, and Augustus rubbed his face.

Patro stiffened as he focused on the space behind me.

"Wait—is that the *bitch* that was working with Theros?" Patro pushed past Achilles. "Why the fuck is that scum not in the dungeon? Why is she standing behind Alexis . . . *What* is going on here?"

Ceres whimpered and curled in on herself. "I didn't help him," she whispered. "I know it—even if I can't remember everything."

I straightened to my full height, shielding her with my body.

Nyx smacked her lips together as she snored around my waist. *Helpful.*

"I've freed Ceres," I explained.

Patro looked over at Kharon and Augustus with incredulity. "And you two are *okay* with this?" Achilles glowered beside him.

Hot rage scorched my chest.

"It . . . *doesn't* matter what they think," I whispered. "She's innocent." *And suffering from trauma-induced memory loss.*

Patro laughed cruelly. "Well, if you're *so* sure, then let me touch her and see if she's telling the truth."

Ceres flinched back.

"Good idea," Augustus said.

"No w-way," I said. "She's traumatized."

Patro moved toward me and Ceres with predatory slowness.

I stepped forward, blocking his path.

The temperature between us plummeted, ice wafting off him as he halted before me.

We were almost eye level, and in the moonlight, his handsome features looked like they were carved from marble.

"Careful, Alex," he whispered. "You're playing a *dangerous* game." He flicked my nose before I could react, angry eyes glinting.

"Don't c-call me that," I said as Augustus shouted, "Get away from her!"

Kharon lunged for Patro. "Don't you *ever* fucking touch her again."

Achilles moved in front of Kharon, stopping him. They stood chest to chest, bristling, snarling at each other like animals—Augustus shoved himself between them and tried to force them apart.

Patro didn't seem to notice the commotion. He just kept staring at me, his eyes searching my face for answers—the scent of frost intensified—Poppae crouched, jaguar tail swishing back and forth with agitation.

It felt like I was back at Corfu.

Patro was mocking me again, *hindering* me.

"What are you d-doing?" I asked, the sound barely audible. "You don't even like me. Just leave me alone—let me make my own choices."

Patro smiled, and the effect was so breathtaking that it was deeply disturbing. "Are you . . . *sure* about that?" he asked softly.

He stepped closer into my personal space, our faces inches apart.

Goose bumps pebbled my arms.

"You chose *us* as your partners, *Alex*." Patro's voice deepened. "So let me and Achilles help you."

"I don't like that n-name," I whispered.

Dark memories played. *Alex, you stupid fucking bitch, I told you to stay outside where you belonged.*

"Isn't that too bad," Patro said, ice wafting off him. "We can't all get what we want . . . and when we do, we *don't* always like it." Emerald eyes flashed. "Yet here we are—Alex."

The temperature between us plummeted.

My heart raced. *Why does it feel like we're talking about something else?*

"Step aside and let me interrogate Ceres," Patro said coldly.

I lifted my chin. "No."

A muscle ticked in his jaw. "Alex," he said warningly.

"*No*," I repeated. "She's suffering from m-memory loss, her mind is broken—just leave her alone, *please*. She needs to heal."

"You think you would have learned by now *not* to fight me." He ran his tongue over his white teeth.

"Same," I said.

A few feet away, Kharon shouted something derogatory at Achilles, and Augustus struggled to separate them.

Patro's chest bumped against mine, the icy sensation spreading as he arched a dark brow mockingly. *He's such a dramatic bastard.* I planted two hands on his shoulders and shoved him back with everything I had.

Patro chuckled, unmoving.

"Careful, *mentee*," Patro whispered.

I dropped my hands and took a step back, fingertips frozen.

"Let Patro question Ceres!" Helen shouted.

Patro stepped out of my personal space, and I gasped. I hadn't realized I'd been holding my breath.

Everyone turned to Helen. *What is she doing?*

I backed further away from Patro.

"But—" Helen said slowly. "You can only ask her if she assisted Theros. Nothing else."

Patro stared at Helen for a long moment.

"Fine," Patro said.

"Only that q-question," I said. "Please. *Promise?*"

Patro tipped his head back, muttering a prayer to Kronos. When his eyes met mine, they were blazing.

"I promise, Alex."

Eye twitching at the nickname, I stepped aside.

Patro rolled his eyes as Ceres cowered, but he asked, "May I touch you?"

Ceres nodded quickly.

With surprising gentleness, Patro bent down to her level, placing his hand on her dirty shoulder.

The whites of his eyes filled with crimson. "Have you assisted Theros in *any* way?"

Ceres opened and shut her mouth, lips trembling, as she wheezed like she couldn't breathe.

Tears streamed down her dirt-streaked face.

Patro frowned. "*Answer* the question."

"No," Ceres croaked, the sound unnaturally scratchy; her vocal cords were ruined.

She turned her face away like she was trying to crawl into the marble wall and disappear.

For a long moment, Patro said nothing as he towered over her emaciated form—he dropped her arm and stepped away.

"She's not lying," he said reluctantly.

Helen and I sighed with relief.

Patro's eyes sharpened as he glared at me. "It *doesn't* mean she's innocent—some people are experts at deception. Maybe she hasn't assisted him. Maybe she was the *leader* of the entire operation? You can never tell—I want to question her. Extensively."

I stepped back in front of her. "You *promised*."

Patro clenched his fists. "Alex," he said, his jaw working like he wanted to say something else.

I held his gaze. "Leave."

Patro backed away from me and turned to Achilles, signing rapidly, "That bastard almost killed her, and this bitch probably helped—we can't let them free her. It's not safe."

I swallowed down the urge to argue.

Can't you see she's suffering? She's not a threat, you heartless bastard.

When the men had forcibly taken me and Charlie from Montana, back to Sparta, we'd agreed to hide that we knew sign language from the others so we could collect information. It felt safer that way.

It was getting harder to hide that we could communicate, but I was glad for our subterfuge, because it meant I could understand moments like this.

Achilles looked back and forth between me and Patro. "You promised her," he signed slowly. "If you want her to trust us, you can't change your mind."

Patro swore viciously. He rubbed at the back of his neck.

Wait, why do they suddenly care what I think?

"You questioned her. Can we all go to bed?" Helen whined. "I'm tired."

Augustus's face immediately twisted with concern. "This is settled for now. We can discuss it at dinner tomorrow. Everyone, go back to bed!"

Wow, she's good.

Patro turned slowly and stared at me, his eyes piercing.

I squirmed.

There was something different about the way he was looking at me, something *unsettling*.

Achilles glanced between us, tensing.

Is he angry?

Patro grabbed Achilles's arm. "You're all trusting fools—something is suspicious about her . . . I can *feel* it." He muttered something about Ceres being shorter than he remembered.

I swallowed a retort as they stalked away down the hall.

"Tomorrow morning," Augustus said, voice sharp with danger. "Be ready—*Alexis*."

He once again said my name like it was a threat.

Kharon's frigid eyes sharpened. "Good night, wife."

Helen and I flanked Ceres, holding her on either side and shielding her from the men with our bodies as we escorted her down the hall.

Augustus and Kharon didn't move as we passed; they both just watched.

By the time we made it to the bedroom next to Helen's—which shared a connecting door with hers—I was trying not to throw up from anxiety.

"Just rest for now," I whispered to Ceres as she tentatively crawled into the grand four-poster bed. "Shower in the morning. You need to heal."

Her panicked eyes met mine as she settled under the covers, quivering, covered in dirt and blood.

"I remember recent events," Ceres said shakily. "But the years before that, my childhood, it's all a blur. I need to remember where I came from. I need to know who I am . . . I need . . . I need . . ." She trailed off with a strangled gasp.

Her trauma was tangible.

"I can bring you Spartan books," Helen offered. "About our history, *your* history. It will help you . . . regain what you've lost."

For the first time, Ceres relaxed, her guard lowering. "Thank you," she whispered. "I like to read—it should help . . . I can't thank you both enough—what you've done is . . ." Her voice cracked as she trailed off, staring at me with tear-filled eyes.

"Of course," I said, even though apprehension twisted my stomach. I'd felt the fear and acted anyway.

So had Helen.

Eventually, the consequences would come for us. Until then, we'd bring Ceres whatever books she needed until she got her memory back.

Helen and I turned to leave.

"Wait! I recall . . . one thing," Ceres blurted.

We turned back to her.

Her lavender eyes were wide and haunted. "Zeus."

Talons of fear scraped down my spine. "What . . . about him?" I asked as a high-pitched ringing started in my left ear.

Ceres looked dejected. "I can't remember."

Helen and I backed away into her bedroom and closed the door. We crawled into her pink bed and turned onto our sides, facing away from each other.

Fraught silence stretched.

"You don't want to mess with Zeus."

It took me a second to process Helen's quiet voice.

"There's a reason," she said, "that the Great War was so fatal for Olympians *and* Chthonics. Have you ever wondered why no one talks about it?"

I dug my nails into the "C+A" tattooed on my forearm.

Everything about Sparta was convoluted.

"Three words," Helen whispered.

I squinted, confused what—

"Mutually assured destruction."

Paralysis stiffened my limbs. *Rigor mortis.*

Helen fell asleep first, whimpering and kicking under the

covers. When I finally joined her, I dreamed of a cloaked grim reaper watching me.

"Be careful, darling," Death whispered darkly into my ear, twirling one of my curls.

It's just a nightmare.

A mouth brushed softly against my forehead, lips warm and disturbingly real. The hair on the back of my neck stood on end.

The grim reaper stared down at me.

All night, he didn't move.

Death stood hunched over my side of the bed, staring without blinking, hovering inches from my face, his breath hot against my cheek.

Watching.

Mutually assured destruction played on a loop inside my head.

6

GUNS AND OTHER FOREPLAY

*ALEXIS: SIX DAYS UNTIL THE
FIRST TITAN ASSIGNMENT*

Nyx was a heavy, snoring scarf around my neck.

"Holy Kronos, I *can't* do this," Helen said as she sat on her bed, waving one of her bedazzled "emotional support" guns in the air.

Dragging my hands over my face, I closed my eyes and imagined Carl Gauss praising me for my work on the Riemann Hypothesis. Emmy Noether smiled as she looked over my calculations. Tension melted out of my shoulders at my heroes' approval.

"What in Kronos's land am I going to do with Ceres?" Helen wailed despondently. "What have we done?"

My eyes shot open—Carl and Emmy were dead.
Welcome to Hell.
"I did it, technically," I said. "Not you."
"We're *both* in so much trouble." Helen waved the gun at me.
At least everyone's staying calm.
I took a deep steadying breath.

Knock. Knock.

I jumped and Helen pointed the gun at the door.

"Alexis, we have to go right now before Augustus murders us!" Drex shouted from the hall.

Funny story, Drex, you're actually in more imminent danger than you think.

Helen stared up at me, face contorted with pure panic. She didn't lower the gun.

"It will be fine," I lied.

"We can do this," she lied back.

Nothing in life was more powerful than two women affirming each other's horrible life choices.

A few seconds later, I ran out into the hall.

Drex grabbed me. "We're supposed to meet in the villa's training complex right now. If we don't hurry, we'll be late."

"How far can it be?" I asked.

Our eyes widened with terror as we both realized I'd just cursed us. *Crap.*

We sprinted out of the villa into the rain.

Nyx sputtered on my neck. "Ughs—I'm melting." She slithered underneath my clothes.

Lightning flashed.

The electric fence towered thirty feet into the air. Small silver boxes protruded from its base. *Spartan solar-powered generators.* Sparks sizzled.

Drex pointed at a rock-colored hatch.

Fluffy Jr. pushed his wet nose against my leg. I glanced down at him. *What?*

He picked up a twig and held it in his mouth.

Don't you dare. I don't have time for this.

He choked it down.

Wagging his tail, his tongue lolled out of his mouth—it was covered in bark.

Drex opened the door, revealing a dark stairwell that led into the earth. My kidneys twinged with phantom pain—bomb shelters in Montana were infamously used to store harvested organs.

Drex grimaced. "Ladies first."

Fluffy Jr. sprinted down the dark creepy steps, tail wagging as he gagged.

I made the sign of the cross and followed him down.

Finally the dark stairwell opened up and I stumbled to a stop. Drex ran into me. "What is it—"

He gasped.

A cavernous concrete bunker bigger than multiple football fields spread out before us.

Flickering overhead lights covered everything in shades of green, as a chrome Spartan generator sputtered loudly in the corner.

Pockets of fake trees, mimicking a dense forest, were positioned around piles of junk cars, and a quarter of the room looked like an old movie set, crumbling brick buildings standing as tall as the trees.

It was a training course, designed to kill (literally).

Case in point, on closer inspection, the dotted pattern covering everything wasn't a design choice—they were bullet holes. *Oh nice.*

Five masked figures stepped forward from the fake trees.

Each of them held a short dagger.

White tank tops, white exercise pants, and white ski masks completed their ridiculous ensembles. If they were trying to disguise themselves, it didn't work.

Agatha crossed her arms, propping up her boobs, one of which was bigger than both of mine combined (a devastating observation).

Next to her, Poco sat on Augustus's shoulder, eating his long two-toned hair.

Kharon's skeleton tattoo stretched across his right arm, and gruesome chest scars peeked out from beneath the scoop of his tank.

At the other end of the line, Patro was wrapped possessively around Achilles.

He winked at me.

Does he have something in his eye?

Achilles only wore the top half of a mask; his lower face was covered by the muzzle.

They stared at us, creepily silent.

Drex shuffled closer to me as he cleared his throat. "So, what are we doing—"

"Pick up your weapons and strap on your holsters." Augustus pointed at the Spartan guns lying at the bottom of the steps. "NOW!"

We both jumped and obeyed.

"Oh—this is going to be *so* much fun," Nyx hissed (our ideas of fun were not the same).

"Here are the rules." Kharon stepped forward, a dagger swinging between his skeleton-tattooed fingers. "We hide . . . You shoot." He lazily stretched his arm. "Simple. Any questions?"

My mind blanked.

"Why are you all in white?" Drex asked as he glanced down at the plain black exercise togas we'd both been given to wear. "Why the dagger?"

Kharon spun his knife. "Your goal is to hit us—white will show the blood." He grinned evilly. "The knife is my Titan claws. *Boo.*"

"But . . . what if we hurt y-you?" Drex took a step back.

The Chthonics burst into laughter.

Augustus shook his head. "You won't hit us. That's *why* we're here . . . We have a lot to cover in only six days."

He smiled.

"This simulation is about shooting accuracy. When it comes

to Titans, a Spartan gun is your best defense. Your powers are secondary."

He lifted Poco up from his shoulder and gently placed him on the ground.

"Protectors head over there for safety." Augustus pointed to the dark alcove behind the stairs we'd come down.

Poco screeched and put his hands in the air like he wanted to be picked up.

Nero and Poppae trotted over obediently. Hell and Hound followed, their bony skeletons appearing every couple of steps.

In contrast, Fluffy Jr. jumped high, wildly throwing his back legs up into the air in a full donkey kick. Apparently, the motion got things moving—he hacked loudly and threw up a twig.

Everyone stared at it.

"I'll get that later," I mumbled (I wouldn't).

Nyx sighed as she slithered off my shoulders. "I'll go make sure the obese horse doesn't choke to death." I was both grateful and offended.

While Fluffy Jr. chased his tail (it was hard to watch), Augustus gave Poco a treat. He waved his cookie at me as he waddled past.

What a cutie patootie.

I waved back and he chittered while covering his crumb-covered face.

When all the animals were safe behind the stairs, Kharon pulled his mask up and held the hilt of his dagger between his teeth. He clapped loudly and everything plunged into darkness.

Drex and I both gasped with awe. *I thought clapper lights were just a myth.*

"This is a level-one simulation." Augustus's silky voice echoed strangely in the pitch-black. "We will not harm you—we are only using evasive maneuvers. This is to assess your shooting accuracy in the field."

"THREE," Kharon yelled abruptly, and lights flicked on in the floor, casting strange shadows across the room.

"TWO."

There was a loud hum and fog billowed out around us.

"ONE!" Kharon (Karen) cackled.

BOOM.

BOOM.

BOOM.

Explosions flared all around the course; the floor shook; fires raged in all directions; smoke mixed with fog.

All five Chthonics disappeared like ghosts.

There was a loud staticky noise as Titan screeches echoed over speakers.

Drex looked at me with panic. "These people are *actually* mental."

"Cults!" I yelled louder as the sound of machine guns popped. "I told you."

Another explosion rocked the room.

"Run—or I stab the boy." Breath blew against the shell of my ear. "Carissima, you better hunt us down. *Now.*"

Whirling around, I aimed, recoil vibrating through my arms as gunpowder burned my nose.

A tattooed hand with black painted nails waved mockingly ten feet away. "Come and get me," Kharon taunted.

He made a V with his fingers and held it up to his lips. He wiggled his tongue suggestively.

My face heated.

Pervert.

I lunged forward, firing at Kharon as he disappeared into the ruins.

What felt like hours later, but could have been minutes, Patro's voice rang out from behind a car that was on fire.

"Are you even trying, Alex?" Patro taunted.

"Don't call me that name." I raised my gun.

Patro moved in a blur into my blind spot, too quick to track.

He leaned a few feet away. "So—now that you've chosen us as partners, we should probably get to know each other."

I fired.

He chuckled.

The scent of ice filled my nose.

"Why are you d-doing this?" I whispered, feeling off-balance with his personality switch.

Emerald eyes were shockingly vivid behind his mask as he stepped in front of me.

"Doing what?" he taunted.

"You know."

He cocked his head to the side, mask gleaming in the firelight. "Know what?"

"Stop with the games!" I waved my gun.

"Grow up—Alex," he sneered. The cruel man who'd tormented me was back. "There's a lot at stake. Stop pretending you don't feel it too."

Wait? Feel what?

I fired, but he'd disappeared.

Time dragged on as I ran through the course.

Two rows of buildings, in what appeared to be a movie set, towered around me.

I walked the path between them, scanning the darkness.

White flashed.

A large shadow sat atop a building.

I pointed my gun at it.

Achilles kneeled on top of a structure, the first one in a row of ten. His burning eyes smoldered as he stared down at me silently—the muzzle obscured his features. A sharp dagger glinted in his hand.

I fired.

He leapt impossibly fast, crouching on a roof three buildings down.

I pulled the trigger as quickly as I could.

Achilles stood on top of the tenth building, hair escaping his man bun as he slowly shook his head like he was disappointed.

Annoyed and exhausted, I lifted my middle finger.

He lifted a square device, pressed a button—the building next to me exploded in flames.

Concrete chunks flew everywhere.

I was flung back.

Blinking into awareness, I slowly took in my surroundings.

My left ear was ringing painfully, and I was lying on the path under a pile of—I picked up a slab of the building and brought it close to my right eye—*Styrofoam* painted to look like concrete.

Rolling my eyes, I got to my feet and kicked the material away. Little white pieces drifted in the air around me like snow.

Heat warmed my face—the rest of the buildings were on fire.

A muzzle filled my vision.

I screamed.

Achilles loomed before me.

He cracked his neck like he was preparing to attack; Patro's name was tattooed down it.

Is he mad that Patro keeps talking to me? Everyone knew how possessive he was.

I stepped back, terror clawing at my lungs.

Achilles took a step forward.

Smoke billowed around him, the scent of fire and ash filling my nose.

He's going to attack me. No one's ever going to find my body.

Titan screams echoed over the speakers and another building exploded in a spray of Styrofoam and fire.

I turned and ran for my life.

An indeterminate amount of time later, I leaned against a metal pole in the fake forest and panted.

I couldn't hit any of the Chthonics. They were too fast.
Metal scraped.
I whirled around.
A white mask stood a foot away.
"Do you need water?" Augustus asked, his long black and white hair blowing in the fog, voice drifting in and out as my ear rang. "Are you feeling, okay? Please, let me know if you need—"
What a thoughtful, nice man.
I fired at his face.
Not.
Augustus moved in a flash.
He was gone.
Groaning, I resumed jogging around the course.
Heaving for air, vision blurry, lungs aching from exertion, I stared down at my gun and turned it so the gold WSDL flashed: *War, Sex, Death, Lies.*
"Make them fear you, daughter." Hades frowned down at me. "No one fears the weak."
These people were highly competent monsters.
Unlike them, I'd never been particularly adept at physical fitness. I was good at calculating obscure mathematical problems and writing scintillating (inappropriate) fan fiction. I was a true Renaissance woman.
Gunshots echoed.
A tall figure jumped down from above and landed silently in front of me.
Skeleton-tattooed fingers raised a knife.
It was pointed directly at my heart.
"It's like you're *not* even trying, carissima," Kharon drawled, his tone cruel.
My gun clattered to the ground.
Kharon grunted with surprise as he clutched at his stomach.
"You're supposed to shoot it—not *throw* it at me, darling." His eyes went cold. "Pick it up."

I raised my chin. "No."

Kharon held himself unnaturally still. "You have *three* seconds to pick up your weapon and apply yourself to the simulation that I spent hours creating just for you, or else . . ."

I scoffed.

"Three." His voice vibrated with violence.

Does he have a counting kink or something?

"Two."

My breath caught and I pressed my thighs together.

Wait . . . Do I?

I raised my arm up, opening my hand like a puppet. "*One*," I said, before he could, chuckling at my joke.

Icy fingers wrapped around my throat—he pushed me back until I was pressed against rough metal. He wasn't laughing.

Kharon squeezed the delicate pulse points of my neck as he held me against a fake tree.

In slow motion, his masked face moved to eye level.

He pressed harder and cut off oxygen to my brain.

Foreign thoughts filtered through my head, a mix of emotions and images in a confusing jumble.

Mine. She's mine. Need to claim her. Control her. Possess her. Own her. Destroy her. Taste her cunt. Tie her to me. Protect her. Punish her. Need to watch her submit to Augustus. Devour her.

Scarlet-filled eyes contrasted with the white of his mask.

I gasped.

Kharon was using his Chthonic powers—I could *hear* what he was feeling.

Blood rushed from my face.

He was more animalistic than I could have ever imagined. The level of obsession flowing from him was incomprehensible.

Karen was truly feral.

"If you don't take this seriously, shoot me." His fingers tightened mercilessly. "You won't sleep for a week—we'll hold you hostage in this training room."

"Physical . . . Nothing m-more," I whispered.

His feelings took a dark turn.

Kharon ripped himself away from me with a strangled sound.

"You're wrong." He pressed the gun into my palm.

Fuck you.

"No, I'm not." I aimed for his handsome face.

Kharon twisted to the side and dodged; the fake metal tree exploded where his head had been.

"Closer, baby," he taunted. His raspy laugh echoed, and it had a cruel brittle edge. "If it was just physical, I would have fucked and discarded you like I've done with dozens of other—"

Pop. Pop. Pop. Pop. Pop.

I fired, dread crawling up my throat at the mere thought of him with other people.

Kharon laughed louder as I stalked after him, fire, explosions, and Titan yells echoing all around.

Screaming, I followed him deeper into the darkness. It was where we both belonged.

"Alexis, where are you going?" Augustus's voice cracked like a whip.

To go drown myself in the shower. Obviously.

"Stop!"

I halted. Drex and Agatha disappeared into the bunker's locker room.

Slowly, I turned.

Kharon glared at me. "You're not dismissed, *darling*." He said the endearment like an expletive. "They get the showers first, and you get to explain yourself. Drex grazed one of us— you hit none."

Patro and Achilles stood beside them, both staring at me with angry expressions.

Wonderful, everyone's mad at Alexis. It's a party.

I flipped them all off in my head.

"Do you care to explain your performance?" Augustus asked slowly, the harsh planes of his face unmoving.

I didn't want to speak, so I didn't.

Kharon narrowed his eyes, and Augustus twitched like he was having an aneurysm.

Sure, I had the potential to be physically fit and athletically competent. The problem was, I didn't want to be. I enjoyed sitting. *A lot.*

Also, I was partially blind and deaf, so there was that.

"ANSWER ME!" Augustus bellowed.

"Don't speak to my mentee that way," Patro snapped as he crossed his arms over his chest. "We'll deal with her performance issues in private. She chose us after all."

I choked at the double entendre.

Kharon turned with a snarl. Achilles cracked his knuckles, *DEATH* tattooed across them.

"Do you people ever shut up?" I asked with a mumble, genuinely curious.

Kharon stilled. "What was that?"

I turned and walked away from all of them, collapsing on the bench outside the locker room to wait in peace.

Augustus followed and sat down on my left, in my blind spot.

I stared straight ahead.

Kharon chose that exact moment to aggressively shoot at a target across the training room. My bad ear rang with sharp feedback as a headache pounded in my temples.

"How come your aim is so off?" Augustus asked quietly.

I kept my expression blank. "No idea."

Augustus made a noise of disbelief, and the side of my face prickled under his intense gaze.

I glanced over.

His midnight eyes were narrowed with suspicion.

It felt like he was staring through me, straight into my soul. *He doesn't know about your eye and ear. Don't panic.*

Patro and Achilles were having a tense conversation at the edge of the metal forest. Achilles signed something about "Alexis, patience, trust" and "needing a plan."

Do men think they're subtle?

When Agatha and Drex finally emerged clean and in fresh clothes, all five of us awkwardly moved toward the showers.

Patro and Achilles glared at my husbands.

Kharon raised his gun.

"Careful," Augustus said darkly. "I'm still the eldest heir." His eyes filled with blood, and a few droplets dripped down his cheek, trailing across his scar.

Tension increased.

"Fine—" Patro spat after what felt like an eternity. "We'll wait . . . this time. But don't forget, she chose us." He smirked mockingly.

I made a face at him. *Stop antagonizing them.*

Achilles scowled.

Kharon elbowed Patro as he stomped over and shoved past him into the changing room. Augustus and I followed.

The room was smaller than I expected. About a dozen lockers filled with folded clothes faced a bench with towels.

The other side had a narrow hall with two shower stalls positioned across from each other.

I stared at them suspiciously.

Showers were a luxury I was still getting used to, but I was pretty sure they normally had doors—only the one on the left did.

Augustus saw where I was looking and explained, "It's because Hermos is a Gorgon. They're notoriously bizarre about their privacy. We added the door for him so he'd stop complaining about nudity."

It took a second for me to process that he thought the one *with* the door was the weird one.

Maybe the sirens are right, and I am a prude?

Kharon muttered about Hermos being ridiculous as he walked past me—butt-ass naked.

A small smear of blood contrasted with the pale, unblemished skin of his left thigh.

But his right leg was a patchwork of burns, welts, and ruined skin. The scars were different from the ones across his chest, but no less painful looking.

Kharon was a shocking amalgamation of fury, tattoos, and old wounds.

He stepped into the open stall and turned on the water.

His expression became guarded as he saw me looking at his leg, and he roughly grabbed bottles.

Guilt filled me, because I'd noticed his limp back in Corfu, but I hadn't thought much of it. I never could have imagined the awful extent of his injury.

Augustus sauntered past, also sans clothes, and I momentarily lost the ability to think. Black and white hair hung loose against his bronze skin.

His chest was unbranded, smooth with a light smattering of hair, but there was also blood streaked across his thigh, and silver glinted in the head of his thick penis.

Wait—what?

My gaze shot to his face.

Augustus arched a dark brow as he stepped into the shower beside Kharon.

God save me.

The drawings of genitalia on the Spartan Lifestyle Page were clearly fabricated because *none* of them had a piercing—I would have remembered.

Shaking my head, I ran into the stall that had a door and closed it tightly behind me.

Being the world's first introverted perverted prude is surprisingly exhausting.

I hastily stripped down.

The divinely hot spray almost made me forget about the two naked men an arm's reach away.

Almost.

"Are you okay in there?" Kharon crooned mockingly, an edge to his tone.

I shouldn't have stared at his leg. He was clearly self-conscious about it, even though, if anything, the scars made him more impressive.

"Is the shower up to your standards, *princess*?" Kharon called out, clearly trying to get a reaction out of me.

"Don't c-call me that." I furiously rubbed soap all over my sweaty skin.

"But it's true," Kharon said. "You're the *princess* of the great House of Hades."

"We know," I muttered under my breath. "It's why you married me."

The silence that followed was charged.

"That's not the only reason," Kharon said sharply.

I scoffed.

Kharon's pale feet appeared outside my door. "Alexis, you're being a *coward* hiding from—"

"And *you* only married me b-because of my heritage."

"I married you—" Kharon's tone was dangerous "—because when I saw you, I immediately wanted to *ruin* you . . . body and mind."

A primal part of my brain recoiled with horror.

Save yourself; get away from him.

"Is that what you wanted to hear?" Kharon asked harshly. "Does that make you feel better, princess?"

"No."

It really doesn't.

Turning off the water, I quickly wrapped myself in a towel and wrenched the door open.

"It's *not* just physical." Kharon bared his teeth as he glared down at me, his naked skin glistening with water.

If he was trying to look remorseful, he failed.

He looked cruel.

I pushed past him, my arm tingling where we touched as I grabbed the first training clothes I found in a locker and pulled them on. When I was fully dressed, I turned back to him.

Kharon had found pants.

I was a devastated woman (read: pervert).

"I admit the urge to stalk you is—" Kharon wet his lower lip "—unbearable."

I took a step back. What was someone supposed to say to that?

"When it comes to you, my desires are even . . . darker than usual." His voice was gravelly.

The queasy sensation returned.

Augustus stepped out of the shower in a cloud of steam with a towel slung low on his hips. "We both enjoy control," he said casually. "I tend to praise—while Kharon is more viciously inclined. One could say he's . . . cruel."

I choked.

WARNING: DANGER.

Red lights flashed in my mind.

Kill them and run before they can hurt you.

"Do you understand what we're saying?" Augustus asked, his voice velvet wrapped in steel.

Praise?

Cruel?

"Carissima," Kharon said with sinister gentleness. "Tell us that you understand." Tendons strained across his tattooed neck. "Now." He pinned me with his gaze.

My mouth went dry.

Shadows clung to Kharon's sculpted face as his expression

turned sinister. A vein bulged in his forehead as he pointed at me. "TELL ME RIGHT NOW THAT YOU—"

"I GET IT!" I yelled back, desperate for him to shut up.

Augustus stepped toward me. "Oh, Alexis," he whispered darkly. "I'm so glad you comprehend what's happening here. That's . . . my *good* girl."

Kharon seethed and Augustus smiled.

My nervous system shut down.

Acute full body paralysis, all systems failure.

There was no cure.

Never, in all of history, had a woman ever been so unequivocally screwed.

7

The Lover

Patro

Augustus and Kharon stepped out of the locker room, Alexis sandwiched between them with flushed cheeks and dilated pupils.

Chthonic crowns gleamed atop their heads.

Emotions choked me.

Alexis was *my* mentee.

I was the one who'd housed her, clothed her, and guided her through the crucible. She was my charge. I'd helped her first. I'd introduced her to Sparta.

The SGC was this August, only a few months away, and since Alexis was still technically our mentee, her performance would in some ways be a reflection of us. We should be the ones by her side, preparing her.

Sure, in the beginning we'd been slightly hostile, me especially. And yes, she was *nothing* compared to Achilles. But there was still something between us—a nascent spark—*potential energy*.

Alexis wiped at her face, flashing her hideously expensive diamond.

It was a kick to the teeth.

A reminder.

I was standing before three Spartan royals, and I was . . . nothing.

A nobody.

Heart hammering painfully in my throat, I tasted the past.

Patroclus, your human heritage makes you weak. Stop struggling. The Gorgons are going to fix you. They'll break the bitch out of you.

I was a spoiled human child, arrogant and haughty. Showered with toys and told I was superior because of my wealth and breeding.

Then Aphrodite came to collect me.

I was a tortured Spartan teen.

My fourteen-year-old self screamed inside my head.

He'd never stopped.

Torture makes the man was the infamous Gorgon tagline.

Sometimes I wondered if it would have been better to be born in rags because the fall would have hurt less. A pampered child doesn't suffer well. Better to be nothing all along, than to think you were a somebody and have it all ripped away.

Alexis made a noise, and I came to a halt—I'd been stalking toward her mindlessly.

Two-colored eyes narrowed as she tilted her head to the side like she recognized something in me that I didn't want her to see.

Shivers prickled down my spine. I felt sick.

Augustus slowly draped his arm over Alexis's shoulders. There was a warning on his face. He reeked of danger.

Kharon smirked beside them as he pulled on his black creature cloak. "The locker room is all yours, *honeys.*"

His familiar greeting was acid on the open wound that once was our friendship.

How far we'd fallen.

"*Fuck you,*" I mouthed.

Kharon bared his teeth and reached for his chest holster.

Achilles moved in front of me protectively, and Alexis frowned as she looked between the three of us.

Skin crawling with sweat, I shoved past all of them and threw open the door, eager to wash the filth of training away.

Kharon's taunting chuckles rang behind me.

Ripping off my clothes, I turned the shower up until it was scalding and scrubbed as hard as I could, digging the washcloth deep into my skin.

It wasn't enough.

The dirt remained.

When the past rose up to choke me, as it always inevitably did, the only thing that ever helped was cleanliness—it was my religion, the only piece of my spoiled self that I had left. I'd always been obsessed with feeling put together.

Grinding my teeth, I scrubbed harder, reaching for more soap.

It was basically empty.

With a desperate groan, I chucked the bottle onto the tile floor.

I raised my fist to the wall and swung—Achilles caught my wrist.

Vermillion eyes softened as smoke rose out from his muzzle, water spraying across our naked flesh.

He smelled like fire and rage, like *home*.

Knuckles cracked as he gripped me tighter—*DEATH* was in stark relief across them. I flexed my hand—*LIAR* stared back at me.

I tried to yank away.

Achilles slammed himself forward, pinning me against the shower wall with his body.

Our chests heaved together.

Eyes locked.

He raised his hands between us. "You're getting yourself all worked up," he signed angrily. "It's not worth it."

I laughed miserably, choking on disbelief and angst as water sputtered off my lips. "You said you wanted her too."

"I said," he signed, "that I cared and viewed her as ours . . . our mentee." His fingers moved slower. "I do, but you're falling apart. *You're* my priority. Not her."

"So, you're just giving up on us?" I scoffed, shoving against his wide, bronzed chest.

He flexed and leaned into my touch, his skin scorching hot.

"They're our brothers!" His fingers slashed perilously close to my face. "You're having nightmares about the Gorgons, you're barely eating, you're a mess—you need to stop this . . . before you get bad again."

Fiery despair exploded in my gut.

Stifling a sob, I pushed him back with all my might.

He banged against the shower wall, bronze skin heaving as he stared down at me.

Hands fisting, his tattooed cock stood erect against his chiseled abs.

The beast of the House of Ares was back.

He'd never really left. He just liked to pretend that he was someone else, someone nicer, someone with morals.

I clicked my tongue. "You're *so* predictable."

Achilles moved in a blur, pinning me with my back against the wall and my hands above my head, as hot water sprayed over both of us.

Reaching down with one hand, our gazes locked together—faces millimeters apart—he squeezed my aching cock. His touch tethered me to reality. The anguish abated.

I tipped my head back.

He stroked me expertly, hard and fast, then shallow and slow, just the way I liked. Our hearts pounded through our sternums; our chests were pressed flush against each other.

He released me abruptly.

I cried out, needing him close.

Eyes smoldering, he picked up the discarded soap bottle and turned it over. He banged it against his palm, then squeezed, veins standing out along his forearm.

Thick liquid slowly poured into his hand.

His hair was loose, plastered across his wide shoulders, and his muzzle dripped water. It smelled like something was burning.

Achilles arched his eyebrow.

He didn't have to speak; I knew exactly what he wanted.

Slowly, I turned around and widened my stance.

Wet hands trailed down my spine, his nails pricking lightly against my skin, as he caressed the sensitive skin at the top of my ass.

His hands drifted lower.

Soapy fingers danced across my hole.

I shivered, breath catching.

He slowly worked the digits into me, and I groaned with pleasure, widening my stance.

There was a pop as he pulled his fingers away.

His muzzle pressed against the side of my face as he leaned closer, blanketing me with his body. His breathing was ragged and loud against my ear.

He was so close, yet so far away.

Another wave of anguish washed over me.

"You said you wanted her too," I whispered, the leather of his muzzle digging into my cheek as he pressed against me from behind. "You're taking their side. You're abandoning me—"

Achilles wrapped his hand around my throat and squeezed, cutting off my words.

Familiar hardness pressed against my entrance.

Achilles thrust forward without warning, seating himself fully.

I bellowed, the fullness so intense it bordered on pain, as I stretched to accommodate his size.

He stilled.

We stood, locked together, breathing in tandem, drowning in heavy emotions.

His fingers loosened around my neck.

"We're going to have to marry someone because of that stupid law," I whispered hoarsely, trembling all over. "I don't want to marry some Olympian stranger." My voice cracked. "It will ruin what we have—"

Achilles's fingers tightened, so once again, I couldn't speak.

My head spun.

He expertly shifted his hips, pulling back at an angle as he thrust—I saw stars as he hit my prostate—his rhythm pinning me against the tiled wall, pleasure mounting.

Our hips slapped together, the sound wet and obscene.

He reached around and squeezed my cock.

I shuddered as I came, leaking all over his hand.

Achilles dragged his thumb against my sensitive head.

He brought it up to my mouth, rubbing it across my parted lips, then his hips flexed, hardness pulsing, as he also came. Leather creaked as he fought against the muzzle.

Slowly, his hand dropped away from my face.

He didn't pull away.

We stayed connected, pressed against the wall, drifting down from our pleasure, as the shower sprayed down on us.

Achilles massaged my shoulders.

I leaned my forehead against the wall and reached back to grab his thigh. My nails dug into his skin, eyes closing in the afterglow.

When he finally pulled himself out of me, he grabbed my hunched shoulders and turned me around, gently cradling me against his heaving chest.

His heart pounded thunderously against my ear.

"I don't know what to do," I whispered, tilting my head up to him. "She respects our love—what we have. I thought maybe . . ."

I trailed off, unable to verbalize my tangled thoughts as the scent of fire intensified. Any other person would want Achilles for themselves. They'd try to take him away from me. *He's the only family I have left.* He was all I had. There was no one else in my life who truly cared.

Achilles studied my face.

A part of me was already crumbling to pieces, my soul cracking at the thought of another person trying to ruin what we had.

There was a fire in his eyes—a promise—that *we* would be okay.

Tattooed fingers slashed through the hazy air.

I jolted.

His words hung in the air between us, explosive and slightly deranged.

"For you, my love—she'll be ours."

8

MEN WHO KNEEL

*ALEXIS: ZERO DAYS UNTIL THE
FIRST TITAN ASSIGNMENT*

Moonlight reflected off the still lake outside and filtered through the villa's windows.

I closed the bedroom door gently behind me and Nyx snored around my waist.

The week had passed in a blur of shooting simulations, but my aim had barely improved.

Today we were going into battle against Titans.

I would have been depressed, but since I also had to fight to the death in the SGC this summer, I felt nothing at all.

Fluffy Jr. crouched at my feet; Poco sat on his neck, holding his ears with tiny black fingers, like they were reins.

Wait, shouldn't he be with Augustus?

Shrugging, I moved down the gilded hall toward the atrium where we'd all agreed to meet. The predawn hour was fraught with anticipation.

Crack.

Smoke rose around a short figure in a green toga with long curly blond hair. Her shoulders slumped as she sighed with relief.

"I'm so glad I caught you, daughter," Persephone said as she stepped in front of me, a sleeping dragon on her shoulder.

Fluffy Jr. wagged his tail and Poco chittered a greeting.

"Hello, M-Mother." The word was unfamiliar and foreign in my throat.

What is she doing here?

Persephone opened her arms wide and waited, eyes glittering with tears. "I didn't want to burden you with . . . our heritage," she whispered. "The federation doesn't want you to know the truth—but I realize the burdens are already there."

I stepped into her embrace. Her warmth engulfed me as she held me tightly, rubbing my back. It felt right.

Her dragon shifted and its leathery wing poked the side of my face.

Persephone's power was a living, prickling thing, and she smelled like wet earth tinged with hunger.

I breathed in deeply.

"You have the blood of the House of Hades *and* the House of Demeter," she said into my curls. "Do you know what that means?"

I tried to reply, but there were no words inside of me.

"It means you're *my* daughter, and our power is . . . unique."

"Because of my grandfather—Iasion?" I whispered the name of the infamous dark creature who had sired her.

She squeezed me tighter and nodded.

Nyx grumbled about being crushed to death.

"It's why Demeter disowned me," she said quietly. "Why the federation exiled me, and why Hades had to take me in. Sparta prefers it when people fall into neat boxes."

She'd claimed the land on Crete. The earth itself had responded to her.

Persephone pulled back and looked at me, her eyes twinkling with something mischievous.

"Remember—" She leaned closer like she was letting me in on a secret. "It's *much* easier to wield power that is insignificant. If it's difficult to harness, that's how you know it's going to be good."

She winked, then glanced down at her watch with a sigh. "I have to leave. The federation can't know I'm here—be strong, my daughter."

Crack.

Persephone disappeared in a haze of smoke.

I stared at where she'd stood.

In a daze, I staggered forward through the villa. Nyx hissed as she slithered around my shoulders.

When I finally made it to the atrium, the sky outside the grand windows was a never-ending sea of stars. Their twinkling light reflected off the shadowy black marble floors.

Assembly of Death members were all getting ready, adjusting their weapons and buckling harnesses. Protectors sat next to them, half asleep.

Time had run out—the Titans were waiting.

Fluffy Jr. plopped down, belly up on the marble. His tongue lolled out of his mouth, as Poco lay next to his head, playing with his floppy ears.

Nyx hissed something in her sleep about murdering everyone.

Dragging my hands over my face, I calmed myself by humming a classical tune and mentally working through a differential geometry problem that would hopefully make Carl Gauss proud.

But he's not here and you're a soldier, not a scholar.

I sat down on the hard marble (collapsed from exhaustion that had nothing to do with sleep deprivation) and retied my combat boots.

A shadow fell over me and I looked up.

Augustus stared down, the harsh planes of his face even more severe than usual as he held out a black pager. "Press this button if you get into *any* trouble. We'll come immediately."

Before I could respond, he crouched in front of me with the device. It was similar to the pager General Cleandro had used to summon mentors during the crucible.

Augustus breathed out heavily as he knelt before me. Long sooty lashes surrounded eyes as black as a starless night—he was so close that I could make out every jagged edge of the scar that intersected his cheekbone.

I had a bizarre urge to run my fingers over it.

He tucked the pager into the pocket of my cargo pants.

I shivered.

"Please use this," he said. "Even if you're not sure but you feel threatened, use it . . . We'll be there." His hand lingered, fingers spanning across the top of my thigh.

Ozone and musk filled the air.

His hand flexed possessively across my leg and he leaned forward, until our faces were close.

"Alexis," he whispered as he pressed his forehead against mine.

I wanted to collapse into his arms and let him shield me from the world.

There was no doubt in my mind that he'd protect me. He'd always been vocal about women not having to fight. The idea of sitting back and relaxing while someone else handled everything was intoxicating.

But the world didn't work that way.

You had to save yourself.

Always.

"Please—promise me, Alexis." His baritone voice was smooth as silk, dark eyes flashing. "I hate that we can't be there to protect you—I *hate* . . . that you're fighting at all."

He clenched my thigh, nails digging through my cargo pants. "You should *not* be in the Assembly of Death. It's fucking ridiculous."

He didn't think I was made for this.

Neither did I.

Sometimes what we were made for was different from what we wanted. The lines were blurring, and I needed to remember.

Pulling my head back, I squared my shoulders.

"I can look after myself." I didn't stutter.

All traces of the gentle, caring man disappeared. If he'd ever existed to begin with.

His face was a dangerous mask. "Let's agree to disagree, *wife*."

The devil incarnate was here to see me off to battle.

Augustus pressed his forehead against mine and our breaths mingled. The gesture was wrathful.

"You *better* keep yourself fucking safe." His voice vibrated. "If you need to leap to safety, do it. Do you understand? Protect yourself at all costs . . . No one else matters. Only you."

Zap. Our bond fired.

"Take care of yourself," he said quietly. "Or there will be consequences, my carus."

It was a threat.

He pressed a gentle kiss to my forehead. His lips were featherlight—my skin burned, breath catching, as a fever spread through me.

"My precious wife—familia ante omnia." Augustus kissed my forehead again.

I leaned into his touch.

Family over all.

"I think I just fell in love," Nyx hissed dreamily.

He waited for my response.

Words bubbled up, but they died on my tongue. Augustus didn't pressure me to speak, instead he offered me his hand and he pulled me to my feet.

My fingers tingled where he held them.

"Alex will be fine with me." Patro's voice broke the trance we'd both fallen under as he sauntered over with his arm wrapped around Achilles.

The muzzled man was glaring at me. *Again.*

"Don't worry." Patro smirked as he adjusted the buckle on the back of Achilles's armpit harness. "She'll be completely safe with us—we're her mentors. Just like old times. When she used to live with us. You remember?"

Augustus straightened to his full height, looming above Patro. "Oh, I remember," he said. "How you called her spoiled and pathetic."

"People change." Patro yanked harder on Achilles's holster and repositioned a gun.

WSDL glinted on the handle.

War. Sex. Death. Lies.

It was all so disturbingly fitting.

Augustus's expression was cold as he focused on me. "They're young—they can't protect you. Remember to use the pager and leap to safety."

"Interesting," Patro sneered, a cruel edge to his voice, like he was going in for the kill. "I've never heard a complaint about the Crimson Duo's fighting ability before. We're not losers." He pointedly rubbed at his chest. "Unlike *your* partner."

"Here, put these on," Kharon said abruptly, breaking the tension.

I jumped.

He was standing in my blind spot, and I hadn't heard him approach. It was as if he'd been summoned. *Like Satan.*

Hell and Hound sat at his feet, shaking their bony tails, and Fluffy Jr. threw himself at the dogs in greeting, the three of them pouncing on each other (wrestling violently).

Patro turned, giving us his back.

Achilles rotated with him, but he looked back over his shoulder, eyes blazing as he glared at me.

What is his problem?

"Here." Kharon held out leather holsters filled with knives and guns for me to take.

I pointed to my already loaded chest and hip holsters.

"You need more," Kharon said, his tone leaving no room for argument. "Put them on now. Also, you need these handcuffs if you capture a Titan."

I opened my mouth to argue.

Patro had already told me not to worry about handcuffing any Titans because he and Achilles would handle it.

My jaw clicked shut, and I held out my hands for him to give them to me.

Kharon ignored my outstretched arms. He moved into my personal space, fastening the buckles around my waist and thighs, black nails flashing.

The scent of a rainstorm made it hard to think.

Augustus watched us both with a heated gaze.

When Kharon *finally* stepped away, I gasped for air like I'd been running.

"This is a little overkill." I was now a walking arsenal.

Pale features tensed, and for a second, Kharon reminded me of the grim reaper. The one I had nightmares about; the one that watched me sleep.

"*I'll* decide what's necessary for your protection," Kharon said. "You're the newbie and a woman. We've been soldiers for years."

"That's sexist," I said.

"Exactly." Kharon smirked and arched his brow, not even bothering to deny it.

I sputtered with outrage. He was such a walking red flag it wasn't even funny.

I shook my head. "You're horrible."

A sinful grin split his face. "Carissima—when have I *ever* said that I was a good man?"

Flushing with a heat that I refused to identify, I turned and walked away from him.

I moved around Agatha, who was in a full front split touching her face to her thigh, and stopped beside Drex.

"How do you feel about a suicide pact?" I asked casually. "Also, on a completely unrelated note, do you want a gun? I have extra."

Kharon said something muffled behind me (most likely derogatory), and Nyx hissed something in response (most likely sexual).

I fantasized about throwing her at him.

Drex chuckled, then his expression became deadly serious. "I'm in."

"Thank God."

Drex shuddered. "I am *not* feeling good about today. It's very—"

Crack.

A woman leapt into the atrium and Drex stopped talking as glittering red mist spread out and filled the room. It felt like a blanket of terror.

Arthritis (Artemis) was back.

"I'm here because Hades is indisposed," Artemis said coldly. "He and Ares are still tracking an abnormal Titan sighting in Australia."

"Agatha and Drex—there's been a sighting in the mountains of Canada." Artemis pulled a small piece of paper from her toga pocket and handed it to Agatha. "Here are your coordinates."

Artemis turned to face the rest of us.

Fear was sour on my tongue.

"Augustus, you and your partner are going to South America—we've tracked one into the Amazon." She handed another set of coordinates to Augustus.

Kharon's face went blank as she approached.

Artemis didn't glance at him, but her mist thickened and surrounded him, pulsing, like it was attacking. The scarlet avoided Augustus completely.

Kharon's expression was blank as he was engulfed.

She's tormenting him.

Artemis clapped her hands.

"Patro, Achilles, and . . . Hercules, I mean—Alexis." She looked at me suspiciously, like it was my fault that she wasn't sure what to call me.

"We changed your initial location. You three lucked out—you're now staying close," Artemis said flatly. "A Titan was just spotted in Rome."

She handed the coordinates to Achilles, who took them with a nod, but like Augustus, the mist didn't surround him. He was untouched by her power.

Is Artemis afraid of the children of the House of Ares?

Why?

Patro furrowed his brow. "Are you sure it was *within* the city—inside the protected zone?" He scoffed with disbelief.

Artemis's face twisted with malice. "Yes." Her brown hair stood on end with power. "As you've been told, there's been a change in their behavior. That's what Hades and Ares are investigating. You *will* handle this."

Patro bowed low. "Of course."

Artemis ignored him. She reached into her pocket and pulled out what looked like multicolored tags. "One more thing." She walked around the atrium handing them out. "The federation has passed a new decree for us to follow—going forward, whenever you capture a Titan, you have to tag it."

The gold tags were cool and heavy between my prickling fingers.

I looked at one. "Hercules, House of Hades" was engraved in black on one side, and on the back, there was a thick pin.

"Once you have your Titan cuffed, put this tag through their lower lip. That way it's easily identifiable who captured them."

I put the tags in one of my cargo pockets. *No way am I doing that.*

"Good luck, soldiers," Artemis said, her voice emotionless. "Because of Medusa, the federation is watching all of us closely. *Don't* return until you've captured your Titan."

Everyone nodded.

"Medusa has ruined our plans to surprise the Olympians. War is already escalating. These are dark times for Chthonics . . . Beware."

I struggled to inhale.

Artemis bared her teeth. "May Kronos bless your hunt. Crush your enemies . . . or you better die trying."

Crack.

Artemis leapt away.

Smoke swirled around the atrium as the glittering scarlet disappeared, but this time the terror remained.

9

POISONED TONGUES

ALEXIS

"Don't worry, just stay behind us. We'll take the lead and handle this because it's your first mission." Patro winked. "Just observe and learn."

Oh great, men making all the important decisions.

I was worried.

Steeling my nerves, I focused on staying calm as we crept down the street.

The late May morning air was crisp.

Achilles led the three of us through a narrow alley on the outskirts of Rome, eyes narrowed with concentration as he stalked silently, checking around corners before waving us forward.

Nero walked at his heels, Fluffy Jr. whined beside me, and Poppae slunk after the three of us quietly, ears back, long tail low. Nyx was quiet on my shoulders.

Dawn was slowly creeping over the horizon—the sky was streaked with orange rays and bricks glistened with morning dew—but the city was deathly quiet.

It wasn't sleeping.

Rome's population had been decimated by Titan attacks decades earlier, and like the rest of the world, it had never recovered.

Ancient architecture crumbled next to the ruins of modern buildings.

Past and present were both dilapidated.

Something feels sinister.

There was an energy in Rome that I'd never felt in an empty Montana field.

Faded maroon handprints streaked across doors, bones poked out from beneath piles of bricks. Human teeth dotted the path as we moved through the ruins.

Death had visited.

You could taste the tragedy in the air.

"If Titans are within this p-protected zone," I whispered to Patro as we stopped at the end of yet another alley and Achilles looked around the corner, "shouldn't we be able to locate them? Aren't they . . . loud?"

Patro shrugged, looking completely unconcerned.

"Titans haven't been inside a protected zone in years," he said. "I'm not convinced that Artemis didn't have faulty intel."

I rubbed at the golden cuff that covered my scarred wrist. "And if she was r-right?"

Patro waved his hand in the air. "Don't worry so much—we've done this thousands of times." His tone was patronizing and dismissive.

Hot rage filled my chest.

Patro paused when he saw my face. "Sometimes Titans don't always announce themselves," he sighed. "Some of them move quietly. Every Titan is not the same—it's not that deep. Stop panicking."

My jaw hurt from how tightly I was clenching my teeth.

I'm not.

Achilles turned his head, watching us with an inscrutable expression.

Another burning stick protruded from the grates of his muzzle, and the veins in his neck popped, like he was clenching his jaw.

Patro smacked me on the back, and I jumped.

He laughed. "Buck up, Alex. We're not gonna let anything happen to you. Just follow our lead and relax."

I turned to him. "Don't call me that."

Patro didn't respond as we followed Achilles through the city's side streets toward the Roman Colosseum, the ancient Spartan structure towering over the ruins of modernity.

Crash.

I stumbled over a pile of bricks and . . . I blanched—*human bones.*

Patro reached out and steadied me, his hand wrapping around my forearm. "There's something I need to tell you," he said quietly as we stood, eye to eye. "I've been wanting to discuss it with you."

Achilles turned around and shook his head at him.

Ice wafted off Patro while Achilles reeked of fire. The two dichotomous scents created a toxic combination.

"Why are they acting so weird?" Nyx hissed as she slithered around my neck.

Did they bring me out here to kill me?

Were the Titans all a ploy?

I yanked my arm out of Patro's grip and took a step back.

Nyx tensed like she was getting ready to strike.

Patro sighed heavily, his cocky demeanor gone as he reached into Achilles's pocket, pulled out a cigarette, and lit it. Exhaling a cloud of smoke, he looked at me expectantly. "Aren't you going to lecture us on the dangers of smoking?"

I held his gaze. "No."

These were dark times. If he wanted lung cancer, then that was his prerogative.

"We wanted to tell you." Patro cleared his throat again, smoke streaming out of his nose. "Both of us . . . wanted to tell you this for a while now—but we've had to wait to get you alone so . . ."

He trailed off, glancing at Achilles.

We're going to harvest your spleen and trade it on the black market, I mentally finished.

The first thing they taught us in high school was to always be wary of people who tried to befriend you.

Every year we had an assembly on S.O.R.E., *Snatching Organ Resistance Education.* We all signed a pledge to not sell our body parts to anyone but the government.

It was a tad confusing what their message was.

A bird (government drone) screeched above while Achilles glared at Patro like he was trying to set him on fire with his eyes.

Patro pushed his shoulders back and turned to me.

"Penance," he blurted. "As your mentors."

What?

Achilles shook his head like he was angry.

"We want to make it up to you—how we acted during the crucible," Patro said slowly. "We think the best way to help you is to . . ."

Achilles stepped toward him like he was going to physically intervene.

"Help sever your marriage bond," Patro finished in a rush.

Nyx gasped, and Fluffy Jr. moved in front of me.

I took a shaky step back. *This is about Augustus and Kharon?*

Fluffy Jr. moved in front of me, crouching low and hackles raised.

Patro stared at me—the man who'd spent the past year *laughing* with Kharon as he called me spoiled and pathetic. He narrowed his eyes. "Your marriage is making you miserable."

No, my entire life is making me miserable.

There was a difference.

He rubbed roughly at his jaw. "We've been researching marriage bonds for you." He looked at Achilles as he spoke. "We think there's a way you can break the Spartan oath and effectively . . . divorce them."

The morning haze swirled, leaving a dense fog along the ruined streets.

"What?" I croaked. My mouth was dry, tongue heavy, heart full of lead.

Patro stared harder at Achilles. "From what we understand, if you use your . . . blood powers, then you can . . ."

He trailed off like he was physically unable to say the words.

"I can . . . *what?*"

Patro's eyes glinted like uncut emeralds. "If you bring them to the brink of death, it will break your oath."

Sludge filled my veins.

"You want me to . . . *kill* Kharon and Augustus," I said, feeling faint. "You want me to murder your friends." I pointed to them. "Kill your *brothers*."

Achilles flinched like I'd struck him.

Patro huffed. "Don't be so dramatic. You don't *actually* kill them—just bring them to the brink." He snapped his fingers. "They're strong, they'll recover. Then . . . you'll be free."

I'll never be free.

I could taste the vengeance; I could taste the regret.

Dragging my hands down my face, I pressed my palms into my eyes and tried to stop the racing thoughts. When I finally lifted my head, Patro and Achilles were staring at me expectantly, waiting for an answer.

Aren't we supposed to be fighting Titans? Why would they do this now?

My vision tunneled.

"Why?" I asked as I stared at my mentors like I'd never seen them before.

Patro flicked his cigarette onto cracked pavement and stomped on it. "Because—what they did to you was wrong." He made a face, like he was trying to convey that he was sympathetic to my plight.

He failed.

Numbness washed over me.

Patro fidgeted.

I wish I had his power.

"So, there's . . . no other r-reason?"

Patro rubbed the back of his neck, eyes darting to Achilles. "No."

He was a crap liar. *How ironic.*

The sneaking suspicion became an avalanche, and I'd already played the fool.

"You're both under twenty-six," I whispered. "Right?"

Nyx hissed.

My face twisted. I let them see the angst, the sleepless nights, the dark choices I'd made—two times over.

They had no idea who I was.

Not anymore.

Achilles stepped toward Patro protectively.

"I bet you're looking for a wife," I said. "Someone Chthonic."

Patro's eyes widened as he donned a fake mask of surprise. "What? Alex, that has nothing to do with—"

"Stop calling me that name!" I shouted.

Patro's jaw slammed shut.

His handsome face contorted back into a sneer of hatred, the one I was used to—the one that fit him.

"Just, what the fuck are you trying to insinuate?" he asked.

"*I'm* not insinuating anything."

Achilles stepped closer to him like he was offering him strength.

Two versus one.

It always was with them.

"This is *not* just about us wanting to marry a Chthonic." Patro crossed his arms. "We aren't like *them* . . . We were actually worried about you. Forget I said anything—enjoy your wedded fucking bliss."

I smiled slowly. "So, what else is it really about—if it isn't *just* about me being Chthonic?"

Patro froze as he realized his slip, but he recovered quickly, his face hardening. He was carved from marble and cruelty, just another dangerously attractive member of the House of Aphrodite.

"I'm *sure* Kharon's a real gentle lover," Patro said quietly as he stepped closer. "I'm sure he holds you and whispers sweet nothings after he fucks you. Everyone knows about his more *vicious* sexual tastes. I'm sure you're not *scared* at all—little girl."

We stood face-to-face.

"Go fuck yourself," I whispered.

Patro laughed, the sound loud and manic.

Achilles grabbed his bicep and wrenched him back. "Shut the fuck up," he signed in big slashing motions. "What are you doing? You're ruining everything."

"Careful." I walked around Achilles so I was once again in Patro's face. "You almost sound . . . *jealous*. Do you wish Kharon could have chosen you?"

Patro recoiled.

"Yesss," Nyx hissed encouragingly. "Ruin him. Men don't deserve to feel good about themselves. Make him cry."

Patro ripped his arm out of Achilles's grasp and lunged at me.

I held my ground.

Achilles grabbed him again, stopping him a few inches from my face.

"Aw," I taunted, pursing my lips and channeling my high school bully Jessica. "Do you wish you two could have *married* him? Is that what this is about? Are you mad Kharon chose a *pathetic* girl over you?"

"Fuck you," Patro spat. "You don't know *anything* about Sparta. You're playing a game you can't win. Augustus and Kharon will *never* care for someone as weak as you. Two dominant, *powerful* men like them. You'll always mean nothing to them. You're just pathetic."

The ice inside me became stone.

I'd forgotten how it felt when Patro taunted me, how my heart dropped as he'd mocked me for eating too fast.

How he'd always called me pathetic.

I remembered.

"Shut up," Achilles signed angrily at Patro. "You're losing control and ruining everything. This isn't what *you* wanted. I told you—you should have waited to talk to her at a better time. This isn't at all what you were supposed to say."

My sternum boiled with rage.

"*Please* enlighten me," I said smoothly. "What was his script?"

They froze, their eyes widening as they stared at my hands.

Achilles raised his arms, long fingers moving slowly. "Alexis, how *long* . . . have you known Roman Sign Language?"

10
SIGN LANGUAGE

ALEXIS

My arms dropped to my sides.

In my anger, I'd resorted to old habits and signed as I spoke.

"How long have you known sign language?" Achilles repeated, eyes narrowed with rage as he took a step toward me while signing. "How long? Tell me now!"

My fingers moved quickly. "Since I was a child."

Achilles's chest heaved as smoke billowed around his muzzle. He cracked his tattooed knuckles—one finger at a time.

I'd never seen him so furious.

"Why didn't you tell me?" he signed, his eyes full of heavy emotions.

I raised my chin up and held his gaze, tired of Chthonic men shoving me around. "Because—I was afraid of you."

Achilles reared back like he'd been punched.

"You entitled bitch." Patro reached for my wrist, and once again, his grip was punishing. "How *dare* you say that to him—after everything we've done for you? Everything we've sacrificed."

Achilles had paled behind his muzzle, and he looked sickly.

"You've done *nothing*," I whispered.

Patro's lips curled as he shook my wrist. "We took you in. Clothed you, fed you, helped you survive the crucible. Put up with all your weak woman *powerless* Olympian bullshit."

His eyes filled with blood as he engaged his Chthonic powers, fingers digging into the sensitive skin of my wrist.

"No. You m-made me feel worthless," I said softly. "You made me want to die."

Patro dropped my arm like I'd scalded him. He staggered back, disengaging his powers.

From his reaction, it was the truth.

For the first time since I'd met him, Patro had nothing to say.

The Crimson Duo stared at me, guarded and hostile.

Turning away from them, I stomped from the narrow street into what looked like a dilapidated town center. Fluffy Jr. trotted beside me, an oversized white blur as tears spilled down my face.

"Don't cry, kid," Nyx hissed, her tongue flicking against my cheek. "I could kill them with one bite. Give me five seconds, and they're dead."

Swallowing a sob, wishing I could argue without crying, I rubbed furiously at my eyes.

"Don't kill them," I said miserably as I jogged forward blindly.

Nyx clicked her teeth.

"Not yet."

Nyx hissed proudly. "That's my girl."

I clutched at her dry, smooth scales.

"It's them," a young voice rang out, echoing off the ruins.

Twenty feet away, three young boys were pointing at me with tattered book bags slung over their shoulders.

Rome wasn't as dead as it appeared.

They gasped as they looked at something behind me.

I turned.

Achilles and Patro approached, their faces hard, as Poppae and Nero slunk low beside them.

"Holy crap, it really is the Crimson Duo!" one boy yelled, practically bouncing with hero worship.

"I want to be you when I grow up," another shouted. "I love your muzzle!"

Patro laughed, a forced rusty sound. "Stay in school."

The boys tittered and sprinted away to tell their friends.

I pivoted away and stomped down a different city street. Cars were overturned on either side and a tree grew smack dab in the center of the lane.

Patro huffed behind me, but didn't say anything.

I was over Chthonic men.

From what I could tell, they were all emotionally stunted. I'd met organ snatchers who were more well-adjusted than them (there were some good, hardworking harvesters out there).

Now, as the three of us marched in stony silence, my mind turned to thoughts I shouldn't dwell on—*poisonous blood and fractured marriage bonds.*

The silence between us grew more strained.

After an hour of walking through the mostly quiet city, we'd seen about a dozen people and nothing else.

There were no signs of monsters.

We'd gone in a giant circle.

Artemis must have had faulty intel. There are no—

Shadows moved in my blind spot. I whipped my head.

Air whooshed.

Thud.

A figure had dropped down from the top of a four-story building and landed in the street directly in front of me, a few feet away.

Thud.

A second figure landed beside it.

The fog cleared—both stood up to their full, grotesque heights.

Screeeeeech.

The birds went dead silent.

I froze mid-step.

Oh.

My.

God.

Two Titans—*with wings*—stood framed by the Roman Colosseum in the background, its ancient facade towering high above the crumbling modern street.

The scene was haunting like an oil on canvas by the artist Alexandre Cabanel.

Fog thickened, swirling between us in an eerie haze. *Since when did Titans have fucking wings?*

Ten feet separated us.

"Holy . . . *fuck*," Nyx hissed as she reared back on my neck.

I could feel Carl Gauss's ghostly presence—we'd be meeting soon.

The Titans tilted their heads down, zeroing in on me, an amalgamation of hollowed corpse-like features, bulging black veins, and sharp talons.

Fluffy Jr. whimpered.

I slowly took a step back.

Each Titan had a twenty-foot wingspan.

The leathery appendages were a patchwork of mismatched puckered flesh that appeared to be sewn together—the seams where skin connected were swollen, oozing with infection.

Mary Shelley herself couldn't have dreamed them up.

"I'm going to be sick," Nyx hissed.

The Titans smiled in sync, too-wide mouths crowded

with razor-sharp teeth, black blood pooling in their unblinking eyes.

Fluffy Jr. crouched in front of me, growling protectively, teeth bared as he tensed.

They both lunged for me.

I couldn't move.

Ghastly black talons approached, air whistling as they swiped for me and—

Poppoppopopopopopopopopopopopopopop.

Hot liquid splattered across my face.

In slow motion, I brought my fingers to my wet cheek as the Titans were flung backward through the air by bullets.

Blood covered my hand—it was black.

Achilles and Patro stalked forward, smoking guns raised, gunfire spraying.

My left ear rang with sharp feedback.

In a blur, the Crimson Duo dropped empty cartridges, reloaded, and kept firing.

Shakily, I made the sign of the cross.

Even though I walk through the valley of the shadow of death, I will fear no evil, for You are with me; Your rod and Your staff, they comfort me.

Poppae and Nero leapt forward, snapping at the downed Titans as the monsters crawled backward in the assail of bullets.

Amen.

Gunpowder mixed with the putrid scent of gore.

Fluffy Jr. stood in front of me growling protectively. His head swiveled back to me, like he wasn't sure what he should do.

My feet were rooted to the spot.

One Titan stopped crawling. It stood up and straightened to its full height, bullets clattering to the pavement as its body healed and expelled them at a terrifying rate.

Achilles shot at it with two guns, one in each hand.

Ligaments popped as the shadowy wings spread up from the Titan's back—it leaned forward and let out an *unholy* screech.

Gnarled wings flapped and the Titan shot forward with impossible speed.

There was no time to react.

Thud.

The monster rammed into a body.

Patro sailed through the air, slamming into the wall of a townhome—his head cracked loudly and debris crumbled around him. His neck was turned at an unnatural angle, and crimson painted the bricks behind his skull.

He lay collapsed in the rubble, unmoving.

Achilles's eyes widened with horror.

The Titan who'd rammed Patro stood in the middle of the street—and was now focused on me.

Achilles was between me and the Titan, smoke rising around his head, staring at Patro with his weapons lowered.

With shaking fingers, I unholstered my Spartan guns.

Long, tension-filled seconds stretched, seemingly endless.

The other Titan joined its brethren. The monsters stood side by side, both once again focused on me.

Aren't they solitary hunters?

Achilles took a step toward Patro.

The Titans screeched.

Turning, I pivoted on my heels, and in my peripheral vision, Achilles sprinted toward Patro.

I ran down the street in the opposite direction.

"FASTER!" Nyx screamed in my ear.

Gunshots echoed.

I glanced back—Achilles knelt over Patro, shooting at their retreating forms.

It was too little, too late.

The Titans were headed for me.

Achilles threw down his weapons, then lifted Patro's limp body and met my gaze—his eyes were aflame.

Crack.

They leapt away.

There was a whooshing sound as the Titans shot straight into the air and took flight—a scream ripped from my throat.

I was alone with monsters.

Again.

11

THE DRAGON

ACHILLES: ONE MINUTE EARLIER

Fyodor Dostoevsky once said, "Above all, don't lie to yourself."
Did he know what this moment feels like?

He couldn't have.

Only Kronos himself could understand the terror ripping through my chest.

In the middle of a decrepit city street, Titans with wings—*when did that happen?*—stalked past me as the man who owned my soul lay broken and bleeding, his neck bent at an unnatural angle.

For the smallest second, I glanced away from Patro.

Alexis, the girl we were supposed to protect, was staring at me with a resigned heaviness reserved for Sisyphus himself.

There was no hope in her two-colored eyes, just acceptance.

My psyche was disintegrating.

I turned back to Patro, unable to look anywhere but at his ruined body.

Leather chafed against my jaw as I tried to open my mouth

and scream. My jaw cracked as the material refused to budge. The fucking muzzle had enough give so I could eat or smoke, but not enough that I could unleash my powers. If I could use my Kronos-given talent, the Titans would be handled. *Easily.*

But the federation had neutered me.

They'd damned me to this misery.

I'd never regretted anything more than taking the Spartan oath not to take it off. Oaths, like protector bonds, were forever.

A lifetime of imprisonment in the Underworld would have been preferable to this torment.

Seconds were bleeding out around me.

There wasn't time.

Patro's chest wasn't moving.

Spartans could survive extreme physical damage, but we weren't invincible. If his spinal cord was severed, lungs punctured, blood pooling internally, he could fall into a perpetual coma.

If Patro perished, so would I, as I refused to exist in a world that didn't have him in it.

He was the reason I woke up, the reason I bothered to breathe, the source of any joy I'd ever found in this miserable wasteland of a civilization. He *was* my beating heart.

Time seemed to slow.

Both Titans paused mid-step.

Alexis's curls stilled around her face.

Falling bricks hung suspended in the air above Patro's body.

Everything funneled down to this moment as my thoughts raced.

Patro was obsessed with claiming Alexis; the girl standing in the middle of the street in imminent danger. She'd lived with us for months—she *fit*—she didn't disrupt the obsession, the devotion we had for each other. He thought she could become more to us, and he just wanted a chance for us to have the happy ending Sparta didn't want us to have.

But Augustus and Kharon were unyielding.

And they'd claimed her first.

Now Patro was having nightmares again. He was unraveling, and I couldn't help him. I couldn't give him what he wanted—her.

My madness was rising in response.

Dark possessive *inclinations* pounded through my soul. The urge to lock Patro away and keep him safe from all harm was becoming harder to ignore.

The passion—the possessive *rage* of the House of Ares—seethed inside of me, day and night. I tried to hide the feelings, but they wouldn't stay buried.

How Augustus maintained his facade was beyond me. To the world, he was calm, stoic.

I still remembered how Augustus had sobbed, spit falling from his lips, tears dripping from his eyes, as he screamed in agony while Ares slashed his face with a poisoned Vulcan blade, the metal forged to scar immortals.

Growing up, Augustus could never hide his madness.

I was made in his shadow, and I followed his example.

But somewhere along the way, Augustus started hiding his wrath, and I stopped being able to contain mine.

Now I had a decision to make. Patro would want me to help Alexis, he was convinced she was our salvation. I cared for her; I did.

Do not lie to yourself.

What I felt for Patro was unfathomable.

Maybe in the future I could care enough for Alexis, but not now.

There was no choice. Not if I was an honest man.

The Titans screeched, heads turning, as everything snapped back into motion.

I sprinted, kneeling over Patro protectively as I fired at the Titans.

You're losing time. Stop pretending.

I threw the weapons down with disgust.

As gently as possible, I picked up Patro's ruined body.

Alexis was running away, glancing back over her shoulder.

I expected tears, a look of betrayal.

Her expression was blank.

The acceptance on her face was worse than anything I could have ever imagined. She understood—she saw my ruined soul better than I did.

She was running for her life, abandoned by the mentors who were supposed to shield her from harm, but she was strong, she'd be fine.

You're a dishonest man.

It was an unadulterated lie.

Domus.

I was so powerful I didn't need to say the word aloud to leap away.

Rome disappeared, replaced with sterile white walls and medical equipment covered in the symbol of Spartan healing, a staff with wings—the Rod of Asclepius.

Tenderly, I laid Patro down on a gurney.

Alexis had just learned the harshest truth of all.

Agony had a second name—*Chthonic.*

Either we were the loneliest beings on earth, or we loved obsessively, with our entire soul.

Complete devotion or *nothing.*

There was no in-between.

Dostoevsky was wrong; it was not the liar who suffered, but the man who accepted the truth. No one else could know such damnation.

Olympian doctors swarmed around Patro, and I fell to my knees beside his hospital bed.

Head bowed. Hands clasped together. Tears streamed down my muzzle as I prayed to Kronos for the life of the man who owned my soul.

And the woman I'd left behind.

12
Fighting to the Death, and Other Womanly Pursuits

Alexis

Sprinting, I veered left down a narrow opening between buildings.

Titans were on my heels, and guns were clutched in my hands.

I should leap away, but then Augustus would be right that I needed men to look after me.

These days, all I had was spite.

I'm a strong independent woman.

I jumped over rubble and skeletons. Stumbling, scraping against jagged bricks, I righted myself and ran faster down the alley.

The Titans screeched above, flapping gruesome wings.

Actually, I feel like men should be handling this.

"Move!" Nyx hissed with panic as her scales slid like she was looking up. "*Faster.*"

I skidded out from the safety of the alley. Arms pumping, I headed straight for the sheltered walls of the Colosseum.

A boom echoed and the ground shook.

Both Titans slammed down into the grass park that surrounded the ancient structure, directly in front of my path.

Their tattered wings slowly folded in.

What a nice day to die.

Stumbling back, I raised my weapons.

They stalked forward in a slow approach. Fluffy Jr. barked, the sound loud and harsh, as he once again stood in front of me defensively.

I unclicked the safeties.

"You need to get out of here," Nyx hissed. "Right now."

I nodded in agreement.

A light flashed brightly and a camera clicked.

Both Titans stopped moving, their heads tilted to the side—they focused on something off to my left. In tandem, they opened their mouths, razor teeth glinting. Saliva oozed as they licked their mangled lips with long black tongues.

I mentally focused on leaping to a safe destination.

"Dom—"

Someone whimpered.

I turned my head, heart dropping—I'd missed them in my blind spot.

A group of a dozen elderly men and women were frozen with horror, seated at concrete chess tables set up in the grassy park. One of them lowered a camera.

The Titans were zeroed in on the people, their intentions clear.

"Leap away, Alexis!" Nyx shouted. "Go—save yourself while you still can!"

I tipped my head back.

"Were the human casualties avoidable?" Persephone whispered in my ear.

I raised my guns and fired.

Bullets peppered the Titans' flesh; they shrieked, but their attention remained locked on the group of people.

Arms wide, I jumped in front of the humans protectively.

"Pater noster, qui es in caelis," someone cried out in Latin. *Our Father, who art in Heaven.*

The Titans prowled toward me, talons extended, mouths open.

Amen.

I raised both guns and kept firing.

Poppopopopopop.

Some bullets hit, some missed, but the monsters kept advancing, slow and steady. They were toying with their prey.

Ten feet away.

Poppopopopopop.

Five feet.

Poppopopopopop.

Two feet.

Poppop—Click. Click.

A ferocious growl echoed as Fluffy Jr. leapt forward, slamming into one of the Titans. The beast tried to shake him off, but my protector held on, his teeth locked around its throat.

It crumpled to the ground—Fluffy Jr. had ripped out its throat.

Jerkily, I reloaded both guns, raised my arms, and fired at the second screeching Titan.

In a blur of white fluff, Fluffy Jr. launched himself at the remaining Titan, but it was quicker, raising its forearm. He bit down on its arm.

I lowered my guns, unable to get a clear shot.

"Adveniat regnum tuum, fiat voluntas tua," chanted frantically behind me. *Thy kingdom come, Thy will be done.*

Sobs became wails.

"Genuine question," Nyx hissed. "Are we trying to die? Because if not, we should be *running* away right now!"

"I just need a plan," I whispered.

Gritting my teeth, sweat burning my eyes, I bounced back and forth on my toes as the Titan spun, trying to dislodge my protector.

My thoughts raced desperately—*a times x squared plus b times x plus c equals zero.*

New plan: never think again.

Reciting the quadratic equation was not helping anyone.

I threw my guns down because the weapons were barely doing anything.

Try visualizing your success—a dead Titan morphed into the triangular function graph of Collatz conjecture.

I grabbed the hilts of the long daggers strapped to my thighs—the pair Kharon had insisted I wear—and pulled them both free.

All I had was poisonous blood and an unhealthy amount of theoretical math knowledge.

So be it.

I pointed both daggers at the Titan that was still on its feet, trying to shake off Fluffy Jr., and careening closer.

"Don't you dare." Nyx clicked her teeth. "Alexis, I have not raised you from a hatchling for you to throw it all away for some random humans."

I bent my knees, weapons ready.

"Fine. You better survive." Scales scraped—Nyx launched herself off my neck.

Bite marks bloomed across the Titan's face as it spun, Fluffy Jr. gnawing on its arm.

Eyes narrowed, my fingers tingled. *Closer.*

The Titan turned as it struggled, its front wide open.

I leapt forward, stabbing both daggers into its blackened chest cavity. It shrieked and staggered.

I'm doing it!

I'm actually amazing at fighting!

A terrible slicing sensation exploded down my back—the Titan used its free arm to shred my spine.

There was no resistance.

I screamed.

Never mind, I'm not doing it.

"Alexis!" Nyx called.

Everything went fuzzy, the world blurring at the edges as I loosened my grip.

The monster spun.

All pain cut out, as if a switch had been flipped.

Eyes closing, I drifted into the peaceful dark, calm settling over my limbs.

"ALEXIS!" Nyx yelled.

My eyes shot open.

I was barely holding on to my daggers, bloody grip slipping and fingers burning, as the Titan stumbled, trying to shake all three of us off, its face purple as Nyx strangled it.

Repositioning my hold, I dug the knives deeper into its chest.

Fluffy Jr. growled louder, gnawing on its right arm, which was now partially hanging off below the elbow.

Good doggie.

Engaging my triceps, I hoisted my weight up, pushing on the hilts of my daggers for leverage—*crunch*—the blades ripped down from chest to navel.

Inky blood drenched my front as black organs unraveled between us.

My blood pooled with it.

Fresh pain exploded in my chest as I engaged my powers.

The Titan let out a strangled screech, talons falling away from my ruined back. Foam dribbled from its lips as it convulsed.

Mozart played the piano, fingers dancing, head flung back, eyes closed in ecstasy.

The monster careened backward into the grass—Fluffy Jr. and I fell forward with it.

In the grass, Fluffy Jr. went for its throat. I raised my daggers high, ruined back screaming in protest, as I slammed them down. Black gore sprayed as I stabbed again and again.

Pausing, I wiped blood from my face with my forearm.

The Titan was lifeless beneath me, a mangled mess of stab wounds. Its right arm was hanging at an angle, face swollen and covered in snake bites, mouth dripping with foam.

With shaking hands, I groped at my belt, fingers still tingling.

The pain in my back was slowly becoming a fire. The titanium cuffs wouldn't unlatch. Tears streamed down my face, and it was getting harder to see as I fumbled with the cuffs.

Crunch.

Fluffy Jr. growled as he got to his feet beside me.

A few feet away, the other Titan's head snapped back into place. It sat up, an empty ravaged cavity where its throat used to be.

No. No. No.

The Titan stood tall, blotting out the sky.

Wings unfurled wide.

I dropped the stupid cuffs and tried to stagger to my feet, groaning as my back throbbed with pain.

There was a split second—a flash of wings—darkness exploded.

Air whooshed and my stomach dropped, there was a horrible pressure on my arms, a fresh burning sensation streaked down my spine.

The Titan had slammed into me.

Two taloned hands were wrapped around my biceps. Its monstrous face hovered in front of mine as it held me up—and I realized we were shooting straight up into the air.

I screamed.

The Titan opened its mouth, emitting a raspy whistling noise as the muscles in its ruined neck contracted.

Fluffy Jr.'s barks grew distant. Nyx was down there with him, still wrapped around the fallen Titan.

My hair whipped against my face.

Mangled black wings whooshed as they pumped and we rushed past the top of the Colosseum, hurtling toward gray clouds.

I looked down, head lolling from the force.

People were crowded on the side of the street across from the park, peering up as if they'd all come out to watch me fight a Titan. Multiple cameras were pointed up at me.

The crowd became little dots as we flew higher.

My ears popped as the pressure and temperature plummeted.

The Titan squeezed its hands together, crushing me. There was no way to move, no way to infect it with my blood.

I wheezed as black spots filled my vision. Charlie, Helen, and Ceres were waiting for me to return to the villa.

The bowl of the Colosseum grew smaller.

There was nothing left. Last time I'd been trapped, I had the option to leap. Now there was nothing to do but— *Wait. Could I?*

My gut told me no, my injuries were too severe.

The Titan squeezed harder and my bones creaked as I screamed louder.

You're dead anyway.

I focused on the concrete chess table in the middle of the park.

Might as well.

"Domus," I shouted.

Everything went black.

We slammed down into the empty table—taloned hands released me and concrete broke beneath us.

Smoke was everywhere. *Pain.* The Colosseum once again towered above.

Chess pieces dug into my hands as I crawled blindly through

the smoke. Coughing and slipping on blood, unimaginable agony scoured my spine.

Fluffy Jr. launched himself at the Titan as it rose beside me.

With unfocused vision, I pushed up to my feet.

The elderly gaped, huddled together in a tight circle.

"Get out of here!" I couldn't hear my voice over the ringing in my left ear.

The humans remained frozen, crouched with fear around an elderly woman with short spiky white hair. "Lucia," they cried out as they touched her red-covered skin. *Blood.*

There was a long slash across her chest. A chunk of concrete had sliced her.

"Were the human casualties avoidable?" Persephone held my shoulders as she screamed in my face.

I collapsed to my knees next to Lucia. Leaning over, I desperately gathered pieces of her ripped shirt and pressed them against her wound.

My chest ached with pain as I tried to staunch the bleeding.

She said something, but I couldn't hear it.

I couldn't see anything; panic, desperation, and exhaustion beat against me. I pressed tingling fingers against her chest like it could save her.

The group sobbed and chanted in Latin.

Screeeeeeech.

The hairs on the back of my neck stood on end. Choking on remorse, I shouted, "Put pressure on the wound," as I pushed myself to my feet and staggered away.

It's my fault.

I had to protect the rest of them.

Stumbling, I turned toward where Fluffy Jr. was still attacking the first Titan. It was all a blur.

"Salvator!" an old man cried out in Latin behind me. *Savior.*

Knees buckling, I leaned over and puked, unable to handle the agony coursing through me.

The second Titan rose from the ruined table.

I wiped bile from my bloody lips.

You survived the crucible. This is nothing.

The first Titan let out a hideous screech and violently flung Fluffy Jr. off—he yelped as he rolled across the lawn toward me in a blur of white, then he stood up on all fours by my side.

Nyx hissed weakly from somewhere nearby.

Hunched over, I reached into my pocket. Bits of mangled metal filled my hand as I pulled out what was Augustus's pager—it was completely crushed. I dropped the pieces onto the grass.

There was nothing left to do.

Both Titans stood taller, their bones crunching back into place.

Blindly, I grabbed at the extra holster Kharon had given me—I pulled out a Spartan gun with my left hand and a hunting dagger with my right.

Nyx slithered up and around my shoulders.

The Titans stalked toward us.

Acceptance washed over. I couldn't go far, but I could still try.

"Domus," I screamed, pushing my right leg out so that Fluffy Jr. was touching it, as I was stretched into a million little pieces.

I blinked—we'd leapt across the lawn.

Thirty feet away, the Titans ran into each other in a blur of talons as they swiped at where we'd stood a second before.

Squinting, I fired.

Pop. Pop. Pop. Pop. Pop.

The Titans turned with confusion, black blood spraying as bullets hit them—they zeroed in on where I stood.

Wings unfurling, they leaned forward to fly at me but stumbled and looked back—their appendages were torn with bullet holes. Shaking their heads with frustration, the Titans hobbled forward at a rapid clip.

Well, this has been fun.

The pain in my back was unbearable; the ringing in my ear was now a high-pitched wail.

Might as well go out with a bang.

The Titans lunged for me at the same time—I pressed my leg against Fluffy Jr. and focused on a spot across the grassy park, one hundred feet away.

"DOMUS!"

The world shattered in agonizing darkness.

Crack.

I landed with my knees in the grass, a moan gurgling from my throat. Fluffy Jr. whined and sniffed at my face as bile dripped from my lips.

The Titans shrieked.

I was only fifty feet away, not as far as I'd hoped.

Everything was on fire.

Nyx screamed something in my ear, but I couldn't hear her.

Mentally, I designed my grave—nothing tacky, just a mausoleum with a small crypt and a ten-foot bust of my face. *Here lies the introverted pervert who had two husbands.*

Chuckling madly, blood sputtering from my lips, I dug tingling fingers into the lawn and heaved.

Standing was an act of God, and I bellowed as I staggered up to my feet. I'd lost my gun in the leap—the dagger was still clenched in my fist.

The Titans screeched and hobbled toward me.

My old friends.

I opened my arms wide (I'd lost my mind).

Come to dance?

My protector bond flared inside my chest, exploding with power.

Fluffy Jr. leapt forward. Midair his body expanded, legs and neck lengthening, lumps on his spine protruding—this time when he collided with a Titan, he threw the monster backward with his size.

Did Fluffy Jr. just . . .

I blinked in shock.

The second Titan swiped its talons at my face. *Whoosh.* I leaned my head back on instinct.

The tango, a classic.

I took the opening, stabbing my dagger deep into the Titan's ruined chest with both my hands. Nyx lunged.

Grinning, I leaned into the sick embrace, bleeding all over the monster.

Die, bitch.

A fresh wave of throbbing agony filled my sternum.

The Titan collapsed onto the grass beneath me, foam once again on its lips. It convulsed violently, arms flailing—I yanked back as a talon swiped in slow motion, but I was too late.

Agony exploded, warmth gushing down my neck.

A mangled ear fell to the grass, one that should have been *attached* to me.

The Titan convulsed again, its taloned hand slicing through my fallen ear, cutting it to ruin.

I guess I didn't really need it anyway.

The Titan stilled.

A few feet away, a now oversized Fluffy Jr. growled savagely as he rolled, still fighting the other monster.

Zap-zap-zap. Electric shock waves pulsed through my marriage bond with increased intensity, like it was keeping my heart beating.

I gasped weakly, half lying on top of the still Titan.

Snap. Crunch. Bones shifted beneath me as it came back to life.

I stared blankly down at it. *Fine, you win.*

The Titan bucked.

I tumbled off, sprawling brokenly in the gore-covered grass. A conspiracy of ravens flew past. *How fitting.*

Government drones were the last thing I'd ever see. I smiled weakly as emotions bubbled in my chest.

Nyx slithered over and flicked her tongue against my cheek. I tried to raise my hand and feel her scales, one last time, but I couldn't find the strength to move. I turned my head, resting my cheek against her face.

"I . . . love . . . you," I whispered between gasps. *I love you, Fluffy Jr., Charlie, Helen, Drex, and maybe—*

A whistling sound cut off my potentially disturbing revelation.

Pops, grunts, shouts, and slaps echoed.

It took a second to decipher the blur of bronze skin.

Augustus stood over the Titan.

His black and white hair was undone, blowing behind him—he strangled the Titan with one hand wrapped around a metal chain, and fired a gun with his other, pumping its chest full of bullets.

Has ambidexterity always been so hot?

Splattered with black, teeth bared, crimson dripping from his eyes, Augustus looked positively feral.

Maybe it was the blood loss.

Maybe it was the pain.

Maybe it was the fact that Augustus was *disturbingly* capable of eliminating evil.

But suddenly, I couldn't understand how I'd ever thought I was asexual.

The chain was attached to Augustus's hip, the end tied around a third wingless Titan—it was trussed up with a tag stabbed through its bottom lip, and he was using the middle part of that metal chain to choke the Titan that had been attacking me.

Whatever this is, I'm into it.

Augustus holstered the gun, buried two knives into the Titan's eyes, then resumed firing from point-blank range.

A hand grabbed my face, turning me away from the carnage.

Kharon tipped my chin to the side and froze, staring at what felt like a hole in the side of my skull.

Oh yeah, my ear's on the ground somewhere, chopped into tiny pieces.

His eyes hardened into chips of unyielding ice. Kharon reached for his holster and raised up a wickedly sharp dagger.

Wait . . .

He sliced the blade clean through his left ear.

Someone screamed silently in horror.

It was me.

With a determined expression, Kharon pulled a small box out of his cargo pants.

A needle and thread glinted.

Augustus came back into view as he stalked across the lawn.

His gun was raised high as he fired at the last Titans. Poco perched on his shoulder with narrowed eyes—his fluffy raccoon arm was raised, pointing at the Titans, his thumb flexing rapidly.

Wait, is that a finger gun?

Kharon leaned down and blocked my view as he brought the needle and thread up to the left side of my face.

I tried to speak, but I couldn't; I tried to tell him with my eyes not to do it.

Kharon bent closer, his jaw clenching with resolve as he sewed his appendage onto the side of *my* head.

"Per angusta ad augusta, carissimus," he whispered.

Through trials to triumph, my dear.

Augustus appeared and Kharon leaned back to give him space. They patted my pockets until they pulled out two tags engraved with *Hercules*.

A single droplet fell from the sky, splattering across the golden name.

Augustus leaned down.

He pressed a gentle kiss to my forehead. I couldn't feel a thing, yet my skin tingled where his lips brushed. He smelled like gunpowder, lightning, and sin.

Poco patted my cheek.

As they pulled away, the heavens opened up and rain drenched the world.

Kharon resumed sewing.

I was alive when I should be dead.

The Roman Colosseum loomed above, an ancient reminder—this was Sparta, and for better or worse, we were the gods of this new dark age.

13

The Hunter

Kharon

The world hissed as rain poured down, mud gathering beneath my knees.

Gunshots echoed, Titans screeched, chains rattled, and Augustus grunted as he fought behind me.

Soaked to the bone, pain throbbed across the fresh wound on the left side of my head.

All that mattered was *her*.

Alexis Hert was lying in the muddy grass covered in blood, looking ruined and ethereal.

My wife is injured.

It was nothing short of devastating.

With perfect precision, I stitched my ear to the side of her head.

In, out, in, out.

Fixing Alexis was the only thing of consequence.

The fucking Titan had sliced her ear into pieces, and I had a perfectly good one that she could use. It was that simple.

I was also no stranger to stitching appendages back on. I'd lost fingers, toes, and even an entire hand once in battle.

Spartans couldn't regenerate anything that was hard tissue, like appendages and limbs, but we could fuse.

If you stitched an injury within a few hours of receiving it, our bodies would re-heal the damaged appendage, and the same applied to the body parts donated from other Spartans.

My wife's body was going to accept my ear. It didn't have a fucking choice.

Hell and Hound prowled protectively around us, flame eyes flickering, ready to maul anyone who dared approach.

A Titan screeched close by, but I didn't turn and look.

Augustus would handle it. I trusted him with my life, and hers.

But when the fuck did the Titans start mutating into bats?

I finished the last stitches as Alexis drifted in and out of consciousness.

Rain splattered across bronzed skin, and her golden curls were a tangled halo around her head as she lay in a muddy puddle of pink.

Even for a Spartan, even for a Chthonic, she'd suffered *grievous* injuries, and yet she was somehow still breathing.

I'd never seen anything like it.

She'd single-handedly fought off two Titans that could fucking *fly*. It was mind-boggling.

Achilles and Patro were also missing, which meant they'd abandoned her.

If they aren't already dead, they will be soon.

Alexis gasped brokenly and I used the hem of my shirt to wipe away the gore around her ear.

Tracing my finger over the stitches, I inspected it closely for signs of rejection—the pale skin color was already turning bronze. Her body was accepting it.

I could do nothing but kneel beside my wife as I waited, shaking, my tears mixing with rain.

Alexis rolled onto her side and coughed jerkily.

My heart stopped as I stared down at the damage on her back. It was so much worse than I'd initially thought—skin flapped unattached and the white knobby bones of her spine were visible. Her back was torn to absolute shreds.

There wasn't enough skin to even pretend to stitch up.

"*Don't move!*" I ripped my shirt off and pressed the fabric against her ruined flesh.

"Shut u-up." Alexis struggled in the mud.

I tried to stand to stop her, but I slipped and fell to the ground with a grunt. The Titan we'd captured in South America had left talon marks through my thighs, and for some reason my back was also hurting. I had more wounds than I'd realized.

"How—" Alexis coughed as she turned her head. "You know . . . come . . . here?"

Rain dripped from her long lashes.

"We were *always* coming back for you."

Hell and Hound sat down next to her, whining as they nuzzled at her side.

It didn't escape my notice that neither of them were worried about helping me.

Alexis laughed weakly, her ruined back shaking. "Good . . . doggies."

The deadly class six beasts wagged their bony tails, preening under her attention, licking her face as she giggled.

Alexis coughed, blood dripping from her lips. "Save . . . yourself . . . leave . . . me."

Our mud-covered faces were inches apart.

Something dark and sinister awoke inside me. "Do you know *who* I am?" I asked.

Her gaze darted to the bloody side of my head, and she blanched.

We were physically connected, forever.

Perfect.

"I'm *yours*," I said as the rain roared around us. "You can break my legs, but I'll still crawl after you. If you're injured, I will carve myself to pieces to make you whole . . . every . . . single . . . time. This is not a temporary arrangement. We will be together. Forever. Or I'll be dead."

Two-colored eyes widened.

"Do you understand what I'm saying, *princess*?"

Her breath hitched.

"*Tell me* that you don't feel it." I leaned closer—our mouths touched. There was nothing sexual about the kiss; it was all possession and rage. "If you don't feel it, I'll give up," I whispered against her lips. "I'll still protect you, but I'll stop . . . trying."

I breathed in, inhaling her, like a dying man.

Her pupils dilated.

"I . . . feel it," she said quietly. "But it d-doesn't . . . mean anything."

I opened my mouth against hers, tongue sweeping out. *Devouring*.

Her tongue fought back.

"What the fuck is wrong with you two?" Augustus shouted. "Why do I keep finding you like this? You're both *kissing* as you bleed out?"

I dropped her chin like it burned.

Long seconds passed as Augustus studied us in the rain. His hair was drenched, sticking to his arms and back like a second skin, and Poco sat on his shoulder shivering.

He shook his head. "Can either of you stand?"

"No," I said, at the same time Alexis whispered, "Maybe."

We glared at each other.

Augustus took a deep steadying breath. "None of us are in any shape to leap—we have to get to a safe house."

There was a loud whine, then a monstrous creature nuzzled Alexis's face.

I reached for my gun.

"Don't . . . Fluffy Jr."

I gaped at the white beast, which now had the build and height of a small horse, but the body of a dog. A strange lump protruded from its back.

"What the fuck happened to him?" Augustus asked, aghast.

"Just . . . growing."

Great, my wife is a lunatic.

Before I could lecture her on animal safety, Augustus nodded like he was steeling himself for something.

"Let's go," he said. "I know a safe house in this city—I'll carry you both."

Alexis looked at the three Titans chained around his waist with disbelief.

I nodded in agreement. The House of Ares was the House of War for a reason. Its heirship was earned through unfathomable pain and endurance.

A few minutes later, mud splattered as Augustus stomped forward.

He held Alexis against his chest bridal style, I leaned against his arm for support, and chains clattered as he dragged three Titans behind him.

Alexis mumbled as she lulled in and out of consciousness.

Augustus didn't falter. A muscle in his jaw ticked, the only sign that he was in pain, as he continued to stalk forward, a stoic behemoth.

When we made it to the edge of the grassy park, two figures stepped forward in the rain, blocking us.

Augustus clutched Alexis tighter to his chest.

I grabbed my gun.

"What are you doing with her?" an elderly woman demanded. Her chest was drenched in blood and she swayed like she was seconds away from passing out.

"Lucia, be careful. They're Spartans," an old man warned her.

"I don't *care* what they are." She glared at me. "Where are you taking her?" Her voice warped strangely in my missing ear.

Augustus gaped down at her.

Humans didn't approach Spartans. *Ever.*

"Excuse me?" I asked, stunned by her hubris.

Another woman stepped up next to her and pointed at Alexis. "She saved us—so *what* are you doing with her? Answer the question. We won't let you hurt her."

I chuckled sarcastically. "She's our *wife*. She's none of your concern."

More people sidled forward, standing behind the idiots blocking our path. They crossed their arms and scowled up at me like *I* was the problem, not one of the men who'd just *saved* her.

"Move aside." I raised my gun.

I'd mow them down for the audacity of thinking they had a right to her.

"Put your weapon away." Augustus's voice was clipped as he shook his head at me.

The world hissed in the downpour as I slowly lowered my weapon but didn't re-holster.

Fine, I'll just kill them all with my bare hands.

Augustus cleared his throat, tension melting off his face, as he donned his mask—the nice guy, the eldest heir, the leader.

"Don't worry, folks." His voice rang with sincerity as he addressed the growing crowd.

Dozens more people spilled out from side streets and buildings to block our path. *Where the fuck did all these humans come from?*

There were so many of them. It was disgusting.

"On my honor as the eldest heir of the House of Ares," Augustus said. "I promise that I'm taking Alexis Hert, heiress to the House of Hades, to get medical treatment. No harm will come to her under our care. I solemnly swear, she is ours to protect."

Forever.

The elderly woman huffed as she peered at my missing ear suspiciously.

I glared back.

She frowned. "She's better than the rest of your Spartan lot—you never care about us. Not like she did . . . She's different."

She made the sign of the cross with her gnarled finger.

"Angelus Romae," a man called out from the crowd, his voice shaking like he was addressing someone of greatest esteem.

The Angel of Rome.

Augustus bowed his head respectfully.

The crowd parted for him, and as we walked forward, humans of all ages reached out and lightly touched Alexis.

They spit on the bound Titans, and a few even kicked them.

Cameras flashed.

"*Angelus Romae!*" Humans chanted with hero worship as we moved forward. Instead of dispersing, people flooded out of crumbling buildings, lining the rainy streets.

Skin prickling as I limped forward, I studied Alexis's features.

The humans weren't wrong.

Even in the rain, her golden hair curled around her head like a halo. She looked like the paintings of their divine creatures.

The problem was the humans were calling her *their* angel, and I'd claimed her first; the only person I'd share with was Augustus.

Everyone else could go choke.

I bared my teeth to the crowd, growling with my hellhounds at anyone who touched her.

The chant grew louder, and the urge to scream at them to shut the fuck up increased.

For now, the humans could pretend she was their hero.

They would learn.

At the end of the cobbled street, a loud crack echoed. Smoke billowed.

A figure stood in the ruins of a townhome. Fresh blood was

smeared across the brick wall, sheltered from the rain by a broken slab of concrete.

We halted.

Augustus clutched Alexis tighter against his chest and she grumbled incoherently.

The figure walked forward out of the shadows.

"How *dare* you show your face here!" Augustus shouted, his face twisting with fury.

Achilles took a step toward us, eyes wide as he stared at Alexis. Rain dripped off his muzzle.

"You abandoned her." Blood streaked down Augustus's face, washing away in the rain. "You left her TO DIE!"

Achilles took a guilty step back, shoulders rounding.

Augustus straightened to his full height, the sharp planes of his face ruthless and unforgiving. "You disgust me, brother."

Crack.

Achilles leapt away, eyes haunted with regret.

He deserved far worse.

14
THE ELDEST HEIR

AUGUSTUS

Adrenaline burned me alive.

How dare Achilles show his face after he abandoned her.

The House of Ares, the House of War, had no place for cowards.

Stomping forward through the pouring rain, I navigated the side streets of Rome.

I needed to get her medical care. *You should have given her to Achilles to take to safety.*

My grip tightened around her limp form. Over my dead body would I entrust him or Patro with her care. Never again.

A strange agony coursed down my spine, and a sharp ache throbbed in my right knee, but I easily ignored the pain.

Weakness wasn't allowed. Greatness or nothing—there was no in-between.

The clouds hung low and ominous as I marched through puddles, scanning the ruined city for threats. Cold rain dripped off my nose, and Poco was huddled on my back, chewing on my wet hair.

The humans had dispersed.

Chains tugged at my waist holster, but I refused to slow as I stalked forward, fuming, dragging the three bound Titans behind me, their skulls cracking satisfyingly against the cobbled street. They shrieked behind the gags I'd made from my shirt.

When did Titans sprout fucking wings?

The rain splattered against the ruined cobbled street with an angry hiss as two hellhounds stalked ahead of me, glitching in and out of focus, leading the way to the safe house.

Kharon was heavy against my left side, his grip painful as he clung to my arm. His state was rapidly deteriorating. Half-unconscious, he mumbled nonsensically, a mangled ridge where his ear used to be.

He'd done the unthinkable.

Determination flared hotter in my chest. I would save them both or die trying.

Poco dropped my hair and chittered at Alexis with concern, shivering with matted fur, as he reached down and patted her pale cheek with his tiny black hand, but she didn't wake.

He mewled sadly.

I agree.

Fluffy Jr. limped to my right—the size of a pony—and nudged Alexis's feet with his head. She was covered in so much blood that the downpour couldn't wash it away.

I picked up the pace, dragging Kharon with me.

Minutes later, the hellhounds finally stopped in front of the safe house's tall decorative wall.

I pushed on the corner of a dark-colored brick, unlatching the secret door. Shoving forward, I checked over my shoulder to make sure we weren't being followed.

The small structure sat plain and unobtrusive, hidden by dense foliage, so it blended in with the rain, almost invisible.

There were no windows, just a solid brick facade, reinforced by a thick sheet of titanium.

I kicked aside the welcome mat and gingerly bent down, balancing Alexis and propping Kharon against the wall, as I picked up the silver key.

If for some bizarre reason an Olympian discovered this safe house, they'd look for a more advanced point of entry, like a keypad or finger scanner.

The key under the mat was surprisingly effective.

Hefting Alexis against my chest, I fumbled with the door, shoving the key into the lock. Multiple clicks echoed.

Titanium unlatched.

I pushed my way in, out of the rain, pulling in Kharon and the Titans behind me. Once all of us were inside, I flipped the locks and shoved the steel door jammer into place.

The air was chilly and stale.

It was mostly dark, only a sliver of light came in through the peephole, but I knew where everything was.

All Chthonic safe houses had the same layout and amenities.

A king bed filled the small carpeted room, and there was a galley kitchen behind it. The white door led to a bathroom with a shower and two sinks; the black door led to a cellar.

The three dogs—if the two hellhounds and Alexis's lumpy protector could even be called that—flopped down onto the carpet.

Gently, I laid Alexis on the bed.

Poco climbed off my shoulders, sitting beside her, chittering as he smoothed curls from her forehead.

My heart clenched.

Kharon groaned. I shrugged him off my shoulder, and he collapsed beside Alexis.

I needed a plan.

Stalking over to the small kitchen, I opened and closed drawers until I found the bottle of matches. There was no power in any of the safe houses because solar generators were visible with infrared lenses.

I lit the candles scattered around the room, chains clattering as they stretched.

I yanked open the cellar door, dragging the three chained Titans roughly down the narrow stairwell. They thudded against each step, rolling at unnatural angles with muffled shrieks.

At the bottom, I tightened their gags, checking to make sure they still had the tags pierced through their lips. The two winged Titans I'd given Alexis's golden tags, because by the time we'd arrived, they were mostly defeated. She deserved the credit.

One by one, I grabbed them by their bound hands. Their shoulders cracked as I wrenched their arms up and back, attaching their cuffs to the titanium hooks bolted into the ceiling.

Once all three of them were secured, I hurried back upstairs and studied Alexis and Kharon.

You need to see the damage. Clean them, then wound care.

I went into the bathroom and turned on the shower, limping slightly. It took a minute, then steamy water sprayed out from the well that was located far beneath the building's foundation.

I paused before the mirror.

What the fuck.

Blood was still dripping from the corners of my eyes, even though I wasn't using my Chthonic powers.

My headaches were also getting worse, and my gut was telling me that something was happening to my power. It was *changing*—I just had no idea how.

I gripped the cool porcelain sink.

The dark circles around my eyes were almost black, stained with streaks that matched the scar slashed across my face; stubble covered my lower jaw, and purple veins protruded from my neck.

What the fuck is happening to me?

The sink cracked beneath my fingers.

Shaking my head, as if I could jostle the madness away, I tried to smile to soften my features. It came out as a snarl.

Stalking back over to the bed, I stopped pretending to be something I wasn't.

I slapped Kharon across the face. "You need to shower—wake up," I ordered. "Stop feeling sorry for yourself."

Kharon moaned, "Oh fuck off." But he stretched his arms and cracked his neck, eyes still closed, like he was readying himself.

Turning away from him, I shook Alexis's shoulder as gently as possible. "Can you stand, sweetheart?" I whispered into her ear.

Eyelashes fluttered open, but her gaze was glossy and distant, then she closed her eyes with a sigh.

"I need to take off your wet clothes," I said. "Just to get you warm and prevent infection—I won't look. I promise."

For some reason, I felt the need to add the last part. Nudity was as natural to Spartans as wearing clothes, but Alexis always rushed to change in the locker room.

I didn't want her to feel uncomfortable.

"Is that okay?" I asked, stomach sinking at the thought of causing her any more angst.

Eyelids fluttered, and she rolled to her side. "It's . . . fine," she whispered sleepily.

I pulled off her soaking bloody rags as efficiently as possible, swearing as dried blood tugged on open wounds.

Some guns and knives clattered to the floor, much fewer than what she'd started with.

I lifted her in my arms, her heart resting against mine as I carried her into the shower. Her skin was frigid and she vibrated with shivers.

Luckily, the bathroom was made specifically with wounded Spartans in mind, because the fully stocked marble shower was double the size of a usual one, with a built-in bench for sitting, and nozzles that sprayed water from the ceiling and sides.

Still clothed, I gingerly sat down on the bench, trying desperately not to jostle Alexis.

In the steamy dark, she groaned and flinched under the hot spray.

"Shhh, don't fret," I said, voice cracking. "I got you . . . You're safe now."

Repositioning her so she was seated on my thighs, I reached for soap and a washcloth.

Alexis was a tall woman, but I was still a much larger man. She weighed next to nothing compared to Kharon (I'd carried him and cleaned him after a Titan battle more times than he'd ever admit) and it was easy to position her.

As gently as possible, I scrubbed off the dirt and blood that covered her like a second skin, so thick the rain hadn't been able to clean it away.

Even in the dark, I could see that the water ran black as I scrubbed.

"You're so strong," I praised, whispering into her hair as I cleaned every inch of her body.

I kept muttering, desperate to put her at ease.

"You're so brave . . . You're the strongest Chthonic I've ever seen . . . You're so powerful . . . You're so intelligent, a math prodigy . . . I've never seen a more impressive warrior . . . You're so resilient . . . so good . . . You're going to change the world."

I meant every word.

Once the water ran clear, I turned to her messy mane of curls. Dumping shampoo into my hand, I gently leaned her forward, holding her with one arm around her midsection as my other hand lathered her hair.

I dug my fingers deep into her scalp, scrubbing at the base of her head.

Alexis moaned groggily, this time with pleasure. Her shivers subsided and it felt like I could breathe again.

"You're so perfect," I whispered.

My beliefs were cracking around me and I didn't know what to think.

Women shouldn't have to fight in war. It was fundamentally wrong, but it didn't escape me that Alexis had nearly decimated two Titans with *wings*, all by herself.

How someone so delicate could be so powerful was beyond my understanding.

I struggled to get my thoughts in order.

Instead, I scrubbed at Alexis's scalp for long moments, as if the tenderness could replace the last hour of her life, and the memories that would surely haunt her.

She tilted her head to the right, and I stilled my ministrations as she looked at me through heavy lashes.

"Thank . . . you," she whispered, her voice hoarse from screaming.

I smiled softly. "Of course . . . I'll always be there to take care of you."

She sighed at my words, eyes closing, her head once again lolling forward as she trusted me to take care of her.

Her back was a mess of ruined skin.

And she was thanking me.

The smile fell from my face. Eyes blurring, I cleaned her hair gently, biting down on my lower lip to stifle a sound of distress.

Angelus Romae, indeed.

The humans had seen the truth of her. I'd seen it in their reverent expressions and heard it in their choked voices. They'd seen her for what she was.

Unlike most Spartans, Alexis cared for others, even to her own detriment.

She protected everyone—but who protected her?

We should have.

Tears streamed down my face.

Months ago, Kharon and I had immediately recognized her goodness.

I'd seen it during the crucible.

She'd spent every free minute hunched over a textbook, calmly helping Drex understand Thagorean.

She'd been much smarter than the idiot Olympian boys, but she never bragged, even though she had the type of mind that scholars searched for centuries to find.

Pine would never admit it aloud, but while half starved and delirious, she'd solved complex Thagorean problems that even he couldn't. And he'd spent over a century teaching Thagorean at the *highly* competitive Rhodes Olympian University.

Her intellect was astonishing.

Pine had whispered with awe that she was a prodigy, the likes of which he'd never seen.

Alexis was an enigma.

An angel.

So, we'd manipulated, tricked, and trapped to get exactly what we wanted. *Her.*

Regret crushed my chest, a heavy weight of shame.

I moved Alexis, so she was leaning back on me, and grabbed some conditioner, slowly working it through her long tresses.

"We don't deserve you," I whispered, as if saying the truth aloud could atone for what we'd done. "Angels don't deserve this . . . You're so much better than us."

"No shit—*ow*—fuck." Kharon stumbled naked into the dark shower, collapsed onto the bench beside me, and tipped his bloody head back, groaning as he leaned against the wall under the spray. "We'll never deserve her as long as we live."

I glared over at him. "Stop shouting."

He rolled his eyes and tapped his missing ear.

"Figure it the fuck out. Don't agitate her."

Instead of getting mad, Kharon raised an eyebrow. "Get out of your head—I can practically see you thinking from here."

Gritting my teeth, I focused on separating her curls with conditioner. "We're bad for her," I said, the words hanging heavy in the hazy darkness. "She deserves someone . . . nice."

Kharon laughed, a harsh cruel sound. "Oh, fuck off with your melodramatic, self-loathing, eldest heir bullshit."

His voice was too loud in the quiet shower, his words jarring.

My fingers stilled.

"Excuse me?"

"You heard me." Kharon dumped the bottle of shampoo over his hair, hissing as the suds burned his wound.

When he'd finished grunting through the pain, he looked at me pointedly. "Alexis is *our* wife. No, we aren't good for her . . . We're cruel, possessive, aggressive—"

"I got it," I snapped, cutting him off.

Kharon sprawled with his legs wide on the bench, and our knees knocked together as he lathered soap across his scarred chest.

"The point is," he said darkly. "She's too good for *all* of Sparta, not just us. Achilles and Patro fucking *abandoned* her."

We both fumed.

They'd be dealt with. *Brutally.*

"So—what do we do with someone who's too pure for this world?" Kharon's white teeth flashed in the dim. "We protect her. We make her so irrevocably ours that everyone is *afraid* to look in her direction."

I shook my head. "That's a fool's dream."

"No." Kharon's voice rose. "That's what Hades did with Persephone. No one dares look at her wrong, and we need to do the same."

I paused.

He had a point.

Kharon reached over and wrapped one of Alexis's curls around his finger.

"She needs monsters," he said, turning his head to reveal the mutilated side of his head. "Precisely because she's not one."

His smirk was rabid, a carnivore in the body of a man. "That's why she has us."

I cleared my throat.

"So, you . . . gave her your ear."

"I did." His eyes flashed as they met mine. "Do you have a fucking problem with that?"

I raised an eyebrow at his hostility. "Just an observation."

He smirked with satisfaction.

"So," I said. "Do you want to talk about why you—"

Kharon slumped over and fell onto the shower floor. Water splattered on his naked sprawled form as steam rose.

He was out cold.

I sighed.

Thirty minutes later, Alexis and Kharon were dry, warm, and asleep in the middle of the bed.

I'd given them each a shot of purified adrenaline mixed with an insanely expensive sleeping agent. It was the newest Olympian technology and there'd only been two vials in the medical kit. It would send them into a light healing coma, but they'd wake up almost fully healed.

Afterward, I'd sprayed a healing mist on all their wounds, the Rod of Asclepius golden on the sides of the container, signifying it was Olympian medicine. Finally, I'd wrapped them both in fresh bandages and placed them under the covers.

Taking my time, I tucked the covers under Alexis's toes and legs, just like Helen always liked.

I tossed the other side haphazardly over Kharon.

He snored, wrestling a pillow from my hands in his sleep, and then he turned over, wrapping his arms around Alexis. He held her like he was afraid someone was going to take her away.

Poco clambered up onto the bed. His gray fur was still wet and plastered to his little form, and he was shivering.

"Come here," I said, and he held up both his hands like he wanted to be picked up.

I obliged.

After another thirty minutes in the shower, this time scrubbing Poco's fur with shampoo until he was clean, I wrapped him in a towel and sat him on my lap, then brushed him in long strokes until he was fluffy.

When I was satisfied he was clean and I dry, I carried him back to the bed. He looked up at me, black eyes wide and trusting, as I raised the corner of the blanket up for him.

He snuggled under the covers, chittering with contentment as he wrapped his little black hands around Alexis's neck.

I tucked him in with only his little gray ears peeking out, just like he preferred.

Satisfied that everyone was taken care of, I quickly stripped off my clothes and scrubbed myself clean as fast as possible.

Rushing, I pulled on a pair of sweatpants stashed in the bedside table, then I dug through my discarded clothes, found the two loaded Spartan guns, and tucked a sheathed dagger into my waistband.

With guns in both of my hands, I leaned back against the front door. Eyes wide, mind alert. If anyone tried to mess with the lock, I'd feel it immediately.

No one was getting inside.

Not under my watch.

I stood guard as Alexis, Kharon, and Poco slept peacefully in the bed. Head fuzzy with exhaustion, I ignored the aches in my body.

On the floor, the hellhounds were curled together around Fluffy Jr., the lump on his back quivering.

Some beasts underwent molting transformations, but none looked remotely like he did. *Another mystery.*

One, two, three, four, five, six.

I counted the rise and fall of Alexis's chest, watching every breath she took as the candles burned low.

As the hours passed, calm descended, the kind that only occurred when purpose met passion.

Duty was melting away into something new.

Alexis was going to be okay, because there was no other option.

I was going to make sure of it.

Warmth filled my chest, and for the first time since it painfully settled into place, the marriage bond hummed with contentment.

"Flectere si nequeo superos, Acheronta movebo," I whispered into the shadows. "For you, my carus. Always."

It was a promise.

If I cannot move Heaven, I will raise hell.

15
SATAN'S TOUCH

ALEXIS: THREE DAYS LATER (POST-HEALING COMA)

"I watch you." Satan's breath whispered tantalizingly against the shell of my ear. "Every . . . *single* . . . night."

The sleep world was fading into reality, but I kept my eyes shut.

"That's," I whispered, "not healthy." I squirmed deeper into the cozy warmth.

Fingers tangled in the curls at the base of my skull, pulling my head back.

"Fuck healthy," the guttural voice rasped. "I fantasize about—" lips pressed against my jaw "—ruining you so thoroughly that you forget your own name."

Butterflies fluttered in my stomach.

"I want to chain you to my side. I want to punish you for driving me crazy. I want to show you just how much you mean to me . . . body *and* soul. Do you know what that's like?"

I do.

One hand yanked my head back further as his other wrapped around my hip, pinning me in place.

A masculine groan vibrated, desperate and needy, the tortured sound of a ravenous man.

Goose bumps pebbled, heat pooling between my legs.

"You're going to obey me," Satan ordered as he kissed my jaw.

"I won't," I whispered back, eyes still squeezed shut.

The hand in my hair tugged. "You *will* obey." The hot mouth trailed lower to my neck.

I shivered with delight.

"No," I panted.

Satan sucked against the column of my throat, just hard enough to leave marks.

My face flushed. The fever was spreading.

He held me tighter, breathing roughly, like he was losing all control, and the scent of a rainstorm filled my nose.

A silky-smooth male voice echoed from across the room. "Fuck, she likes that. Don't stop."

My stomach dipped with heat.

Satan lifted his hips, rigid heat pressing flush against me.

He kissed my neck hard, sucking my skin between his teeth, then gently peppering the abused flesh with delicate kisses, as if in apology.

I fisted the sheets, back bowing with pleasure.

You're in grave danger.

Sticky warmth dribbled as velvety hardness pressed against my upper thigh.

"Mine," he whispered hoarsely as he kissed my collarbone.

The fever stoked higher as fingernails trailed across my stomach, flesh burning in their wake.

"Wake up, carissima," Satan ordered harshly as he sucked my nipple into his mouth. I shifted—there were bandages wrapped around my entire torso, everywhere but my breasts.

Pain twinged in my back, but I ignored it as heat streaked straight to my core. I peeked through my lashes.

Muted candlelight highlighted his strikingly refined features, as Kharon hovered above me, glacier eyes hooded, ink rippling as he swallowed.

His hips rolled, the length of his hardness pressing against me like a brand.

I whimpered.

"Hello, princess." Kharon tangled his hand deeper into my curls, pulling my head back.

"Hello." I tangled my hands in his short silky hair. "*Karen.*"

He stilled, blue veins standing out against his pale skin.

Skeleton-tattooed fingers reached up and gripped my chin—Kharon slammed his mouth against mine, tongue diving deep.

He kissed me like he was punishing me. *Does he have an oral fixation?*

I yanked at his hair and arched my back off the bed, whimpering as my nipples dragged across the scarred ridges of his chest.

My back twinged at the movement; a mostly healed wound pulled.

I ignored the pain.

Kharon groaned, calloused hands trailing from my face down to my neck, dancing across my chest.

His touch was reverent.

The flush spread lower, my core pulsing.

He palmed my breast, his hand covering it as he tweaked my nipple with his thumb—I whimpered, dragging my nails across his scalp and rolling so our bodies were flush together—velvety hardness settled between my legs, stiff against my dripping core.

"Do that again," Augustus ordered across the room. "She likes it."

Kharon obeyed.

I threw my head back with a moan.

"You're mine." Kharon swore, hips jerking.

"Good girl," Augustus praised. "You're so responsive."

Wetness pooled between my thighs.

"Alexis," Kharon said darkly, his voice scratchy.

"Yes?" I asked, licking my cracked lips, my voice still hoarse from screaming. I tugged on his silky hair.

Memories of shrieking Titans, claws through flesh, and sobbing people played at the edge of my subconscious as I kissed his shockingly soft lips, chasing the thoughts away with pleasure.

Our tongues tangled.

Powerful thighs flexed beneath me as his legs spread wider.

"You're going to take me," Kharon ordered.

My toes curled at the deepening register of his rough voice.

"I'm going to fuck you so hard—you'll *crave* it for the rest of your life."

"Mmm-hmm," I sighed into his mouth, my hands trailing down over his chest. *Lower.* Ridges trembled as abdominal muscles clenched under my touch.

I peeked through my lashes.

The mellow candlelight danced across smoldering blue eyes, pale edges, and messy black hair. Kharon stared at me hungrily, burying his hand deeper in my curls.

His dick was pressed fully against the length of my core, and if either of us shifted, he'd be inside me.

Sweat streaked down my chest.

"What are you going to do—Karen?" I taunted, lust making me bold.

His eyes flashed. "*You're* not the one in charge here, princess."

I pressed my thighs together.

We both groaned as his velvety hardness slipped lower, closer to my entrance.

I smirked.

Kharon clenched his jaw and flexed his hips—his cock slid slowly through the folds of my heat.

A spasm fluttered and I bit down on my lower lip, face flushing.

He looked smug.

I tightened my thighs again, and Kharon's features sharpened, blood pooling in the whites of his eyes as he activated his powers.

His emotions slammed into me—*fuck her for hours, consume her, going to tie her to the bed, destroy her, need to be inside of her.*

Masculine pleasure joined mine, sensations exploding through my skin, as every hair on my body rose. Sweat beaded and the fever became an inferno.

Augustus made a harsh sound, his eyes hooded with lust as he watched us from the end of the bed.

"Can you feel how hard his cock is for you?" His silky voice had a biting edge.

Kharon panted, his jaw clenching like it was taking all his self-control not to push himself inside of me.

"Alexis—answer me," Augustus ordered.

"Yes," I whispered, sparks dancing in my vision as my fingers sprawled across Kharon's scarred chest.

"Good girl," Augustus drawled. "So obedient. So perfect for us."

His praise washed over me, head spinning, everything becoming hazy.

Kharon dragged his blunt tip through my folds.

We both gasped.

"Tease her clit," Augustus demanded.

Reaching his hand between our bodies, Kharon grabbed the base of his dick and dragged it back and forth over the sensitive bundle of nerves.

I closed my eyes and tipped my head back, nails digging into his flesh, as pleasure mounted in white-hot waves. I clenched around nothing, desperate for more.

"Look at me," Kharon said harshly. "Look me in the eyes as your pretty cunt gushes all over my cock."

He pushed the tip down, hovering in front of my entrance.

I stopped breathing.

"No," Augustus said as he sauntered around the bed and stopped beside me. "You've both been in a healing coma for three days. She's too injured for that. Not right now."

He couldn't have said something earlier?

Kharon groaned, face twisting, but he pulled his hips away.

I barely stopped myself from reaching for him.

Augustus leaned down, eyes hooded. He made a finger gun with his thumb and two fingers—then lowered it between my thighs.

His thumb made circular motions around my clit while his two fingers slid inside, stretching as he pumped.

Kharon leaned forward and kissed my lips. "You like that?" he whispered against my mouth as Augustus thrust his fingers inside me faster.

Nodding, I saw stars as Augustus bent the tips of his fingers just so, rubbing a sensitive spot deep inside of me.

"Come for us," Kharon ordered as he kissed me. "Now."

Augustus pressed on my clit, and I bowed my back—flutters pulsed through me in crashing waves as I came on his fingers.

Augustus held my gaze, working his fingers in me as he wrung out the surges of ecstasy.

Slowly Augustus pulled his hand out of me, then he brought his glistening fingers up; Kharon leaned forward and licked them.

I shivered as both of them stared at me with hungry, greedy eyes.

Aftershocks waned as the glow of my orgasm abated.

Kharon rose with a lazy smirk and climbed off the bed, unbothered by his nakedness. Scarred skin stretched across chiseled sinew; a skeleton sleeve was stark against his pale skin.

My gaze traveled lower.

I inhaled swiftly.

There's no way that's fitting inside of me.

The pink tip of his weeping cock bobbed against the V of his Adonis belt.

Kharon moved his head quickly, and winced with pain.

He tried to hide it, but it was too late, and dread replaced the heat of arousal.

The dim candlelight illuminated the white bandages covering the side of his head.

Dark spots danced in my vision, and I couldn't breathe—there was a new crushing pressure inside my chest, pinning me to the bed.

Memories played—*Kharon kneeled over me in the pouring rain, his eyes flashing with incandescent fury. He lifted a knife past his cheek, held my gaze, and . . . sliced.*

"You . . ." I pointed with a shaking finger to the side of his head.

Kharon smirked casually. "Yes, I gave you my ear. It's not a big deal."

My jaw clicked as it opened and closed.

"My l-left ear," I breathed out with horror.

My vision went black.

He'd sewed his ear onto the side of my head that had *irreversible* internal damage. The side that was deaf.

"What have you done?"

Covering my face, I burst into tears.

"It's really not a big deal." Kharon's voice was laced with confusion. "You needed an ear, and I had one. It's an old Spartan tradition, and I like . . ." He cleared his throat. "I like that I could give you a piece of myself. It's an apology for how we trapped you in marriage—*acta non verba.*"

I sobbed harder.

Deeds, not words.

"Deep breaths. You're okay," Nyx hissed from where Fluffy Jr. was lying on the floor. She slithered onto the bed, invisible scales wrapping around my waist. "Don't blame yourself—it's not your fault he's an idiot."

My heart cracked with regret, because I should have stopped him. I should have said something.

Kharon wouldn't have done it if he'd known I was partially deaf. No one in their right mind would have.

"Please . . . don't cry." Kharon crawled onto the bed and kneeled beside me, his face twisting with panic.

Augustus gently pushed curls off my forehead.

I sniffled, gasping for air, as I wiped at my nose and gathered my courage.

Taking a deep breath, I looked straight into Kharon's eyes. "My left ear was . . ."

"Your left ear was—what?" His brows furrowed.

Augustus kept gently stroking my hair away from my face.

I closed my eyes.

"I'm partially deaf," I blurted, ripping the bandage off. "Your sacrifice was useless—I can't hear out of this ear anyway."

Augustus's hand stilled on the top of my head.

It was dead silent.

I peeked open my eyes sheepishly.

Kharon's face was swathed in shadows, a vein in his forehead pulsing, and Augustus was frozen, a bronze statue of harsh lines.

Suffocating silence stretched.

"How?" Augustus asked with deadly calm.

I shrugged, desperate to break the tension. "It was just some physical damage, not a big deal at—"

"Who?" Augustus cut me off. "Who did it?"

"That's n-not the point." I took another deep steadying breath and focused on Kharon. "You shouldn't have given me your ear. It's a waste."

Kharon closed his eyes, dark eyelashes fanning across sharp cheekbones; Augustus's hand curled, nails scraping against my scalp.

"Who . . . did this to you?" Kharon asked. "I want a name."
"I misspoke . . . I fell . . . and injured myself."
Augustus clenched his jaw.
Kharon smiled, a hateful expression. "You're a shit liar."
"I'm not lying."
They both glowered at me.
I rolled my eyes.
Their fury mounted and I couldn't hold back an inappropriate, watery laugh.
"What's so funny?" Kharon asked with confusion.
Oh.
Out of nowhere, the truth hit me. "I'm not afraid of you two anymore."
Augustus grimaced. "My carus, Sparta is a violent place, and we're . . . *not* good men. You don't know what we're capable of."
Yes, I do.
Kharon's face twisted with pity.
My laughter died, replaced with indignation.
"Maybe," I said, "you two don't know what *I'm* capable of."

16
YOUR PAIN IS MINE

Alexis

"Maybe," I said, "you two don't know me at all—and you *never* will."

Kharon's eyes narrowed into dangerous slits. "Is that a threat?" A muscle in his jaw ticked. "*Princess.*"

"I don't know." I glared up at him. "Is it? You tell me."

The moment stretched.

"I'm too tired for this," Augustus said, raking his hand through his long hair. "It's been long enough since I last leapt—I'm going to deliver the Titans." He turned and wrenched open a narrow door. "Try not to kill each other before I return."

He stomped down the stairs.

Chains rattled and there was a muffled screech.

A crack echoed as he leapt away.

Shivering, I climbed out of the bed. My back throbbed with pain as I quickly pulled on a sweat suit that Augustus had laid out on the bedside table.

Nyx hissed as she slithered around my ankles, climbing up my body, and wrapping herself around my stomach.

I pulled the sweatshirt down on top of her.

Crack.

Augustus reappeared in a cloud of smoke. "Are you strong enough to leap the three of us back to the villa?" he asked as he stared at Kharon's missing ear.

Kharon scoffed. "Clearly."

I could leap us back.

No one bothered to ask me.

Kharon held out his skeleton-tattooed hand, waiting for both of us to take his arm.

Augustus and I obeyed as the hellhounds stood, their bones clattering as they sat at Kharon's feet. Fluffy Jr. pushed his muzzle into Kharon's stomach and looked up at him with wide trusting eyes. Poco climbed up onto Fluffy Jr.'s back for purchase and he laid his little black hand on top of Kharon's finger.

Crack.

The safe house disappeared.

Smoke filled the villa's atrium, the muted morning light dancing off gilded walls and decorative olive trees.

I pulled my hand away like his touch was toxic (it was).

The sacrifice Kharon made for me was heinous—it was the most generous, worst thing anyone had ever done for me.

"My carus," Augustus whispered.

Both of them stepped toward me.

I was drowning in them. *Again.*

"I'd do it a million times over." Kharon gestured at the side of my face. "Stop overthinking."

We weren't good without words, and we weren't good with them, or maybe I just wasn't right for them.

They called me princess. They wanted a good Chthonic girl to coddle and protect. *To obey.*

"I don't think we work," I said, cradling my arms in front of my stomach, a subconscious instinct. "This thing between us . . . isn't . . . healthy."

The tension stretched to a breaking point.

"Alexis—" Augustus's voice was uncharacteristically quiet, and the golden rays softened the sharp angles of his face. "I don't think you understand—there's *no* going back. We're trying to be better . . . for you."

There was a strange pressure around my heart.

I opened my mouth to say something, anything, but a sharp zap coursed through our marriage bond.

Both Augustus and Kharon straightened to their full height, shoulders pulled back as they spread their legs wide—faces cruel.

Dread washed over me.

"You're . . . okay, thank Kronos—we were so fucking worried, we were about to go get . . ." Patro's voice sounded behind me, his words echoing off the marble atrium.

The hairs on the back of my neck stood on end as understanding coursed through me. I froze, rooted to the spot. I didn't turn around.

Augustus stared over my shoulder at the newcomers, his mask of civility disappearing; Kharon never wore one to begin with.

They were both ready for war.

Hell and Hound bristled. Poco stood up on Fluffy Jr.'s back, flashing a mouth of razor-sharp teeth, and chittered viciously.

Poppae hissed behind me, and Nero growled.

Patro cleared his throat. "Alexis—I'm so sorry. I told Achilles he shouldn't have left you. I can't believe—" His voice lowered. "It's my fault."

I wanted to turn around.

If Patro was here, then so was Achilles.

I wanted to confront him, but right now, my mentors were the lesser threat.

DANGER DETECTED.

Sirens wailed inside my skull.

The House of Artemis and the House of Ares had never looked so volatile.

The heartless Chthonics were back.

The killers.

I held up both my hands pleadingly to my husbands. "Wait—let's talk about this. There's no need to overreact."

Neither acted like they'd heard me.

Their gazes were laser focused on the men standing behind me.

"Oh shit . . . it's about to go down," Nyx hissed with excitement, nudging against my chin as she poked her head out the top of my sweatshirt to get a better view.

I wanted to glance behind, but I was certain if I took my eyes off my husbands for even a split second, there would be unholy carnage.

My mind raced. I needed to defuse the tension.

"I f-forgive them." I looked at Kharon imploringly. It wasn't true. Not really. But I needed to do something. "It's okay—I'm *fine*. It all worked out in the end."

Nothing worked out.

Augustus's eyes darted to my ear, then back to the men behind me, and a vein in Kharon's forehead pulsed.

That was my only warning.

Air whistled against my cheeks as my curls lifted and whipped across my face—in complete silence, too quickly for my eyes to track, Kharon and Augustus moved across the marble.

I turned in slow motion.

"Stop it!" I shouted, as Nyx hissed, "PAINT THE WALLS RED WITH THEIR BLOOD."

Augustus threw himself at Achilles.

Kharon tackled a heavily bandaged Patro to the floor, and Patro's metal neck brace clanged.

Nails clacked against marble as the protectors all leapt into action, sprinting after their owners, joining the chaos.

One hellhound tackled Nero and the other tackled Poppae. Guttural growls echoed as the four predators rolled about on the floor, and Poco hissed from within the fray.

"*STOP IT!*" I yelled at the top of my lungs, because I was so tired of the never-ending violence.

Kharon pinned Patro to the floor, crawling over him viciously to get purchase as he shouted in his face.

Achilles tried to get to Patro, but he fell to his knees as Augustus engaged his power and stared into his eyes.

Kharon bellowed with frustration as he looked down at an injured Patro like he was going to strike, but at the last minute, he held himself back, punching the marble floor instead.

Sharp pain flared through my hand. I covered my mouth.

I just felt . . . Kharon's punch, like it was my own.

Across the room, Augustus stood over Achilles with glowing Chthonic eyes.

White lights exploded in my vision—a fresh stabbing sensation pierced behind my eyes—I swallowed a whimper of pain as a migraine slammed into me.

Headaches had recently become an issue for me—*around the same time that blood started leaking from Augustus's eyes.*

Clammy and weak, I stood up straighter.

Kharon got to his feet, limping as he backed away from where Patro struggled on the floor, looking near death.

Augustus staggered away from his brother.

Achilles crawled toward Patro.

I ran forward to try to help Patro—Kharon turned with surprise and his elbow slammed into my solar plexus.

All three of us came to a stop.

Kharon clutched his stomach in shock and Augustus also grunted—no one had touched either of them.

Our gazes locked.

Sick realization dawned on their faces.

"Our bond. We're connected," Augustus said. "By . . . *pain*." He blinked at me, then keeled over and threw up.

Kharon's face twisted. "Can you . . . feel . . . ours?" he asked me with a look of horror as he glanced down at his ruined knee.

I took a deep breath. It would be just another reason for them to coddle me.

"No." I cleared my throat and schooled my expression. "Why? Can you feel mine?" I didn't stutter.

Augustus and Kharon visibly relaxed with relief, shoulders slumping, breath whooshing.

A dark memory surfaced. *"Father killed her," I said calmly to the police officer.*

They thought I was a bad liar.

I wasn't. Not when it really mattered.

On the floor, Patro struggled to sit up as he looked at me. "I'm . . . so sorry. For everything," he whispered brokenly.

For the first time, Patro looked so young.

He was only twenty-two years old.

We were about the same age.

I tried to tell him it was fine, but the words got stuck in my throat. My back was still wrapped in bandages, and Titans were still shrieking in my ear.

Instead, I looked around the room. "Stop fighting. All of you."

"Why, Alexis?" Augustus asked, his voice strained with confusion. "They *left* you to die."

"Because—" I took a deep breath. "I won't treat any of you like you treated me."

Taking a step back, I put more space between us. "I won't be another reason for your violence—I won't be like you two."

"And just . . . *what* are we, carissima?" Kharon's tone was poisonous, shadows crawling across him.

"Belligerent," I said as I held up my fingers and ticked them off. "Misogynistic, cruel, hyperaggressive, despotic megalomaniacs. You don't even *know* what happened, yet you would attack Achilles and Patro."

As I spoke, Fluffy Jr. moved so he stood in front of me protectively, and Nyx slithered up my leg.

Augustus glanced down, then back up to me, face paling like he'd seen a ghost.

"Poco," he whispered.

The raccoon climbed up my back, then stood up on my shoulder with his tiny fists resting on his hips.

Kharon's face dropped as his hellhounds slunk across the atrium to flank me. Bony tails lowered as they growled menacingly.

I reached down, one hand resting on a hellhound's surprisingly warm head.

"We . . . protect," the hellhound said in a garbled voice.

I smiled with gratitude, then straightened.

"Let's go." I gestured to Fluffy Jr., my voice echoing in the atrium, the meaning clear.

Kharon made a strangled sound.

"*Wait*," Augustus whispered.

Achilles helped Patro to his feet, the two of them watching us silently.

I shook my head.

My husbands looked on with devastation as I walked away with their protectors at my side.

17
The Hunter

Kharon: Early June

Thud.
 Whoosh.
Thud.
Whoosh.

The heavy punching bag swung in the dark as I pounded my taped fists against it.

The clock on the training room wall read six in the morning, but time didn't matter when you didn't rest.

My nights were spent standing over Alexis, watching her sleep.

Every morning at five, I ripped myself away from her side and took out my aggression in the gym.

Missions had been paused after the Rome incident, aka the worst day of my fucking life.

There was nothing to do but run through Titan simulations, stalk Alexis, and prepare for the SGC.

August was fast approaching.

We'd started incorporating battle weapons into our daily exercises, mostly sword and dagger work, since guns weren't allowed in the Dolomite Coliseum. The modern weapons dishonored the Kronos blessed sands—only knives, swords, and fists were allowed. Alexis did okay, but she was a novice, and it would take *years* to master a blade.

We didn't have years. We had weeks.

On top of all that, Alexis hadn't talked to us since we'd fought with Patro and Achilles a few weeks ago.

She hadn't said a *single* word.

Not one.

The Crimson Duo had fucking left her to *die*. We'd saved her, and yet she was mad at both of us.

Little did she know, we'd shown them mercy.

They were still alive.

Bouncing on the balls of my feet, I kicked out. The bag careened violently to the side, spinning. I kicked it back in the other direction. The need to slaughter, kill, hurt, was a constant urge.

Thud-thud-thud.

I jabbed with all my might.

Bloody prints smeared the bag's surface as my knuckles split.

I punched faster.

The sound was muffled strangely without the shell of my left ear, but I hadn't lied when I said I was glad Alexis had it. If she'd been permanently marred by the fucking Titans, Achilles and Patro would be dead right now.

I kicked harder, my ruined knee on fire.

It was a Kronos damned miracle that Alexis couldn't feel my or Augustus's pain. *Thank fuck* the connection only went one way. Embarrassment churned inside my gut at the mere thought of Alexis knowing how I felt.

If she knew just how weak I was, how much my leg hurt daily, she'd be disgusted.

She'd think I wasn't good enough to be her husband.

At this point, I'd do *anything* for a single word from her. I'd strip naked and crawl. I'd stab myself in the heart.

At night, I found myself delicately tracing her cheeks, her nose, her eyebrows, with the tips of my fingers, desperate to connect with her.

"Fuck!" I screamed as I kicked, and the chain snapped. The punching bag flew across the room, slamming into the wall in a cloud of chalk.

I fell to my knees.

"You need to come to our room and see this!" Augustus shouted down from the entrance hatch. "*Now.*"

Neck prickling at the uncharacteristic fear in his voice, I staggered to my feet.

A few minutes later I stood in front of a black computer screen, as Augustus rapidly clicked buttons on the keyboard.

"What am I supposed to be looking at?" I asked, as I dragged my bloody hands down my face and attempted to wipe away my exhaustion.

Augustus didn't answer, stabbing at the keyboard like he had a personal vendetta against it.

The screen flickered on.

It was a grainy video with the watermark of a popular Spartan chaser. I rolled my eyes at the crowd of elderly humans on the screen. "What did the stupid bastards film now—"

The camera panned to the Roman Colosseum, where two Titans stood tall on the grass in front of it, their wings larger than I remembered. They looked revolting.

The camera turned, zooming in on the humans again.

Both Titans were headed straight toward them.

They were dead.

Shots echoed off screen and the cameraman gasped, the picture shook—Alexis lunged out of nowhere and threw herself in front of the humans with her arms spread wide.

I leaned closer.

She raised both her guns and fired.

Hair blowing behind her back, face determined, she held her ground like certain death wasn't stalking toward her.

The bullets barely slowed the Titans.

I waited for her to leap away; I waited for her to save herself.

In a blur of white, Fluffy Jr. jumped on one of the Titans and tackled it to the ground. The usually docile creature, who seemed to constantly be suffering from digestive issues, was more vicious than I could have ever imagined.

But there was still one Titan standing.

"Why isn't she leaping away?"

Augustus's frown deepened. "Oh—just you fucking wait."

I didn't like his tone.

Hands fisted, I watched the winged fucking monstrosity approach my wife until it was close enough to kill.

I gritted my teeth. "Tell me she leaps away right now."

Augustus scowled and shook his head, his eyes locked on the screen.

"WHY isn't she saving herself?" I asked, unable to watch, but unable to look away.

Alexis reached down and unsheathed two of the knives I'd given her.

My breath caught. "No . . . she doesn't." I'd assumed she'd gotten her wounds because the Titans had tracked her down, ambushed her before she got away.

Never in a million years could I imagine *this*.

"Yep," Augustus said.

My jaw dropped as my barely trained wife leapt *toward* the Titan with two daggers raised, stabbing it at point-blank range.

The creature shrieked in pain as it spun, trying to dislodge her. She held on.

I covered my mouth as talons sliced through her back, exposing bone. I waited for her to fall back, to pass out, to collapse.

Alexis shook her head and tightened her grip. Somehow, with

her back torn to shreds, she held on and dug her knives deeper into the Titan, dragging them down through its belly.

The Titan collapsed and she straddled it.

Two-colored eyes wide, black blood splattered across the delicate bridge of her nose, Alexis stabbed at the creature without mercy.

She was the most powerful, beautiful thing I'd ever seen in my fucking life.

Without help, Alexis had incapacitated a Titan that was more powerful than any we'd ever seen. It was limp beneath her. She reached for her cuffs. *She's doing it.*

The camera panned to the side.

The other Titan was getting to its feet.

No.

Alexis's hands slipped as she desperately fumbled with the cuffs. She didn't have time, and she was badly injured.

"RUN!" I yelled at the screen.

The Titan was on her before I could blink.

She was gone.

The camera tipped back. Alexis was rising through the air, locked in the Titan's grasp as it flew straight up—higher and higher, until she was nothing more than a dot in the sky.

Human voices screamed with horror as they pointed.

Crack.

A concrete table exploded as Alexis and the Titan slammed into it.

The camera zoomed in on where my wife was crawling through the smoke and rubble.

"What the fuck?" I whispered.

"She somehow leapt from midair to a controlled spot on the ground," Augustus said, pure awe in his voice. "While she was badly injured . . . *with* a Titan."

"That shouldn't be possible."

"No fuck."

"And it's such a short distance—how is she doing that?"

"I have . . . no idea."

The House of Hades was known for its might, but this was next level. We both watched in shock as our blood-covered wife stumbled to her feet. She focused on the pathetic humans, like she was more worried about them than herself.

Then she was kneeling over an injured woman, the camera view mostly blocked by other people.

What is she doing?

"Savior," the humans called out as they cried and prayed.

She staggered to stand again. Golden curls were messy around her head, resembling a halo.

What the fuck is she doing?

"She's an angel," someone shouted.

"A hero."

"She saved her."

Another voice said, "The Angel of Rome."

The picture shook and there was a watery gasping, like the cameraman was sobbing.

Humans prayed loudly. From the sound of it, they were praying *to* her.

Alexis said something weakly, then she threw up.

Everything got blurry as the picture swung back and forth between the two Titans who were both standing up.

It focused back on Alexis. Her expression was determined even though she had deep wounds.

Augustus looked at me, and the unspoken *holy fucking shit* hung between us.

Our wife was a beast.

I forced my gaze back to the screen.

Again, she leapt across the field—*Crack!* Then she leapt *again*. She kept fighting, long past when she should have passed out from blood loss.

I didn't look away until we appeared on the screen.

I didn't look away as I sobbed over her in the rain, cut off my ear, and sewed it onto her.

I watched as Augustus carried Alexis against his chest, Titans dragging behind him, as I hung off him half delirious, glaring at all the humans.

I didn't remember there being such a crowd.

The camera panned out.

There were *hundreds* of people.

"Angelus Romae," echoed loudly as the young and old chanted for her.

When the screen went black, long moments passed as Augustus and I stared at it in silence, neither of us knowing what to say.

"She's fucking insane," I croaked hoarsely, when I finally regained the ability to speak. "She's . . ."

"Perfect," Augustus whispered reverently.

I nodded in agreement.

"The problem is—" Augustus's voice hardened "—all the humans think so too." The keyboard clicked as he toggled between screens.

The Spartan Lifestyle Page came up, the bane of all our existences. But instead of the usual images of Achilles and Patro, the page was covered in pictures and videos of *our* Alexis.

"The Hero We've Been Waiting For" spread across the top of the page in big bold letters.

Augustus clicked.

Image after image of Alexis in the fight popped up. There were also drawings of her. Paintings. *Sexual* paintings of her falling from the sky with wings. Thankfully, they were fully bullshit and looked nothing like her—but it was the principle of it.

We weren't the only ones obsessed.

Everyone wanted her.

They can't have her.

"We have to earn her trust," I said. "We *have* to do something to show her how we feel. She won't accept jewelry, clothes, or money. We have to come up with—"

"I'm already ahead of you." Augustus stood up and rummaged through a dresser drawer until he pulled out a sleek black box.

He opened it and I grinned. "That's genius."

Augustus smiled back, the first time in weeks that he'd made the expression. "We're going to get her back." His eyes dimmed. "We have to . . ."

Or we won't survive was left unsaid.

Either Alexis broke the silent treatment and spoke to us, or we perished.

It was just a matter of time.

Muted rays streamed in through the windows as doves cooed outside, heavy clouds hanging over the choppy waters of Lake Como.

Morning had arrived.

It was time to train.

Augustus sighed heavily and rubbed at the stubble on his jaw. The circles around his eyes were darker than they'd ever been. He was as ruined as I was.

"Let's go," he said.

"Where?"

"To get our wife."

I cracked my knuckles. It was about time.

18
The Price of Power

Alexis

I limped into the villa and headed toward Helen's room.

Hell and Hound prowled in front of me, and Fluffy Jr. walked at my side with Poco on his neck.

I was exhausted and drenched to the bone, because for the last sixteen hours, Augustus had led all of us on a punishing run through the rain (he was a homicidal maniac).

When night had fallen, and we'd *finally* stopped, I slipped out while everyone headed to the training center to shower.

Only Achilles had noticed me walk away. In fact, he'd been staring at me a lot lately.

Lightning flashed, illuminating the villa's entrance, and my right knee buckled—I grabbed blindly to steady myself.

I was holding on to the fifteen-foot-tall bronze statue of a naked warrior that decorated the corner of the atrium. The man held a stone in his right hand and was strangling a monstrous snake with his other—the beast's mouth was wide open, curved fangs bared.

"You *really* need to bulk up," Nyx said unhelpfully from around my neck.

Releasing the sculpture, and ignoring my bruised pride, I limped out of the atrium and made my way down a long corridor.

"Carissima."

Thunder cracked as Kharon's voice echoed darkly off the walls.

I slowly turned around.

Augustus and Kharon stood at the end of the hall I'd just limped down. Soaking wet, their workout clothes were plastered to their sculpted bodies.

Their narrowed eyes glowed faintly in the dark, like they were creatures from Hell.

It's an ambush.

Winged Titans would have been less imposing.

Augustus cleared his throat. "We have something for you. A . . . gift." He held up a black box. "Please, take it."

Never again.

I shook my head.

Kharon's jaw clenched. "Take it," he said quietly, his posture rigid. "Please," he bit out, like it physically pained him to say the word.

I pulled my shoulders back, mimicking his stance.

"No."

Kharon ground his teeth together.

A beat passed, then he and Augustus stalked toward me, their footsteps silent as they approached.

Run for your life.

I widened my stance and held my ground.

The storm raged outside.

"Leave me alone." My voice rang down the hall.

Kharon's face twisted. "I can't do that." He clenched his jaw. "*Anything* but that."

"You looked tired during the run." Augustus studied me

from head to toe, searching for injuries as he stalked closer. "Are you feeling okay?"

Sure, if okay means like a cadaver.

They were only ten feet away.

Nyx clicked her fangs. "Tell them you'd feel better if they crawled and kissed your feet." She paused like she was thinking about it. "Also, they need to be naked. That part is crucial."

I really can't keep living like this.

They were almost in my personal space.

I reached my hands down and touched the animals who sat at my feet.

Kharon made a strangled sound as he realized my intention—he grasped for me.

"Domus."

Black-painted nails swiped like claws, centimeters from my face.

CRACK.

I collapsed onto a pile of sparkly dresses, groaning—smoke billowed—I was back inside Helen's empty room. I'd done the impossible again; I'd leapt a short distance mid-panic.

Apparently, I had no innate sense of self-preservation. *Yay?*

Tripping over pillows and boxes of makeup, I threw myself against the door, shutting it as I turned the locks.

Heaving, I leaned against it and slumped with relief.

My gasps echoed in the quiet.

I was alone.

Safe.

No one was going to bother me.

Finally.

I just needed some time to—

"Alexis." Kharon's voice echoed through the door, vibrating with menace.

I shrieked.

How did he move so fast?

I backed away into the room. A string of pearls on top of a

bejeweled purple gun wrapped around my ankle and I fell to the ground.

"You could have gotten hurt leaping," Augustus said in the hall.

"What did I say would happen if you injured yourself?" Kharon asked coldly. "I believe I was very . . . explicit."

Something about tormenting me for all of eternity?

Too late.

There was a dull popping sound like Kharon was cracking his knuckles.

"Wait, are you threatening me?" I asked, half outraged, half disturbed (mentally).

"No," Augustus said too quickly.

Kharon chuckled, cadence severe and mocking. "Obviously—Alexis."

My heartbeat pounded in my ears.

"Go away," I said as I crawled on hands and knees across the floor, desperate to put more space between us.

"We're trying to apologize." Augustus sounded remorseful and sincere.

"I'm fucking sorry," Kharon said belligerently. "I demand you forgive me, Alexis." He paused. "Right now!"

I choked.

Does he really think that's going to work?

How I'd managed to find a man *more* socially inept than myself should be studied.

"Tell them that you'll accept their regret," Nyx hissed. "But *only* if they give you a sexual favor. Woman's choice."

I looked longingly at the gun.

Kharon swore viciously in the hall, like he'd just realized verbally attacking his wife was not yielding a positive result.

I crawled into the attached bathroom.

Fluffy Jr. whined (neighed?) in the bedroom, too large to fit, but the skinnier hellhounds followed me inside, the blue flames in their eye sockets flashing red—I blinked—they once again flickered an innocuous teal.

Did I imagine it?

I blew a kiss to Fluffy Jr. and shut the door.

Kharon yelled something, but it was blessedly muffled.

Dozens of flickering pink candles, wrapped with white bows, sat along the rim of the bathtub, dripping wax.

Nyx slithered off my shoulders as I climbed into the tub, reached up, and yanked on the spray.

Fully clothed, I looked down.

"C+A" was stark across my forearm—I traced the letters of the messy tattoo.

Sparta was a tangled web of politics and power.

Kharon shouted something louder.

Do it for Charlie.

I dug my right fingernail into the palm of my hand.

Blood trickled out of the shallow cut as a prickling sensation tingled my fingers.

Water fell around me in slow motion.

I raised my arm higher and imagined the bloody streaks forming a protective shield or hovering in the air like fog.

Claim your power, daughter. Hades's voice echoed in my head.

Nothing happened.

Everyone else in the Assembly of Death controlled their abilities—mine was inert—it was wielding *me*.

Even Drex could tap into his stamina at will.

"Don't panic," Nyx hissed as I did just that. "Let's play the alliteration game."

Nostalgia hit me. Nyx came up with it when I was a young child, and we'd continued the tradition through high school. We used to play late at night when the hunger pangs were so sharp that I couldn't sleep, and there was nothing to do but wait for the sun to rise.

"Audacious anguines annoy Alexis," I whispered.

Nyx cackled. She'd always loved the game. "Adders almost *ate* Alexis."

"Alexis anticipates agita," I said, already feeling calmer. "After another archaic *agonizing* anticlimactic athletic action."

"Now it's the hellhounds' turn," Nyx hissed.

I sighed. Lately she'd become unhealthily obsessed (murderous) when it came to the dangerous creatures.

Pulling aside the shower curtain, I looked at the skeletal hounds. "Nyx wants to know if you want to play the alliteration game with us." I found that it helped my subconscious to speak hellhound if I was looking at them. Talking to Nyx was way easier, probably because I'd known her most of my life.

They nodded aggressively.

A long minute passed as they came up with their answer.

"Alexis . . . big . . . girl," Hell garbled, bony jaw flapping.

Hound chortled. "Good one."

Over the past few days, it had become abundantly clear that they *weren't* the brightest.

I wasn't in any place to judge.

"What did they say?" Nyx asked excitedly. "Tell me."

Being a translator was surprisingly exhausting. "They said—Alexis is an awesome animal."

Nyx scoffed. "Tell them that's not how the alliteration game works and they're pathetic stupid idiots . . . Also, I will kill them to put them out of their misery."

I rolled my eyes.

"Tell them right now—do it," Nyx demanded impatiently. "I want to see their faces."

I looked at Hell again. "Nyx says you're very smart and she's impressed by your alliteration."

Hell sat up straighter and preened. "She big right."

"Smart dog!" Hound announced proudly as she bumped her shoulder into Hell's with a clatter.

"Why do they seem so happy?" Nyx asked suspiciously.

"They want to die," I said dryly.

Nyx clacked her jaw with excitement. "So—can I try and kill them now?"

"No."

"So, yes."

"No."

"No, as in maybe?"

I stared up at the multiple water faucets. "Asking for a friend—can snakes drown?"

Nyx hissed but fell silent as she slid up my body and twined around my arm.

A few minutes later, I stumbled out of the bathroom and dressed for bed. From the peaceful quiet, my husbands had left.

I slipped into the adjoining room.

Ceres was asleep under the covers, which were covered in the Spartan history books that Helen kept giving her.

A pen was still clutched between her ink-stained fingers, like she'd fallen asleep taking notes, desperately trying to regain her memory.

In the bright moonlight, her features were soft and doll-like—she furrowed her brow and whimpered, looking impossibly young in the grand four-poster bed—there were ink smudges on her cheeks.

Lavender eyes blinked open and Ceres yawned, pointing to a book open at the foot of the bed. "I think . . . I'm finally remembering."

She closed her eyes and turned, snuggling under the covers as she fell back asleep.

I peered down at the book she'd pointed to. Words were scribbled at the top of the page in her cursive handwriting.

"Zeus + Vyco. Hercules? Assassination?"

My stomach dropped.

What do I have to do with her memory?

Also, Vyco was the man who claimed I'd been attacked by Titans as a baby.

The scar on my sternum tingled.

I looked closer at the book. The text appeared to be archaic symbols in different colors, and was like no history book I'd ever seen.

Ceres had underlined sections and written in the margin, "Need to remember that day."

How can she read this?

I backed away.

Tensions in Sparta were high.

Just yesterday, "Medusa manhunt picks up steam, Federation plans to start interrogating Chthonics" was printed across the top of the daily *Falcon Chronicles*.

I need to run away while I still can.

I rubbed at my wrists.

Hades believes in you.

I stumbled back into Helen's dark bedroom.

Helen and Charlie were both asleep.

During my shower (protracted mental health episode), the two of them must have returned from their night tutoring session.

Charlie was asleep on the floor in a pile of pink pillows, a healthy glow to his cheeks. His features had been filling out since he began his stay at the villa.

Kohl was smudged around his eyes. *Definitely Helen's.*

Smiling more and scowling less, Charlie stuck to Helen's side since they had classes together all day. They often were giggling with each other at some joke the rest of us didn't understand. He wrote on a notepad and was constantly showing it to her, then hiding it from everyone else.

I'd even caught him signing with Achilles at dinner.

There was no evidence of the aggressive boy who was constantly getting into fights. He'd shed his old, starved self like a second skin.

I wished I could do the same.

Charlie smiled in his sleep. Fluffy Jr. lay facing him, their arms (and hooves?) overlapping.

Sighing, feeling like I was twenty going on one hundred years old, I slid under pink silk sheets.

Almost instantly I dreamed of the grim reaper standing over me.

He caressed my cheek. "I'll be back," he promised darkly. "Don't worry—I'll *always* return."

My eyes opened and I sat up with a gasp.

Death was gone.

Did the door just close? Was there a shadow moving? Was there—

The bed dipped as a fluffy gray creature waddled across it. Poco climbed toward me until his whiskers tickled my face.

"I told you that we can't keep doing this," I whispered.

He patted his tiny hand against my cheek as if telling me not to worry, then he curled up into a furry ball, his back pressed against mine.

I pulled the covers up over him, so he was fully covered with his ears sticking out, just how he liked.

His gentle purrs vibrated through me.

I closed my eyes.

For the first time in weeks, nightmares didn't plague me.

The grim reaper was gone.

Knock.

Knock.

Knock.

For the second time, I jolted awake.

From the moonlight, only a few hours had passed. The soft raps continued. Poco purred. Helen and Charlie shifted in their sleep.

"Alexis—are you up?" Patro whispered through the door. "We need to talk."

19
DEMONS IN THE DARK

ALEXIS

My heart dropped.

I hadn't spoken to Patro and Achilles for a reason—the reason being *betrayal* of the highest order.

Lingering childhood abandonment issues aside, leaving a person alone with mutated monsters was simply unprofessional, even for cult members. *No one has any class these days.*

Knock.

Knock.

Knock.

Charlie huffed on the floor, turning over in his pile of pink bedding.

"Stop," I called out as quietly as I could. "People are *resting*."

Helen mumbled into her pillow, unconsciously reaching for the bedazzled pink Beretta on her bedside table.

She wouldn't shoot me in her sleep, right?

"I don't care. Come out—or I'll wake the room," Patro threatened coldly from the other side of the door. "Now."

He knocked again, louder.

Helen sat up and raised the gun—eyes still closed—and clicked off the safety.

Blanching, I quietly slid out of bed.

Poco woke up with a sleepy chirp. He climbed up onto my shoulder as I pulled a snoring Nyx out from under the pillow, and wrapped her around my neck.

"Go back to sleep, you stupid cow," she hissed at me.

Hell perked up on the floor.

Helen mumbled in her sleep, waving the loaded weapon around the room before she pointed it directly at my forehead.

Oh nice.

I backed toward the door, tiptoeing around Charlie.

Fluffy Jr. was next to him whimpering in his sleep, and the large hump on his back was . . . quivering?

I leaned closer.

Patro rapped sharply. "Alexis—are you coming or not?" He sounded haughty and arrogant.

I miss when he was unconscious with a snapped neck.

Helen pointed the Beretta at the door, then she aimed it back at me. Apparently, her sleep self had decided I was the bigger threat.

A little flattered, but mostly afraid of imminent friendly fire, I slipped out into the candlelit hall with Hell following.

The door creaked shut behind us and I walked straight into an unmoving mass.

I looked up slowly.

Arms were crossed over a wide chest, an unlit cigarette hung from the grates of a muzzle. Achilles stood right outside the door, blocking me.

I stared at him and waited.

Neither of us moved.

Lungs turned to stone in my chest.

Titans screeched, talons sliced through my spine, humans sobbed, blood everywhere, suspended in the air above the city, "Domus."

Weeks later, abject terror still left a bitter residue in my mouth. I understood *why* he did it, but something about the way Achilles hadn't bothered to apologize set my teeth on edge, especially since he knew I would understand his signing. If anything, he acted like he was mad at me.

During workouts, I'd constantly find him glaring at the side of my face, glancing between me and Patro with open distaste.

"M-move," I whispered.

A growl echoed from my feet, bones pressing against my leg as Hell tensed next to me protectively.

Achilles didn't budge.

Hot resentment mounted. "Fuck you," I signed, before I could stop myself.

He jerked, eyes flashing, then he raised his hand—I just barely stopped myself from flinching back.

The temperature in the hall increased as Achilles leaned toward me. "You *should* have told me you knew sign language." His fingers moved, deliberate and accusatory.

It smelled like something was burning.

"And *you*," I signed back slowly, "shouldn't have *left* me to die."

Achilles flinched. His hands bunched into fists, knuckles cracking.

He still didn't apologize.

"Get the fuck away from me," I signed jerkily. "*Now.*"

Leather cracked as his muzzle stretched, and Achilles finally stepped to the side, revealing Patro.

Candlelight danced over the sculpted planes of his perfect face; his emerald eyes were startlingly bright in the shadowy hall.

"What the h-hell are you doing?" I whispered, deeply unsettled by my standoff with Achilles.

Patro arched his eyebrow, dress pants and shirt impeccably

pressed, hair perfectly coiffed. He was a superiority complex in the flesh.

"We've been trying to get you alone," Patro said slowly. "But it's been impossible lately—especially with Kharon at night."

What about Karen?

I shook my head and focused on the problem at hand—Patro.

"*What* do you want?" I asked.

Patro's lip curled as he looked me up and down.

The infamous courting gift—aka Kharon's oversized skeleton sweatshirt, which I refused to give back or feel sorry about wearing because it was so cozy—hung to my knees, and the marble floor was chilly beneath my bare feet.

"Nice hat," Patro snickered.

Poco hissed from where he sat, heavy, fluffy, and warm on the top of my head.

Patro muttered something about me being "ridiculous and hard to take seriously."

I turned to go back inside—Achilles blocked me, *again*.

Poco pulled at my scalp nervously, and my spine prickled with warning.

"Wait." Patro grabbed my arm and turned me to face him. "*Please*—we want to apologize . . . for Rome." He looked at me pleadingly.

With a deep steadying breath, I met his gaze. "Achilles was always going to choose you."

It was the truth.

Patro dragged his hands over his face. "No," he said. "It's not like . . . that." LIAR was written across his knuckles. He couldn't meet my eyes.

"It's done," I said. "I don't want to talk about it." *There's nothing more to say.*

Patro dropped his hands.

"Leave me alone."

"I can't," Patro whispered, like he was sorry.

I stepped back and bounced against Achilles's unmoving chest.

Turning in a rush, I struggled to breathe.

Achilles raised his hands, as if dealing with a skittish animal, and moved to stand beside Patro.

"Our initial offer still stands," Achilles signed, the end of his cigarette burning, smoke curling around his face.

A sharp pain stabbed behind my eyes. *Is Augustus using his power right now?*

"Do you accept?" Patro asked.

I looked between them with confusion. "What are you t-talking about?"

"We'll help you." Patro stepped closer, his icy scent contrasting with Achilles's heat. His voice dropped to a low whisper. "Use your powers to . . . you know . . . *break* the marriage bond with your husbands."

I stepped back, banging against the door.

"No way," I blurted.

Why on earth would I want to do that?

You're supposed to be getting revenge.

Not like that.

Patro sighed. "You'll just *almost* kill them—just use your power and bring them to the brink."

I shook my head.

"Kronos." Patro raked his hands through his short curls, messing up their perfect placement. "Why are you *always* so difficult?"

Angry words gathered on the tip of my tongue, but they wouldn't come out.

"Then *we'll* do it for you," Patro said. "Since you're too afraid to do it yourself."

"Leave m-me alone."

Patro studied my face like he was searching for something.

Light flashed at my feet. I glanced down. The flames in Hell's eyes were bright red, instead of their usual teal flame. *What the heck?*

Patro grabbed my arm gently. "This will just be a pinch," he said. "It will all be okay, I promise."

"What—"

Patro jabbed a needle with an Olympian vial into my skin, and the tube filled with scarlet. In a flash, he removed it, pocketing my blood. "You're welcome. You'll thank us." He nodded like he was trying to convince himself.

Panic paralyzed me.

Poco hissed and swiped—Patro dodged his claw and backed away from me with Achilles at his side. Something that looked like regret glimmered in his eyes.

"I'll make you pay for this."

Patro smiled sadly. "All you have to do is give us a signal. We're on *your* side."

Hell growled, the sound filled with warning.

"I'm just trying to protect you," Patro added. "By the way, Ceres is playing you. I can tell when someone is lying. You don't know the danger you're in and I can see she—"

"*Don't*," I signed, cutting him off. "Stay away from her."

Everything was spiraling out of control.

Patro frowned. "I'm only trying to help you."

Hell stalked toward him, bones flickering, serrated teeth bared.

"Drop dead," I signed jerkily.

Achilles yanked a hurt-looking Patro behind him protectively. Hell crouched low between us.

"You're both cowards," I signed.

Achilles held my gaze, unflinching, as they turned and disappeared into the shadows.

Gasping, I staggered into the silent room and climbed into bed. Poco chirped mournfully.

He wrapped his little fluffy arms around my neck, and I hugged him back, my tears dripping into his fur.

Hell jumped up, resting a bony skull on my lap. "You . . . sad?"

I nodded.

Hell growled. "Me . . . kill."

I shook my head no.

Nyx woke up around my neck with a yawn. "What did I miss?" she asked.

"Hell wants to murder people," I whispered.

Poco chittered and curled up next to me, and Hell repositioned so he was resting on the bed at my feet.

Nyx huffed. "How does he feel about his own personal demise? Is he terrified of me?"

I picked up a sparkly pillow and crushed it against my face.

"Alexis, ask him for me," Nyx hissed. "Ask him *now*."

I silently screamed.

20

The Eldest Heir

Augustus: That Same Night

The night was dark and sinister outside our bedroom window. Emotions choked me as my skull pounded.

So much fucking rage.

Every second that Alexis refused to talk to me, the madness grew.

Seething inside my chest, the urge to slaughter, destroy, *maim* was mounting. There was nothing that could put out the fire, and it was becoming harder to pretend that I was a reasonable man.

Kharon stalked inside the room.

His pupils were blown, eyes full of fury, because he wasn't going to be able to watch Alexis sleep tonight.

We both pretended he didn't have a problem.

"You ready?" Kharon asked as he stared at my hands. "The plan's still on?"

I dropped the gasping Olympian doctor to the floor.

The purple owl of the House of Athena was embroidered on his white coat; dark hair was a tangled mess around his withered face; green eyes darted around wildly.

My finger marks were stark around his pale throat.

"Last chance," I said calmly, as I flexed my knuckles. "What have you heard about why the Titans are mutating? What do the Olympians know?"

The doctor shook his head. "I told you. *Nothing.* Nobody knows why they—"

I engaged my powers.

His head rocked back—eyes exploding—limbs sprawled as he slumped unconscious.

Kharon arched his brow.

I smiled.

For the first time in weeks, my headache abated, and a sense of peace settled over me.

"Whatever." Kharon stepped over the Olympian. "Let's go."

He held out his tattooed arm—I grabbed it.

"Domus."

It took a second for my eyes to adjust to the new brighter light.

The sun hung low on the horizon, setting in streaks of vibrant pink. Birds flew overhead, and insects chirped. The air was crisp and scented with wet earth.

Location: *trailer park, bumfuck Montana.*

I cracked my neck with anticipation. The site was a reminder—Alexis hid from us that she was partially deaf. Someone was going to pay.

My headache started up again, worse than before.

It was time to get answers, and where Alexis grew up was the perfect place to start.

I wiped wetness off my face, my fingers covered in scarlet.

All this time, Alexis couldn't hear out of one ear. During the fucking crucible, we screamed at her while she—

I needed to stop thinking about it.

Struggling to breathe, to calm myself, to tamp down the madness, I tried to focus on our mission.

Golden hair blowing as she raised a gun and a knife, glaring at the Titans with determination.

Alexis wasn't weak. She didn't need my pity.

Kharon palmed a gun. *Click.* He slid in a cartridge and flicked off the safety.

"What are you doing?" I snapped.

Ignoring me, Kharon stomped down the gravel road toward the row of dilapidated trailers, gun raised and his black cloak trailing behind him.

I stalked after him.

Sighing, I reached down my hand to offer—

Poco isn't with you anymore.

My heart squeezed.

Kharon banged on the door of a trailer, scoffing at the hand-painted sign hanging above it: *Private property, organ harvesters beware.*

"Open the door," Kharon shouted. "Or I'm kicking it in."

The various metal sheets, patched together to create the front of the trailer, rattled like they were going to fall apart.

The door flew open.

A portly middle-aged man held up a crowbar. "I'm gonna fucking whack you, you goddamned—"

Kharon smiled with his teeth.

"S-S-Spartans?" the man whispered in horror, crowbar dropping as he stumbled back.

Since we stood taller than the peeling door frame, we had to duck our heads to keep him in our vision.

Have humans always been so puny?

I pulled out the pictures of Alexis and Charlie that I'd secretly taken at dinner last week.

"What can you tell me about this girl and boy?"

The man blanched and shook his head, his eyes darting around. "I d-don't know them."

"You're lying." Kharon held the gun up to his head.

Whimpering, the man's mouth opened and closed with a wheeze. A woman appeared.

Gray-haired, wearing hole-riddled clothes, she cleared her throat as she pointed to the picture I was holding. Her arm was covered in fresh bruises.

"Alexis and Charlie," she whispered. "Those rug rats lived behind the tree line . . . Good kids. Everyone in town knew about them—especially Alexis . . . She was a prodigy. We heard she's a Spartan." Her voice filled with awe. "Is it true?"

Kharon worked his jaw back and forth. "*Why* . . . did no one help her?" he asked.

"Shut the fuck up, Katie." The man whirled toward the woman. "Don't say another goddamn word or I'll—"

Thud.

He dropped to the floor with a splattering sound.

Wincing, because I'd only meant to knock him out, I nudged him with my boot.

Cerebral fluid leaked out of his ears.

Not my best work.

Katie gasped, raising her bruised arms in front of her face protectively as pieces of the man's brain oozed from his nose.

Fresh rage filled my chest, and I wished I could kill him a second time.

"Really?" Kharon looked at me.

I focused on Katie. "Madam, you're safe now. This man can't hurt you anymore."

Slowly, she lowered her arms, wide eyes staring up at me in disbelief. "Why . . . why would you help me?" She looked confused.

Alexis's admission about her ear echoed in the back of my mind.

"Men who hurt women don't deserve to live."

Katie made a strangled noise.

Gazing around the decrepit trailer, I patted down my empty

pockets with increasing frustration. "I'll come back with some healing paste and money so you can—"

"Here." Kharon pulled a Spartan gun out of his holster. "You should be able to pawn this for money. Right? Also, you can use it to protect yourself if anyone else tries to hurt you."

Katie blinked in disbelief as Kharon placed the gun in her hand.

Kharon wiggled it. "*Careful*—don't shoot yourself."

Katie jumped.

I slapped Kharon across the back of the head. "Sorry, madam, he doesn't get out much."

"It was just a joke," Kharon grumbled, but he stepped back and gave the woman space to hold her new weapon.

"Do you have anything else you can tell us?" I asked her, letting my desperation show on my face.

She shook her head no, and stared down at the gun with awe.

I tasted bile.

Her face morphed into Alexis, then Helen, then back to Alexis.

I left as quickly as possible, needing to get out of the trailer. Kharon followed without a word.

"Wait!" Katie yelled from the door.

We stopped.

I couldn't look over at her.

"The rug rats—we couldn't help them, because rumor was . . ." She lowered her voice. "Someone threatened to make grizzly food out of any folk who helped them—that's all I know. *Swear to God.*"

"We appreciate it," Kharon said calmly, even though his eyes flashed with wrath.

Katie disappeared inside her trailer.

Both of us scowled.

Dark emotions were rising between us—killing wasn't enough—we needed to hold Alexis as she told us every bad thing that had ever been done to her, then avenge it all.

"When she said grizzly—" Kharon bit out. "Does she mean the antique semiautomatic weapon I was researching for our initial prototype bodies and—"

"It's a type of bear," I said.

Kharon made a face.

An hour—and four dead men—later, we'd learned Alexis and Charlie had once lived in a trailer with two supposed parents, but the father was arrested for killing the mother, and they were homeless orphans.

Also, this trailer park had a problem with men hurting women.

The only men who seemed nonviolent in the park were a group of elderly guys who lived at the edges, and a young man named Paul who wouldn't stop talking about birds and . . . *government drones*? He wasn't well.

"I can't believe someone threatened them to let kids live in the fucking *woods*, and they all did nothing." Kharon kicked a rock, and it shattered against a distant tree. "Why the fuck would anyone do that? Do you think it was their foster father?"

I clenched my teeth. "The scars on Alexis's wrists and her ear."

"They're old injuries." Kharon stilled. "She must have been a child because her Spartan healing hadn't kicked in yet . . . We need to pay a visit to the prison."

I nodded in agreement. "That one woman said something about a tattooed man helping them—let's find out."

The last trailer, positioned at the edge of the forest, was maintained better than the rest.

As we moved toward it, Kharon's face became blank, the whites of his eyes filling as he activated his Chthonic powers. He stopped walking.

"What are you doing?" I asked.

He didn't answer.

Seconds stretched into minutes as I waited for him to do or say something.

Just when I was convinced he needed medical help, the blood receded and his blank expression disappeared.

His expression was livid. "We have a problem," he said darkly.

I pointed to the last trailer we needed to investigate. "Save it—we need to finish what we started."

Kharon looked like he was going to argue, but he eventually nodded and stalked forward.

"Open up or we'll *shoot*!" Kharon kicked at the front door.

The door swung wide immediately. "How can I help you gentlemen?"

The man who answered was about our age, slightly shorter, and his face was covered in satanic symbols.

He smiled pleasantly.

Without preamble, I stabbed my powers into his mind.

Solid darkness greeted me. He had mental defenses, *extremely* strong ones.

I pressed against them, searching for weak points, but they were heavily fortified. Animalistic growls echoed in my head each time I pushed against the solid rock. The only minds I'd ever felt that were somewhat similar were—

I withdrew from his mind. "Shoot him," I ordered.

Kharon fired, but it was too late.

Smoke billowed and there was nothing but empty space where the man had been standing.

He'd leapt away.

"*What* the fuck?" Kharon turned to me. "Who was that?"

"Not who—*what*."

Kharon stomped into the trailer, opening drawers and pulling shit apart as he searched for a clue. "Was it an Olympian?"

"He was primordial—*ancient*." I shook my head. "I think . . . I think he was part creature. His defenses were animalistic, but he was strong. Extremely so."

No one had ever fully stopped my mental attack.

Minds were breakable.

Always.

Kharon threw down the letters with frustration. "Why would a powerful ancient creature be living *here*?"

"I don't know."

"Fuck!" Kharon kicked at the trailer wall; his foot dented the metal. "I don't like this—I don't like this at all."

"Me neither," I said. "We need answers."

Kharon straightened his dark cloak, determination on his face. "Well, then let's get them."

Crack.

White flurries fell furiously through freezing air and I exhaled an icy cloud—a white-covered concrete building towered before us with a tall barbed wire fence surrounding it.

The only human prison in the Northern Hemisphere.

Snow crunched beneath our boots as we walked up the path to the guarded entrance.

The human guards paled as we approached.

"We're here on official Spartan business," I announced. "We're looking for a prisoner."

They blinked up at me.

"My name is Augustus. I am *the* heir to the House of Ares. I suggest you open the door for me. Now."

The gate rose.

Kharon's cloak whipped behind him as he stalked forward, a jagged ruby crown gleaming on his head.

It was time to avenge our wife.

The next morning, I stomped up the steps leading out of the villa dungeon with Kharon trailing behind me.

Both of us were vibrating with fury.

"Her stepfather *bragged* about hurting her as a child," Kharon said. "Fuck this shit—we need to kill him."

I nodded in agreement.

He injured little Alexis. He needs to die.

We both turned and had made it down a few steps before I gathered my wits about me.

"No," I said as I grabbed Kharon's back, pulling him out of the dark stairs into the brighter hallway. "We agreed." I shoved him against the wall. "We *need* to earn Alexis's trust . . . We'll leave him for her. *She's* the one that's been wronged—she can decide what she wants to do with *her* foster father."

"She's gonna forgive him or some fucking bullshit," Kharon spat.

Seething, I nodded in agreement.

"We have to kill him."

FUCK.

No.

I stopped both of us from leaving the hall.

The protective urges—*the unholy madness*—was making it hard to think. I was being torn to shreds.

Kharon placed a hand on my shoulder. "I . . . understand," he said through gritted teeth. "What you're saying."

His support grounded me, allowed me to think, to focus. "We have to show Alexis that we respect her," I said hoarsely. "That means we respect her wishes . . . whatever they are."

Kharon nodded sharply, then his chest caved in like he'd been punched. He gasped as he hyperventilated. "I can't do this—I need to kill someone. It's too much. It's—"

I wrapped my arms around him in a hug, holding him upright.

"Breathe," I coached as we inhaled at the same time.

He relaxed against me.

Neither of us moved, silent understanding coursing between

us. We were doing this together; we would be better men for Alexis, or we'd be nothing at all.

Footsteps sounded around the corner.

"No way," Alexis's voice echoed.

"Oh, *come on*," Helen replied. "Just open it—it's probably an expensive necklace or something pretty. Everyone knows that Kharon loves blue diamonds—rumor is the House of Artemis has an entire vault *full* of them. I'm jealous. The House of Aphrodite prefers pearls, which is so *boring*. My life is not fair."

"You gotta just open it to see," Drex said.

Kharon stiffened in my arms, and I released him.

Alexis and Helen are heading to breakfast.

They were going to pass us in the hall.

Standing up straight, I wiped my bloody knuckles on my black pants hastily.

Kharon adjusted his wrinkled shirt. He ran his hands through his hair, desperately trying to pat it down, but somehow looked messier after he touched it, strands sticking out in every direction.

Then, he relaxed his shoulders and smiled, like he was practicing looking approachable—his teeth were covered in blood.

I pointed at them, and he scrubbed them clean with his finger.

"What are you doing?" I whispered. Kharon had struck a dramatic pose, leaning against the wall, knee bent, arms crossed.

"Act casual," he said out of the side of his mouth.

I put my hand on the wall and leaned toward him like we were talking.

Alexis, Helen, Drex, and Charlie stopped as soon as they turned the corner. A small horse (Fluffy Jr.?) and two hellhounds halted beside them.

They stared at us.

Helen froze mid-motion—she was holding out a black box to Alexis. It was the gift we'd left outside the door for her. The one I'd spent months working on. I'd gotten it commissioned the day after our marriage day, after Alexis leapt away.

Awkward silence stretched as the group cautiously moved forward down the hall, straight toward us.

Nothing to see here. Just two men hanging out by the entrance to a dungeon.

Alexis had purple smudges under her eyes.

Is she sleeping?

I swallowed down the urge to beg her to talk to me.

She crossed her arms over her stomach and purposefully looked away from us as she got closer.

It felt like I'd been slapped in the face.

"So, um," Kharon said. "Augustus—how did you . . . sleep?"

"What?"

"How did you sleep?" Kharon repeated.

I stared at him with incredulity.

He knew we'd been out all night killing and torturing people for our wife.

Kharon narrowed his eyes and tilted his head in Alexis's direction.

"Amazing," I deadpanned as I realized what Kharon was doing. "I feel *so* well rested."

Kharon stretched his arms above his head in an imitation of someone waking up. "Same—I think I got a full ten hours last night."

Real smooth.

Helen made a sound as she she neared, openly staring at the scar on the side of Kharon's head where his ear used to be. The fucking *Falcon Chronicles* still hadn't stopped writing articles about what Kharon had done.

The headlines called it "the most romantic sacrifice of the century."

They should have been working on finding out *why* the fucking Titans were mutating, not glamorizing my wife's suffering.

Heart thudding painfully, I turned to Alexis, mouth opening to ask her to—

My jaw clicked shut.

Poco was sitting on Fluffy Jr.'s back, holding his ears like reins, and his gray fur looked more unkempt than usual.

Is anyone spritzing him with water? He clearly needs a trim. What are they doing?

"Is anyone brushing Poco?" I asked. "He needs four brushes a day."

Helen laughed. "Yes, we do it constantly. His fur just looks puffy because he keeps wrestling with Fluffy Jr."

Since my wife's protector was borderline obese, that did not make me feel better.

Poco chittered shrilly as if agreeing with her.

I glared down at him. "Don't you *dare* take that tone with me, mister."

Poco crossed his gray arms and stuck his nose into the air, staring up at the ceiling.

I leaned down and got in his little face. "No fish treats for you."

His black eyes widened and he shook his head as if he didn't believe me.

"I already *threw* out the bag."

Poco tipped his head back and screeched like he was dying.

I'd actually just paid a seven-figure sum to have a box of them personally shipped from the other side of the world because global supply chains no longer existed, and I was stooping to bribery to get him back.

"Yep," I said. "That's what happens to bad raccoons who don't take their afternoon naps."

Poco wailed mournfully, still stuck on the treats.

Someone laughed.

It took me a moment to realize everyone had stopped moving and was staring at me.

Flushing with embarrassment, I stood up straight.

"Open the box," Kharon said as he quickly snatched my gift out of Helen's hand and held it out for Alexis to take.

She stared at it, but didn't move.

"Please," I said.

The urge to fall to my knees at her feet and beg for forgiveness was mounting. My legs shook.

I would do it.

I'd do *anything* if it meant she'd look at me without a pained, guarded expression.

"Please," I repeated. "I promise, it's not jewelry."

Alexis reached out and gingerly opened the box. She peered over the side.

Helen frowned. "Ew—what is that? No girl wants—"

"For me?" Alexis's lips parted with awe as she stared at the black item.

"It also has a built-in recorder," I said, desperate to keep the smile on her face as I pointed to the button on the side. "I had it custom made, so if you don't have a pen or paper, you can still record your findings and play them back. And a cable port to hook it up to a computer and transfer your findings."

"Thanks, Augustus." She smiled at me.

Kharon puffed up his chest. "I designed the metal holder—it's bulletproof titanium."

Alexis stared at him like she couldn't tell if he was joking, then she shook her head and beamed at us.

Her smile was as breathtaking as sunshine on a cloudy day. The pounding in my skull lessened.

I'd had to pay our weapons manufacturers a small fortune to create one from scratch, because they'd had to consult with an Olympian lab, but it was so worth it for the joy on her face.

"Can someone please tell me *what* in Kronos's kingdom is that ugly thing?" Helen asked with a huff.

"It's a graphing calculator," Alexis said reverently, her fingers trailing over her name engraved in gold on the back.

"Wow," Drex said as Alexis held it up for him to see. "I didn't know they still made those."

They don't.

Alexis grinned at Drex, and I cleared my throat, tamping down the urge to slaughter him violently.

"Thanks again." She glanced up at me through long lashes. A single curl hung against the delicate column of her neck.

"Anything for you," I said, feeling faint.

Alexis turned back to the calculator and resumed walking toward the dining room, Charlie and Drex following.

Helen leaned close as she walked past. "You're acting *pathetic*," she whispered. "It's embarrassing me."

I nodded dumbly, too busy trying to remember how to inhale.

Seconds later, we were once again alone in the hall.

Kharon's face twisted, sharpening into cruel edges. "I just remembered—I've been waiting to tell you what I saw while we were away."

"What?"

"Achilles and Patro . . . want to take her from us."

"What the fuck are you talking about?"

"Alexis," Kharon said. "Let's go." He whirled around and headed down the hall.

I scowled and followed.

No one messed with our wife.

21
OMENS AND WARNINGS

*ALEXIS: THE NEXT MORNING,
ONE DAY UNTIL THE INITIATION MASSACRE*

"Alexis?"

I woke up with a start.

A storm raged outside, making the morning unusually dark, as rain streaked drearily across the window. The hellhounds, Fluffy Jr., and Poco slept in a big pile on the floor.

The room was quiet except for a strange muffled rattling.

Helen and Charlie were absent, probably already at their morning class, but the rest of us had the day off from training because the initiation massacre was in one day.

"Alexis?" Ceres called.

Groggily, I pushed myself out of bed, wrapping a sleepy Nyx around my neck as I went into the adjoining room.

Ceres was sitting on the floor, chewing on a pen, her pink hair askew, surrounded by piles of ancient tomes.

She held up a blank page with a squiggly symbol on it. "Can you believe it?"

"Believe . . . what?"

She pointed to the two dots on the top of the symbol. "This umlaut! It's an extremely rare configuration that is seldom seen in this ancient language. Yet *here* it is. Right in front of me all along. So obvious!"

"What l-language?" I asked, struggling to follow her words because she talked faster than anyone I'd ever known.

Wait, what does this have to do with getting your memory back?

Lavender eyes sharpened. "The words of predestination."

A sense of foreboding slithered down my spine.

"I've seen this umlaut before," Ceres said in a rush. "I remember—it was crucial, a rare moment of clarity. The pieces all fit together, and it made sense. It was clear. It's *never* clear. And I realized that I'm on the right track. I have to be. Because . . . *Guess* which ancient Olympian House book I found this symbol in? Guess. Please guess. Guess. You must guess."

She blinked up at me expectantly.

"Um."

Ceres made me realize that I was a very *low*-energy person.

Wait, am I anemic?

"Guess a House," she demanded. "Guess. You gotta guess. Just do it. Do it quickly." She practically vibrated with excitement.

"The House of . . . Zeus?"

"You got it!" She slammed the page down and picked up a heavy tome, flipping through it. "I'm right, I know I am. The House of Zeus had something to do with *your* disappearance and my memory loss."

She beamed at me.

"But it's *so* satisfying because my memories are *finally* coming back. It's Plato's cave—I'm in the dark, then I'm turned to the light and suddenly I can see. Duh, right?"

"Sure?"

I felt stupid.

"This girl needs so much help," Nyx hissed.

"Want to sit here while I read?" Ceres offered slowly,

suddenly looking self-conscious. "It's nice to have someone around."

I nodded.

She nudged my shoulder as I sat down next to her on the floor. Her smile made me feel warm inside.

I'd never had a girlfriend. Now I had her *and* Helen.

A few hours later, there was a ringing in my bad ear and a cramp in my lower back. Ceres was reading a book in silence.

With a groan, I stood up to leave.

"Alexis—" Ceres grabbed my arm to stop me and I startled. Her lavender eyes were shockingly bright. "Have you seen this symbol before? It matters tonight." She ripped a page out of her book and held it up to me.

The cream-colored page had a single drawing on it.

The symbol was extremely crude. It was a straight line with a circle at the top, and a squiggle over the line, with two puffy clouds floating on either side of it.

I squinted. It looked familiar, but I couldn't place it.

"Maybe . . . I'm not sure," I said, confused what was going on. "What's tonight?"

She tilted her head and stared like she was studying me, uncharacteristically silent.

"Ceres . . . Wh-why?" I repeated, feeling increasingly awkward.

In a flash of movement, she crinkled up the piece of paper

and threw it aside. She turned back to her book and resumed reading like nothing had happened.

"Uh—Ceres," I said, "why did you j-just crumple up that symbol? What do you mean it matters tonight? What were you—"

"What, Alexis?" She smiled. "Sorry, I've been lost in thought while reading."

"The symbol you just showed me," I whispered, deeply unsettled. "What was it?"

"The umlaut?" Ceres asked.

I reached down and picked up the wrinkled piece of paper and did a double take—the page was blank.

"I think that was just scrap paper." Ceres went still. "Wait—Alexis, can you see something on it?"

I stared at the empty page, feeling sick.

"No, n-not anymore. I swear it just had a . . ." I shook my head. "Never mind. I must be tired. Sometimes when I'm exhausted, I imagine a man is watching me sleep. My mind runs away from—"

"Stop, Alexis." Ceres stared up at me. "All we are is what we perceive. Right or wrong, real or not. Predestination speaks in a language that no one truly understands." She pressed a hand to her heart. "It's a feeling—and if *you've* felt it, you need to believe in yourself."

I backed away, dropping the paper.

"I'm just t-tired."

Ceres looked grave. "You need to trust yourself. I trust you, with my life. You need to do the same. Believe in yourself, in your abilities."

I backed into the other bedroom.

"I just need to rest," I said, shutting the door before she could reply.

Falling into Helen's pink bed, I pulled the cover up over my head, then grabbed my pocket graphing calculator.

Dragging my fingers over the shiny buttons, I admired the linear equation I'd been working on.

"Dear Diary," I whispered into the microphone. "Ceres is acting strange, and my recent graph supports that the Riemann zeta function has its zeros not only at the negative even integers but also with complex numbers with real halves."

I paused.

"Also, I think I'm going crazy. I'm seeing things. A strange symbol. The grim reaper. And I feel like I'm *dying* every time I think about my husbands." I clicked it off.

Knock.

Knock.

"The heir to the House of Hades has been requested to meet in the dining room," a servant called through the closed door. "It's urgent."

I groaned.

Is a single day of rest really too much to ask for?

Less than a minute later, I cautiously pushed open the door to the dining room with the animals all huddled at my feet.

I peeked inside.

Spooky.

It was midday, but the curtains had been pulled, and the dining room was dark. The only light was from the smoldering fireplace, its flames burning low, and the scent of smoke was sharp.

Wind howled outside, as sheets of rain slammed against the long windows.

The storm was picking up.

Cautiously, I slipped inside with the animals in tow.

"Uh, I was s-summoned . . . Is anyone in here?"

Lightning flashed.

The door shut behind me with a bang.

"Welcome . . . *wife*," Kharon said quietly.

He stood at the middle of the long table, twirling a dangerous hunting knife between his fingers. "We've been waiting for you."

I blinked.

Not dramatic at all.

Augustus was next to Kharon, leaning his hip against the table, like he was blocking something, arms crossed over his chest, expression stony.

"Uh," I said eloquently, not sure what the best practices were when it came to dealing with deranged men.

Something clattered loudly.

Kharon and Augustus stepped away from the table.

Lightning flashed—Patro was bound and gagged; Achilles was tied to a chair next to him.

My mentors turned their heads toward me.

Patro shouted, the sound muffled behind a gag, as he kicked and struggled.

Achilles sat perfectly still beside him, eyes narrowed with rage, trussed up in silver restraints. They were the same kind of chains they used to secure Titans.

Kharon pointed his knife at a single seat on the other side of the table. The rest of the chairs had been removed from the room.

"Please sit, *wife*," Kharon said calmly. "Join us."

Nyx hissed as she slithered from my waist and coiled tightly around my arm, ready to strike. Fluffy Jr. crouched low, and the hellhounds and Poco silently stared at the men.

I straightened my shoulders and held Kharon's fierce gaze.

"Or . . . what?" There was no way he'd hurt me.

I knew better.

Do I?

Kharon pointed the knife at Achilles's face, then he hovered the blade over his left ear. "If you don't, I will *avenge* the wrong perpetrated against you."

I inhaled sharply. "You wouldn't."

Kharon's smile was pure sin. "Want to test me?" He pressed

the knife into the skin above Achilles's ear, features twisting with mania.

Patro screamed and kicked his bound feet at the table leg next to him.

Achilles stayed perfectly still.

Shock morphed inside my chest into something dangerous and seething.

Kharon's face sharpened. "Please—sit. We have . . . important matters to discuss."

Augustus stood silent.

With careful measured steps, angling my body to keep them in my sight, I walked in the opposite direction around the table to the chair.

I stared across at them.

Kharon laughed harshly, a familiar mocking sound. "Smart choice."

"Sit," Augustus ordered.

Indignation kindled inside my stomach.

I remained standing.

Midnight eyes narrowed into slits. "Sit," Augustus repeated with more force.

Kharon bared his teeth. "You're outnumbered and you have no weapons. Don't do anything you'd regret, carissima. You have no other choices."

How dare he.

I raised my right arm toward my husbands, finger pointed, thumb cocked.

Kharon tipped his head back and chuckled mockingly.

Black scales shimmered into existence as she became visible—Nyx's head hovered over my pointer finger, mouth wide open, fangs on display. She coiled tighter on my arm, ready to strike—vibrant purple snake eyes watched Kharon.

Thunder cracked.

Everyone in the room froze.

Kharon opened and closed his mouth, no sound coming out.

"Alexis," Augustus said with menacing softness, his gaze locked on Nyx. "Please tell me that snake doesn't have purple eyes . . . because that would mean you're pointing a venomous *echidna* at us like it's a gun."

22
Enemies Who Crawl for You

Alexis

Nyx rose higher, opal fangs distended and glistening with venom.

"Is this . . . *enough* of a weapon for you?" I asked sarcastically. "Husbands."

A single droplet of blood spilled from the corner of Augustus's eye, tracking down his scarred cheek. "Put the venomous beast down," he said slowly. "And step away."

I brought Nyx up to my lips and kissed her head.

"No."

Kharon lunged forward like he was going to dive across the table, but Augustus grabbed the back of his collar and yanked him away.

"We need to save her!" Kharon said.

Augustus glared at me like he didn't know what to make of the situation. "How long have you had a . . . pet echidna?" He choked over the last word like it physically pained him to say it aloud.

I shrugged. "Forever."

Augustus inhaled deeply. "Of course you fucking did."

Kharon pulled away from Augustus, straightening his cloak and crown, serrated hunting knife still in his hand; a raised patch of scar tissue where his ear used to be.

"That's a class *seven* dangerous beast." Kharon's voice was so deep it was barely more than an animalistic growl. "It's ranked as dangerous as *Titans*."

He slashed his knife through the air.

Whatever he saw on my face made his eyes narrow. "Do you even know—" Kharon overenunciated each word "—what class seven means?"

I shook my head no, curious to see how he'd mansplain Nyx to me.

Kharon glared at Nyx with pure disgust. "Class seven beasts are designated *kill on sight*—it's a crime to harbor one in Sparta, a threat to the safety and well-being of all sentient life, penalized with a lifetime of imprisonment in the Underworld."

Augustus's scowl deepened.

"Echidnas are uncontrollably dangerous," Kharon continued mercilessly. "Their toxin can kill full-grown Spartan children and put adults into comas . . . forever."

Spartan boys screamed as they fell away from me, dying in the sand of a gladiator stadium.

Nyx's head lowered, her eyes not meeting mine as she gently squeezed my arm. Black scales disappeared as she went invisible.

"I'm so sorry, kid," Nyx hissed quietly. "I should have told you. I just . . . You could talk to me and my kind is almost extinct. I was . . . lonely."

I tried to remember what she'd said about being bonded. I'd assumed she'd meant she was someone's protector. What if it was something else? Was she bound by a Spartan oath? Was it something more sinister?

"Put the echidna down," Kharon said. "Just put it down and we'll handle it. No questions asked."

Nyx made a wounded sound.

Head spinning, I sat down in the chair and leaned back with a shaky exhale.

"That's it," Kharon said. "Now just take the echidna off your arm and put it on the table. You're doing great."

"No questions asked?" I whispered.

Kharon nodded. "No questions asked."

Dragging my hand over Nyx's scales, I pulled my forearm to my chest, my left arm positioned in front of her protectively.

"No questions asked." I chose my words carefully. "It's a good thing then—" I leveled a glare at all the men across the table. "That none of you saw anything."

Kharon slapped his hand on the table. "Alexis—give me the monster."

Covering her with my arms, I said, "Never. Drop it . . . Or else."

"Are you threatening me?" Kharon seemed flabbergasted.

I arched an eyebrow mockingly. "Obviously, *Karen*."

He clenched his jaw, looking equally impressed and furious.

Nyx sniffled.

Augustus met my gaze, his face stony. "Is that what you want? Are you sure, Alexis?"

I nodded.

Lightning flashed.

Augustus took a deep steadying breath. "Fine—it's settled." He paused pointedly. "We will respect her wishes. None of us saw anything. If anyone dares say differently—" he glanced down at Patro and Achilles "—I'll gut you myself."

"But it's *not* fucking safe," Kharon argued.

Augustus glared at him. "We didn't see anything."

Warmth filled my chest.

Deeds, not words.

Kharon tipped his head back and closed his eyes. "Fine."

"Let's move on to the *purpose* of this meeting." Augustus

straightened and pulled a familiar vial of blood out of his pocket. "They want you to *murder* us—wife?"

Lightning flashed again and shadows flickered through the dark dining room, as Patro and Achilles struggled in their chairs.

Augustus held the vial up—blood sloshed back and forth. *My blood.*

Kharon pointed his knife at me, looking betrayed.

"So it's come to this," Augustus said, his words clipped as he glared at my mentors. "They want you to use your power to free yourself from the marriage bond . . . *from us.*"

I opened my mouth to deny it, to explain that I was never going to do it, then clicked my jaw shut. *How dare they act like I'm the one at fault.* It was Patro and Achilles's plan, not mine.

I was done apologizing to men.

They could beg for my forgiveness or go fuck themselves.

Kharon smiled cruelly as he stepped back from the table—Hell and Hound left my side and sauntered over to Kharon, flanking him—crimson filled his glowing eyes.

His protectors' turquoise gazes also changed—their flame eyes flickered a vibrant red.

Kharon straightened, his face unnaturally slack—he opened his mouth, and so did his beasts.

"I *am* my hellhounds." His words echoed strangely around the room as all three of them spoke at the same time in a growling cadence. "What they see—I see."

Ringing increased in my left ear.

His stalking was even worse than I'd thought.

Kharon bared his teeth and nodded, so did his hounds; a puppet master and his puppets.

"I heard your discussion with Patro," Kharon's garbled deep voice projected eerily around the room. "I saw your *longing* for what they were offering—wife."

Fluffy Jr. growled next to me.

The blood slowly receded from Kharon's eyes and his

hellhounds looked back and forth between the two of us like they didn't know who to choose—after a long moment, they slunk away and lay in the corner of the room.

Kharon lazily twirled his hunting knife, waiting for my reaction.

Dark emotions churned in my gut, but I wasn't going to give him the satisfaction of showing that I was afraid.

"So . . . are you going to *kill* me?" I asked softly.

Augustus's smile was sinister. "Oh no—wife. You've got it *all* wrong." He turned, revealing a drink cart. He picked up two empty whiskey glasses and placed them gently on the table.

Kharon held my gaze and he stuck out his tongue.

Wait.

He brought the sharp edge of the hunting knife up to his open mouth.

I shouted as he violently slashed it across his cheeks, lips, and tongue. Scarlet poured down his chin.

Augustus uncorked the vial with a pop and dumped my blood into the two crystal glasses.

They wouldn't.

"Don't worry," Augustus said silkily, his midnight eyes predatory. "We're going to give you *exactly* what you wanted, my carus."

Kharon handed the knife over and picked up the glass of my blood. "Cheers, Alexis."

Kharon threw back my blood and swallowed. Augustus stuck out his tongue, cut himself with the knife, then drank from the second cup. They both smiled—revealing *my* blood mixing with theirs, covering their teeth.

They did.

"Fuck you," I whispered with horror, gripping the arms of my chair. My sternum ached as my power reacted.

"Well, wife." Kharon arched a brow, licking his mutilated

lips wickedly. "Go for it. Break the bond—free yourself from us. I fucking *dare* you."

I shook my head and gritted my teeth, chest heaving as I fought to try to calm myself.

Patro jerked and I met his panicked gaze. He was trying to tell me something with his eyes.

What did he say to me back in the gladiator sands? Calm my breathing?
I gasped for air.

Excruciating pain burned inside my chest. For the past weeks I'd been trying to access my power in the shower, and now it wanted out.

Kharon and Augustus sauntered around the table.

Wood scraped against marble as I turned my chair to keep them in my line of sight.

My vision blurred.

They stopped in front of the hearth, and the orange haze behind them created the illusion that they were standing in front of the gates of Hell.

Cheeks flushed, their eyes were unfocused, and glazing over with agony. *They're feeling my pain.*

There was fifteen feet of open space between us.

Too far to touch; close enough to kill.

All three of us gasped for air like we were suffocating.

They swayed slightly as they also fought an invisible battle.

Patro shouted something louder behind his gag and the table shook as he kicked it.

None of us looked over.

"*Do it*, carissima." Kharon's voice dropped an octave, eyes hooded as he spit blood onto the floor. "*Take* your revenge—I know you want to. I saw your face. Just go for it . . . Man up, sweetheart, and pull the trigger. For once, *hit* your fucking target."

His words were fire, and I was the oxygen.

Pain exploded in my chest.

Lightning flashed as I reared back in my chair.

"After all . . . isn't this exactly what you wanted?" Augustus arched a dark brow, his scar an angry slash. "Don't tell me you're backing out now. Not when we're giving you exactly what you want. Take the offering. Have your divorce . . . MURDER US!"

"Or were you waiting for the *men* to handle it?" Kharon pointed across the table at my mentors. "And now you're too afraid to do it yourself?"

There was nothing left of the man who'd knelt beside me in the pouring rain.

He was heartless. *Brutal.*

"I guess," Kharon taunted wickedly, "you really are just another *pathetic* girl who's never had to do anything herself. It's a real shame—the House of Hades lineage was wasted on the likes of you." He pursed his lips and mimed rubbing away fake tears. "Poor little Alexis needs Patro and Achilles, the big, bad Spartan men to save her because she can't do it herself and—"

A scream ripped from my throat.

Kharon and Augustus fell to their knees, shoulders shaking, foam dripping from their parted lips.

Even as they convulsed, they held my gaze, their smiles sad.

White stars danced as my vision tunneled, their pain mixed with mine, and I felt it all.

I was killing them.

And myself.

"That's my woman," Augustus praised softly, tears glimmering as he crawled forward. "We're so—" he groaned "—fucking sorry for trapping you . . . in this marriage . . . Take your revenge," he gasped. "Please."

No.

Kharon gazed up at me with resignation. "I'm so sorry—" the tendons in his neck stood out as he also crawled "—I wasn't good enough—" he coughed "—for you . . . wasn't strong enough, or . . . what you wanted. You deserve . . . better."

A tear streaked down my face.

The devils were on their knees—coming straight to me.
Groveling at my feet.

"I don't deserve you," Kharon mouthed as foam dripped from his quivering lips.

"You can be with them." Augustus's voice cracked as he collapsed onto his stomach. "Now."

The agony receded.

Kharon face-planted next to Augustus and curled into the fetal position, gurgles and moans falling from his lips.

I breathed easier.

For the first time in months, my headache completely disappeared and the throbbing in my knee was gone.

Our bond was breaking.

They were dying.

Because of me.

Augustus cradled me against his chest as he carried me through the Roman streets. Kharon hovered over me, his left ear missing.

A broken sob ripped from my throat.

No.

I didn't want this. I wanted to *feel*.

I wanted to know when Kharon was pushing himself too hard, and I needed to live inside Augustus's broken mind; I wanted them to talk to me; I wanted to know where the three of us were heading.

"Breathe, Alexis," Nyx hissed into my ear as she slithered around my neck. "You can control this—you're in the driver's seat. It doesn't control you."

Kharon and Augustus inhaled shakily, their fingers stilling.

I held my breath.

"Stop fighting against yourself." Nyx tightened. "Some of us are lethal, and that's okay."

Just like when Patro had coached me with Theros—the pain in my chest receded as I calmed myself down—I gathered control, and the poisoning stopped.

I don't want to hurt them anymore; they've been hurt enough.
Tingles climbed up my fingers to my palms.
I was in command of my powers.
A strange white light emitted from my fingers—my hands glowed brightly; the skin lit from within.
I don't want to kill them. I want the three of us to figure this out.
A loud wheeze echoed.
"Alexis," Kharon said hoarsely as he pushed up from his chest onto his knees, and wiped at the cut on his face.
My right knee spasmed.
Eyes still glossy with the remnants of pain, he slowly crawled across the floor toward me.
He bowed his crowned head—I gripped my chair—he kissed the tops of my feet. "Angel," he whispered.
I reached down for him with glowing hands, gently touching his head.
He stared up at me like I was his deliverance.
The brilliant light intensified until it hurt my eyes, and a strange feeling washed over me.
Nyx hissed something, but I couldn't hear her.
The warmth flared brighter, light becoming pain.
I was boiling alive.
Kharon shouted something and pulled away, breaking our connection.
The light under my tingling fingers faded, as stars receded from my vision.
Kharon sat back on his haunches, still looking up at me with awe.
Augustus laid weakly on the floor, his chin lifted. "Are you . . . okay?" he whispered to me.
I wasn't sure. Long seconds passed as I struggled to process what had happened.
"Did . . . you . . . see that?"
Both men nodded.

In high school, we'd watched a historical early 2000s documentary about deep-sea anglerfish—*A hideous creature, it lures prey in with its glowing bioluminescent antenna light, then eats them. It also exhibits extreme sexual dimorphism.*

Dread sank its talons into my chest.

My blood was poisonous. Maybe this was how it worked. I attracted people with my light—then violently slaughtered them.

I also had no idea what sexual dimorphism meant, but from how awkward things had always been for me, I probably had it. I stared at my shaking hands (antennas?).

"Breathe, carissima," Kharon said hoarsely. "Don't panic. You're going to figure out what it means."

I already have—*I'm a hideous fish.*

As I stared down at the floor in shock, the full weight of what had just transpired crashed over me.

Strange, dangerous glow aside, I *hadn't* killed Kharon or Augustus.

I'd done it.

For the second time in my life, I'd controlled my power.

We were *still* bonded.

Tears mixed with my chuckles as I leaned back into the chair with exhaustion.

"Wait? I can still feel—" Kharon's eyes widened.

He tried to stand up but collapsed back onto his knees.

Augustus panted, still splayed on the floor. "Why?" he asked. "It doesn't make any sense . . . We gave you an out."

"We gave you the divorce that *you* wanted." Kharon frowned. "But you stopped. Why?"

Rubbing my face tiredly, I looked anywhere but at them.

"Alexis," Augustus said, his voice tight. "*Why?*"

"I want to . . . give us a chance," I whispered, feeling lightheaded. "It's just physical now, but . . . maybe we can be . . . more . . . some day?"

A muffled shout echoed, and the table rattled.

Augustus held his side as he sat up, and Kharon shifted at my feet.

The air crackled with tension.

Wait, what is happening?

"Carissima," Kharon purred, eyes half-lidded and smoldering, as he wiped at his bloody face, revealing smooth unmarred skin. He grabbed on to the table. It creaked against his weight as he hoisted himself to his feet. "I'm *so* sorry for everything I've done to hurt you—you deserve better than me."

I gripped my chair for dear life.

Kharon loomed over me, blocking out the rest of the room as his breath fanned against the shell of my right ear.

"If what we have was just physical," he said quietly, "I'd lay you out on this table and kiss your lips. Then I'd stroke myself as Augustus did the same."

My nails dug into the arms of the chair.

Kharon breathed heavily. "And while Augustus was busy with your lips, I'd kiss your mouth."

I jerked, face heating as I realized what he'd meant.

"*Then* . . . Augustus and I would sit down in two chairs across from each other—we'd pass you back and forth, fucking you on our laps, for *hours*."

Kharon paused as he smirked down at me. "We'd fuck you until you couldn't walk, and they couldn't look you in the eyes without picturing us thrusting *deep* inside of you."

I shivered.

Abruptly Kharon pulled back.

He flexed his fingers, then fisted them as he cleared his throat. "That's what I'd do—if this was just physical. But that's . . . *not* what this is. This is me apologizing."

He stepped to the side.

Augustus got to his feet and walked toward me with awe

like I was his benediction. Crimson dripped from the side of his mouth, the cut on his tongue still bleeding.

He reached for my face, cupping my cheek.

"My carus." He leaned forward until his warm lips hovered over mine.

The kiss was featherlight; I felt it in my soul.

He pulled away.

I touched my tingling lips.

A gagged bellow echoed, chains clanking. Patro's emerald eyes were wide and pleading, his expression distraught as he struggled harder, desperate to free himself.

Achilles sat still and watched us.

"We are *devoted* to you," Augustus said solemnly.

Kharon rested his hand on my shoulder, as if bestowing a blessing. "There is *nothing* in the world we wouldn't do for you, Alexis."

Their promises hung heavy in the air, depraved in their vehemence.

They meant exactly what they said.

That's the problem.

23
The Hunter

Kharon: The Night Before the Initiation Massacre

An agonizing headache throbbed in my skull. I breathed harshly as I focused on Alexis's sleeping form and not Augustus's pain.

Moonlight gently kissed her delicate features.

It was quiet in the bedroom. The spring storm had died down hours ago, the rain finally stopping.

Everyone in the villa was sleeping.

Everyone but me.

I rubbed at my mouth where there was no longer a mark—our marriage bond was making us more powerful—I'd never healed so quickly before.

I used to think the bond, the increased Chthonic power, was everything I'd ever wanted.

Now I loathed it.

It was the reason Alexis didn't trust me, the reason her intriguing eyes became guarded in my presence.

Even amongst Spartans, Alexis was special.

A few hours ago, I'd crawled to her, fully prepared to die so she could be free of me.

But she hadn't done it.

Instead, Alexis had saved me, her fingers glowing with pure bright light, like she was the sun itself. I'd never seen anything like it.

She was giving us another chance. It was everything I could have ever dreamed of—nervous energy turned my stomach—the pressure was immense.

I couldn't afford to fuck this up. Not again.

So here I was, standing over her, watching her sleep, holding a black-and-white rose that I'd hand cut from the garden because it reminded me of her eyes.

The groundskeeper was going to murder me.

You need to stop stalking her.

Knowing something was technically wrong was one thing, but *actually* stopping the behavior was another.

Alexis discarded the roses I left on her pillow every night, but she still bothered to pick them up. She touched them. She looked at them. She gave them attention, and that had to mean something.

I still had a chance.

If she didn't care at all, she wouldn't bother to look at them. She'd just ignore them.

I can still win her over.

Mine. My woman. Mine.

The primitive part of my brain had latched onto Alexis Hert, and it couldn't let her go. I needed to watch her sleep just like I needed air.

Augustus understood the obsession.

We both felt the pull.

I needed to know that she was safe, especially at night. My protective instincts were screaming at me that it was the most dangerous time of day. She was unguarded. Anyone could sneak up and attack her, and there would be no way to react in time.

But when I watched her, no one could hurt her because they'd have to get through me and my hounds first.

I was her shadow. The *monster* that stood behind her.

Augustus said Helen told him that people who loved each other gave each other space when they needed it.

Those people sounded like actual idiots.

I wanted to crawl under Alexis's skin and learn everything about her. I yearned to hear every thought she ever had. I needed to ask why she slept with her calculator on her pillow next to her head, and how she came to have a pet echidna.

It physically hurt to be parted from her.

Mine. Mine. Mine, the voice chanted in my head.

Maybe I'd spent too many hours in the forest hunting prey; maybe I was born messed up; maybe my parents' lack of affection had broken something inside of me; maybe it was just how I was.

Space was not something I could give Alexis. *Ever.*

Pink bedding rustled as the object of my every desire sighed heavily in her sleep, an errant curl blowing off her lips.

Stop being a coward. Do it.

I stepped out of the shadows and leaned over Alexis.

Her face twisted as she whimpered in her sleep.

I wish I could take away your pain.

This time, I had another gift besides the roses. Perhaps they weren't flashy enough for her, weren't enough of a statement of what she meant to me.

It was time to do more.

I pulled the long glittering strand out of my pocket and carefully draped it around her neck. The strand of priceless blue diamonds danced in the moonlight. Gently, I hooked the fastener.

Alexis mumbled, turning her head to the side—I held my

breath—she pursed her lips together and made an agonized sound, but didn't wake.

She hadn't had a nightmare this bad since she'd fought the Titans.

What's wrong, carissima?

I traced my fingers gently over the row of glittering gems.

Dark possessiveness filled my chest.

My woman.

The rare blue diamond was the official stone of the House of Artemis. Our vaults were overflowing with them, and since the jewel matched my eyes, it was the only type I ever wore.

Seeing *my* stones around Alexis's neck made something primal and unhealthy rear up inside of me, even more so than usual.

Augustus could give her calculators and books. He understood her love of academia in a way I never could.

I was a simpler man.

Diamonds, roses, weapons, and blood were my love language.

Amor gignit amorem.

I laid the black-and-white rose next to her pillow, hoping it was true that *love begets love*.

Augustus's headache abruptly stopped as I stepped back into the shadows.

I barely noticed the lack of pain because *nothing* in life compared to the agony of of my unrequited love for Alexis.

24

The Eldest Heir

Augustus: That Same Night

Marble cracked beneath my fingers as I gripped the sink, the bathroom spinning.

Drip.

Drip.

Drip.

Scarlet splattered violently across the white sink as it fell from my lashes.

The madness of the House of Ares was breaking free, and it only wanted one thing—Alexis.

When I'd crawled across the floor toward my wife with regret, lust, and emotions smoldering inside my chest, my headache had sharpened into a razor blade.

Now a dagger's edge hovered behind my eyes. The point was slowly scraping across the front of my skull, demanding to be released.

Panting, I raised my head.

I didn't recognize the man in the mirror.

The scar across my face was a deep maroon, dark circles rimmed my black eyes, and my hair was disheveled.

Pressure mounted and it felt like the invisible dagger was pushing through my forehead and cracking bone.

Unblemished skin mocked me.

The marriage bond zapped hotly inside my chest, and it was all too much.

With a shout, I pulled my fist back.

Crack.

Shards of mirror exploded outward. In slow motion, they flew toward me, a hundred broken versions of myself reflecting in glinting silver, each man more ruined than the last.

Abruptly, the pain in my head vanished, *gone* as if it had never existed.

The shards dropped to the floor with a clatter.

I stood amidst the ruin, chest heaving, as I waited for the pounding to start up again in my head.

It didn't.

Equally relieved and horrified, I engaged my mental abilities. I felt the same, but my gut was telling me something was off.

My power was irrevocably changed.

I slowly turned, broken glass crunching beneath my boots.

The man who walked out of the bathroom was not the same man who'd entered.

25

A MASSACRE OF POWER

Alexis

I sprinted out onto the dark lawn.

Barbed wire fence glinted menacingly in the moonlight.

I turned the corner—straight into a warm body.

Kharon grunted with surprise as I bounced off him and stumbled right into Augustus, who grabbed my arms to steady me.

"Sorry," I said as I tried to catch my bearings. "I didn't see you—"

Kharon crowded me and Augustus until we were both pressed against the side of the villa.

The Milky Way glittered behind his handsome face, a cloud of stars in the night sky.

"Alexis," Kharon said softly as he leaned forward, his arms on either side of my head. "It's really you." He inhaled shakily.

Augustus was hot against my back, and I melted into him.

The night breeze was chilly, but both of them radiated fierce heat.

There was a rushing in my ears, a flush in my cheeks.

From the way they were breathing heavily, I wasn't the only one affected by the proximity.

In slow motion, Kharon reached forward and traced his fingers over my jaw, his touch a trail of fire. I gasped as his thumb lingered on my mouth. He licked his lips, gaze ravaging.

"Kharon?" I breathed out softly.

He closed his eyes, his chest heaving. "Carissima," he said, his voice gravelly. "I want to devour you—"

"Please do," I whispered.

Kharon pulled his hand away from my face and wrenched himself away from me. He pressed his tattooed knuckle into his mouth and bit down as he stared at me through hooded eyes.

His expression was feral.

Augustus's fingers tightened on my arm, his hips pressed against me, and something hard dug into the lower curve of my back.

"You know the sinful things we want to do to you," Augustus whispered silkily into my ear. "Right?"

I gulped. "Uh, y-yes."

"Are you ready . . . to take both of us?" Augustus's stubble grazed against the side of my face.

He cocooned me with his larger body as Kharon stared down at me hungrily.

"Yes," I breathed out, heat mounting inside my core.

Augustus inhaled deeply. "Good girl," he growled into my ear.

I jolted as his grip tightened, turning painful. My gaze locked on the scar tissue where Kharon's ear used to be.

A confusing jumble of emotions welled up. Before I could identify them, Kharon had stepped back more, and Augustus released me.

"You're not ready for us," Kharon said cruelly, his face morphing into a skeleton.

Augustus scowled, blood pouring from both his eyes. "You could *never* handle the both of us."

Kharon pointed his hand at my face, his fingers in the shape of a gun.

He pulled the trigger.

Sharp pain exploded through my skull.

I jolted upright in bed, gripping my forehead as sleep dissipated.

The sharp agony in my skull was gone, and there wasn't so much as a headache, just blissful peace.

It was just a dream.

A nightmare.

Morning light warmed my face, and I flopped back onto Helen's frilly bedding.

Fluffy Jr. stood next to the bed—we made eye contact—he jumped up and jabbed oversized paws (hooves?) into my stomach.

I coughed, barely surviving my protector's affection (violent assassination attempt).

Struggling for air, I turned my head—a fresh-cut rose stared back at me.

Gently, I traced my fingers over the thorns.

He's visiting you at night. You know it's not the grim reaper. It's your—

I shook my head, refusing to think about it.

At this point, my life couldn't get any worse.

Knock. Knock.

"We have to go to the initiation massacre in a few minutes," Drex yelled from the hall. "Everyone ate breakfast and is waiting for you in the atrium."

Never mind, it's worse.

"Shut the fuck up and end yourself," Nyx hissed at Drex from somewhere in the covers. "I'm sleeping."

She was not a morning person.

A horrible thought struck me. "Were Patro and Achilles at the table?" I asked with growing trepidation.

"Yes," Drex called back.

"Were they . . . chained to their chairs?"

"Uh—no. Wait, why would they be? Alexis—*what* are you doing in your free time?"

"Nothing."

He made a sound of disbelief.

Ignoring Drex's judgmental energy, I busied myself putting the new rose in the vase where I'd started collecting them.

Fluffy Jr. wagged his tail and ran in circles as I hurried around getting ready. His excitement for life was endearing, and also highly annoying.

"Simmer." I pointed at him. "We're all going to die."

Fluffy Jr. jumped and kicked his back legs up with enthusiasm.

I tried.

After I finished getting dressed in the outfit Helen had left out for me, I wrapped Nyx around my neck.

"Careful," she hissed. "The diamonds are cold."

I moved to the mirror. "What are you talking about? There are no—"

My jaw dropped.

A necklace of glittering blue diamonds hung around my throat like a choker.

Oh.

My.

God.

"Kharon?" I whispered with dawning horror as I fingered the gems, entranced by how much they sparkled. Sighing heavily, I searched for the clasp. "I can't wear these."

"Why?" Nyx asked as she slithered down my arm.

"Because it's *too* much and I—"

"Didn't you agree just yesterday to give Kharon a chance?" Nyx cut me off.

"I mean . . . I didn't kill him?"

"Exactly," Nyx hissed. "Accept the pretty jewelry. Don't be ungrateful—it's tacky."

My fingers stilled.

She had a point.

I dropped my hands, determination filling my gut. *I can forgive my husbands and prove myself to Sparta.*

Either I was turning over a new leaf, or I was completely delusional. Only time would tell (it was definitely the latter).

Drex smiled with relief when I stepped out the door. He grabbed my arm and dragged me through the gilded villa. Fluffy Jr. barked and ran beside us while Toucey flew above our heads, his metallic feathers grazing the high ceiling.

We came to a stop in the bustling atrium.

Everyone turned to me.

The leaders and heirs were all present, including Helen and Charlie. The only person missing was Ceres. At least she would be safe in the villa, protected from the Olympians.

Persephone and Hades smiled at me with pride—I smiled back at them.

In contrast, the side of my face prickled under the heavy weight of Achilles's and Patro's death glares. From their expressions, they were *not* happy with me.

On the other side of the room, Kharon smirked with pure male satisfaction as he stared at the jewelry on my neck.

"Who are you all looking at?" Nyx hissed. "Creeps."

"Let's go," Hades ordered.

Why are Augustus's right knuckles wrapped?

Everyone placed their hands in.

"Domus," Aphrodite shouted.

Crack.

Smoke rose—protectors crouched low at our feet with anticipation—the tunnel of the Dolomites Coliseum towered around us.

I'd been here before.

Stone vibrated and dust fell as people stomped above our heads. Most of Sparta would be in attendance today.

"Amor fati, memento mori . . . Amor fati, memento mori!" chanted through the air.

Remember death, love your fate.

I reached into the layered loose folds of my toga and clutched the cold metal of my emotional support calculator.

Nyx slithered tighter around my arm.

Fluffy Jr. picked up a rock with his mouth and crunched down on it. *Yep, that's a horse.*

Ares, Aphrodite, Artemis, and Hades took the lead, walking up a narrow spiraling stone stairwell built into the rock, and we all followed behind them.

Augustus looked back over his shoulder at me as he walked up the stairs. Poco hung off his back eating his hair.

His eyes seemed sharper, *brighter* than usual.

Kharon walked behind me, his hand lingering on my lower back, pushing me forward. His fingers drifted up my spine and traced across the blue diamond necklace. *Did he slip it on in the dining hall, or did he visit me in the middle of the night?*

I wanted to ask, but nerves were twisting my stomach, and the tension between the three of us was mounting.

We emerged from the narrow staircase into the stadium—gray clouds hung low, a stiff breeze whipped back and forth eight colorful Olympian House flags, each section was full of a few dozen House members in matching regalia.

Augustus and Kharon moved so they flanked me, each with a hand resting on my lower back. It was the lightest of touches, but I struggled to focus on anything else.

Yesterday, they'd crawled to me, begging.

Their heady scents—lightning and rain—filled my nose.

I discreetly turned my head to the side and breathed deeply as I scanned the crowd, spotting the lion of the House of Zeus.

Amongst the Houses were pockets of different creatures I

hadn't noticed my first time here. I recognized a packed section full of sirens, and Erebus sat with dozens of men in similar cloaks. There were other creatures I didn't recognize.

In the center of it all, the arena sand was empty.

The contestants hadn't arrived yet.

"Amor fati, memento mori . . ." Spartan voices trailed off as every head turned to stare at our group.

The black silk of my toga blew against my legs and my wedding ring felt like a brand on my finger.

The Chthonic leaders turned back to look at us, their expressions cold and regal. Power strummed tangibly around them in glittering mist and fog.

Ares nodded, a ruby halo shining creepily around his black irises.

Stomp.

Clap.

Stomp.

The stadium vibrated beneath my feet as the Olympians slammed their feet against stone with anticipation.

Hades had coached me on this moment.

The flag ceremony at the initiation massacre was apparently a centuries-old tradition. It was a great Spartan honor.

Augustus moved from where he stood beside me and walked forward, tailored black suit stretching across his wide back as he raised the charging Minotaur flag of the House of Ares.

Wordlessly the crowd watched, all eyes focused on him.

Augustus's long legs flew as he ran up the steps, two at a time—he held the House of Ares flag proudly above his head.

The stadium stomped faster.

Kharon stepped forward next.

With a grim expression, Kharon raised the rabid horse flag of the House of Artemis, his face hardening into sharp angles.

As he walked past Artemis, mother and son made eye contact.

She'd secretly disowned him, but publicly, he was still the heir of the House. After all, there weren't any other children left.

Artemis stared at his missing ear, then down to his visible protectors, her mist glittering as something like surprise flashed in her gaze.

Kharon looked away first, his face emotionless as he sprinted up the steps with his flag.

Hell and Hound ran beside him, teeth bared to the crowd. Olympians gasped and recoiled as they pointed at his protectors.

Murmurs of monsters and a missing ear echoed around the stadium.

From the reactions, most Spartans had never seen a hellhound in the flesh, since they were usually invisible.

The murmurs died down as Patro stepped forward.

He had one hand wrapped around the black swan flag of the House of Aphrodite, but Achilles raised it high, his grip taking the brunt of the weight.

Both men looked at me as they walked past.

I raised my chin—*it's not my fault you got caught, it was your plan, not mine*—I silently let them see my annoyance.

Patro's jaw clenched.

Achilles straightened.

They turned to each other and raised the flag higher, running up the steps in perfect tandem, side by side; Nero and Poppae trailed behind them.

It was my turn.

Hades nodded his head to me. Next to him, tears glimmered in Persephone's eyes. "You can do this, daughter," she mouthed with a hand over her chest.

The stadium shook with stomps.

I pulled my shoulders back.

I will make my mother proud.

Raising my right arm—Nyx invisible around my forearm—I held the long black staff above my head.

"Bow before us!" Nyx hissed for dramatic effect.

With my head high, I sprinted up the vibrating steps. Sparta blurred around me.

The skeleton hellhound flag of the House of Hades fluttered above.

My House.

My lineage.

Goose bumps broke out across my skin.

My power.

I would figure out what the tingling in my fingers and glowing light meant; I would figure out just *who* I was.

With Fluffy Jr. on my heels, an ancient war cry echoed through my mind. My ancestors ran with me—I could feel their pounding feet and racing hearts—their hopes and dreams were strumming through my veins.

Their power lived on inside of me.

My lungs expanded.

I will make my bloodline proud.

Even if it killed me.

"The lost heir to the House of Hades," Olympians whispered as I ran by. Their bird protectors screamed, wings fluttering with distress—they were afraid of me—the animals and the Spartans.

I straightened as I sprinted.

They should be afraid.

Black flag above my head, arms tensing, I waved it back and forth with all my might.

"Angelus Romae!" someone called out near the top of the stadium, and there was a responding wave of nervous murmurs. *Angel of Rome.*

I stumbled, nearly tripping over a step.

I was no angel.

Adrenaline and pride drained away as I came to a stop at the designated Chthonic section and took my seat.

There was nothing left to do but wait.

All too soon, the massacre began.

One hundred boys leapt into the arena sands—then, they fought to the death.

Fluffy Jr. lay at my feet, whimpering. Helen and Charlie huddled together with Drex not looking, and my husbands sat rigid on either side of me.

A gruesome legacy to bear.

The chanting had died down as the first body dropped, and now screams from below echoed through the silent stadium.

Hades and Zeus stood together on a podium watching the death match.

Kharon and Augustus sat on either side of me.

I stared down blankly, head full of static.

Last year I'd been one of the bodies crawling through the muck and inky fog. I'd been throwing punches, amped up on adrenaline, delirious with blood lust.

Kharon leaned toward me, like he could read my thoughts. "How did you . . . survive?"

My hand drifted to the warm scales wrapped around my arm. "Nyx. Without her, I never would have made it. She . . . saved me."

A forked tongue flicked against my skin.

"I'm . . . glad then," Kharon said softly. "That you have her."

"Me too."

Nyx slid off my forearm onto him—Kharon jolted, his eyes wide as he stared down at where the sleeve of his suit indented.

"I always knew he would be a good mate," Nyx hissed as she twined up his arm. "He smells like blood and death."

If that doesn't sum up my life.

Kharon sat up straighter and smirked at Augustus. "The killer snake likes me more than you."

"False." Nyx slithered over my lap to Augustus, and he grunted with surprise.

"I like the muzzled one best," Nyx said. "And the raccoon

mother second best. I prefer men who don't speak. Men should be seen—slaughtering and protecting—not heard. I've always said this."

If a massacre wasn't happening before my eyes, I would have laughed at her ridiculous name for Augustus.

But it was.

Charlie and Helen were now cowering in front of me with their eyes squeezed shut and their hands covering their ears. Drex was pale, his face turning green.

I forced myself to watch as Hades's fog retreated, and ten boys were left standing, eighty-three broken bodies splayed around them.

A familiar elderly woman with white hair and purple eyes walked out with a clipboard. She wore rainbow-covered rainboots and a ridiculous yellow hat.

Fate, they called her.

Ten Olympian men jumped down from the stadium and Zeus announced their assigned mentors.

Patro glanced over at me, his expression caught somewhere between pleading and a sneer.

I looked away.

With electricity dancing across his skin, Zeus droned on about unity in the face of darkness.

"Rest assured, Medusa *will* be captured." Zeus's voice crackled as it broadcasted boomingly through the stands. "But until then—for everyone's safety—the federation has made a decision to break with tradition."

Augustus and Kharon stiffened beside me.

The stadium held its breath.

"The SGC will now start tomorrow. All Chthonics will stay at the Dolomites stadium for the twelve-day showcase. They will also be extensively questioned by the federation to make sure they have no association with Medusa's disappearance."

My heart stopped.

It was June.

The SGC wasn't supposed to start until August. We were supposed to have *two* more months to prepare.

There was a roaring in my ears as Chthonics jumped to their feet around me. People were shouting. Olympians were screaming about dishonor and war.

The chant, "Kill Medusa—kill Medusa—kill Medusa," rose throughout the stadium.

I covered my mouth to stop myself from throwing up.

Zeus continued, "Any Chthonic who leaps away, or refuses to answer questions about Medusa, will be named an enemy of the state of Sparta—punishable by imprisonment in the Underworld . . . or death."

The shouts increased.

People jostled as fists were raised.

Someone was crying.

I stood up, my knee almost giving out as I struggled to straighten. Charlie and Helen turned—they were grabbing me.

"What," Helen whispered, "are you going to do about—"

"Don't worry," I said, cutting her off. "I'll . . . I'll . . . f-figure something out."

Helen didn't look reassured, her eyes filling with tears. Charlie swayed like he was going to pass out, and Achilles grabbed his shoulder, signing to him, "It's going to be okay."

My brother nodded.

Kharon sidled closer to me. "Stay beside us. We need to stick together while we figure out what the fuck is happening."

I tried to nod to show him that I heard, but my neck wouldn't move.

Our time had run out.

26

CHANGING BEASTS

ALEXIS

A dozen Olympian guards with sparking riot sticks led our section—minus the Chthonic leaders—down winding stairs. Gold laurel wreaths decorated a few of their heads, designating them as heirs, and different Olympian House insignias were engraved into their chest plates.

I needed to talk to Hades, but he'd disappeared with the other rulers. They'd all stalked off as soon as the announcement was made, and last I'd seen, Hades was arguing with Zeus.

Deep down under the coliseum we descended.

To another layer of Hell.

We headed through dark tunnels filled with stringy cobwebs and layers of dust, our protectors prowling beside us.

I shivered as the air chilled considerably, my boots scuffing the dirt floor.

It was a labyrinth of chambers.

Skeletons of all sizes—creatures, beasts, and Spartans—were piled inside rooms blocked with iron bars. As we walked deeper into the maze, the low-ceilinged tunnels were lit with a reddish hue from the rows of copper torches mounted on the stone walls, and we had to duck under the arches that separated the tunnels to avoid hitting our heads.

"Stop!" an Olympian guard barked.

We came to a halt in front of a row of iron doors covered in patina. Thick silver chains hung to the floor on one side of the door frames. Hooks lined the other.

"Because Medusa is still at large, this is where all ten of you will stay during the SGC," a guard said. "As Zeus explained—any efforts to escape will be viewed as an act of defiance against Sparta . . . Treason."

Dirt sifted from the ceiling, motes clouding the air.

"You two first." The guard gestured at Charlie and Helen.

Charlie released my arm, his yellow eyes illuminated strangely in the torchlight. He shifted in front of Helen protectively as the two of them were herded inside a room by an Olympian guard.

"They shouldn't be held d-down here. They're not competing," I said as the door slammed shut behind them.

"We have our orders." The guard glanced at me nervously as he inserted a large iron key into their lock, then he pulled chains across the outside of their door and threaded them through the hooks.

Wait, are we prisoners?

"How dare you," Augustus said. "You're dead for doing this to them."

"Treason," the guard repeated, but he paled as Augustus stepped forward, and held up his hands in a surrender gesture. "Just following orders."

Augustus's eyes filled with blood.

"Are Charlie and Helen going to be okay?" I asked, trying to distract him.

Augustus took a deep breath and nodded, blood receding from his eyes. "It's just fucking politics. The Olympians are trying to make a statement and are using Medusa and the federation to do it—but they wouldn't dare to actually hurt us . . . It would mean war."

Around us, chaos unfolded.

To our left, Agatha and Hermos sauntered into a room, the former blowing a kiss to three of the guards while the latter rolled his eyes like he was used to her antics.

Drex shot me a worried glance as he was pushed into his own room, with Toucey squawking on his shoulder. *Even a government drone doesn't deserve this.*

Achilles and Patro turned to me.

"Alexis," Patro said, overenunciating to make it clear that he was saying my name properly. "You're welcome to stay with *us* . . . during the competition."

The guards grumbled, but Achilles shot them a glare and they fell silent.

Patro held out his hand for me to take. "Stay in our room—let's talk things through. Everything's been very—" he trailed off like he was searching for the right word "—hostile."

His vivid green eyes were full of heavy emotions.

"*Please*," he whispered.

The raw sincerity in his voice made my chest hurt, because he wasn't one for heartfelt apologies.

He looked so lost, so pleading.

I didn't know what to make of this version of Patro. A part of me wanted to help him, to take his hand and make everything better between us. He'd been the one who stepped up and helped me calm down so I didn't kill Theros. For a small period of time, he'd been my friend.

Achilles shifted on his feet.

They left you to die.

I wanted to make things right with Patro, but not like this.

Patro saw something in my face—his hand dropped to his side, knuckles fisting.

"Thank y-you," I said as I glanced between Kharon and Augustus, who were both glaring at Patro. "But I'm . . . okay staying with them."

Patro's face twisted. "Typical," he sneered.

Augustus stepped forward. "*Watch* . . . how you speak to my wife."

"Whatever . . . I didn't *actually* care." Patro tried to scoff dismissively, but his eyes were full of anguish. "I was just offering to be nice, since you're *our* mentee."

Achilles glanced over at Patro with concern, then he shot me a glare. *How dare you hurt him* was written all over his face, and even the muzzle couldn't hide it.

I held his gaze.

"Let's go," Patro said to Achilles. "This hall *reeks* of betrayal." He stalked inside the room, then slammed the door shut behind the two of them, before the guards could do it.

He knows how to make an exit.

Electric riot sticks sparked in the guards' hands as they directed us, and I recognized one of the guards wearing a laurel wreath as Vorex from the House of Poseidon. He'd been Alessander's mentor in the crucible. His gray eyes and the pink ferret on his shoulder were unmistakable.

Vorex dipped his head to me in acknowledgment. "Please wait inside your room," he said calmly. "We'll retrieve you soon for the opening ceremony."

Kharon stood taller, his skeletal tattoos stark in the dim light. "*Don't* tell my wife what to do."

Vorex gulped. "Of course, sir . . . we're just following orders." The riot stick shook in his hand.

I'd remembered him being fierce and intimidating during the crucible.

Augustus studied the men cowering before us like he was making a decision. "Fine," he said coldly, his expression combative as he escorted me and Kharon inside.

The iron door slammed shut behind us with a loud bang, chains clicking as they slid into hooks.

The small windowless stone chamber had a sinister scarlet cast in the torchlight. A wooden door led to a sparse bathroom, and that was the only other space.

Nyx tightened around my neck.

Realization dawned.

Dear God, please don't do this to me.

Kharon and Augustus inhaled sharply as they came to the same conclusion I had.

The object of my certain demise was innocuous, yet it was much more insidious than any weapon or monster I'd ever faced. *Much* worse than staring down the barrel of a gun.

"Unum cubile," Augustus muttered under his breath as he dragged his hand over his sharp jaw.

One bed.

The three of us were trapped in a room with no other furniture and barely enough floor space for our animals. A wave of relief hit me that I hadn't accepted Patro's offer. Sharing one bed with the two lovers would have been *particularly* awkward.

The relief died a swift death as I remembered who I was trapped with—in my mind's eye, the singular bed expanded until it was all I could see.

My husbands shared a long-suffering look. Kharon nodded at Augustus and their shoulders pulled back like they'd come to a silent decision.

They weren't the only ones.

Clearing my throat, I gathered my courage. "I think we should—"

Fluffy Jr. let out a loud whine of distress, then collapsed to the floor at the foot of the bed. His eyes rolled back as his body twitched.

I fell to my knees beside him, trying to figure out what was wrong.

Fluffy Jr. stopped convulsing, but he panted, and his neck hung limply, like he couldn't find the strength to lift it.

The hellhounds sniffed at Fluffy Jr., then backed away warily, while Poco patted his head gently.

"What's wrong with him?" I asked as I ran my hands over my protector, searching for injuries. Kharon and Augustus knelt beside me. "It must be all the excitement . . ."

The lump on the middle of Fluffy Jr.'s spine quivered beneath my touch like something was moving under his skin.

I pointed at it.

Augustus grimaced. "It's probably . . . a tumor."

My heart twisted, shattering inside my chest. "No—there has to be another explanation. What else could cause this?"

Augustus shook his head, pity written on his face. "Alexis, that's probably what it is."

"What else is there?" I snarled.

Augustus stayed silent.

I shook his shoulder. "Tell me—I know you've read a lot. What else is there? What other options?"

"I don't want to give you hope." Augustus closed his eyes, features harsh in the crimson lighting. "There is another option, but it's a long shot and most likely doesn't apply to this—"

"Tell me."

"Molting," Augustus said, like it was self-explanatory, and Kharon visibly startled at the word.

Augustus rubbed at his stubble. "It only happens in certain rare beasts . . . It doesn't make any sense."

I hit his arm, desperate for something. "Explain."

"Certain types of beasts—usually larger, more powerful breeds—have extra appendages."

We both studied my protector, who was half pressed against the wall, barely fitting into the narrow space at the end of the bed.

"He's built large," I whispered.

Augustus winced. "Molting body parts consume a lot of energy to maintain, so they don't fully develop on the beasts until after puberty. But it's only *certain* beasts." He frowned, his scar pulling tight. "They only occur in Griffins, sphinxes, three-headed dogs, unicorns, and Pegasuses."

Fluffy Jr. let out a horrible, pained whine.

"Well—" I leaned down and pressed a kiss to his muzzle. "Which one do you think he is?"

"Alexis, he's clearly not *any* of those creatures."

"No." I shook my head. "He could be—I know it."

"Look at him." Augustus gestured at his furry head. "I can't even tell if he's a dog or a horse."

"He's probably just a mix of the two."

Kharon looked at me with sympathy.

"Mixed beasts are extremely rare," Augustus said, "and when they do survive birth, they're practically . . . feral . . . characterized by extremely low intelligence and hostile tendencies."

"He eats sticks," I pointed out. "He chokes on them. He's never been bright—it's actually something I've been noticing and—"

"That's not what this is," Kharon said quietly, and from his tone, he thought I was delusional.

"You *don't* know that," I said, anger rising. "He's *my* protector—I understand him better than either of you. I'm telling you, something's happening. He's changing. He must be molting."

Kharon ground his teeth. "You need to accept that it's most likely a tumor. These things happen with beasts all the time."

"I don't need to accept anything." A wave of calm washed over me. "He's going to be fine. I know it."

Tears blurred my eyes, but I blinked them away. I would not cry because he was going to be okay. There was no other option.

Fluffy Jr. sighed heavily, eyes closed as he slept.

He looked peaceful.

Poco stroked his ears and Nyx slid off my arm, an indent parting Fluffy Jr.'s fur as she slithered around his neck. She would never admit it, but I knew she had a soft spot for him.

Inside my chest, my protector bond still strummed. It was slightly tinged with pain, but for the most part it was strong.

Fluffy Jr. will be alright.

Toxic fear drained out of me, leaving nothing but exhaustion.

I climbed to my feet, full of hope.

Everything will work out.

I was going to ensure it.

I took a deep breath and regained my composure as I looked around at our extremely tight sleeping quarters. *This won't do.*

Turning, I faced my husbands head on. "Since we're all stuck here, I'll sleep in the bathtub."

They both froze.

"Excuse . . . me?" Kharon asked acerbically. Augustus arched a dark eyebrow, his Chthonic eyes glowing.

"I'll sleep in the bathtub," I repeated with conviction.

"No," Kharon said. "You won't."

27
SEXUAL TENSION & OTHER DRUGS

ALEXIS

"Say that again." Kharon's voice cracked through the room. In the torchlight, he looked satanic.

Actually on second thought, maybe I should have gone with my mentors?

"I'm going to sleep in the bathtub," I said calmly. "I won't sleep in the bed with—"

"Shut up." Kharon slashed his tattooed hand through the air.

The Machiavellian dictator was back.

"*You* shut up," I said. "I make my own decisions."

Kharon smiled cruelly. "Carissima—" His blue eyes reflected the light strangely. "Our wife will sleep in the bed, not in the tub like a fucking animal . . . *End* of discussion."

Augustus stood unnaturally still behind him, and there was something off about the way he was watching me.

His headache was gone.

Something has changed.

"Alexis." Augustus said my name quietly, his voice velvety smooth.

He raked his eyes over me, from head to toe.

I like to praise. One could say he's . . . cruel. Augustus's description of their sexual proclivities haunted me.

Be strong.

I was done running from men who should be afraid of me.

Tipping my chin up, I met Kharon's gaze. "What if I refuse? Are you going to *hurt* me? Break me? Trap me? Crawl across the floor while you—"

"SHUT UP!" Kharon tipped his head to the side, neck straining with pale tendons, a network of blue veins visible across his throat and jaw as he struggled for control.

"No."

Kharon surged forward, crowding me until my back bumped into the unyielding wall—he pressed his elbows against the stone on either side of my face.

I was pinned.

Augustus adjusted himself as he watched us with hooded eyes.

"*Fuck off, Karen,*" I whispered, feeling faint.

Kharon leaned in, the scent of a rainstorm wafting off him. "No—I'll *fuck you, Alexis,*" he purred.

I turned my face, so his lips were a hair's width away. "Aren't you supposed to be groveling for *my* forgiveness?"

He pressed his forehead against mine. "Oh, darling . . . are you asking me to crawl, again? We both know I'm very comfortable on my knees."

Augustus stepped forward—Kharon shifted to the side to give him space—both crowded me; Augustus's hips pressed against the right side of my body, and Kharon's were flush against my left.

Badump-Badump-Badump.

Kharon's calloused fingers rose to my collarbone and feathered over the diamond necklace—he dragged his nails up to my jaw, leaving a wake of fire, then wrapped his hand around my neck.

His skin was burning.

Tchaikovsky waved his conductor's wand, and the cello played.

The sensitive skin on my neck *prickled* where Kharon was touching me.

"Good girl," Augustus whispered hoarsely.

A droplet of sweat dripped slowly between my breasts.

Kharon's fingers tightened around my throat infinitesimally.

Unable to stop myself, I reached up and traced my hand across the hard ridges of his chest.

Kharon groaned, fingers relaxing as he moved his hand down to my sternum, while his lips ghosted over the side of my neck in barely there kisses.

Everything was hazy, in a warmly *delicious*, scream-into-the-abyss-and-tear-at-your-scalp-while-you-spiral, hellacious sort of way.

Augustus wet his full lower lip.

I reached up and tangled my free hand in his long hair. It was shockingly silky.

Augustus surged forward—he kissed my open mouth, his tongue plunging deep—I tugged his hair, and a tortured growl ripped from his throat.

He tastes like lightning.

Kharon dragged his teeth down the side of my neck, then lapped at the aching flesh. My hand dipped lower, trailing over his torso.

Augustus kissed me harder—and I yanked sharply on his hair. He snarled, teeth nipping at my bottom lip.

Kharon bit down on the side of my neck, and I shivered, fingers splaying across his lower stomach—he panted as he kissed the mark he'd left.

It feels like we're fighting.

"Enough." Augustus's voice cracked like a whip as he pulled

away—yanking Kharon back with him. "Alexis will sleep in the bed, and we'll worry about our arrangements later. We *can't* afford to be distracted. We need to rest right now and mentally prepare for the opening ceremony."

I struggled to catch my bearings.

Kharon tipped his head back to look at the rock ceiling. When he lowered it, his pupils were blown wide, black consuming the ice blue of his irises.

An otherworldly solar eclipse.

Augustus tossed his crown onto the bed and raked both his hands through his hair as he shouted a curse, his body taut.

The calm, composed man was gone, and the ferocious heir to the House of War seethed before me.

Kharon frowned, his eyes narrowed as he watched Augustus struggle. In reverse of their usual roles, he grabbed Augustus by his shoulders and shoved him into the bathroom.

The door slammed shut behind them—*crash*—and the walls shook, dust falling from the ceiling in a cloud.

Grunts and swears echoed.

"Calm the fuck down and stop panicking!" Kharon shouted as another crash rattled the wall.

"Not . . . *helping.*" Augustus's muffled voice shook, like he was gasping.

I sagged against the shaking wall. Head spinning, thoughts scattered, I slid down to sit beside my sleeping protector, patting his head.

Poco chittered, his little black fingers touching my arm gently, and I gave him a shaky smile. He nodded his furry head, like he understood that I was trying to keep it together, then he climbed up and curled into a lumpy gray ball on my lap, purring.

The hellhounds lay behind Fluffy Jr.'s butt, pressed against the wall, barely fitting.

"He . . . big dog," Hell said in his strange, scratchy voice as he tipped his head toward Fluffy Jr. "He . . . okay."

Hound nodded in agreement. "We . . . together . . . all good."

"Of course," I whispered to them, infusing my voice with confidence. "Everything is going to be alright."

The whiplash of power, imprisonment, fear, and then lust was making it hard to focus on any one thing.

Sparta will not break me.

There was only one thing to do in this type of situation. I pulled out my calculator and clicked the recorder.

"Dear Diary," I whispered.

"I'm scared Fluffy Jr. is sick. Kharon and Augustus don't scare me . . . but I'm afraid of how I feel around them. The gladiator competition is starting early, and I haven't figured out how to wield my power. Yesterday, my hands glowed with a bright light. I don't know what any of it means."

With a shaky exhale, I pulled the recorder away from my lips.

Toggling through my settings, I found my saved work and lost myself in the numbers. I graphed until my neck hurt and my fingers went numb.

Time lost all meaning.

Guard voices echoed outside—Kharon and Augustus came out of the bathroom, their expressions perfectly calm.

You would never know they'd been fighting.

Clang. The cell door slammed open and Nyx hissed.

I hastily tucked my calculator away and lifted Poco off my lap. Batons sparked brightly in the dim light as guards stood framed in the doorway.

"It's time for the opening ceremony," Vorex said, wreath gleaming atop his head. "Come with us."

28
SOFTLY IT BEGINS

ALEXIS

Augustus pulled me to my feet and Kharon finger-combed dust out of my hair as he straightened my crown. Nyx slithered, wrapping herself around my leg.

"No protectors allowed for the ceremony," Vorex said as the animals walked forward with us.

I stared down at Fluffy Jr.'s sleeping form.

"He'll be okay," Kharon said quietly.

I straightened and held my head high. "I know." I glared at Augustus, daring him to argue.

He didn't.

Deep inside my chest, my protector bond strummed, warm and alive. Everyone else might underestimate Fluffy Jr., but I wouldn't.

Augustus placed his hand on my lower back as he escorted me out of the room and Kharon trailed behind us, his fingers resting possessively on the top of my spine.

My skin tingled from where they touched.

In the dimly lit tunnel, Kharon moved so he flanked my other side, his thumb caressing the priceless necklace.

Four guards marched at our front, electric batons sizzling in their hands.

I glanced back. *One, two, three . . .* Eight Olympians marched behind us.

It wasn't a fair fight—they should have brought more guards.

Vorex wasn't the only one I recognized. Alessander, Titus's crony from the crucible, also marched beside him in a matching blue suit embroidered with the House of Poseidon symbol.

Alessander's gaze flicked to mine. His weapon lowered as he opened his mouth like he wanted to say something to me. Vorex shot him a glare and he pursed his lips shut.

Alessander was shorter than I remembered. *How was I ever afraid of him?*

Augustus's nails dug into my lower back as his fingers tensed. "Are you okay?" he asked in my ear as he followed my gaze. His eyes flashed with recognition.

"Yes," I said, feeling the truth of the word in my bones.

Alessander was no threat to me.

Kharon's calloused thumb stroked the back of my neck soothingly.

My husbands pressed closer to me as we were escorted up through the maze of tunnels, out of the torchlight, into the orange rays of the setting sun.

This time we didn't climb the steps—we were led out onto the sand.

Four Chthonic flags waved in the breeze where they were planted in the middle of the arena. The corresponding leaders stood in front of them, spiky crowns glinting atop their heads.

A long white marble altar sat to the left of the flags. Standing unobtrusively, the block of stone looked distinctly out of place.

People screamed down at us, the coliseum much louder than during the massacre. The siren section was now packed with hundreds, as were the other creature sections. They sat too far away to make out individual people.

The sheer magnitude of the crowd was overwhelming.

It was easy to forget that Sparta was made up of thousands of creatures because of the constant Chthonic versus Olympian politics.

Sharp feedback rang in my left ear, and I swallowed a wince.

Augustus grabbed the side of his head, and he glanced down at me with recognition.

He felt my pain.

I looked away from his too-knowing eyes and studied the packed stadium, where eight Olympian House flags waved in the wind, fluttering with bright colors.

"Non desistas, non exieris . . . non desistas, non exieris . . ." chanted loudly through the air.

Never give up, never surrender.

Dusk painted everything in a muted radiance, and the ancient civilization didn't seem real.

The sun slowly lowered behind the mountain peaks.

The dead bodies had been removed, but the sand was still splattered in blood, the scent of copper lingering in the air.

As we approached the Chthonic flags, my breath caught.

Hades's eyes were bloodred—a menacing scowl contorted his features. For the first time since I'd known him, he looked like he was seconds away from losing control. Inky fog pulsed violently around him.

He scanned the sand, and his back straightened as his gaze landed on me.

I gave him a small reassuring smile.

His fog stopped pulsing, tendrils slowly wrapping around his feet as he visibly relaxed.

Behind him in the stadium, Persephone sat next to Charlie and Helen in the front row. She waved to me and shouted something, but I couldn't hear it.

"Never give up, never surrender." The chant increased in decibel as we were escorted toward the center of the arena.

Augustus and Kharon pressed closer.

To our right, Patro and Achilles stalked forward with three guards standing a distance away from them like they were afraid to get too close.

Achilles looked at me, then turned away.

Patro grimaced.

To the left, Agatha blew kisses at the guards. Behind them, Drex was once again looking sickly as he stumbled forward.

"Form a line!" Vorex shouted over the clamor, as he gestured with his sparking baton to a perpendicular strip of empty sand that faced the altar and half of the stadium.

Kharon and Augustus stopped walking, their fingers curling where they rested against my skin, and scowled at him.

"Uh . . . please," Vorex amended with a wince as he looked down, unable to meet their gaze.

"Watch your fucking self," Kharon warned Vorex as he pulled me closer to his side.

The three of us lined up next to the others.

Hades, Artemis, Ares, and Aphrodite stepped away from the flags and joined the end of our line.

Sparta chanted all around.

There was a thud as a cloaked figure jumped over the edge of the stands and landed in the arena.

Erebus stood to his towering height, a sinister white bone mask obscuring his features. He straightened his tattered cloak, shadows clinging to him as he stalked across the sand.

The poster hanging in Helen's room failed to capture his *terrifying* aura.

Erebus came to a stop at the end of our line and Aphrodite leaned up to whisper something in his ear. His masked face snapped down to hers, posture sharp.

Fear sank its teeth into my spine.

If the leaders were unnerved, then I needed to preemptively exit left (die).

Hades leaned forward in the line. "It will be okay," he mouthed silently as he stared at me. "Don't be afraid, daughter. You are the best of both of us."

I wasn't so sure of that.

"Welcome, Chthonics." Zeus's voice projected as he walked out onto the sand, electricity jumping across his skin.

The crowd went wild.

Fate walked beside him with a clipboard in her hand—rage filled me—*Why did you deliver Charlie to that toxic trailer?*

She glanced my way, and a small knowing smile curled her lips.

I let her see my hatred. *Someday, you'll pay.*

She smiled wider.

The roars from the crowd increased tenfold as the seven other Olympian leaders walked out behind Zeus, oversized laurel wreaths heavy on their heads.

"Never give up!" the crowd chanted with growing excitement. "Never surrender!"

Stomp.

Clap.

Stomp.

Sand vibrated, and as the Olympian leaders neared, their crests identified them.

Hera walked behind Zeus in a shiny silver toga. Tall and willowy, the severe bun at the base of her neck gave her a waspish look.

Hermes stood out beside her, short and skinny, his lime-green suit studded with diamonds.

Athena followed behind them in a glittery purple toga—she was shorter than Hera but much more muscular. Her dark bronze skin shone like she'd rubbed herself in shimmering oil, and her wavy brown hair fell down her back in a glorious wave.

Two men flanked her.

Poseidon walked to her left, extremely tall and muscular, in a navy suit. He had long white hair and a matching beard, clear green eyes, and tan skin—from his fierce scowl and size, he looked more like a Chthonic than an Olympian.

On her left was a man in a yellow suit: Apollo.

The rumors of his attractiveness didn't begin to do him justice.

It was hard to look at Apollo—his bronze skin and long curly blond hair were both so bright, he practically gleamed. As he neared, his eyes were a light shade of golden brown that I'd never seen before.

He sneered as our gazes met. *Rude.*

At the back of the procession Demeter and Dionysus walked together.

Demeter was a short woman with curly blond hair and icy gray eyes. Her pale skin was covered in freckles, matching the rhinestones that dotted her brown toga. She was beautiful in a familiar, ethereal way. *Persephone's mother.* She looked more like her sister.

Her head snapped and she scowled at me, her expression severe. *Grandma?*

Something told me she would *not* like it if I called her meemaw or gammy.

Demeter's gaze traveled across the Chthonics and landed on Hades. The death glare she shot him was sharp enough to kill. Slowly, she drew a threatening finger across her neck.

I was intrigued.

I'd always wanted to be involved in family drama, and this seemed *extremely* promising.

Dionysus walked beside my meemaw. He was a brawny Black man with long wavy purple hair that matched his suit.

He turned his head to look at us and his eyes were a shocking shade of white.

I swallowed a gasp.

Is he also secretly blind?

The Olympian House leaders positioned themselves in a line across from us on the other side of the long altar.

Thirteen of us.

Eight of them.

There was a heavy aura surrounding the leaders on both sides.

Power tingled across my tongue.

No one looked physically old, but they all *felt* ancient—it was something I couldn't put my finger on—a sixth sense was screaming at me to run for my life. It was an innate terror.

These were the leviathans of this dark age.

The Olympian leaders focused on Kharon, their eyebrows rising. Athena leaned up to Poseidon and I read her lips, "He really did give her his ear. How . . . romantic."

Poseidon scowled down at her. "It's deranged."

He's not wrong.

Athena shook her head in disagreement.

Kharon reached up and rested his hand once again on the back of my neck, his thumb shifting my necklace so the blue diamonds caught the light.

Territorial and overly possessive, the action would have been demeaning coming from any other man, but there was something about Kharon—an animalistic energy that matched his hellhounds—that was intrinsic to his being.

I couldn't stop myself from leaning into his touch.

Demeter's scowl deepened.

Meemaw's not happy. I fought the urge to wave at her.

Hostility radiated between the two groups.

Suddenly, I wasn't sure the great war of Sparta had ever ended—it felt like we were standing in the middle of a ceasefire, both sides waiting for the other to take the first shot.

There was no love lost, no empathy, no . . . *anything.*

Just open hatred, and barely concealed violence.

Tension stretched, energy mounting, as Chthonic and Olympian House leaders sized each other up, waiting for someone to make the first move, so they could slaughter each other freely.

"Never give up, never surrender." The stadium clapped and stomped, clumps of dried bloody sand shaking.

Zeus walked up to the altar—he raised both his hands up in the air, electricity sizzling on his skin—the stadium fell dead silent.

No one moved.

"Let us begin." Zeus made eye contact with me, sparks leaping from his gaze.

The scar on my sternum prickled.

Fate smiled.

It didn't take the power of premonition to know that things were about to get *extremely* unpleasant, for me.

29

OPENING CEREMONIES & GORE

ALEXIS

"The historic Spartan Gladiator Competition showcases Chthonic power." Zeus's voice projected, sparks dancing across his lips as he stood before the altar, his arms raised.

The stadium roared.

Olympian leaders glared behind him in their line.

Kharon scoffed on my left. "It's a humiliation ritual," he muttered under his breath, his thumb still stroking my neck.

Augustus's nails dug into my lower back as he flexed his fingers.

He'd tried to rebuild his calm facade, but it wasn't as convincing as before—cracks were showing. His eyes shone a little too brightly, his expression a little too sharp.

It was almost as if his headaches had stifled him, and now that he was pain free, his true nature was breaking free.

"This year there are thirteen Assembly of Death competitors," Zeus said, looking over each of us. "Per tradition—we will have a thirteen-day contest starting tomorrow. One day for each Chth . . ." His gaze stopped on Drex, and he grimaced, like he'd forgotten about him. "Contestant."

Drex tilted his chin up high like he was unaffected, but his face paled.

"Thirteen days of Spartan showmanship with no guns allowed," Zeus continued with a golden smile. "Spartans, knives, and protectors only . . . just as our ancestors fought on these sacred sands. This is our modern ode to them."

I shivered.

Only thirteen days?

From the way everyone talked about the competition, and the snippets of extreme bloodshed that played on the Spartan Lifestyle Page, I'd assumed it would be a month-long affair.

One day.

I just had to survive a single day.

Easy, you can do this.

Zeus rambled on about honor, violence, and the pride of showing off Spartan power.

Kharon and Augustus glanced down at me, faces twisted with concern—I'd subconsciously grabbed both their arms and pulled them closer to me—with a deep breath, I forced my fingers to relax.

"Don't," Kharon whispered under his breath. "Don't stop touching me . . . please."

I retightened my grip.

His jaw worked back and forth, and he was staring down at me like a starving man, eyes smoldering.

My heart sped up.

We were standing in front of the powerful Spartan leaders who ruled the world, preparing to compete in what was rumored to be the most dangerous competition on earth, and my husbands were eye fucking me.

My face flushed.

Are there support groups for perverts?

Augustus's dark lashes fanned across his tan skin. "Are you okay, my carus?"

I nodded.

Nyx slithered up from where she'd been sleeping on my leg, and tightened around my arm. "You should have sex with them already—it's getting weird."

No, it's been weird.

Feeling exposed—and like a deviant with a man problem (both were true)—I tried to ignore my husbands, but their hands on my neck and lower back were like brands.

The sun sank fully behind the mountains.

"We will now begin the ceremony—" Zeus paused, and torches lit with a whooshing sound throughout the arena "—with the revelations of the victors and reading of the labors."

I jumped as claps echoed thunderously all around.

"*Labors?*" I whispered.

Augustus leaned down. "The number of labors is how many competitors we have to face during our fight—we all fight once, but the more labors you get . . . the more rounds you have to survive. The rounds get progressively harder, physically and mentally."

Oh, how wonderous.

This entire experience (my life) was becoming increasingly more unfortunate.

Maybe I should just leap away. How bad can treason and imprisonment really be? Guilt hit me. Ceres would beg to differ.

Zeus pulled a small velvet pouch out of his coat pocket and dumped two gold dice onto the altar.

"We welcome Ajax of the illustrious House of Hermes, this year's honorable enforcer." Zeus pointed to a guard wearing a small laurel crown.

Ajax stepped forward, rainbow peacock crest sparkling on the lapel of his black suit as he stepped up beside the altar.

Why do they need an enforcer?

Fate put on a pair of purple reading glasses, and held her clipboard out.

"Will the Chthonic leaders please step forward?" Her voice boomed around the stadium. The tenor was even more commanding than Zeus's.

The crowd quieted.

Hades, Artemis, Erebus, Aphrodite, and Ares stepped forward and slowly sauntered as a group up to the other side of the altar.

"Per tradition," Zeus said as he held up a die, showing off the five dots. "As there are five of you, do you each accept your labors—will you each fight against five adult Cyclopes?"

"We do," Hades said calmly, fog swirling around his feet.

Augustus leaned down again and whispered in my ear, "The leaders always fight five Cyclopes to start the competition. They're so powerful that it's more ceremonial than anything else."

I nodded up at him, grateful he was giving me some context.

Hades had planned on giving me a debrief of the SGC the week before the competition, but that was before the accelerated timeline.

"Now—their revelations!" Zeus spread his arms wide, face up to the sky.

I looked up at Augustus for an explanation, but he was staring at Kharon with a nervous, worried expression.

Purple eyes flashed as Fate tapped her clipboard. "Artemis."

Artemis smirked. She grabbed the V-neck of her toga, turned in a circle so everyone in the stadium could see, and . . . ripped the material wide, exposing the bare, unblemished skin of her sternum.

Scarlet mist glittered around her in a dangerous shimmer.

"Revelation," Zeus announced. "Zero defeats."

Artemis looked smug as she tied the ripped top of her toga so it covered her chest, and walked back to stand in our line, a haughty sneer on her face.

"Ares," Fate called out.

The infamous leader of the House of War stepped up and unbuttoned his suit jacket. Folding it neatly, he placed it on the altar, then deftly unbuttoned his white shirt and shrugged out of it.

His head was shaved down the middle, and the crimson rings around his irises flared. Layers of bronze skin rippled as he slowly turned in a circle.

Long jagged scars slashed across his lower back and the thick ridges of his stomach, matching the scar across his lips.

"Revelation—zero defeats!" Zeus shouted.

Hades was called forward, and he also shrugged out of his suit jacket. I looked away, because I didn't want to be scarred for life, and Zeus announced he also had zero defeats.

"Erebus!" Fate yelled.

Kharon stiffened, his grip tightening around my neck.

Erebus stepped up to the altar, his mask gleaming menacingly in the golden light of dusk.

He parted his cloak, revealing combat pants and a plain black T-shirt. He was probably the only person in the stadium not dressed in ceremonial clothes.

Erebus gripped the neck of his shirt and ripped down.

The stadium gasped.

Every inch of Erebus's pale lithe torso was covered in old and new raised claw marks. It looked like he'd been attacked by hundreds of wolves, *repeatedly*.

"Revelation." Zeus cleared his throat like he was composing himself as he stared at Erebus warily. "Zero . . . defeats."

Erebus turned swiftly, cloak parted, ripped shirt fluttering off his ruined torso as he stalked back to the line.

Between the claw marks and bone mask, I understood why the poster of him on Helen's wall said, "Beware: this creature is more beast than man."

"Look at me—over here, Erebus!" Nyx hissed loudly as she slid invisibly along my arm. "Stay sexy, you absolute *monster.*"

She made a seductive clicking sound that would haunt my nightmares, and I whimpered.

Kharon looked down at me, and I shrugged, because a little male harassment never hurt anybody.

Womanhood was complicated.

Men could never understand the lifestyle.

"Aphrodite," Fate called.

The stadium fell unnaturally quiet as everyone collectively held their breath and stared at her with rapt attention. Olympians and creatures alike.

Aphrodite's curvy figure was clothed in a diamond-covered silk toga.

Augustus covered his eyes with his right hand. *That's his mother.* It was easy to forget.

Unlike Artemis, Aphrodite didn't rip the neck of her toga.

She lifted her long ruby-covered braids—they tinkled as the gems clacked together—and exposed her graceful neck.

Poseidon licked his lips; Athena's eyes widened; Zeus stared across the altar at her like he was possessed; Hera's face twisted with malice.

With every eye on her, Aphrodite slowly spun in a circle. Long lashes fluttered and her electric green eyes practically glowed. She pulled one silk sash of her toga off her shoulder; it slipped across her arm.

Somehow, the silence got quieter.

Another silk sash was removed.

The top of her toga fluttered down, exposing dark unblemished skin and a dozen sparkling diamond necklaces, nestled between the most impressive cleavage I'd ever seen.

I blinked, and Aphrodite was covered, the sashes of her toga once again concealing her chest.

She blew a kiss to the crowd—there was a commotion in the stands as men and women, creatures and Spartans, passed out.

"Um." Zeus coughed, looking extremely flustered. "No defeats . . . I mean zero . . . uh, revelations."

Hera scowled at Aphrodite, as she glared at Zeus and glided back toward our line, her hips sashaying beneath silk.

All eight Olympian leaders watched her hungrily.

"Now *that* is a woman," Nyx sighed dreamily. "Are you sure you went through puberty?"

"Everyone is beautiful in their own way," I mumbled under my breath.

Nyx's scales slid smoothly against my skin as she slithered around my arm. "Whatever you need to tell yourself to sleep at night."

I huffed.

Nyx sighed. "Ugly people can be *so* sensitive."

Everyone is beautiful in their own way, I repeated to myself.

Zeus raised his hands again and announced, "The younger, *weaker* Chthonic contestants will now reveal their scar status and be assigned their number of labors." He said *weaker* like he was making a threat.

"Agatha!" Fate announced.

Agatha stood tall, hands clasped together behind her back, as she walked up to the altar like she was walking toward the gallows.

"*Empusa scum!*" someone shouted and the crowd laughed.

Zeus stared at her expectantly.

Ajax took a menacing step toward her, his hands raised. "Expose your sternum," he demanded.

Agatha ripped her toga and revealed the top of her pale chest—she had two detailed circular scars on her flesh.

They looked familiar.

Kharon's grip on my neck tightened painfully.

"Revelations—" Zeus shouted, sparks jumping off his lips. "She has been dishonored by *two* of her labors."

A few boos echoed from the crowd. Hateful comments were screamed about her heritage.

Augustus leaned close and whispered, "They brand you with a Vulcan stamp. The metal is specially designed to scar any immortal."

My stomach rolled as I glanced over at Kharon's stoic face.

Agatha pulled her toga back together, holding the ripped parts closed with her hands as she held her head high.

Zeus picked up the two dice. "This SGC, Agatha will face . . ." He threw the dice onto the altar.

Agatha stared down, her expression paling.

"FIVE LABORS!" Zeus shouted and the stadium clapped and hollered. "TWO rounds in the arena."

Augustus rubbed my lower back. "If you roll four or fewer adversaries," he whispered against the shell of my ear, "then you have to survive one round in the arena. If you roll more than four, you have two rounds. If you roll more than eight . . ." He grimaced. "Three rounds."

Agatha stalked back to the line.

"Unlike the leaders, our competitors are a surprise," Augustus continued to whisper. "Their labors are for show—ours are for punishment . . . and humiliation."

"How long is a r-round?"

Kharon leaned close. "Until you defeat your labors," he said darkly. "Or they defeat *you*."

"So, if you're defeated, it just . . . ends?" I asked.

Kharon gripped my neck tighter, his eyes hardening. "It doesn't *end* until you drag your broken body out of the arena and—"

"And then they brand you," Augustus said quietly.

"What if . . . you can't leave the arena?"

Kharon and Augustus stood up straighter and refused to meet my eyes.

This is barbaric.

"Hermos."

He walked forward calmly. A single snake trailed out of his head like hair, rattling, as he ripped open his shirt, showcasing multiple brands.

"Revelations—he has been dishonored by *six* of his labors," Zeus shouted as he rolled the two dice.

The crowd held its breath.

"One round," Zeus announced. "Three labors."

The crowd booed with disappointment. "Snake scum!" someone screamed. "Abomination. Your kind isn't wanted in Sparta!"

Hermos smiled as he walked back to the line and Agatha grinned at him.

There was a one in eighteen chance of rolling a three with two dice.

Lucky.

"Patro," Fate said.

My mentor sauntered lazily across the sand.

At the altar, he slowly opened his shirt, and everyone stared enraptured. The Olympian leaders leaned forward like they were all trying to get a better look.

He truly was his mother's son.

Patro casually revealed his impressive, muscled physique—he appeared as if he was carved from bronze, the statue of David in the flesh—and showed off a single circular mark in the middle of his chest, right over his heart.

The dice clattered across marble.

"Revelations—he has been dishonored by *one* of his labors." Zeus's lips twitched into a frown. "One round—two labors!"

The crowd clapped.

Another lucky roll.

Catcalls echoed as people whooped and hollered, begging him to look in their direction.

Achilles relaxed with visible relief.

Patro shot me a smug grin when he was within earshot. "Enjoy your time with your *husbands*," he mocked. "I hope you don't *regret* your choice."

I nodded back, too nervous to engage, and Patro looked bewildered.

Achilles glared over at me as he ripped his shirt open, buttons popping and falling to the sand, then he stalked toward the marble altar.

"Revelations—" Zeus announced. "Zero defeats."

The stadium cheered, and everyone got to their feet. "*Achilles . . . Achilles . . . Achilles*" was chanted all around.

The people's hero.

As Achilles stood tall, glowering at Zeus and awaiting his fate, Hera openly fanned herself while Apollo admired his exposed chest.

Is everyone in Sparta a pervert?

I was starting to sense a theme.

Zeus threw down the dice, electricity sparking off his fingers onto the table.

An evil smile curled his lips. "EIGHT LABORS!" Zeus shouted and the stands erupted. "TWO rounds in the arena . . . *without* his muzzle." The cheers were thunderous.

Sharp feedback pierced my left ear.

Achilles turned around to walk back to the line, open shirt fluttering to reveal a thin trail of dark hair over the deep grooves of his stomach.

"Yep, that's my type," Nyx hissed unhelpfully.

Achilles's eyes met mine—they narrowed with malice.

From the disdain wafting off him, he wasn't happy with my choice to stay with my husbands, and he wasn't going to be getting over it soon.

I leaned into Kharon's touch.

Fate tapped her clipboard. "Drex!" she called out.

There was a smattering of applause and a buzz of conversation. From the sound of it, Sparta didn't know what to make of an Olympian mutt competing in the SGC.

With clumsy fingers, Drex unbuttoned his shirt and showed off the unmarked skin of his chest, face flaming red.

Zeus grimaced as he rolled the dice. "One round—two labors!" There was relief in his voice.

Thank God. An extremely lucky roll.

I exhaled and so did Drex.

"Kharon."

My left side went cold as he disappeared, his hand falling away.

As he prowled toward the altar, the crowd quieted.

Kharon ripped off his shirt—revealing his tattooed, mutilated chest.

He turned in a circle with his hands wide, face apathetic.

The stadium fell dead silent.

Zeus cleared his throat, eyeing Kharon like he was a wild animal that might attack at any moment. "Revelations—he has been dishonored by . . . eleven of his labors."

Kharon bared his teeth.

Augustus's stubble brushed across the side of my face. "In Kharon's first games," he whispered, barely audible, "he was just eighteen and hadn't come into his full powers . . . He drew eleven labors . . . the most anyone has *ever* faced—they were all Minotaurs."

I jerked with shock.

What?

Kharon smirked—he appeared completely impervious to the Olympians' judgment—but I could feel the pain radiating up his leg in hot waves.

An image of a younger him, defeated, crawling through the sand away from monsters, flashed inside my mind.

He deserved so much better.

The dice rolled. "One round . . . three labors," Zeus said, his frustration evident.

There was a smattering of nervous applause.

Kharon stalked back toward me with piercing pain streaking up his leg and his tattered shirt fluttering.

When he made it back, he buried his shaking hand at the base of my head, fingers tangling roughly in my curls as he breathed deeply to steady himself.

"Fuck the Olympians," he whispered.

I nodded. "*Screw* all of them."

The corner of his mouth twitched into a smile.

Augustus's name was called and he casually untucked his shirt and undid the buttons as he walked forward with a pleasant, calm expression.

His posture was relaxed.

He looked like he didn't have a care in the world.

"Revelations—" Zeus shouted. "Zero defeats."

Sparta cheered loudly.

People stood up and clapped as they chanted his name.

The Olympian leaders smiled at Augustus as he spun lazily in a circle, showcasing the unblemished tan skin of his chiseled chest.

He wasn't just the Chthonic golden boy—*everyone* loved him.

Augustus's black, soul-consuming eyes locked on mine as he turned, and they radiated danger.

How did he deceive them all into thinking this version of him is real? The hostile, depraved glint in his eyes was unmistakable.

Couldn't they see it was all an act?

Zeus stared down at the altar. "Two rounds—six labors!" The crowd cheered louder.

I felt sick.

Augustus sauntered back over to us, his expression affable. The shirt hanging open revealing the deep grooves of his Adonis belt was slightly distracting.

I blushed as his hand settled on my lower back, fingers splaying possessively.

"Our last competitor," Zeus announced with a smirk.

"Hercules!" Fate called.

Once again, the crowd fell silent.

It took me a second to remember—that was me.

I walked quickly toward the altar—Zeus's gray-eyed stare was intense—Ceres's warning washed over me.

I bumped against the edge of the altar and stumbled back.

The weight of everyone's stares was suffocating; the quiet was oppressive.

Zeus cleared his throat.

"Expose your sternum." A voice growled to my left and I jumped as Ajax appeared in my blind spot.

It was strange being slightly taller than a man, since I was used to looking up at Chthonics; I'd forgotten that I was a large woman.

It was a nice reminder.

Stepping away from Ajax, I pulled at the high neck of my toga. Right. I just needed to show my clavicle. *Easy.*

The fabric didn't budge.

"Fuck." Swearing under my breath, I tugged, but my clammy hands slipped across the silk, which was surprisingly durable.

Of course I'd get the toga made with exquisite craftsmanship.

Dear God, why do you keep doing this to me?

"You can do it," Nyx hissed encouragingly. "Just tense your core and rip."

Face flaming with heat, I pulled harder and nothing happened. Panic and embarrassment were an inferno inside my sternum.

This was hell.

I stared down at the layers of my toga and started to pull my arm from a sleeve. I just needed to get a different angle.

RIPPPPP.

It took me a second to process that hands were violently holding the top of my toga open.

Air blew across my stomach.

Ajax held the torn fabric, exposing the lacy pink bra I'd borrowed from Helen all the way down to the bow on the top of my underwear.

His knuckles were pressed against my exposed chest.

"Release me," I said.

Ajax snarled something in my face, but I couldn't hear it over the rushing in my ears—I grabbed at the silk, roughly pulling it from his hands.

The dice clattered across the altar. *Wait, why are they sparking with electricity?*

"THREE ROUNDS—TWELVE LABORS!"

Zeus's voice was like a gunshot in the too-quiet coliseum. *What?*

Ajax said something and stepped toward me, but I couldn't hear him over the whooshing in my ears.

He reached for me.

I raised my fist to throw a punch, twisting my hips for power and—

Ajax's neck snapped to the side.

My fist hung suspended in midair.

Kharon was holding Ajax's twisted head—he threw the limp body down—Ajax's skull hit the side of the altar with a loud crack. Augustus moved in front of me protectively.

"Oopsie," Kharon said. "My bad. I slipped."

The crowd screamed.

"I've always liked that *Karen* man," Nyx hissed sarcastically as she slithered around my shoulders.

Hermes lunged at Kharon, but Hera held him back.

"Oh please," Kharon said as he gestured to Ajax's crumpled body. "He'll be *fine* . . . He dishonored my wife—he's lucky I didn't decapitate him."

He kicked Ajax.

Something cracked.

"I slipped again," Kharon drawled.

I hunched over with my hands on my knees, and Augustus gently grabbed my chin and tilted my head up. "Alexis, *breathe*. You're going to be okay, darling—we'll make sure of it. Everything is fine."

"It was a statistically *unusual* event," I said with a gasp, needing Augustus to understand. The mathematical odds were truly devastating. There was a one in thirty-six chance of rolling a twelve, which meant there was less than a 0.05 chance.

Ceres was right about Zeus. I saw the dice spark.

Also, Kharon just snapped a man's neck.

Nothing was fine.

"THIS IS UNACCEPTABLE!" Hades shouted as he stalked across the sand toward Zeus. His Chthonic eyes were bloody, and fog pulsed angrily around him. "My daughter ca*nn*ot face *twelve fucking labors.*"

I'd never heard him swear before.

Persephone jumped over the edge of the stadium, landing gracefully. She sprinted toward the altar, her hand raised, finger pointing at Zeus.

"Fix this!" she screamed.

Zeus held his hands up in a surrender gesture. "I agree! This is wrong—I would never want my niece to have to face this."

He's such a liar.

"Roll it again," Persephone demanded as she came to a stop beside Hades, who was now covered fully in rolling inky fog. "Now."

"I would." Zeus's expression was pleading as he looked between them. "But it's written into the laws of Sparta—you both know I can't. I swear I want to. The odds . . . This is *horrible*."

Déjà vu washed over me as my parents argued with Zeus in the middle of the stadium.

Ceres said the best plans were simple—ours was one of deception, not force.

I needed to get Zeus alone, and I needed to get him to talk. That meant he couldn't suspect that I *knew* what he'd done. I wasn't completely sure about the details, but I had a growing suspicion.

However, entrapment was easier said than done.

Twelve labors.

I'll die on the sands.

Ceres was waiting for me back in the villa, and she believed in me.

With visceral terror pounding through me, I stood tall. "Zeus is right!" My voice rang, strong and clear.

Zeus turned slowly. "I . . . am?"

Everyone looked at me.

I needed to play the naive idiot, one last time.

"I'll be fine." I stared at Hades and Persephone, mentally pleading with them to trust me one more time. "I've been training—I'll face the labors, all . . . twelve."

"Are you sure?" Zeus asked, his gray eyes wide with what looked like concern.

I forced myself to act casual. "I can handle him . . . I mean *them*."

Zeus's expression didn't change, but the corner of his mouth twitched down like he was confused. For the first time, he looked unsure.

Persephone nodded as she studied my face—she saw through me in a way that only a mother could. She grabbed Hades's arm and whispered in his ear.

Murmurs erupted in the stadium.

I widened my shoulders.

Nyx hissed, "Oh, now *this* is going to be fun."

No one fears the weak.

I would play Zeus's game, until it was time to play mine.

30
THE ELDEST HEIR

AUGUSTUS

Poco was wrapped around my head, purring soothingly, and I leaned into his touch. I'd missed him so much that it hurt to think about our time apart.

Wall sconces burned low, and shadows crawled across the ancient coliseum stone.

We'd been locked in the room for hours, all of us lying in the one bed.

Alexis lay stiffly pressed against my back, her breathing shallow and harsh—buttons clicked as a faint green light illuminated the screen—she pressed her calculator while muttering about statistically unlikely events.

Kharon grumbled and shifted.

We were on either side of her, half hanging off the much too small mattress.

It should have been heavenly—it was tortuous.

The urge to wrap my arms around her and pull her close was driving me mad.

I wanted to touch, kiss, *caress* her.

But I also wanted to respect her—she thought what we had was just physical; I needed to prove to her that it wasn't. She could have severed the bond between us with her blood, she could have chosen to stay in the room with Patro and Achilles—but she'd chosen *us* each time.

I couldn't ruin the trust that was growing between us by being too sexually aggressive.

I had to keep my more physical nature under wraps.

For now.

Kharon swore under his breath as he punched at his pillow, and Alexis poked faster at her calculator.

She had to survive three rounds and twelve fucking labors; it was Kharon all over again, but somehow *worse*.

None of us could sleep.

Fluffy Jr. made a pained sound and kicked the bed in his sleep—my head jerked—the steel bed frame slammed against the stone wall. He'd been doing it for hours.

Alexis tensed, focusing on her calculator.

Something was seriously wrong with her protector, but at this point there was nothing we could do to help him. At least he was resting.

Poco chittered as he gnawed on my hair.

On top of the imminent danger that my wife was facing, she'd also been exposed against her will in front of the entirety of Sparta. I hadn't missed the way the Olympian leaders had stared at her flesh hungrily, and they hadn't been the only ones.

Catcalls and whistles had echoed around the stadium.

I'd memorized the face of a male siren who'd shouted, "Ride my face, Angelus Romae," from the front row of the stadium.

He would die by my hand. Soon. Gruesomely.

To calm myself, I made a mental hit list.

Ajax was number one.

He'd dared to touch my *wife* in front of me.

If Kharon hadn't snapped his neck, I would have done *much* worse.

I took a deep breath.

We had to play the federation's game.

The Great War had ended because of a "peace agreement," but everyone knew it hadn't *really* ceased. Olympians and Chthonics were still battling, as we had been since the dawn of Sparta.

The power struggle never ended.

All we had to do was outlast the Olympians. Sparta was a giant game of combat chess—you had to strategize and play the long game, while being shot at.

Poco's whiskers tickled my cheek.

Alexis cleared her throat. "I did something . . ." she trailed off in the quiet.

Kharon stopped swearing under his breath.

My heart skipped a beat at how pained she sounded.

I wanted to turn to see her, to hold her, but there was no room on the stupid bed.

It didn't help that the soft tenor of her voice made blood rush to other parts of my body. Images of her obeying, kneeling, bowing before me, made it hard to breathe. She was so beautifully submissive.

Every second in her presence was torment.

Fluffy Jr. whimpered and the bed once again slammed against the wall.

"A while ago . . ." Alexis shifted between us. "I made a choice—a dangerous one . . . You're both going to be . . . angry with me."

There was a long pause.

She audibly gulped.

"I forgive you," Kharon and I said at the same time.

"No—you *don't* understand," Alexis said with agitation. "It's bad . . . *really* bad. It has larger consequences for all of Sparta and—"

"No, princess," Kharon cut her off. "You don't understand. We don't care if you went on a murderous rampage—you're forgiven . . . you're our wife."

"We're *always* on your side," I said.

Alexis pressed against my back as she shifted. "Don't lie—please . . . you're both going to loathe me," she said.

"Never," I said with vehemence.

"Carissima," Kharon chuckled harshly. "We're fucking *obsessed* with you. In fact, it's taking every ounce of control I have to not ravage you right now. Stop talking nonsense and go to sleep. You need your rest."

Alexis sputtered. "You really want to ravage me . . . now? Aren't you stressed? We need to be on top of our game for the SGC and—"

"Oh—I'm always on top," Kharon said.

There was a long pause.

"You're ridiculous." Alexis hit him with her calculator.

"For you, I'm many things. You can call it whatever you want, carissima."

"Can we please concentrate on the *fighting to the death* that we have to do?" Alexis asked.

Kharon and I both froze.

"Don't . . ." I warned softly, unable to verbalize the devastation.

"No one is *dying*," Kharon snarled. "Do you understand me, Alexis? We will wage a war on Olympians before we let them kill you."

Alexis made a sound like she didn't believe us. "Oh please."

"We're not joking," I said.

The three of us breathed heavily in the dark, no one speaking.

"There is *nothing* more important than your life," Kharon said, breaking the growing tension. "That's all we give a fuck about. So, STOP talking about other issues . . . Your safety is the only fucking issue that we care about."

"Exactly," I said.

Alexis gasped like she was suffocating.

This was our exact problem—we didn't know how to love softly. While Alexis was spiraling, I couldn't stop creating a mental hit list, imagining all the painful ways Ajax would die.

"Stop worrying," Kharon said. "You need to rest and stay focused. The competition starts tomorrow. If you murdered an entire village, we would take your side. Every. Single. Time."

"You're actually mad," she whispered.

Kharon clicked his tongue. "You're *just* realizing that now?"

"Personally . . . I've *never* liked villagers," I said.

Alexis relaxed back into the bed, and shifted around, fidgeting with her pillow.

"Go to sleep," Kharon ordered.

"*You* sleep."

"I can't," Kharon said through gritted teeth. "I have insomnia."

"Well, *Karen*, I can't sleep either," Alexis taunted him. "I guess we're both fucked."

The narrow bed bounced as Kharon shifted. "I've noticed this new swearing trend. I like it, but . . . why?" His tone changed to contemplative.

Alexis went still. "I'm trying new things . . . conquering old demons."

"Wait—" Kharon tensed. "Didn't you also used to stutter? When did that also stop?"

"*Wow*," Alexis said. "Way to be sensitive about it."

"When did it end?" Kharon pressed. I leaned closer, interested in the answer.

"When I stopped viewing you two as a threat."

"And . . . when was that?" I asked softly.

"When you drank my blood to break the bond . . . when Kharon cut off his ear and gave it to me."

There was a long, silent pause.

"Oh, princess," Kharon purred wickedly. "That's *not* the only thing I can give you."

Thud.

There was a loud yelp.

"Creep." Alexis huffed.

I turned over on the bed as there was suddenly a bunch of empty space. Kharon groaned from the floor.

Alexis had shoved him off.

She looked at me, her lips pulled up in a small smile.

My breath caught—she was fierce, intelligent, *glorious*.

Two-colored eyes searched my face. "You know, you really don't need to make a hit list," she said quietly. "Ajax was already punished."

I scoffed. "No—he wasn't."

She shook her head like I was a lost cause.

Kharon grumbled from the floor as he got up and repositioned himself at her back.

She shifted to let him in, and the faded edge of the too-small pajama shirt that the Olympians had left in the room bunched up, revealing her ribs.

A perfectly circular white ridge was raised across her bronze skin.

It took me a second to process what I was seeing. When it clicked, a rushing sound filled my ears and everything narrowed, until all I could see was the circular mark—the *cigarette burn*—on my wife's body.

There was no way that it was accidental. Feeling like I was underwater, I reached for her.

"Alexis." I traced my thumb across the cicatrix, wishing I could make the history behind it disappear. "*What* . . . happened to you?"

Kharon sat up and looked down at where I was touching.

His gaze hardened as he came to the same realization I had. He gently brushed her curls off her forehead, his fingers trembling.

From the way Alexis stiffened, she understood exactly what I was asking.

With careful slowness, she pulled down the shirt, covering her midsection and the heinous scar, but she didn't pull away from either of us.

Long seconds passed, and finally, she whispered, "I can't talk about it—*not* yet."

The angst in her voice made my heart ache.

Suddenly, I was glad I hadn't yet killed the fucker who raised her—the one currently rotting in our villa's dungeon. If *he* was responsible for this, he would know a torment the likes of which man had never faced before.

Unable to speak, without demanding she tell me *exactly* what happened and when, I forced myself to nod at her calmly. Instead of shouting at the top of my lungs, I opened my arms.

Alexis moved into my embrace, and I tucked her under my chin.

She sighed heavily and I squeezed her three times in a row, communicating with my body the words I wasn't quite yet ready to admit out loud.

Kharon remained sitting against the headboard, his face frozen in a scowl. Blue veins stood out across his neck as he ground his teeth together, all while his hand tenderly stroked locks of Alexis's hair, gentle so she wouldn't know he was losing it next to her.

His eyes flashed down to mine—our gazes locked.

I nodded at him as Alexis sighed again, shifting to get comfortable as she snuggled deeper into my embrace.

Kharon and I were on the same page.

Blood would be shed and the wrongs perpetrated against our wife would be avenged, *eventually*. For now, just holding her was enough.

When I finally calmed down enough to sleep, darkness pulled me under swiftly. As my eyes closed, a single stray thought lingered—*How did she know I was creating a mental hit list?*

31
THE GAMES BEGIN

ALEXIS: SGC DAY 1

I stared at my fingers and imagined light coming from the tips. Nothing happened.

"What are you doing?" Kharon asked, his eyes narrowing. "Why do you keep staring at your fingers?"

"No reason," I said hastily.

His lips pursed with suspicion.

I clapped loudly.

Nothing happened.

Darn it, so much for the clapper light theory. It was worth a shot.

"What the hell was that?" Kharon asked.

I leaned against his shoulder instead of answering. His arm wrapped around me like a steel vise, his grip a little *too tight*.

He held me like I was his hostage.

So dramatic.

For some reason that I refused to acknowledge, I didn't pull away.

The day was blustery and chilled.

Even though it was June, the mountain breeze had a crisp edge as it whipped through the Dolomites Coliseum, and too-bright sunlight reflected off the stone walls of the arena.

I once again found myself seated between my husbands in the Chthonic section of the coliseum, but the stadium had changed.

Fear took root at the base of my spine.

Solar generators hummed around the top edge of the arena walls—a domed web of electric lines arched over the entire stadium. High above, the neon-green network shimmered faintly in the sunshine and descended all the way to the sand.

"What is that . . . net?" I asked as electricity prickled across my skin.

"A force field," Augustus said. "One of the House of Zeus's inventions. No one can leap into it—or out of it—without suffering extreme electric shock."

"It's to make sure no one . . . interferes," Kharon said coldly.

I shifted in my seat.

Fluffy Jr., Poco, and the hellhounds slept at our feet in a pile of bones, black and gray fur, and lumpy protrusions. Every few seconds Fluffy Jr. twitched with a spasm and Poco smoothed a hand over his forehead.

Please God, let him be okay.

An unsettling war cry punctuated my prayer.

Below the shimmering force field, Arthritis (Artemis) rode her muscular black stallion onto the sands surrounded by a scarlet mist.

The stadium chanted, "*Vivere est militare . . . vivere est militare . . . vivere est militare!*"

To live is to fight.

The stallion reared back, and the crowd went wild.

Artemis smirked atop her steed and framed her black chest plate with her hands, drawing attention to the crest displayed across it.

Rubies gleamed in the sun, forming the rabid horse crest of the House of Artemis.

Her long brown hair was plaited into a complicated braid down her back, her aristocratic nose pointed up with pride, and her spiky crown sat tall and regal on her head. A bow was slung loosely over her shoulder next to a holster full of arrows.

Spartan guns were banned altogether, but apparently the Olympians let you choose from an armory of blade weapons, all of which I could barely wield.

The Montana education system had failed me.

Did we really need that sex education course on the mating rituals of nuclear-radiated Canada geese? My gut reaction—*yes*.

I couldn't help but feel like I'd learned something invaluable from that course. Do not try to pet geese, *especially* if they have more than three eyes (they will destroy you).

Augustus shifted closer, draping his arm over mine and Kharon's back so I was tucked between the two of them.

The scents of lightning and rain smothered me as they pressed against me like they were trying to burrow under my skin.

I was in the middle of their storm.

Nyx was twined around my neck, and Augustus flinched as her scales slid against his arm.

Drex looked back over his shoulder, worry on his face, and I tried to give him a small reassuring smile, but it ended up as more of a wince.

He grimaced in agreement, then turned back to watch the show. Helen and Charlie watched the proceedings next to him with cautious interest.

In front of them sat the Chthonic leaders and Persephone, their heavy crowns looking out of place with the sparse, sleeveless, short black exercise togas we'd all been given to wear.

"*Vivere est militare!*" The chant thundered all around the stands as the Spartan crowd screamed with bloodthirsty excitement.

A hand flashed in my peripheral vision.

Charlie was signing something to Achilles, who sat further down the row. Most surprisingly, Achilles was signing back.

Charlie nodded passionately and Achilles's shoulders shook like he was silently chuckling.

I've never seen him laugh before.

They were signing rapidly to each other like they were close friends.

Patro glanced back at me—his eyes narrowed on where Augustus was rubbing my bare arms, trying to warm me.

If he was trying to intimidate me, it wasn't working.

I made a face at him, and Patro made a show of turning around, giving me his back.

Augustus rubbed my arms faster, and Kharon dragged his skeleton-tattooed fingers slowly over the bottom half of my exposed thigh.

Goose bumps exploded as they caressed my flesh.

Kharon and Augustus touched me so casually, as if it was the most natural thing in the world to them, but the intimacy made my face flush and stomach pinch.

Down below, Artemis lazily spun in a circle, keeping her eyes on the five monstrous beasts that surrounded her.

Apparently, I'd been so distracted by my husbands touching me I'd literally missed the arrival of *thirty-foot-tall* Cyclopes.

Their heads came up to the top of the wall that surrounded the arena.

Ratty loincloths, larger than the flags that waved above the stands, fluttered over their portly, dirt-covered, stout bodies.

The Cyclopes' faces were horribly misshapen; sharp yellow teeth jutted at odd angles from their mouths, and their forehead skin bunched grotesquely to make space for their disproportionately large, singular eye.

The five beasts stomped as they walked in a circle around Artemis—the stadium vibrated—their mammoth fists raised high like they were ready to attack.

"Don't worry." Kharon leaned close. "The leader fights are just for show . . . They're too powerful to be actually contested."

The Cyclopes bellowed.

"Do they consent to this?" I whispered.

Kharon's breath fanned against the side of my face. "What?"

I ignored the flutter in my stomach. "Do the Cyclopes *want* to fight?"

Kharon furrowed his brows as he stared at me.

Augustus shook his head as he tucked me tighter against his side. "They quite literally yearn for violence. They're carnivorous beasts with the intelligence of rocks—I taught you this."

He tsked like he was scolding me, and for some reason the heat in my stomach increased.

"They're barely classified as creatures," Augustus continued. "If they could, they'd murder us all and use our bones as toothpicks."

Kharon winked.

Down on the sands, Artemis tipped her head back and laughed as the Cyclopes stomped at her and missed.

I frowned as a thought struck me. "How do you . . . lose in this competition?"

It seemed crucially important, yet no one had bothered to tell me.

Kharon's smile fell.

He looked away.

Artemis scowled as a Cyclops slammed a meaty fist down, barely missing her body.

Augustus sighed heavily. "Three ways: you pass out from blood loss, fall into a coma, or—"

"Die," Kharon finished.

Augustus nodded curtly.

"Tell her the other way," Kharon ordered, his voice loud and harsh.

Drex and Helen glanced back at us; they blanched when they saw Kharon's expression.

Kharon leaned closer, his voice dropping. "There's a fourth way to lose."

I didn't like the gleam in his eyes.

"You can defeat all your labors, but if both your legs are broken, the pieces of your kneecap sticking out of your skin . . . you can crawl across the sand . . ."

His nostrils flared as he paused like he was lost in memories.

"You can drag your bloody, ruined, weak body out of the arena . . . and still be branded a loser." His eyes sharpened. "Winners walk out of the arena on their two feet. Those who crawl . . . get branded."

His ruined knee and the scars on his chest.

This was Kharon's story.

"But that's not fair—you beat them," I said with outrage. "You beat all eleven of your labors—how could they count that as a loss?"

Kharon's lips curled as he stared down at me. "Because Olympians *hate* Chthonics. They live to humiliate us . . . to brand us. To mark us. It's all about power . . . and to wield it over others . . . you must break them."

Skeletal fingers dug into my thigh.

"I won't let them do it to you." Kharon's nails pressed harder. "I won't let them—"

Boom.

We all turned.

The sands were covered in shimmering scarlet as if a bomb had gone off. Artemis sat on her steed in the middle with her arms raised.

Pure terror filled my throat as her mist traveled up the stadium, glittering and deadly in the bright sunshine. The electric force field hissed as the fine droplets traveled through it.

All five Cyclopes shrieked in unison, a terrible sharp sound.

Artemis's black horse reared back, whinnying as its front legs kicked powerfully through the air, and she cocked her bow.

She fired two arrows at a time—in different directions. *How is that possible?*

Two Cyclopes collapsed, long metal shafts protruding from the stadium shook beneath us from the force of their falls.

"YES," Nyx shouted around my neck. "Slaughter them!"

Artemis fired in a blur.

Cyclopes dropped and the stadium rocked so aggressively, stones cracked.

Dear God, please let the stadium collapse and kill us all. Thank you.

The shaking died down and the structural integrity of the coliseum was left unscathed.

Disappointing.

Her mist dissipated and five Cyclopes lay in the sand, blood pouring from arrows embedded in their eyes. Their dirty limbs in a tangle.

The force field hummed.

"Are they . . ." I swallowed thickly, unable to say the word.

Augustus nodded.

The Olympian crowd went wild, screaming and chanting at the top of their lungs: *"Monsteress of the Hunt . . . Monsteress of the Hunt . . . Monsteress of the Hunt!"*

I clasped my cold fingers together.

Artemis stood up on her rabid stallion's back and raised her bow to the sky with a smirk.

She balanced as her steed jumped over the fallen Cyclopes, sand spraying behind as they galloped out of the arena.

The crowd clapped and screamed louder.

No one could say Arthritis (Artemis) doesn't have flair.

Augustus pressed a gentle kiss to the top of my head. "Now we have the symposium. It's in the coliseum."

I turned to him with surprise.

"Not the same one you attended," Augustus said. "It's in the same room—but it's where all the competitors, leaders, House heirs, and some of the most important Spartan creatures and dignitaries mingle and eat during the competition."

"But there are still some . . . *explicit* activities," Kharon muttered, a muscle in his jaw ticking.

Relief filled me.

If the Olympians were going to make us fight to the death, the *least* they could do was put on a performance. Flash a penis, show a boob.

"Why are you smiling?" Kharon asked suspiciously.

"I'm not."

"That!" Kharon pointed at my mouth.

I bit down on my lower lip to try to look less like an awkward sexual degenerate.

Kharon narrowed his ice-blue eyes. "So *help* me Kronos, Alexis, if you try that little strip routine again, I will—"

"I wasn't going to do anything, *Karen*." I rolled my eyes (I'd been considering it).

He breathed roughly through his nose like he was having an episode.

"She'll be fine." Augustus grinned at me. "We'll take care of her. She has us by her side now, right, my carus?"

Scales slithered around my neck. "Oh yeah, I'm sure he'll take care of you with his—" Nyx paused for dramatic effect "—throbbing, engorged cock."

I choked. "*Never* say that again."

"Never say what?" Nyx clicked her teeth together. "Cock and balls?"

Kharon scowled. "What is the echidna saying? Why are you hissing like that and making that face?"

"Nothing," I said quickly. "I'm just a pervert."

They narrowed their eyes like they couldn't figure out if I was joking, or if this was a cry for help.

It was both.

32

ELECTRIC ENERGY

Alexis

The symposium buzzed with energy.

Cameras flashed.

Spartan reporters captured Olympian leaders smiling and mingling with creatures in their finery.

It almost appeared like a normal affair. *Almost*, because guards milled about, glaring at us and holding up their sparking batons in warning.

I scowled back and Nyx hissed every time one got too close, gliding across my shoulders.

Beside me, Augustus and Kharon observed the party like they were plotting. Helen and Charlie had been sent back to their room, where food would be delivered because the event was apparently "adults only."

I was waiting for the nudity and aggressive humping to start, in a purely intellectually tortured, eighteenth-century poet dealing with their sexuality sort of way.

Unfortunately, it hadn't.

Entertain me, peasants!

Sighing from the fact that I was actually suffering from a mental breakdown and needed to seek urgent medical help, I leaned against a pillar.

Kharon and Augustus stood next to me, and our protectors were asleep at our feet.

I grabbed a glass of ambrosia off a tray and threw it back.

The liquid burned.

Heat spreading down my throat, I observed the celebration.

I'd seen the younger Chthonics at a booth somewhere, but since tensions were still high with Patro and Achilles—because my husbands had violently bound and gagged them—we stayed separate.

Artemis was the center of attention.

She sat at a table in the middle of the room with her legs spread wide, eyes roaming lazily over the crowd—her armor was still splattered in Cyclopes blood—Ares, Aphrodite, Erebus, Hades, and Persephone sat around her.

Artemis watched the partygoers with open contempt as they whispered and pointed at her.

A siren poured from a bottle of ambrosia into their glasses with a low bow, then backed away like her life was on the line. She turned, shoulders slumping with relief as she served the Olympian leaders at the next table.

Apollo smiled up at her as she poured for him, and she blushed.

He winked seductively, popping a grape into his mouth.

The siren stumbled like she'd almost fainted.

Spartans and creatures constantly approached the Olympian table, bowing low and kissing the top of the leaders' hands.

Zeus didn't pay them any attention.

His gaze was locked on the Chthonic table, sparks leaping from his eyes. At his feet, his lion swooshed its tail back and forth with agitation.

Lights flashed across Zeus's face, cameras shuttering.

Why is no one naked yet?

I was bored.

And a little drunk.

Where is my granny (Demeter)? I pouted when I couldn't find her because I really wanted to give her a big hug.

Worst-case scenario, meemaw killed me; best-case scenario, meemaw killed me.

It was a win-win.

While the scene wasn't openly hedonistic, dim sconces cast shadows across the dozens of people dressed in finery, and there was a strange undercurrent in the room.

Hooded gazes.

Licked lips.

Lingering fingers.

On second thought, this would be a *very* awkward place to meet up with a grandma. I prayed we did NOT cross paths.

An Olympian heir approached all three of us, unbuttoning his shirt as he neared.

"Don't even fucking try it," Kharon warned him, stepping in front of me protectively.

"We should see what he's working with first," I said, just to annoy Kharon. "Before we turn him down."

From the death glare Kharon shot back at me, he did not find this funny. *Men just don't understand comedic timing.*

The Olympian smirked, undeterred. "Don't worry . . . I'll do a foursome. I love to share." He winked.

"We're open to it," I told him (we definitely weren't).

Kharon gently kicked me.

"Pull his pants down so we can see his penis," Nyx hissed.

I kicked Kharon back, not gently.

"We are *not* open." Augustus's tone promised violent dismemberment.

"How would you describe yourself in the bedroom, introverted or extroverted?" I asked the man, like I was taking a sexual survey.

"He'd describe himself as . . . violently slaughtered," Kharon said casually.

Kharon chuckled as the Olympian turned and melted back into the crush of bodies like his life depended on it (he definitely could not handle all three of us).

"He probably had a small penis," Nyx hissed as she twined slowly around my neck. "That is not good enough for us."

"There is no *us* in this scenario," I hissed back.

"If we were men," Nyx said, "I'd have a bigger dick than you."

Before I could think of an appropriate response (*amicide*—killing a friend), a woman in a pink toga and small laurel crown sauntered up to Kharon with a coy smile. The matching pink bird perched on her shoulder squawked with agitation in my direction.

"Leave," Kharon ordered.

"Nice government drone," I said.

The woman looked at me like I was deranged, then shook her head and recovered her composure.

"Hello," she purred at Kharon and Augustus as she leaned forward, impressive breasts spilling out the top of her toga.

"Get out of here!" Nyx clicked her teeth. "Skanky whore."

I choked on the two lamb sticks I was attempting to eat at the same time (I didn't remember grabbing them off a tray).

"You *can't* just say that to people," I whispered down to Nyx. "It's so misogynistic." A chunk of meat fell out of my mouth.

The woman looked at me again like she suspected I was crazy. She was very astute.

Nyx sighed and slithered down to my waist. "Please—women have already reclaimed the word *whore*. It's not rude. It's a fact."

I squinted. "Wait . . . when did we reclaim it?"

Nyx made a noise like she thought I was the biggest idiot. "Uh, during the *apocalypse*. Where have you been, Alexis?"

Hell stood up from the floor with a yawn. "Belly . . . rub?" he asked me.

"Kharon will do it," I said back.

"Walk away—or my hellhound will bite," Kharon threatened, his eyes cold. "I'm a one-woman man . . . and she's standing beside me."

"Rub . . . now?" Hell growled with excitement, getting worked up at the thought and lying on his back.

The woman stumbled back in a scared rush.

Kharon bent down and patted Hell's rib cage. "Good boy—way to scare the mean lady."

I was surrounded by idiots.

"I'm going to try and murder them again," Nyx hissed as she slithered off my shoulders. "Wish me luck."

I did not.

Kharon turned to me slowly as our animals tussled violently (mine strangled, while his wagged their tails).

"Why . . . weren't you mad at that woman?" Kharon asked.

I shrugged. "Uh—why would I be?"

Kharon turned so I was pressed back against the pillar, his body covering mine. "I will *only* do monogamy . . . My mother might be cruel, but the House of Artemis does *not* sleep around in relationships. We are absolutely devoted—or we are *nothing*."

I struggled to speak, my brain fuzzy from his proximity. "Technically, isn't monogamy a one-to-one ratio of—"

Kharon slammed his lips against mine.

"Quiet, Alexis."

I opened my mouth to argue, and he plunged his tongue inside.

His taste was headier than the ambrosia and the effects more pronounced.

"Enough . . . Do this later," Augustus said gruffly. "You're causing a scene."

Kharon pressed his hips against my core and turned me, so my back was pressed flush against Augustus and my side was against the pillar—he made a guttural sound and grabbed my hips from behind.

Kharon fisted my curls and tilted my head back harshly.

Augustus jerked his hips against my ass.

I melted (a small voice in my head wondered if meemaw was watching, and if Sparta had a witness protection program).

Augustus leaned down and pressed kisses to the sensitive skin below my ear. His voice dropped an octave. "If you keep kissing her like that against me, I'm going to lose all control and slaughter everyone in this room for watching. Then I'm going to fuck her on the floor."

Kharon stilled, his breath ragged as he pulled his lips away from mine.

He swore under his breath as he stepped back, icy eyes full of heat.

Augustus flexed his hips one last time, then released his grip on me.

All three of us were struggling to breathe.

Augustus made another harsh noise as he raked his hands through his hair, messing up the long two-toned locks.

"That wasn't a funny joke," I said, my mouth swollen from Kharon's aggressive kiss, neck tingling where Augustus had pressed his lips.

Augustus's midnight eyes hardened. "What are you talking about?" His voice was gritty.

I rubbed the back of my neck. "The killing everyone and then . . ." I trailed off, unable to say the words.

I discreetly squeezed my thighs together.

"*Fucking* you," Kharon purred as he dragged his thumb across his lips, Adam's apple bobbing as he stared down at me hungrily.

"Yeah, that."

Augustus frowned. "Who said I was joking?" A vein jumped

in his temple and his hands shook as he clasped them behind his back.

He looked undone.

I forced out a laugh. "Har, har, very funny."

"It wasn't a joke," Augustus said softly, the quiet tenor of his voice more disturbing than if he'd yelled. "I meant what I said."

He took a step toward me.

Ozone filled my nose.

Someone tapped me on the shoulder, and I turned away from my husbands. My head was fuzzy, and it had nothing to do with the ambrosia.

Lights started flashing blindingly in my face.

Click. Click. Click.

Fluffy Jr. whimpered with distress, and I acted on instinct, dropping to my knees on the floor, covering his face, as I glared up at the two reporters.

"Hercules—what's wrong with your protector?" one shouted.

I winced at the loud feedback in my ear.

"He's fine," I said defensively, hating the way they were looking down at him with disgust. *How dare they judge.*

Kharon and Augustus shielded us with their bodies.

"Don't speak to our wife," Augustus ordered, his voice dangerous. "Leave. Now."

"Or we'll make you." Kharon pulled up the hood of his cloak.

Lights flashed in quick succession as the reporters backed away. "Are you aware that the video of you slicing off your ear and giving it to Hercules has gone viral with the humans?" one asked provocatively. "Are you concerned humans will view us as barbaric because of your . . . *extreme* action?"

Kharon clenched his jaw. "No. I don't give a fuck what they think. I'll do *much* worse for my wife . . . Nothing is off-limits."

The reporters stepped back. Lights flashed.

"Do you want to make a statement?" the other asked.

"Yes," Kharon said icily. "I'd cut off my fucking head and give it to Alexis if that's what she needed. I'd also cut off *yours* if that's what she wanted." He chuckled darkly.

The reporters visibly paled, but they kept their cameras held high.

"Did you have something to do with Medusa's escape? She's your sister," the female reporter taunted, refusing to be intimidated. "We heard a rumor that the Chthonics broke her out of the Underworld, and you all are harboring her—"

"That's false." Augustus rolled his shoulders back. "You should know how . . . *dangerous* rumors can be."

Kharon cracked his knuckles.

"We got all we need," the one reporter said with a glare. They turned their cameras to the Olympian table.

I sagged with relief, still kneeling beside my protector.

Sparta was exhausting. Everyone was so *hostile*.

Augustus offered me his hand.

I laid my fingers in his and our marriage bond sparked inside my sternum.

All three of us gasped.

Calluses scraped against my skin, and for a second, he did nothing but flex his much warmer hand around mine as he stared down at me.

Augustus yanked me up to my feet.

"Uh . . . wow," I said eloquently.

Their expressions didn't change.

If you ever need to make an awkward situation more uncomfortable, I'm your girl.

I leaned across Kharon to grab a glass from a tray—he rested his hand on my lower back, and my skin prickled with awareness—I threw the ambrosia back.

Once again, the liquid burned my throat deliciously and I let out a moan of enjoyment.

Augustus swore under his breath, and I peered over at him in confusion; his eyes smoldered, jaw tensed.

Why is he so worked up?

Kharon pressed against my back and led me to a booth—the three of us slid in—they scooted in on either side of me.

Under the table, both their hands settled on my upper thighs.

Shadows concealed us.

My breath quickened as Kharon's fingers slowly pulled back the fabric of my toga, tracing a circle on the sensitive skin of my inner thigh. Augustus just palmed the top of my left thigh, his nails digging deep into my flesh.

They were so warm it was overwhelming; my thoughts turned hazy.

The ambrosia made it hard to think.

It was nice.

Augustus dragged his nails up my leg, until his fingers lingered dangerously close to the fabric at the juncture of my thighs. Both their hands touched as they stroked me like they were playing an instrument.

Augustus pressed a soft kiss to my temple, then pulled away with a groan like I'd scalded him.

Skeleton-tattooed fingers grabbed my chin harshly and pulled my face close. "You're playing with fire, carissima," Kharon whispered, his voice gritty.

The ambrosia settled into my stomach, bringing the heat to a fever pitch.

If I'm going to die in this tournament, I might as well live.

Music played.

The room buzzed with energy.

We were hidden in the shadows where no one could see us.

A horrible, brilliant, disastrous idea struck me.

"I want you both to fuck me," I blurted out eloquently.

Kharon's long lashes fluttered, cheekbones sharpening, as his fingers tightened around my chin.

"Excuse me?" Augustus straightened, his pupils expanding, as he searched my face for answers. "What did you . . . just say?"

"Fuck me," I repeated, louder with the confidence only a drunkard could muster.

Kharon's grip became painful. "Why?"

My peril is imminent and I'm horny.

Since saying the truth would most likely *not* go over well, I settled with a casual "We might as well."

Kharon searched my face, disappointment flashing in his eyes. "No." He dropped my chin.

I almost fell over.

Augustus's hands studied me.

Whoa. Everything was spinning.

"Why not?" I giggled into my palm as both men glared at me.

"You're not ready for us," Kharon said harshly, and it didn't sound like he was just talking about sex.

Augustus's stubble scraped against the side of my face as he leaned close. "You'll also be sober when we make love to you."

"Uh—I said *fuck*." I winked.

Neither of them smiled at the joke.

Tough crowd.

Augustus's hand lingered on my thigh, his fingers hovering closer to my core. He was sending mixed messages.

Kharon leaned in. "When you're sober, we're going to dominate you so *thoroughly* . . . that you won't remember your own name."

"So much talk." I clicked my tongue. "No action."

Kharon's smile was all teeth. "Don't worry, darling. I *will* punish you. For hours."

I grabbed at the edge of the table as the room started to spin. "Blah, blah, blah. All Karen does is make promises he can't keep."

He muttered something about sadomasochism and bondage. *Boring.*

Reaching into my pocket, I pulled out my calculator—I clicked the side.

"Dear Diary," I whispered into it. "Karen is saying weird, perverted things, but he refuses to have sex with me. I think he's a creep. Also, I need to find a Spartan man who is willing to—"

Kharon snatched it out of my hand. "Dear Diary, if Alexis touches another man, I will disembowel him in front of her and—"

I grabbed it back. "Dear Diary, fine then. I will find a Spartan *woman* to have sex with. Also, I think—"

"Dear Diary," Kharon yelled into the speaker as he tried to wrestle it out of my hands. "If Alexis touches *anyone* who is not me or Augustus, I will kill—"

"Dear Diary, don't listen to that rat bastard! This is *not* his diary—"

"Dear Diary, it is now. I'm commandeering it because Alexis is the most *infuriating*, stubborn woman I've ever—"

Augustus snatched the calculator away. "You're both cut off."

I opened my mouth to retort, but a male siren came by with a tray and placed glasses on the table with a clank.

"Thanks, baby girl," I said to him, then I threw back another shot of ambrosia.

The siren hurried away looking disturbed.

"Be careful. You don't want to drink too much," Augustus warned.

I wiggled my fingers in the air. "They're *antennas*."

Augustus pressed the back of his hand to my forehead like he was checking to see if I had a fever.

"I'm an *anglerfish*." I pushed his hand away. "I've lured you both in with my glow. My blood—it *yearns* to poison you and . . . I'm hideous."

"Shut the fuck up," Kharon snapped.

Augustus hit his arm but tilted his head as he stared at me. "Do you have some type of . . . aquatic obsession? Weren't you going on about a . . . *whale*, or something equally ridiculous, during the crucible?"

I scoffed. "Next time I have a *personal* realization, you will not hear about it."

"Thank Kronos," Kharon muttered.

"Shut up, *Karen*," I said.

"Alexis, if you call me Karen *one* more time . . ." He stared down at me with frightening intensity, his alabaster features sculpted from ice. "I will throw this table at you."

There was a long pause.

"Sure you will . . . *Karen*."

His eye twitched like he was having an aneurysm, and I waited for him to make good on his promise.

I smirked. "I knew you wouldn't do it."

He grabbed the edge of the table and lifted slowly.

Augustus reached across me and slapped him. "Get control of yourself. What the heck are you doing?"

Kharon tried to shove him away and the two of them grappled across me.

I smacked my hands at them (yay, we're fighting).

"Theoretically," I said in the chaos. "If I was selling my kidney, how much would you give me for it?"

They stopped fighting and turned to me.

I kept hitting them (very fun).

"For the last time, you're *not* selling your organs for money!" Kharon banged his fist on the table and the empty shot glasses fell over. "Alexis, what is actually wrong with you?"

My jaw dropped at his audacity. "*Wow*—I'm just trying to have a little financial independence in the middle of an apocalypse."

"You're wearing a three-hundred-million-dollar necklace." Kharon pointed at my neck. "You're financially *independent*."

"Fine," I said calmly. "I'll sell you the necklace *and* my toe. How much do you want? Onetime offer."

Kharon's face turned red as I arched my brow and waited.

"No deal," he spat, then muttered under his breath, "Obviously."

"And *you* run a business?" I said. "More like *into* the ground."

Augustus laughed, then hid his expression behind his hand as Kharon shot him a death glare.

He refused to talk to either of us the rest of the night.

Nyx was right.

Men should be seen, not heard.

I enjoyed his silence.

33

A SIREN'S PROMISE

ALEXIS: SGC DAY 2

As the last standing Cyclops's wail echoed through the Dolomites Coliseum, I desperately wished I was still drunk.

The stadium silently watched the sands with horror. All chants had died out hours ago.

Kharon and Augustus sat ramrod straight on either side of me, electricity humming in a dome above the blood-covered sand.

No one spoke.

One thing was now *disturbingly* clear—Ares was nicknamed the God of War for a reason.

He'd been in the arena for about five hours. Five *long*, painful, heinous hours.

Bright sunlight illuminated the four dead Cyclopes that were strewn around him. Each of them had been tortured to death by his touch.

There was no reason his round was still happening; he could have ended it in five minutes if he wanted to. The problem was, he *didn't* want to.

My fingers tingled as Nyx slithered tightly around my shoulders, her scales warm.

The stale taste of ambrosia was sour in my throat as I watched the heinous show.

A black Spartan helmet with a red spiky middle gleamed atop Ares's head, and it was the only armor he wore.

An ornate golden broadsword was also strapped across his wide muscular back, but he hadn't unsheathed it.

Not once.

Ares had used his *bare hands* to murder four Cyclopes.

Now he was working on the fifth.

The rumor that he could torture people to insanity with a single graze of his fingers was right. He also didn't appear to have a protector. *Are the other rumors about him having an enormous invisible Colchian dragon true?*

Blood dripped from his eyes like tears as he used his powers—his hand rested casually on the arm of the last living Cyclops.

The creature jerked in the sand as it screamed in agony.

Augustus rubbed my back soothingly.

I studied his profile.

Ares is his father.

His eyes were deep pools of obsidian.

"Are you . . . okay, my carus?" he asked softly.

His scar stood out in stark relief across the bridge of his nose and cheek.

How did he get it?

I leaned my head against his shoulder.

"That's my girl." He gently kissed my forehead.

My stomach pinched.

Down below, the God of War let out a battle cry.

Augustus was the spitting image of him.

They had the same tan skin, harsh features, and build. They both held themselves ramrod straight, postures perfect, shoulders wide.

Scars slashed across their faces.

But where one reveled in unbound cruelty, the other had a raccoon protector who sat on his shoulder all day playing with his hair.

I'd forgotten what it meant that Augustus was the heir to the infamous House of Ares. The *leader* of the younger Chthonics.

Augustus wasn't just the son of the psychopath torturing for fun—he was his *prodigy*.

Yet he also spoke about ancient myths with a passion, gifted me a graphing calculator, and gently tucked me into bed at night.

Augustus stared down at me, his gaze intense like he could read my thoughts.

"Don't be afraid," he whispered.

I'm not.

That was the problem.

The death rattle stopped as the Cyclops *finally* fell silent, and I turned to watch. Its single eye was open wide and unseeing.

Ares sauntered lazily out of the arena.

There was a spattering of applause, but the stadium was still mostly quiet—numb shock hung in the air. The fight had been hideously clinical, yet deeply depraved.

There was a sudden clamor of cheers as the Chthonic leaders all got to their feet.

I couldn't look away from the dead Cyclopes.

Were they afraid as they died?

Kharon bent down and said something to Augustus, but I couldn't hear him above the ringing in my ear.

A thick wave of melancholy washed over me.

Did they wonder why so many people were watching, but no one helped?

My eyes blurred.

Time moved at a strange pace.

The guards escorted us to a much more crowded symposium.

Bodies swirled around us as lively harp music played. Hundreds of candles were flickering on the tables, casting the room in a soft light.

Golden celebratory tinsel had been strung along the room's columns and ceiling. Sirens whirled around brandishing platters overflowing with food.

I pushed through the crush to find a table, fighting through a sea of bodies, drowning in tortured feelings.

Familiar pastel eyes peered into mine. "Alexis?" the siren whispered, lips trembling.

I wiped at my eyes, hiding the tears.

"Lena?" I said, a kernel of warmth lighting inside my chest. The festering sadness receded.

I blinked and we were hugging, holding on to each other as tightly as we could in the middle of the dance floor.

Her breath hitched. "You're a Chthonic now."

"I am."

"Everyone's talking about your fight in Rome—how you defended the humans. How *powerful* you are."

"Really?" I laughed awkwardly. "They have it wrong."

Her eyes searched mine. "No, they don't," she said softly, her voice full of sincerity.

I held on to her, feeling weak.

"How . . . have you been?" I whispered.

She shook her head, long hair sparkling. "Better than you . . . Most creatures think this entire operation is a sham. The Olympians are up to something."

Someone made a commotion to the side.

Zeus was pointing at us.

I smiled back at her sadly. "I think they're right."

"How can I help?" She hugged me tighter, squeezing like she was afraid to let me go.

I couldn't forget Ceres's scribbles about Zeus and Vyco. I'd been working on a plan. It was a foolish plan, a *bad* plan, the type of plan that you never told anyone about out loud because it wouldn't work in real life.

Cyclopes screamed in my subconscious, and I steeled myself.

Only cowards are complicit in the face of injustice. You have to at least try to make a difference.

"I need speakers," I said quickly to Lena. "The fancy solar-powered ones. I need to plug a device into them."

I gestured with my hands to show her what the plug-in port looked like.

She nodded, her pastel eyes wide with emotion. "Stay safe—I've heard that they want to hurt—"

"No talking to the sirens!" Zeus shouted as he pointed at us.

Another siren appeared. Lena was pulled away into the dancing crowd, but her gaze held mine.

"Speakers," I mouthed silently.

She nodded back.

"Thank you." I touched my hand to my heart, vision blurring, as tears once again streamed down my face.

A male siren paused with a tray of ambrosia shots. He pushed a glass into my shaking hands and disappeared.

I threw the liquid back.

It did nothing.

I flagged down another server.

The second glass burned—it did a little something.

I stole a drink off someone's table.

The third glass numbed—*everything*.

Someone pulled a chair out for me.

I collapsed into it. I blinked—Augustus and Kharon sat beside me at one of the long wooden tables set up in the middle of the room for the Spartans. They both moved closer to me.

The rest of the Chthonics sat around us.

Patro and Achilles were a few seats down—both glaring.

The former opened and closed his mouth like he wanted to say something, but didn't know what; the latter smoked a cigarette—his hands were clenched into fists on the table like he was stopping himself from signing angrily.

I tipped my head to them.

Patro frowned at whatever expression he saw on my face.

Achilles remained unmoved, smoke tendrils lazily rising around his muzzle.

We were all prisoners these days.

Hades said something about "the importance of solidarity and appearance of unity."

I nodded in agreement.

Kharon placed a slice of meat on the empty plate sitting in front of me, and I shoved it into my mouth, not tasting anything. I'd never turn down free food. *Ever.*

Kharon shot me a worried look. He snapped at a person who passed us without offering me food from his tray. He kept his hand on the back of my necklace.

He handed me a pastry with one hand, fingers caressing the back of my neck with his other.

I ate every morsel he offered.

Augustus stared down at me like he was afraid I'd disappear if he blinked.

Neither of them asked about Lena.

I didn't offer.

A strange energy wrapped around the three of us. It seemed to be growing with every second we spent together sleeping in the same bed, eating at the same table, sharing a stone bench.

Their thighs brushed against mine on either side.

A small touch.

My nerve endings *sizzled*.

There was a clatter as a siren put the day's *Falcon Chronicles* scroll on the table next to the food—Agatha leaned forward next to Kharon and unrolled it, showing off the headline.

The table craned to look.

Literacy was a curse.

"Hercules's protector is seriously ill and unfitting of the heir to the House of Hades—how did she choose so poorly?" Below the news line was a picture of me kneeling next to Fluffy Jr., Augustus and Kharon were a blur, caught mid-motion as they moved to stand in front of me.

Kharon banged his fists on the table and swore vehemently.

Augustus still hadn't blinked.

I reached my hand down under the table, where all our protectors were lying, and pet the top of Fluffy Jr.'s sleeping head.

Poco climbed off my protector and into my lap. He chirped and curled up in a ball, purring.

Agatha unrolled the scroll further—she glanced around with a worried expression.

The next story was worse.

My vision flickered in and out, anxiety mounting with an intensity that even ambrosia couldn't mask.

The headline read: "Zeus and Federation announce their plan to interrogate younger Chthonics after their rounds." The picture was of Medusa.

Hades snatched up the scroll and slammed it shut.

His worried gaze met mine.

Persephone huffed and pushed her chair back. "Excuse me," she said. "I have a reporter to threaten." She smiled at me, her expression serene. "Don't worry—I'll handle this."

I tried to smile back, but my face didn't cooperate.

How can she be so calm?

I wished I had a tenth of her composure.

She walked around the table to me and leaned down, pressing a kiss to my cheek. "It's all going to be okay, daughter. Stay calm—never let the Olympians see you sweat."

I nodded jerkily.

"We're in this *together*," she said softly.

My vision blurred over.

She was everything my childhood self had ever dreamed about.

Persephone straightened. "Kharon, Augustus." She glared daggers at them. "Treat my daughter right." It wasn't a question.

Augustus bowed his head respectfully. "Of course."

"I'd die for Alexis," Kharon said calmly, and Hades raised his glass to him, looking relieved. I'd forgotten he was my father's favorite soldier.

Persephone didn't look impressed.

As my mother disappeared into the crowd, my thoughts raced. There was nothing she could do. This was bigger than all of us. We both knew it.

The danger had reached a tipping point.

The consequences had arrived.

34
THE BATTLES WE WAGE

Alexis: SGC Day 3

Sparta cheered thunderously.

Sitting between Kharon and Augustus, with my buzzing hands clasped tightly between my legs, I prayed to a god who probably despised me.

Far below, the arena was full of inky fog, so thick and dense, it looked as if black tar had been poured over the sand.

Hades—my *father*—stood tall in the middle, his pale hands held high above his head, blood glowing in his eyes.

There was nothing survivable about what was flowing out of Hades. It was a thick vicious flood of death.

Apparently, he'd gone easy on us in the initiation massacre.

The Cyclopes' screams echoed, but they were barely visible in the dark fog. They were nothing but glimpses of hands tearing at skin, of flesh collapsing onto sand, of single eyes wide and terrified.

Blood splattered.

Hades—contributor of half of my genetic material—didn't have to lift a finger as all five of them tore themselves apart.

The whole thing barely took ten minutes.

Nyx slithered around my neck as the fog pulled back into Hades with a whoosh. "That was impressive," she hissed.

I shivered because she was right—his power was magnificently terrible.

It was a startling, graphic reminder of what it meant that I was a Chthonic heiress. What it meant that he'd made me in his image.

The same lethal energy was dormant, waiting inside of me.

SGC Day 4

Yesterday's symposium had passed in a blur. I didn't remember falling asleep at night—one second I was out, the next I was awake, filled with terror.

My teeth chattered as sweat dripped down my back.

I was back in my seat in the coliseum.

Kharon and Augustus were yet again flanking me. Their thighs brushed against mine and I tried not to jolt each time.

Drums pounded and electricity hummed above the arena.

"Today's competitor is . . ." Zeus paused, his voice echoing around the stadium as sparks leapt around his raised arms. He stood on the walkway that jutted out over the arena, an overseer—*an emperor*—commanding destruction. "EREBUS!"

The crowd lost it.

Chants echoed all around. *"Primordial god of darkness . . . shadow hunter . . . nightmare harborer . . . bow before his shadowy plain, or YOU shall be slain!"*

Erebus prowled out onto the sand, bone-white mask gleaming, tattered black cloak fluttering behind his tall figure.

He had no weapons; no visible protector; no armor. The edges of his figure blurred, as if he was transparent, and not a being of flesh and blood.

A man who was rumored to live with wolves.

"He's so dreamy," Helen said in the seat ahead of me as she covered her mouth. Charlie nodded in agreement beside her.

I tilted my head to the side.

I could see it.

"Oh, I could beat him," Nyx hissed with awe as she twined slowly around my waist. "And I'm *not* talking about in a fight."

I choke-coughed violently (apparently, everyone was getting more sexually aggressive these days).

Augustus smacked my back.

Steel rattled as the heavy gate on the other side of the arena slowly rose up—five Cyclopes charged out, growling with their meaty fists raised.

Erebus casually raised his hand and pointed his finger at them.

Oversized shadows distended and morphed behind each Cyclops—pure inky darkness warped and rose from the sand—sharpening into five tangible, vicious-looking knives.

The black blades hovered in the air for a second.

Erebus pulled back his raised arm as if he was tugging on a rope.

The shadows speared each Cyclops through their back, straight through their heart.

Blood sprayed as the Cyclopes dropped like rocks—*dead*—with a thunderous boom.

A horrible thought struck me, and I peered up through my lashes at Kharon.

His features were hard, eyes haunted.

That's his father.

SGC Day 5

Augustus and Kharon sat close beside me. It was Aphrodite's round.

Our thighs were pressed together.

The three of us hadn't spoken since yesterday when Erebus had wielded his shadows on the sands.

Now we were back for more.

Aphrodite sauntered out into the arena.

She wore a Spartan helmet. Her long braids were covered in crystals, which sparkled as she leaned down and deposited her house cat–sized sphinx protector at the edge of the sandy ring.

She patted its head, like she was making sure it stayed out of the battle.

Then she stood back up and moved to the center of the sand with a golden ax slung casually over her shoulder.

"*Fuck me, you sexy bitch!*" a male screamed nearby, and the entire section erupted in laughter. Sexual innuendos and other lewd propositions were shouted with increasing frequency.

Aphrodite appeared completely unbothered as she waited for the steel gate to rise and release the Cyclopes.

The sky was mostly overcast, but humidity made my toga stick uncomfortably to my skin.

Anticipation mixed with electricity.

Everyone in the arena was leaning forward in their seats, waiting to see what Aphrodite—the most beautiful woman to ever walk the earth—would do.

She was nicknamed the Goddess of Sex because her Chthonic power was in her saliva. One kiss, and a person was a slave to her, mindless with agonizing sexual desire.

From the heckles echoing around the stadium, a lot of men would gladly volunteer to be her victim.

Helen sat ramrod straight ahead of me, her legs bouncing. She glanced back over her shoulder at Augustus, worry on her face.

"She'll be fine," Augustus said smoothly, but his eyes crinkled. "Don't worry."

Helen nodded and turned around. Charlie slung an arm around her and squeezed.

A few seats down, Patro nodded in agreement, but his eyes were also full of concern, and Achilles rubbed his back.

She's their mother.

Helen looked like a younger version of her, and Patro was the masculine equivalent. They both had her breathtaking, almost sculpturesque beauty.

In contrast, Augustus took mostly after Ares in coloring and looks. His features were harsher, more biting.

I jolted in my seat as I realized Augustus and Patro were technically also half brothers. From the way they acted, you'd never know.

In contrast, Augustus and Achilles seemed to have some sort of brotherly bond. From the snippets they'd shared, the two of them had grown up together in the House of Ares.

Patro seemed almost . . . *left out.*

My heart pinched as I thought about how everyone in Sparta, including him, had called me an abandoned mutt like it was the worst sort of offense. It must have been hard for him, growing up in a civilization that viewed him as lesser because of his human heritage.

It never failed to surprise me how small Sparta was. It was nothing like the human world, in so many ways.

Case in point, the gate lifted and five Cyclopes charged out.

Aphrodite sprinted toward them, her muscles rippling as she raised the oversized ax above her head.

The crowd "oohed" with anticipation.

Aphrodite leapt through the air and swung her ax with impressive Spartan strength.

Blood exploded.

She landed in a crouch, beside a decapitated Cyclops head—drenched head to toe in red.

The cheers stopped.

Before the other beasts could react, she leapt at them quicker than my eye could track, wielding her ax like an extension of herself.

Chunks of Cyclopes esophagus sprayed.

Aphrodite didn't use her powers, just sheer brute force.

After long minutes of aggressive hacking, the sand was a mess of severed body parts. Aphrodite let out a war cry of satisfaction as she kicked a head, the size of a boulder, and it rolled across the sand.

There was nothing left to kill.

No one cheered.

Her sphinx sat at the edge of the arena, licking its paw with boredom.

Helen visibly sighed with relief and slumped against Charlie.

Down below, drenched head to toe in blood, Aphrodite rose up to her full, majestic height and smiled, diamond braids sparkling down her back.

She blew a kiss to the silent crowd.

She'd silenced the men.

Hades stood up, and we all followed his lead. Our section clapped and cheered loudly, as the rest of the stadium stared at the sand in shock.

Aphrodite scooped up her sphinx, kissed its head, and disappeared from view.

I smiled. Satisfaction unfurled in my gut.

It was the first fight I'd enjoyed.

Guards arrived at our section, and escorted us to the symposium.

When we stepped through the doors, the harp music had been replaced by electric guitars and a scantily clad male singer. I recognized him as a popular human rock artist. He screeched into a microphone as Spartans jumped on the dance floor.

Well, this is unexpected.

More people streamed into the room than usual. Spartans and creatures of all designations had decided to attend.

The space was already close to capacity.

In the unexpected crush of bodies, I got separated from Augustus and Kharon.

Turning, I stood on my tiptoes and looked over heads as I searched.

I bumped into something hard.

Hands steadied me and a familiar voice said, "Alexis, I was hoping to see you."

I stared into the eyes of a tall, skinny boy with flame-red hair—we were the same height—the goat of the House of Dionysus was embroidered on the pocket of his guard uniform.

Oh goody. Not.

Titus, the bully who made my life hell during the crucible, was standing in my personal space, touching me.

"If he does anything, I'm biting him," Nyx hissed into my ear as she tightened around my neck like she was getting ready to lunge.

"No," I said quickly. "I'll handle him."

Titus shifted awkwardly, his eyes squinting with confusion at what was probably a jumble of sibilant sounds coming from my mouth, but he kept his hands resting on my shoulders.

Instead of stepping back, he leaned closer. "I wanted to get a chance to talk to you!" he shouted over the rock music and buzzing sound of conversation. "I wanted to—"

"Get your hands off m-me!" I yelled back. "Now."

Titus dropped them, but he didn't step back.

We were still standing close together, the crowd of people streaming into the symposium swirling around us.

"I wanted to apologize!" Titus shouted louder, offering a sheepish smile. "I was wrong to target you and . . ." He rubbed the back of his neck. "I've been doing a lot of thinking, now that I'm a guard. It's . . ."

He kept talking, but his voice faded away as I stopped listening. I didn't care what he had to say.

I stared at his moving lips, searching my brain for empathy or some deep-seated urge to forgive him. I sank into myself, looking for goodness, for the ability to forgive and heal. This was the perfect opportunity to be the bigger, more mature person.

I stood on my tiptoes, so he had to look up at me.

"Don't t-talk to me." I smiled coldly. "*Ever* again."

I'd found nothing inside—just rage.

Titus's jaw clamped shut, his eyes narrowing, anger sparking in them.

"I'm *trying* to be better," he said through gritted teeth. "I'm sorry for what I did. You were never really an abandoned mutt and . . . I'm really sorry and I would really appreciate it if you accepted my apology and—"

I made a mocking sad face back at him. "Apology not accepted."

So, this is about my newfound heritage. Asshole.

"No." Titus shook his head with agitation, his neck turning a splotchy scarlet as his chest bumped against mine. "You don't understand . . . I'm being *sincere*. I've been working with a therapist. I feel like it's—"

I laughed harshly. "Try a shovel, it's cheaper."

He frowned with confusion. Someone had clearly never heard of the good old whack to the head.

He continued. "Anyway, I feel—"

"It's not my job to care about your feelings."

Titus bared his teeth. "Stop interrupting me. It's—"

"It's annoying, isn't it?" I said. "When someone doesn't give a *fuck* about how you feel."

Titus shook his head, bodies streaming faster around us as more people tried to run inside the room.

"I know what I did was wrong!" He pointed at my crown. "It's important to the House of Dionysus that we have good relations with the House of Hades and—"

"So your *House* is making you do this?" My smile fell and brow furrowed in (mock) concern. "How pathetic."

The scarlet crept up his face. "Why are you acting like

this? You never used to talk so much. You were quiet and you didn't—"

"Don't you dare." I batted his hand away and raised my own finger to his nose. "Don't pretend you know *anything* about me. Just b-because I didn't say it aloud didn't mean I wasn't thinking it."

He ran a hand roughly through his messy red hair. "It's just you're not listening to what I'm trying to . . . Wait, what were you thinking back then?"

I leaned closer. "I used to wish that you were *dead*."

"*Excuse me?*" He recoiled as he stared at my eyes, which must have filled with blood. "What did you just say?" he asked. "You're the heiress to the House of Hades! You can't just speak like that. Where's your honor and—"

"Walk away before you embarrass yourself further. I'll never forgive you because—" I stabbed my finger into his chest "—I *don't* fucking want to."

Rock music blared around us.

Mozart would have hated this.

I smiled wider.

Titus sputtered with outrage. "You Chthonics really are all fucking *crazy*." He made a face. "You probably helped them free Medusa—you're all *murderous* psychopaths."

I tipped my head back and laughed.

From his aghast expression, he didn't think this was how our conversation would go.

There was a commotion around us as three Olympians were physically thrown out of the way to make room.

"There you are," Augustus said. "We've been looking for you."

Kharon stiffened as he realized who I was talking to. "Is he harassing you?" he asked quietly, his voice filled with promises of carnage. "Do you need me to . . . handle him?"

Titus recoiled again, holding up his hands in a surrender gesture. *Pathetic.*

"No." I led Kharon and Augustus away into the crowd. "*I* was harassing him."

Augustus shook his head, but the corners of his lips pulled up.

Kharon smirked down at me with pride. "Excellent work."

For the first time in days, I smiled and I actually meant it.

"A toast!" Zeus shouted a few feet away. The music stopped with a metallic screech and everyone in the room fell silent.

Zeus grabbed a drink off a tray and held it up.

"To the younger Chthonics starting their rounds tomorrow." The glass of ambrosia sparked in his hand. "May you prove yourself *half* as competent as your impressive House leaders."

His gaze roamed over the room and landed on me.

Still smiling, I didn't look away.

Gray eyes narrowed with confusion, like he didn't know what to make of me.

Remember, daughter, no one fears the sane.

Two could play at psychological warfare.

I winked.

35

THE REAL GAMES BEGIN

ALEXIS: SGC DAY 6

Drex huffed on my right, and Charlie leaned against my left side, his other arm wrapped around Helen.

It was a blustery day in the Dolomites Coliseum. The sands were empty, anticipation crackling through the air, and dense, towering clouds hung so low they almost touched the electric lines of the dome.

Lightning struck far off in the distance, bright white lines branching to the ground.

There was a long pause, then thunder rolled. "I feel ill," Drex said with a groan.

"Me too." I nodded. "I'm not ready."

"Personally, I'm very excited," Nyx hissed as she slithered around my waist. "I can't *wait* to get into the arena and bite people."

Not relatable.

Fluffy Jr. whimpered at my feet, and I tried not to look at the distended hump on his back that now had a faint blue hue. *No way am I bringing him out to fight.* He was clearly sick and needed to recover from . . . I didn't know what.

Drex's knee knocked against mine as he fidgeted with nerves. "We're *so* dead," he groaned. Toucey sat on the floor behind his legs, squawking as Poco tried to poke at him.

I mimed choking myself and Drex laughed (whimpered with manic enthusiasm).

Kharon made a loud, harsh noise behind me.

Peering over my shoulder, I immediately regretted looking—Kharon's eyes were narrowed into slits, nostrils flaring as he stared at where Drex's knee knocked against mine. Augustus frowned beside him.

Thunder boomed, closer.

"Sorry for your loss," Augustus said harshly.

"Uh, what . . . loss?" I asked.

Augustus looked at Drex pointedly.

Drex paled and swayed in his seat like he was going to pass out.

Wait, did he just threaten to kill Drex?

A few minutes ago, when Charlie asked if I'd sit beside him, my husbands had said they understood that I needed to be with my brother.

Now I'd never seen two people who looked *less* understanding in my life.

Apparently grown men and teenage girls had one thing in common: they took seating arrangements *very* seriously.

Charlie linked his arm through mine and I snuggled into him. If he felt Nyx's scales as she slid out from being squished, he didn't show it.

"I've heard rumors," Helen whispered across him. "Zeus is going to interrogate each of you personally after your rounds . . . Are you nervous?"

"No." I forced myself to shrug. "It will be fine."

"How do you know?" she asked.

"Because . . . I enjoy being tortured," I deadpanned.

She narrowed her eyes like she couldn't tell if I was joking, and Charlie smiled, but his arm was tightening around mine with worry.

In six days, Drex would be competing.

In seven days, it would be my turn (to die).

The crowd quieted.

Zeus stepped out onto the platform that extended from the bottom of the stadium. His white silk toga fluttered in the wind, its long train trailing behind him. In his hand, he held a thin white scepter with a golden eagle perched atop it.

Hades sat up straighter in his seat, staring at Zeus, as fog pulsed around him with agitation. The other leaders tensed beside him.

Why does he look like he's seen a ghost?

Zeus held his free hand up to the stadium and electricity leapt across his palm much brighter than usual. "TODAY—THE REAL GAMES BEGIN!" he shouted to the heavens.

Sparta jumped to its feet, a bellowing crowd of creatures and Spartans.

Our section stayed seated.

"You'll do great," Charlie whispered beside me.

Drex whimpered. "We're so dead, it's not even funny."

I nodded in agreement. "*Beyond* dead."

"Wait." I turned to my brother in shock. "Did you just . . . *speak?*" It was the same voice I'd heard calling my name in the woods.

Shadows crept across Charlie's face as his expression changed into something indecipherable. His eyes had an uncanny cast.

"No. Why?" Charlie signed rapidly. "Did you hear something?"

"Uh—no?" I clutched at where Nyx was now coiled on my lap.

Great, I'm consistently losing my mind.

Lightning struck three times in a row on the horizon.

Down below, Zeus still had his hand raised, laurel crown gleaming, sparks coruscating. "I have only one piece of advice to give the younger Chthonics!" His booming voice echoed.

"Nequit homo se reformat . . ."

Zeus paused.

"Absque cruciatu!"

A man cannot remake himself without suffering.

The crowd roared enthusiastically, stomping their feet and clapping in unison.

The clouds darkened, casting the world in gray.

"Lovely message," I said over the clamor. "Very inspiring."

Toucey shrieked at Drex's feet as Poco plucked a metallic feather and held it up to me like a prize.

Grimacing at Drex, I mouthed, "Sorry," and took it. Rolling the stolen feather between my fingers, it accidentally snapped in two.

"That will be my spine," Drex said.

I covered my mouth to hide my laugh. It wasn't funny, but in a very *real* sense, it was hilarious.

Zeus banged his scepter down and the stone podium sparked. "We welcome our first competitor . . . Agatha. Kronos has given her two rounds and five labors to prove her worth!"

"We serve you, Kronos!" the stadium chorused back.

Whenever Father John would shout, "Montana heretics burn in the fires of Hell for all of eternity," we'd respond with "Burn in Hell, sinners!"

This had the same energy.

"*Kronos . . . Kronos . . . Kronos!*" Zeus joined the crowd as all of Sparta was chanting his name.

Agatha walked out.

Everyone stomped, the force field sputtering.

Agatha's long ruby-colored hair hung straight down her back, her pale creature skin almost translucent. She wasn't wearing any armor, but a longsword blade glinted as she spun and raised it up.

She was all alone.

Now that I thought about it, I'd never seen her with a protector. *Is it because she's part Empusa?*

Steel rattled as the gate rolled up.

Four Olympian guards stepped out in full battle armor—golden helmets concealed their faces—each of them held two swords.

She's fighting Olympians?

Thunder boomed, closer than before.

A shocked murmur rumbled through the stadium as they realized some of their own were down there. From the growing sounds of outrage, this was *not* a normal occurrence.

My stomach twisted as the guards approached, twirling their two swords with practiced ease.

Agatha threw her sword down into the sand as she tipped back her head and laughed with giddiness. *What the heck?*

Her laughter turned into a screeching cackle as her features morphed—pale skin peeled away, revealing a skeletal monstrous face—her jaw unhinged down to her chest.

Sharp jagged teeth protruded.

A disturbing clicking noise came from Agatha's distended jaw—it grew in intensity, a metronome of insidious clacks.

The Olympian guards stopped approaching.

They stood up straighter like they were possessed, dropped their weapons, and didn't move. *Are they paralyzed?*

Ruby hair floating in the air behind her, Agatha kept clicking as she sauntered toward the Olympian men.

"She's amazing," Drex sighed dreamily, like he had a crush. *Oh nice, we're both attracted to lunatics.*

Charlie and Helen turned away.

Wait, what do they know? I racked my brain, trying to remember what Empusa did to their prey.

Ten minutes later, I blinked in shock, my mouth gaping as I could do nothing but stare down at the arena.

I should have looked away.

Only Drex was seemingly unaffected—he was still smiling with a goofy, lovesick expression.

The last ten minutes were going to haunt me for the rest of my life (six more days). Numb horror trickled down my neck. Even Nyx was unnaturally still on my lap, like she couldn't process what she'd seen.

It was now crystal clear what Empusa did.

They ate men.

Agatha was covered in bits of gore. The remaining *pieces* of the four guards lay around her, scattered across the sand—mostly just bloody armor and clothes. Apparently Empusa ate *everything* but the stomachs of their victims.

I'd learned this the hard way.

Nyx hissed. "Why can't you be more like her?"

"Because—I have mental health . . . sort of," I whispered (this was a lie).

"SECOND ROUND BEGINS!" Zeus bellowed.

No one cheered.

The gate once again lifted—a man walked out—his hands were bound in front of him, heavy chains trailing behind him through the sand.

He wore a short black exercise toga and a scarlet snake protruded from his bald head.

A collective gasp echoed, and my stomach plummeted.

The Chthonic leaders all jumped to their feet.

"You dishonor Kronos's sacred sands!" Hades roared, pointing at Zeus, who stood calmly on his podium holding his scepter.

I'd failed to notice that Hermos was missing from our section. He was bound, down on the sands, walking toward Agatha. She was his partner.

His . . . lover?

I wasn't exactly sure what their relationship was, but they were partners, and it was obvious that they were very close.

For a second, Agatha's monstrous visage disappeared, and she was once again a beautiful woman. She looked at Hermos with devastation.

Artemis shouted profanities down at Zeus about him taking this too far, and Ares nodded in agreement. Hades's fog was spreading through the stands in screaming tendrils. Olympians whimpered all around.

"What . . . does this mean?" I asked.

Drex shrugged like he also wasn't sure.

Augustus leaned forward. "She has to hurt him as much as possible, until he's incapacitated," he said gravely. "Which will also force him to take the humiliation of being branded once for the defeat—*any* Chthonic loss in the arena results in a brand. No exceptions."

Drex's breath hitched.

Charlie trembled at my side.

Down on the sand, Agatha's skin once again peeled away, and her jaw unhinged.

Click.

Click.

Cli—

The unholy noise stopped as Agatha's skin remolded into the features of a woman. She shook her head no, like she couldn't go through with it, as she stared at Hermos with wide, agonized eyes.

Hermos said something to her.

Agatha nodded in agreement.

They both turned and faced Zeus with mutinous expressions. *They're refusing to fight each other.*

Their courage was shocking.

"IF YOU WANT WAR, WE'LL GIVE IT TO YOU," Hades bellowed at Zeus, backing them, his terrifying fog now filling three-quarters of the stadium.

Zeus's face was disturbingly emotionless as he stared down at the two rebelling Chthonics.

He lifted his scepter, the eagle rising with its wings spread wide.

Electricity blazed across his skin.

CRACK.

The world flashed white, and fiery heat scorched the air. My teeth stung, jaw aching as ozone filled my nose.

My vision cleared.

All around, people's hair stood up with static electricity, defying gravity, as fog curled around them.

Zeus was pointing his smoking scepter down at the arena.

Sand protruded in a jagged, alien sculpture, mere inches from where Agatha stood.

I blinked rapidly, brain struggling to process—lightning had struck Zeus's scepter, and he'd redirected it into the coliseum.

BOOM.

Thunder clapped deafeningly, directly overhead.

The electric dome sizzled.

Agatha and Hermos stood unnaturally still, their lips parted, paralyzed with fear.

Zeus turned on his podium, staring up at Hades. "I do *not* want war, old friend," he shouted. "The games coalition of the federation has assigned each labor based on the abilities and *might* of the competitors. This is a test of HONOR!"

Wind whipped Hades's black toga as he scowled down at him.

The arena was dead silent.

Mutually assured destruction, Helen's warning echoed.

"No one needs to die," Zeus called out, his white toga lit with sparks. "I do *not* want war." He pointed down at the petrified sand. "I spared them."

Hades tilted his head to the side, straining like he was struggling for control. He slowly lowered his hand—fog retreated to him, rushing from the stands, curling around his feet.

Lightning struck off in the distance and the crowd flinched, myself included.

Hades nodded sharply. "On your honor—no one dies!"

Zeus bowed his head low in agreement.

"What—what—what . . ." I trailed off. "*How?*" I whispered.

"Zeus is the only Olympian who can wield his power offensively," Helen said grimly. "A single strike puts anyone who's not ancient in a coma, and most don't wake up from it . . . It's why . . . only the Chthonic leaders survived the Great War."

Charlie gripped my arm hard enough to bruise.

"It's not absolute," Helen whispered like she was trying to convince herself. "He needs to be outside on a stormy day to wield it."

I didn't feel any better.

"RESUME THE FIGHT!" Zeus bellowed.

Hermos moved with shocking speed, wrapping his chain tightly around Agatha's throat before she could react, biceps straining as he choked her with everything he had, his expression determined.

She clawed at his forearms.

Long, awful seconds passed as he strangled her.

Finally, she fell limp to the sand, neck an abused shade of red.

She's immortal, I reminded myself. *He saved her life.*

It didn't feel like it.

Hermos stared down at Agatha's limp body, his expression ruined, as he slowly unwrapped the chain from her neck. He turned away, hands still cuffed like a prisoner, and stalked toward the exit.

He glanced up at Zeus, then quickly looked away.

Zeus raised his scepter—the crowd recoiled. "Agatha has lost," he announced calmly. "She will receive five brands. She failed to defeat all five of her labors."

The stadium remained silent.

Zeus jumped from the platform—through the sizzling force field—and landed in the sand. *Thud.*

Light flared across his skin like the electricity had powered him, and he approached Agatha with a Vulcan metal staff in one hand, the scepter in his other.

Planting the scepter in the sand, Zeus shouted, "FIVE LABORS LOST!" He reached for Agatha's unconscious body and ripped her toga, exposing her sternum.

He pointed the Vulcan staff at it. His arm lit with electricity, and the stamp at its tip turned bright yellow as he pressed the metal end into her chest.

Agatha's unconscious body twitched as she was permanently branded, five separate times.

Sparks radiated from Zeus's scepter, the Olympian eagle glowing.

It looked possessed.

36

SLEEPING ARRANGEMENTS

ALEXIS: SGC DAY 6

Dazed, I trudged with the Chthonics into the symposium, deadly lightning still flashing in my mind.

Rock music had been replaced with tinkling harps and the crowd attendance was more sparse than usual—I missed the screeching guitars.

For how many Spartans and creatures were in attendance, the room was weirdly quiet.

Drex waved us over to where he sat with Achilles and Patro, all three of them looking miserable.

I went to take the chair next to Drex—Kharon pressed his hand to my lower back and guided me to a different seat across the table.

Augustus stood so close his shoulder brushed against mine as we moved.

Awareness coursed through me.

You're in grave danger.

Our new closer proximity was a perilous thing because the abrasive edges of resentment were slowly melting away.

Food trays circulated and Kharon waved down waiters, piling my plate until it overflowed. I ate every piece, and the worry lines around Kharon's eyes relaxed with each bite. The old Spartan adage that hung on a plaque on the symposium wall was correct—*a starving man does not choose his meal.*

Our table ate in heavy silence.

No one spoke about Zeus's calamitous power, but we were all thinking it.

All around, Olympians chatted in Latin with subdued merriment, their extravagant togas shimmering as they spun across the dance floor. Coy smiles painted their lips; long-tailed, vibrantly colored birds sat atop their shoulders.

Strained laughter echoed as lights flashed, the reporters capturing a group of heirs and heiresses.

They'd recovered from their terror quickly.

Zeus is on their side. They feel protected.

Drex slumped lower in his seat across the table, scraping his fork across his plate.

"What's your favorite food?" Kharon asked me abruptly.

I turned to him. "I don't . . . understand the question."

Kharon searched my face. "What type of food do you enjoy eating the most? Sweet, savory, salty? Augustus's favorite is steak. Mine is sweets, like baklava or . . ." He trailed off.

Why is he staring at my lips?

Augustus leaned close like he was interested in the answer.

"I don't have one." I dug my nails into the top of my hand, a strange sort of shame filling my chest.

Both men frowned.

Do they think I'm purposely being difficult?

"I guess . . . I just like any food that you can . . . uh . . . have every day," I said with a forced smile, then changed the subject. "What are your favorite colors?"

Neither answered.

Kharon shared a pointed look with Augustus. Long seconds

passed, and Augustus shook his head, as if to tell him to let it go.

"Gold," Kharon said softly, as he reached up and wrapped his pointer finger in one of my curls—he tugged at it.

My head filled with static.

He leaned closer. "Ask me . . . what my favorite color was before you."

"What was your favorite color?" I whispered.

"Nothing." He stared at me with cold intensity. "I didn't notice colors before you."

I forced out a laugh.

Kharon didn't join me.

"Alexis." Augustus's eyes were dark as a moonless night. "Don't you want to know what my favorite color is?"

"What . . . is it?"

"A shade of pure milky white I've only seen in one place." He lifted his hand to my face, thumb tracing tenderly across my left cheekbone.

I leaned into his touch.

No one had ever complimented me on my injured eye. They said the contrast between them was cool, but no one had looked *only* at my ruined eye and thought it was beautiful.

Would he still think that if he knew the truth?

If he knew it was blind?

"I like yours too," I said, holding his gaze, entranced. "They remind me . . . of the space between stars."

Augustus looked shattered.

I opened my mouth to say something else, but my heart was beating out of my chest.

Augustus dragged his thumb lower and traced my lips.

"*Fuck* us." Hermos threw himself down into the free seat next to Drex, and Augustus dropped his hand, the moment broken. "They're *still* interrogating Agatha about Medusa, like she hasn't been through enough already. Obviously she fucking knows nothing."

Hermos picked up a shot of ambrosia and threw it back, then he picked up another one, and another as he stared down at the grain of the wood, eyes glazing over.

Drex gingerly patted his back, but Hermos gave no indication that he could feel his touch.

Patro and Achilles sat rigid, their expressions blank. *Traumatized.*

I slumped back in my chair, numbness returning.

Symposium, coliseum, or locked bedroom, the results were the same—we were imprisoned.

We retired as a group soon after with Drex half carrying Hermos, who was too drunk to walk on his own.

None of us said anything as the guards held open our cells—we voluntarily walked inside.

Self-determination was a peculiar thing, and for the first time in my life, I wasn't so sure that I possessed it.

In the dim scarlet light of our bedroom, Kharon and Augustus seemed larger, more overwhelming.

They carefully took off their crowns and placed them on the floor next to mine. I hadn't bothered to put it back on this morning.

We stared at the single bed.

Then at each other.

Emotions mixed with lust, crackling between us.

"I'm not s-sure . . ." I said, then cleared my throat and tried again. "I'm not sure . . . I'm ready for more—"

"Shut up, princess," Kharon said softly. "We know—you don't have to explain. We're just going to sleep."

I nodded, the lump in my throat relaxing.

"Can we . . . cuddle?" Augustus asked quietly as he stared down at me. His lips quirked up—he had a dimple in his right cheek.

It was such a small observation, but something seismic shifted inside of me.

"Alexis?" Augustus's smile dropped. The dimple disappeared and suddenly I wanted nothing more in my life than to see it again. "What's wrong, my carus?" He frowned. "Are you okay?"

I reached my fingers up and brushed them across the side of his face.

He closed his eyes, lashes fluttering as he tilted his head.

"You have a . . . dimple."

"Do I?" He smiled wide, showcasing the little indent. "I had no idea—no one's ever said anything."

He glanced away like he was embarrassed by the admission.

How was I ever afraid of him?

My heart cracked as I realized what he'd just admitted. *What did Ares do to you?*

Augustus looked anywhere but at me. "So—can we cuddle?" he repeated.

My fingers pulled away from his face. "Of course," I said.

Kharon climbed in first and pulled the covers back, opening his arms for me. I tentatively lay down, leaving a little space between us, but he pulled me back, so we were pressed snugly together.

Augustus joined us.

I expected him to back in, but he crawled forward, facing my front. He wrapped his arms around me and Kharon so I was sandwiched between them.

"Are you okay?" Augustus whispered, tucking his chin over my head as he draped his thigh over my leg.

"Yes."

Pinned between them, I'd never felt so safe.

Augustus made a deep sound of contentment, his chest vibrating against my heart. Adam's apple bobbing near my face, bronze skin close enough to kiss, I gently nuzzled his neck.

Augustus groaned hoarsely, like I'd done something scandalous, and held me tighter.

Kharon sighed with contentment into my curls, his stomach flexing against my back.

Poco chittered, the covers moving as little paws climbed over the three of us. He paused to sniff Augustus's face and mine, then he wiggled his butt and settled into the space between our hearts.

Immediately, he purred.

"Good night, carissima," Kharon said. "I can't believe . . . this is real."

I knew what he meant.

"Night." Augustus yawned and shifted closer.

"Sleep tight," I said, like I always did for Charlie and Helen.

Augustus pressed a kiss to my forehead.

Kharon's chest vibrated against my back. "I don't sleep, princess. But I'll watch over you . . . I'll keep you safe. I promise."

A gentle zap fired through our marriage bond and it felt . . . tender.

Darkness softly pulled me under.

For the first time, there were no nightmares, only warmth and a fragile sense of peace.

SGC Day 7

*B*ang.
Bang.

Bang.

"It's time to wake up!"

I cracked open sleep-crusted eyes as guards pounded on the door and shouted.

Heat surrounded me.

Still sandwiched between my husbands, I tried to move, but arms tightened around me from behind. Kharon snored, fast asleep against my back, blissfully undisturbed by the commotion happening outside.

Augustus stared at him with a look of awe, then glanced down at me and grinned—flashing his tiny dimple.

The guards banged louder, and his expression fell.

"Kharon, we have to get up." Augustus reached over and tapped him.

Kharon shifted and Poco popped his head up from where he'd burrowed deep under the covers.

I climbed out of bed.

Kharon sat up with a start, rubbing tattooed fingers into his eyes, black hair sticking out in every direction.

He blushed and avoided our gazes like he was embarrassed to be caught sleeping, and instead patted Poco's fluffy head.

My heart skipped a beat. *I'm in grave danger.*

Sleepy Kharon was adorable in the morning, which was a devastating realization.

The door shuddered. "We're leaving now!" an Olympian shouted.

We got ready quickly.

My husbands flanked me as the guards escorted us out of the room. This time, neither of them complained when I sat next to Charlie. However, they did massage my shoulders and rub my back.

It was nice.

The June day was warm and sunny.

Zeus can't use his scepter. I sighed with relief.

The Dolomites towered majestically around the coliseum. They were covered in lush greenery and dotted with Moretti's bellflowers.

Down below, Hermos stalked into the arena with a fifteen-foot-long spear that tapered into a sharp end.

Boos chorused.

Our section cheered.

The gate was lifted and four male Gorgons stalked out—each had a single snake protruding from their bald skulls like hair, but Hermos's was by far the largest—they wielded swords.

The number of snakes and their length symbolize how powerful a Gorgon is. Augustus's crucible lesson on Gorgons came back to me. *Having more than one snake is extremely rare. Their paralyzing bite does not work on their own species.*

Hermos cracked his neck back and forth as the four Gorgons charged in a blur of swinging swords.

"Snake scum!" chorused around the stadium.

Screams echoed.

What felt like forever later, but was probably only a few minutes, Hermos tipped his head back and bellowed with victory.

Pale, blood-splattered muscles straining, Hermos planted the spear in the middle of the sandy arena: four Gorgons were skewered through their stomachs, hanging limp on his spear.

Nyx slithered around my neck. "Okay, now this is *too* far," she hissed, sympathetic for the snakes. I shielded her head so she didn't have to look.

Charlie nudged my side, distracting me from the carnage. "I'm glad you're sitting next to me," he signed.

"Me too."

We leaned closer.

Agatha stood up and clapped in the row before us—our section tensed—she had two black eyes. Thick black and green bruises also covered every inch of her arms and legs. The purple chain marks around her neck were from Hermos, but the rest of the wounds were new.

Agatha had cannibalized her labors without them laying a single finger on her.

The bruises were from her interrogation.

The Olympians had *tortured* her, and it was all because of Medusa.

Head spinning, I fought the urge to retch. Everything became hazy and nightmarish.

Time drifted away from me.

I remembered sitting in the symposium.

The rest was a blur.

Later, I lay beside my husbands in bed.

Kharon fell asleep first.

I woke up in the middle of the night as something moved beneath me. It took me a few groggy seconds to realize I was no longer lying on the mattress.

Kharon had pulled me on top of him like a blanket.

His arms and legs were wrapped around me, holding me in place.

He snored loudly, chest rising and falling.

Augustus grumbled and shifted closer, adding his arms around my back as he pulled us both close against him.

Poco was curled up in a ball on my back. My scalp prickled as he tugged on my hair and chewed on it.

I turned my head.

Augustus was lying in a contorted position, half on top of both of us, and his dimple was showing—he was smiling in sleep.

My expression matched his as I drifted back to sleep.

SGC Day 8

The next day arrived, sunny and bright.
Another miracle.

Down below on his podium, Zeus was once again dressed in all white, and, mercifully, his scepter was missing. Zeus's lightning strike felt unreal, like it had happened in another life.

I sat between Drex and Charlie, holding on to my little brother while Nyx slithered up and down my legs.

Kharon played with the ends of my hair.

I glanced back—Augustus was staring at me. "It will be okay," he mouthed.

Fear filled my lungs. Fluffy Jr. was back in the bedroom because he hadn't woken up this morning, his hump more distended than ever.

"Patro . . . Patro . . . Patro," chanted all around, and Achilles sat ramrod straight beside Drex, watching the arena like a hawk.

Patro stepped out into the sand holding a scythe, electric grid shimmering above him in the sunlight.

The crowd hollered.

Patro flashed a cocky smile, as Poppae walked at his side with her jaguar hackles raised.

The gate opened—gasps echoed—two male Nemean jaguars prowled out.

They were three times larger than Poppae, who was already bigger than a normal jaguar.

Patro calmly twirled his scythe. If he was scared, he didn't show it.

Achilles leaned forward in his seat, hands fisted, knee bouncing.

Patro sprinted forward and raised his weapon with Poppae running beside him.

The opposing jaguars leapt at him, both soaring impossibly high.

Patro jumped to meet them, flying twenty feet up into the air.

They clashed midair.

It happened in a blur—claws swiped, a scythe swung, animals howled, blood sprayed.

A few seconds later, Patro and Poppae stood with the pieces of two Nemean jaguars spread out around them.

There was a moment of silence.

The stadium erupted.

Patro looked up to the stands—he blew Achilles a kiss—then he bowed dramatically.

Achilles sat rigidly.

"He goes next," Drex whispered with trepidation as he pointed at Patro's lover. "Tomorrow—Achilles's muzzle comes off."

We both grimaced.

37

Demons in the Flesh of Men

Alexis: SGC Day 9

A chilly breeze whipped through the coliseum and curls blew around my face in a tangled mess.

Dark clouds concealed the mountain peaks.

Not again.

I'd never view a thunderstorm the same way.

Mist rolled across the sand, and electricity hummed louder than usual, sputtering and sparking in the moisture-filled air.

I searched the stadium, but Zeus wasn't present yet.

The day felt ominous—murmurs filled the arena—there was a strange anticipation bubbling.

Last night, once again, Kharon pulled me on top of him while he slept. He'd woken up with a flustered blush.

I didn't look back at my husbands, but from the way my neck prickled, and my instincts screamed *DANGER*, they were staring at me.

Something was changing between the three of us.

The tension had returned—it was sweeter than before, but still volatile, if not more so. *A dangerous chemistry.*

Sometimes, I didn't know if the three of us were fighting—or flirting.

I wasn't ready to find out.

Charlie interlaced his arm through mine and leaned against my left side, his skin feverishly warm. I snuggled into him. Even back in the freezing depths of Montana winters, his blood had run hot. I used to have to beg him to wear a coat.

Poco was curled into a ball on my lap, looking like a fluffy obese cat.

Such a cutie.

I leaned down and gave his little gray head a kiss. He chittered contentedly.

Nyx's scales tightened around my right arm as she raised herself up. "I want a kiss," she demanded, her tongue flicking out near my ear.

"Are you serious?"

"Yes." Nyx clicked her fangs together. "Kiss me."

I quickly pecked her invisible head.

"Very nice," she hissed.

Drex gave me a strange look. "You know—you're actually a *very* strange person."

I arched my eyebrow. "And *you're* crap at math."

A long beat passed, memories of the crucible spreading between us.

We grinned and elbowed each other.

"I still don't understand how you enjoyed Thagorean." Drex's smile fell as he glanced at the empty seats beside Charlie.

Poppae lay in the aisle, looking despondent.

Where is Patro and why doesn't he have his protector with him?

I hadn't seen him at the symposium yesterday, since he'd been taken directly after his match to be interrogated.

"THE EIGHT LABORS OF ACHILLES—" Zeus's crackling voice resonated throughout the arena as he stepped out onto the podium in a resplendent gold toga—*please no*—a familiar scepter clutched in his hand. "BEGINS NOW!" His lion roared.

The stadium errupted with cheers.

Charlie held me closer, and Drex leaned forward to get a better view.

"*Achilles . . . Achilles . . . Achilles . . . Achilles!*" Sparta chanted. Men and women wailed, half of them screaming, the other half crying.

Nyx joined them.

Humans weren't the only ones who worshipped Achilles. Apparently, everyone on earth was obsessed. He only cared for one person—Patro—and people wanted what they couldn't have.

Achilles stalked out onto the fog-covered sand to a standing ovation.

His short exercise toga bunched as he moved, and a small silver kitchen knife glinted in his fist. That was it. Nero stalked beside him with the scruff on his back raised.

He was heading into battle practically naked.

Achilles turned to look up at the crowd. His large body moved aside and revealed . . . Patro was walking beside him.

What the hell? Why is he down there?

Drex nudged me. "Is Patro limping? Is his ankle bleeding?"

A white bandage was wrapped around Patro's right ankle—a maroon stain was spreading beneath the back of it.

"Why?" I asked dumbfounded. "Even while interrogating him, why would they ever feel the need to . . ."

Patro's Achilles tendon was severed.

They'd severed it the day before *Achilles's* match.

Just like with Agatha, the Olympians were making a statement—it was pure humiliation. A power trip.

I looked over at where Agatha was hunched beside Hermos, still covered in awful bruises. *Zeus had been inches away from striking her dead.*

Terror slithered down my throat.

Charlie rested his head against my shoulder, and I held him close, inhaling his clean scent.

My little brother was safe beside me. We were well fed. Showered and clothed. We'd both survived much worse than this.

Everything would be okay.

Achilles's eyes shone a shockingly bright shade of scarlet as he glanced down at Patro's bleeding leg. Veins protruded from his neck.

The Son of Ares, the Beast of the Crimson Duo, the Killer, had never looked so feral.

Zeus pointed his finger down at them—it looked like he was pointing a gun—and announced, "In compliance with his Spartan oath, the federation grants Patro permission to . . . REMOVE THE MUZZLE!"

The crowd went wild.

Zeus pointed his scepter at a section of the crowd I hadn't noticed before. "TURN OFF THE CAMERAS!"

People screamed with fright, but no lightning struck.

Wait, is all of this being recorded?

What felt like a lifetime ago, I'd watched snippets of the gladiator fights in homeroom before school started.

Dissonance tore through me—past and present collided—the human world was watching.

I felt woozy.

Patro lifted a silver key to the back of Achilles's muzzle. Hand visibly shaking, he inserted it, turning, unlocking the mechanism at the back of the thick leather straps.

The stadium held its breath.

Achilles turned and grabbed Patro's wrist midair, stopping him from pulling the muzzle fully off.

The lovers stared into each other's eyes.

No words were spoken, but Patro's expression fell, his handsome features full of distress for his beloved.

Achilles shook his head, stepping back.

He put space between them, the muzzle still plastered across his face.

Achilles's posture was different—*crueler* than normal. Even from afar, his countenance was harsh.

Patro turned his head, wrenching himself violently away from Achilles, like it physically pained him to leave his side.

Staggering away, tripping over sand and wincing as blood poured from his wound, Patro looked distraught.

Achilles reached to help him, but Patro batted him away and righted himself.

Patro limped away.

Achilles watched him go—his gaze lasered on Patro's severed tendon—eyes flashing.

Cool wetness splattered across my face.

Hissssssss.

The network of electricity sputtered above the arena.

I tipped my head back—droplets peppered my skin—the gray sky opened up, drenching all of us in a deluge. Sparks popped in the air, but the force field held.

The gate lifted up, but Achilles was still watching Patro retreat.

Rain fell faster, pouring down Achilles's face like tears. The muzzle was still on, and for some reason, he wasn't removing it.

Menacing growls echoed as four Nemean wolves slunk out on the far side of the arena. Their coats were a shiny black and each of them was Nero's size or bigger.

It was just like Patro's round.

Nero spun and growled at the incoming threat, his teeth bared as he crouched low in the rain.

Achilles still didn't turn around.

He was watching where Patro had disappeared.

The wolves sprinted, puddles splashing beneath their feet, as they headed straight for Achilles's exposed back.

"What's he doing?" Drex shouted.

The crowd screamed with warning.

Rain pounded down.

The four mammoth wolves pounced—long yellow fangs bared, ears flattened to their skulls—they soared through the rain, straight toward Achilles.

I screamed with the crowd.

Achilles turned.

He dodged in a blur.

Two of the wolves overshot him, and Nero clashed with the third, rolling in the wet sand.

Chilling growls echoed as the two beasts fought.

Achilles didn't pause to watch.

Moving with shocking speed, he drove his kitchen knife straight through the fourth wolf's neck, then he slammed the creature down into a puddle with his other hand.

Blood and water sprayed across his muzzle.

A few feet away, Nero ripped out the neck of the wolf fighting beneath him.

The stadium cheered, but there was no time to celebrate.

The remaining two wolves were already back on their feet, sprinting toward Achilles—one crouched low in front of the other, protecting its neck.

Achilles watched them approach, the knife spinning between his fingers. Nero bared his teeth as he stood over the defeated wolf.

Neither man nor protector moved.

They waited.

Yet again, the two beasts leapt straight at them—Achilles shot up into the air, kicking one at Nero as he grabbed the other with his bare hands.

Crack. The wolf fell limp beside Achilles as he landed in the sand. Its neck was snapped.

Nero once again rolled through the sand, teeth snapping, as he fought the last one.

Achilles stalked over, and quicker than my eye could follow, he slammed his tiny knife straight through the last wolf's skull.

Nero got to his feet and howled.

Achilles stood heaving beside him, leather concealing his face.

The fight had barely lasted a few minutes.

Stones vibrated as the stadium leapt to its feet. *"Take off the muzzle . . . take off the muzzle . . . take off the muzzle!"*

Nyx hissed in unison as she slithered around my stomach.

I gave Drex an incredulous look as he also joined the chant.

"What?" he shouted over the screams. "I'm intrigued."

Rain roared as it fell harder, painting the world dark.

The stomps increased. *"Take off the muzzle . . . take off the muzzle . . . take off the muzzle!"*

Again, the trap door slowly lifted—the second round had begun.

Tall pale skin flashed as four blond men walked out, each wearing an oversized brown garment that was much too large for their lithe frames.

They walked out onto the blood-splattered sand.

They stood silent and soaking wet as they watched Achilles with inscrutable expressions. Something was off about them— *none of them have a weapon.*

Twenty feet of sand, and four dead wolves, stretched between them.

Nero backed up, his tail tucked between his legs, and Achilles moved to stand in front of him protectively.

The stadium went quiet as murmurs of confusion spread.

Charlie stiffened beside me, but I couldn't see his face, his head still resting on my shoulder.

I turned to Drex and asked, "Who are they?" Rain sputtered off my lips.

"No idea."

Kharon swore violently.

Drex and I shared a glance of confusion.

A hair-raising rumble echoed through the coliseum.

Shadows crawled across their four faces, skin rolling, their pale chests widening, layers and layers of muscles bulking onto their figures as they grew in height.

Their faces changed—features morphed—distending and warping.

Thick, curved horns grew out from their shaggy heads as they tipped their heads back and roared.

Sparta screamed.

The Chthonic leaders had all jumped to their feet. Persephone was the only one who remained sitting. She glanced back at me, her eyes full of pity.

I opened my mouth to ask, but she'd already turned back around.

What was that look?

"Are those . . ." Drex trailed off in shock.

I turned to the Chthonic flags whipping back and forth in the aisle—the House of Ares flapped the fastest.

It was fitting. He was the son of the House of Ares.

"*Minotaurs,*" Drex said.

Charlie's arm trembled, and I squeezed him tighter as Kharon swore louder.

"What the fuck is the federation thinking?" Augustus spat.

Zeus stood on the platform at the edge of the arena, watching the sands with hard eyes. Water sizzled as it touched his skin, his scepter sparking.

The four Minotaurs stood in the middle of the arena, almost as tall as the Cyclopes, but much more muscular. Deadly horns protruded from their beastly skulls and their quads bulged obscenely.

There were hooves where their feet used to be.

Augustus's lesson came back to me. *Minotaurs are stronger and faster than Spartans. With a single kick, they can explode all your organs. Their punch—decapitates.*

They were infamous creatures of destruction.

And four of them were here.

Ready to kill.

Achilles raised his arms to the back of his head; the Minotaurs bent their knees.

Slowly, Achilles pulled the leather straps apart.

Sparta stopped screaming—the coliseum was so quiet you could hear a pin drop.

Even the Minotaurs stopped roaring, creatures and Spartans all holding their breath.

Achilles's muzzle dropped into a puddle.

It was worse than I could have ever expected.

Smooth bronze skin pulled across a sharp jaw, framing wide, full ruby lips. Achilles was conventionally handsome, rivaling even Patro for beauty. At least, he would have been.

An X of thick white scar tissue slashed across his lips. Raised and puckered, it reached up to his cheekbones and ended under his chin.

Drex gasped as he also realized.

Someone had tried to *sew* Achilles's mouth shut.

They'd tried to silence him. *Brutally.*

Stomach roiling with nausea, I covered my mouth.

All four Minotaurs leaned forward, their sharp horns pointed directly at Achilles.

Anticipation pulled taut—a razor tripwire attached to a nuclear bomb—as everyone held their breath.

I waited for Achilles to speak, to use his rumored voice powers, and command the Minotaurs.

His lips stayed pressed together in a harsh line and he slowly backed away.

Wind howled as it whipped through the basin, the rain pounding down in harsh sheets.

The Minotaurs watched him move, tense and ready.

Achilles just kept stepping back, putting more space between them. Behind him, Nero curled himself into a ball at the edge of the arena like he was trying to disappear.

Scales slid across my cheek as Nyx leaned forward.

Achilles stopped when he stood in front of Nero, his back to the stone wall.

ROARRRRRRR.

The stadium shook as the four Minotaurs slammed their hooves in unison, wet sand spraying behind them as they kicked back.

The beasts were done waiting.

Achilles stared down at the wet sand, staring at himself in the puddles, as he cracked his neck back and forth.

Boom.

Boom.

Boom.

Boom.

The Minotaurs pounded their meaty fists against their chests in synchronicity and the sound vibrated through the coliseum, a sharp, terrifying warning.

Achilles raised up his head.

Sharp wind gusted—shoulder-length brown hair blew behind him, sticking to the sides of his face. His hair tie had snapped in the last round—and his eyes were brighter than I'd ever seen them.

The X of scars across his lips made him look sadistic.

Slowly, Achilles reached down.

He slashed his knife across the back of his right heel, then rose up to his full height, and pointed the bloody knife straight at Zeus.

Even if he loves him, why would he mutilate himself for . . .
I fingered my left ear.
Not my ear.
The full extent of Kharon's gesture hit me. It was romantic, in the worst way possible. The sentiment was . . . overwhelming.

Steam rose around Zeus, sparks sizzling as he scowled, but he didn't wield his scepter.

Achilles was sending a message back to the Olympians.

This fight was for Patro.

Achilles limped forward, blood washing away in the downpour, but there was no pain in his expression, only rage.

The stadium shook as the Minotaurs charged forward as a unit, their hooves pounding the sand like earthquakes.

Achilles kept limping forward.

His lips parted.

Jaw opening wide, he tilted his head to the side—*fire* exploded everywhere.

Drex, Charlie, and I reared back as heat burned the air. Coughing, the scent of kerosene and napalm scorched my nose as I rubbed at my watering eyes.

Down below, bright scarlet flames were shooting from Achilles's mouth, painting the arena.

Gruesome wails echoed.

The Minotaurs writhed, covered in an inferno. Rolling in the sand, they screamed as they melted to death in an inferno.

"Holy . . ." Nyx trailed off.

The sand itself was lit.

Every single puddle was on fire.

The flames crawled vertically, lighting the rain as it fell.

The gates of Hell had opened wide.

It was the infamous Greek fire, flames that somehow burned water. It was real, and it was coming out of Achilles's mouth.

The Minotaurs were now steaming piles of melted goo.

I made the sign of the cross.

Fire kept streaming from Achilles's mouth as he directed the inferno at the wall of the arena. His eyes were two supernovas.

Zeus backed up along the plank, his expression furious. He still did not raise his scepter.

The fire was traveling up into the stadium; everything that was wet was catching aflame.

Rain continued to pour.

Fire climbed across the electric lines of the dome.

Achilles closed his jaw, but the damage was done.

Everything was burning.

Crack.

Zeus scowled like he was making a decision. *Technically Achilles hasn't disobeyed him. He used his powers and fought his labor like he was ordered to.*

Zeus must have come to the same conclusion I did, because he leapt away.

Crack. Crack. Crack. Crack. Crack.

The crowd screamed, sharp sounds echoing as Olympians and creatures leapt out of the smoldering arena.

Achilles stomped, leaving shards behind him.

The sand was glassing over.

Ares stood up a few rows down, pumping his fist into the air. The other Chthonic leaders stood around him, all whooping and hollering as the rest of Sparta fled for their lives.

Our section was the only one staying in the blazing stadium.

Charlie clutched me and I held him back.

It was the end of days.

Kharon whistled behind us and Augustus chuckled.

I'd gotten a mere glimpse of it during the flag ceremony, but now I truly understood the full weight of just who I was.

To be Chthonic was to wield the power reserved for God.

As the flames sizzled hotter, down below, Achilles stomped

over to a flaming puddle and picked up his discarded mask. The material was fully intact.

"Magic," I whispered.

Augustus chuckled behind me. "*No*—it's the skin of a fire lizard."

Charlie pulled away from me, covering his face protectively as the fiery rain whooshed closer.

One man had caused all this carnage.

A memory niggled at the back of my mind.

Weeks ago, Achilles had cornered me in the hall with an unlit cigarette in his mouth—minutes later, he'd told Patro that he didn't have a lighter, as he sucked on a smoking cigarette.

He'd lit it *himself*. That was why Patro had called him a show-off.

Achilles, the man who smelled like amber and fire, with eyes like coals, could *breathe* Greek fire.

Father John was right again—the devil hid in plain sight.

All along Achilles had been a dragon, hiding in the skin of a man.

Fingers abruptly wrapped around my neck from behind—I jumped in my seat—a calloused thumb scraped down the ridges of my spine.

Panic clawed at my jugular.

"Don't," Kharon whispered gravelly against my right ear, "be afraid, carissima."

It was *far* too late for the warning.

38

SEDUCTIVE PROPOSITIONS

ALEXIS: SGC DAY 9

Drex and I stood next to a marble pillar on the edge of the room, out of the way of the dance floor.

A stack of speakers sat in the corner with an unused electric guitar plugged into it. I stared at it.

A canorous piano melody tinkled through the room, and the musician was good, but not as talented as Kharon.

On the dance floor, I caught glimpses of pastel eyes and long shimmering hair, but whenever Lena came into focus, she was pulled away, disappearing into the crush of bodies.

Olympians, sirens, and all manner of creatures spun languidly to funereal hymns. Sparta was nothing if not morbid.

"Drex, I have pointers for you!" Agatha called from a few feet away, where she was talking to Hermos and Patro.

Patro scanned the room, meeting my gaze—he looked away.

Emotions welled up in my throat.

Drex blushed at Agatha's attention. "I'll be back," he said as he threw back his glass of ambrosia with one nervous gulp and walked away.

Tomorrow it would be his turn in the arena.

Leaning against the pillar, I opened my mouth to tell him to hurry—and erupted into a coughing fit.

Napalm and kerosene still stung the back of my throat.

I rubbed my tingling palms against my toga, vision warping. *The dance floor was on fire, water dripped from the ceiling, the droplets mixed with flames. Heat scorched my cheeks.*

I reared back.

The room was normal. Spartans laughed and danced with abandon.

Everything was fine, except . . . it wasn't.

Little fires burned everywhere.

The battle was raging, and the Chthonics were losing.

Drex, Kharon, and Augustus each had to fight, and then it would be my turn in the arena. *Twelve labors.*

Patro rocked back and forth, listening to something Drex was saying to Agatha—a pool of crimson was gathering at his feet, leaking out the holes of his laces—and there were bloody boot prints across the floor where he'd walked.

Patro glanced at me again, despair in his eyes.

His ankle should have been healing already.

My fingers tingled—I looked down and nearly fell over—a faint glow emitted from them.

"Are you seeing this?" I whispered.

Nyx slithered up my forearm, head resting against my palm. "It's *warm*," she hissed with awe.

We both watched, entranced.

I blinked—the light was gone.

"Do it again," Nyx demanded.

Scrunching my face, I tried to concentrate, but nothing happened. Sweat beaded across my forehead as I remembered the anglerfish. *A hideous deep-sea creature.*

"Make it glow," Nyx ordered.

"I can't." My hands (antennas) continued to stare back at me, the skin a normal innocuous hue.

"False. Failure is not an option—*believe* in yourself," Nyx hissed, scales sliding around my throat as she tightened.

I gasped as I tried to yank Nyx away from my neck. "How . . . suffocating . . . helping?"

Nyx constricted violently. "I'm motivating you," she said calmly.

This was officially the worst pep talk I'd ever received (why was I kinda feeling inspired?).

"Uh—madam?" A short man—a creature with curling horns on his skull—stopped in front of me. "Do you require help?"

I didn't need a mirror to know my face was turning bright purple.

The man's eyes widened as I gasped and asphyxiated in front of him, mouth gurgling unattractively.

"Wait," he said as he looked down at my short exercise toga like he was seeing it for the first time, and his face paled. "You're one of the *psycho* Chthonics."

I smiled at him.

The man turned, running into a siren and tripping over himself in his haste to get away from me—leaving me to die.

Nyx burst into laughter, finally loosening her grip. "Did you see how scared he was of you?"

I held on to the pillar for dear life as I choked. After a while, the imminent sense of certain doom passed, and I chuckled along with her. It was a little funny.

"Is there a reason we just had intense pain around our throats—" Augustus loomed over me, dark eyes flashing.

"What the *fuck* was that?" Kharon asked coldly, holding the two glasses of ambrosia that he'd gone to get for us. "Did someone attack you?"

My skin prickled as I remembered how *he'd* recently squeezed my throat.

I grabbed both shots and threw the contents back swiftly.

"*Why* are you out of breath?" Augustus asked, undeterred. "What was that pain in your neck we just felt? We know it was yours. *Explain*."

I tried to shrug casually but ruined it by having a coughing fit that ended in me gagging with my hands on my knees.

Finally, I came up for air. "Nyx and I were just playing."

Augustus stared at what was most likely a vibrant mark around my neck. "Did she just . . . *strangle* you?" His tone had the deceptive quality that it always did before he absolutely lost it.

"Calm down," I said.

"I *am* very fucking calm!" Augustus slashed his hand through the air.

"Convincing," I said.

"Do you need us to protect you from Nyx?" Kharon asked, his voice deepening. "Are you feeling unsafe?"

I choked, this time from disbelief.

Are these men for real right now?

"We were just *playing*." I overenunciated each word. "It was *funny*."

Nyx twined lazily around my shoulders. "They do know I could just kill them right now if I wanted to—right?"

Kharon's face was turning purple.

I sighed; men could never understand what it was like to have a venomous snake bestie. They just didn't *get* the lifestyle.

Long moments passed as Augustus closed his eyes, muttering a prayer to Kronos in Latin under his breath.

Finally, Augustus opened his eyes, shoulders relaxing. "Okay," he breathed out.

"Okay?"

"I trust and respect your judgment." His face flushed.

Badump-Badump-Badump.

My heart raced, and it wasn't from fear.

"Would . . . you like to dance with us?" Kharon asked through gritted teeth, then he bowed to me, holding out black-painted fingernails.

Augustus also held out his hand.

Badump-Badump.

Dazed, I reached out.

Their hands grasped mine. It felt *lewd*.

The symposium faded out of focus.

No one else existed.

"Let's dance, *darling*," Augustus said, his voice velvet wrapped in silk. He pulled me forward, our chests brushing together.

Kharon moved at my back.

Once again, I was pressed between the two of them.

We twirled around the dance floor.

Augustus held my hand, while his nails dug gently into the small of my back. Kharon clutched my hips from behind.

Four points of contact.

Their fingers flexed, tightening to keep purchase as we spun—stars sparkled in my vision.

Kharon chuckled deeply behind me as Nyx glided off my shoulders onto his.

She was dancing with us.

"Alexis." Kharon's breath fanned against my temple as he leaned closer, his voice rough. "If you don't want to . . . we'll make sure you don't have to compete."

Augustus held my gaze. "I'd rather go to war—than watch you suffer in the arena sands. Just say the word. We'll wage it."

Those words from anyone else would have been over-the-top.

The eldest heir to the House of Ares and the Hunter meant what they said.

My head was spinning, and it wasn't from the dancing.

Badump-Badump-Badump-Badump.

They were speaking of treason—a lifetime incarceration in the most dangerous prison in the world—just because they wanted to spare me from the cruelty of the Spartan world.

Dangerously out of sorts, I leaned forward, resting my head against Augustus's chest. He jolted at my touch. His heart raced, matching the beat of my own.

Music played—it was Beethoven.

A phantom pain scorched the shell of my left ear, *Kharon's* ear.

It would be so easy to accept what they were offering. Of course I didn't want to fight. I *yearned* to sit in a dark room solving esoteric mathematical equations that most likely had no practical implications.

But Ceres was back in a villa, waiting for me to return. She believed in me.

And I didn't want husbands who tore themselves to pieces just to keep me whole.

"No," I said calmly as we spun. "I can do it myself."

Being afraid wasn't a good enough reason not to fight.

Augustus's chest vibrated beneath my ear. "We're here for you. Please don't forget . . . we're *yours*, Alexis. We'll do anything for you."

Kharon made a noise of agreement, his hips brushing against me intimately.

Flushing, a thought struck me—a ridiculously *inappropriate* thought.

I glanced up at Augustus nervously. "Actually . . . there is something."

Midnight eyes twinkled. "What is it, my sweet carus?" he asked.

Kharon's fingers bit harder into my waist.

"If I'm going to die in battle, I want to have sex," I blurted before I lost my courage.

We stopped spinning.

I studied the floor.

"You're *not* going to die." Augustus's fingers tilted my chin up, so our gazes met. "We don't want you to do this because of some misplaced fear of perishing in combat—"

"It's not that," I said in a rush. "I'm *ready*."

"Carissima," Kharon whispered against my temple. "You're playing with fire."

I cleared my throat, a weakness washing over me.

"Oh, for fuck's sake," Nyx hissed as she coiled around my shoulders. "It's just mating—it's not that deep. This is so embarrassing to watch . . . I'll meet you in the stands tomorrow." Scales slid down my legs as she slithered away.

"Wait?" I stared down at the empty space where she'd disappeared. "You can't just leave me?"

"Uh—yes, I can," Nyx called back. "Bye, bitch."

There was a commotion a few feet away as an Olympian tripped mid-spin and threw his male partner to the ground—the two men crashed onto the dance floor.

People screamed as they fell over them.

Nyx laughed maniacally as she slithered invisibly through the symposium.

A siren tripped, tossing a tray of ambrosia into the air.

I sighed and turned back to the men—Augustus was staring at my mouth, his eyes half-lidded. Pure want was written across his face.

He was temptation incarnate, and suddenly, I was a sinner.

"Are you sure this is what you want?" Augustus asked slowly, hardness pressing against my stomach where he leaned into me.

Kharon shifted his hips against the small of my back, pushing into the curve of my spine. "Oh, princess," he said with a vicious bite. "The *depraved* things I'm going to introduce you to."

"Do it," I taunted.

Augustus grabbed my hand—he pulled me off the dance floor; we were heading toward the exit.

Kharon gripped the back of my neck tightly.

I glanced up at him—his eyes were a sharp, steel blue—he wore the same expression he did before he hunted Titans, before he went to battle.

Augustus snapped his fingers at some Olympian guards who were slumped by the door.

"We're going back to our room," he said. "Escort us."

The guards jumped to attention. One got the door for us and held it open, the rest hurried after obediently.

My husbands didn't release me as we moved swiftly through the maze that sprawled beneath the ancient coliseum.

We stopped in front of our room.

A guard fumbled with the key, struggling to open the door.

"*Hurry.*" Augustus's deep voice echoed ominously through the narrow stone tunnel.

The guard paled as he desperately jiggled the key in the lock.

"We have to do everything these days." Augustus stepped forward and took the key, jamming it into the lock, and turning it with sheer brute force.

Hinges groaned as he yanked the heavy door open.

"Lock it up behind us," Augustus ordered as he pointed at the chain hanging on the stone wall.

"Of course—sir," the guards chorused in unison, then bowed deeply.

Who's really captive?

Suddenly, it wasn't so clear.

Augustus held the door open, escorting me into the dim room, lit only by a single copper sconce, burning low on the far wall.

Kharon's hand never left my spine as he walked closely behind me.

The heavy door slammed shut.

Fluffy Jr., the hellhounds, and Poco were squeezed into the narrow space at the end of the bed, snoring in an adorable pile of fur and bones.

The lump on Fluffy Jr.'s back still had a faint blue hue, but he wasn't whimpering, just sleeping soundly. It suddenly struck me that we'd both been glowing lately. *Is it connected?*

Silence stretched.

My husbands were both looming above me, waiting.

I studied the bed, barely big enough for the three of us, courage flagging.

"Now what?" I asked.

"Pick a number," Kharon ordered as shadows settled into the sharp edges of his face. "One . . . or two?"

Augustus clenched his hands into fists.

A sinister aura filled the room.

"Two?" I offered tentatively.

Kharon opened the bathroom door and held it for me, his smile cruel.

"The shower it is."

39

THE PATRON SAINTS OF SIN

ALEXIS

"I need to get something off my chest . . ." I trailed off with a quiver, hugging my knees to myself, words dying in my throat.

Confidence had drained away.

I was fully clothed on the closed toilet seat, afraid if I took off my toga, my flesh would come off with it.

Hair frizzy, I had a narrow field of vision, and a ringing in my left ear. I was *too* quiet, wary of touch, abrasive when I should be soft, gentle when I should be ferocious.

A scalding stream of water sprayed behind us inside the empty shower, sputtering through ancient pipes as a single candle flickered.

Kharon and Augustus dominated the small space; we barely fit.

Sirens flashed inside my mind.

DANGER. Do not touch the predators.

"Speak, carissima." Kharon loomed above me, his eyes a piercing, fatal blue—the shade of frozen lips, stretched across chattering teeth, in a Montana winter. The color of hypothermia. "Say your piece."

I was mute.

"Alexis." Augustus rolled my name in his mouth like he was caressing it. "Darling . . . *please*."

Steam mixed with shadows, casting both of them in darkness. *Merciless, malevolent gods.*

"I'm afraid."

Kharon arched his brow as he stared down at me. His skeleton tattoos were a stark reminder—the sheer depth of his depravation.

"This is who we are," Kharon said coldly. "Who *you* are."

"You're not good men," I whispered.

Kharon's lips curled up, canines flashing. "No—we're not . . . but you already knew that."

Augustus studied me silently.

They offered no platitudes, no promise that they would be gentle, normal lovers.

Kharon tilted his head to the side—there was a puckered scar where his ear used to be.

Terror receded.

Augustus held my gaze, unblinking. "We were fashioned by Kronos to be your husbands—we're one soul, torn into three pieces. Don't be afraid of our love."

I recoiled, porcelain digging into my back. "You . . . *love* me?"

Augustus breathed shallowly, his eyes hypnotizing pools of ink, an unfathomable shade of sin. "I knew it when I watched you battle a Titan, your face determined—at peace—as you *sacrificed* yourself to help some pathetic humans who you didn't even know."

Air sputtered from my lips.

"I knew it—" Kharon said. "When I woke up the day after our wedding. You were gone, the world was colorless, and my heart was missing, ripped clean from my bloody chest."

A rushing echoed in my ears.

Feel the fear, and act despite it.

I released my knees. "I'm ready." I straightened my spine, hoping if I said it, it would become true. "To fuck."

Kharon stood taller. "We . . . won't be *making love*," he said in a low voice. "Until you survive your rounds in the arena."

Augustus wet his lower lip.

"But," Kharon said, seeing the dejection on my face. "We'll give you a *taste* of what's to come after you successfully defeat your labors."

"Do you trust us?" Augustus asked softly.

I shouldn't.

"Yes."

"Stand up," Kharon ordered. "Now."

The air became charged with depravity.

I planted my feet and rose to my full height, tilting my head back, daring him to act.

Slowly, with only centimeters between us, I pulled off the straps of my exercise toga. Cool air blew against my bare back, skin pebbling—the material fluttered to the floor.

Kharon made a raspy, hungry sound.

With lowered lashes, Augustus pulled down his toga, revealing endless planes of rigid bronze—I looked down—his thick cock bobbed against his lower stomach, metal glinting on the tip.

Augustus held out his hand for me to take.

He guided me into the steamy spray.

RIPPPP.

Kharon tore off his toga and followed.

Warmth radiated across my back as long piano fingers traced over blue diamonds. They trailed down my spine, out across each rib, like he was painting my bones.

My nerves screamed at his gentle touches.

Augustus faced me under the hot spray, all wide shoulders and barely constrained power—tentatively I traced my fingers over the network of raised veins that covered his forearms. They were smoother, silkier than I'd thought they'd feel. *Intoxicating.*

Augustus made a sound and jerked.

Emboldened, I explored the firm ridges of his chest, trailing lower over his abs, enjoying how they bunched and flexed beneath my touch.

I brushed lower, glancing across metal and a smooth, weeping head—his dick bobbed against his stomach.

Augustus swore violently as he palmed my breasts, his calluses abrasive against my sensitive nipples—white-hot pleasure shot through my core.

I squeezed my thighs together.

Kharon pressed kisses down my spine, biting gently, then lapping at the tender skin.

Augustus caressed my chest.

He paused as he traced over the thin scar between my breasts—I shook my head, *not now*—his expression promised we'd come back to it later.

Augustus traced across my stomach, lingering on the burn mark, then moved lower to my hips.

Kharon brushed his palms over the globes of my ass, then squeezed, as Augustus casually traced around the patch of curls between my thighs.

Lust made everything blur.

A horribly exciting, ridiculous idea struck me.

With a shaky breath, I rested my hands on Augustus's warm, water-covered chest and gathered my courage.

"Could you both teach me how to . . . pleasure a man?" I whispered, curiosity rising.

Kharon froze behind me, his teeth pausing mid-nip on the sensitive skin where my neck met my shoulder.

Augustus gripped my hips, nails digging into my skin. "Are you sure . . . that's what you want?" he asked hoarsely.

Kharon pulled his mouth away from my neck and stepped back.

I opened my mouth to complain.

He grasped my chin—forcefully turned my head to the

side—and plunged his tongue into my mouth, silencing me. He didn't kiss; he devoured.

When his heated lips finally wrenched away, his hand gripped my jaw tighter, face hovering close enough to count every individual eyelash.

"Don't hold back," I said with a gasp. "I want the *real* you."

Kharon's eyes were completely black, his pupils blown wide. He bared his teeth.

"He's more viciously inclined."

"Carissima . . ." he said softly. "Get . . . on your knees."

Arthur Miller whispered in my ear, "Until an hour before the Devil fell, God thought him beautiful in Heaven."

Augustus cupped my breasts gently—thumbs dragging over my nipples. "Be a good girl, my sweet carus."

"I tend to praise."

"Obey me," Kharon said darkly. "Or we leave the shower, and this is over."

I lowered myself to my knees.

"So obedient," Augustus whispered warmly. "So perfect."

Kharon moved around me, tracing his fingertips along blue diamonds, until he stood beside Augustus.

Water coursed over them; steam tendrilled along their shoulders; they were malefic, ethereal beings.

Kharon looked down at me with a lacerating sneer; Augustus smiled.

They were both exposed before me.

Where Augustus's cock was thick with metal pierced through the head, Kharon's was longer and veiny. One was bronzed with a dark tip, the other ruddy and maroon.

In the faint candlelight, both had scarlet script written across their left thighs.

I squinted at the words, trying to read them—weeks ago I'd thought they were streaks of blood.

They had matching tattoos.

Candlelight flickered, mixing with water, obscuring what the ink said.

"Open your mouth." Kharon overenunciated each word.

I obeyed.

Kharon gripped his dick and pulled it down, holding it above my parted lips.

I leaned forward and steadied myself on his thighs—scar tissue on his right leg, smooth skin on his left.

Kharon gently gathered my wet curls up into a ponytail with his right hand. He held it back from my face, grasping his cock tightly with his skeleton-tattooed fingers—he leaned forward and traced the weeping tip over my lips.

A barely there touch—we both moaned from pleasure.

"Suck. Hollow out your cheeks—*use* your tongue. No teeth." Kharon's pale stomach bunched as he flexed.

It wasn't a question.

Kharon pushed himself into my mouth with tender gentleness.

Holding on to his thighs, I took him deeper, choking on the size as I tried to obey. From his rapturous expression, he didn't mind my lack of finesse.

"You're doing so amazing," Augustus praised as he stood next to Kharon, watching me, while he gripped the base of his dick and stroked slowly along the thickness.

My core fluttered.

Kharon waited patiently, holding himself still as he let me explore. Licking, I traced the silky vein on the underside. Teasing back and forth with my tongue, I enjoyed the velvety soft surface.

Water streamed down my face like tears.

I tried to suck him deep, but choked again.

Apparently, my gag reflex was VERY developed.

Kharon chuckled darkly as I failed to suck on all of him. "Don't hurt yourself."

I looked up at him through the water, holding his gaze.

His hips jerked, and he whispered under his breath, *"You're destroying me,"* like he was praying.

Pulling back, I licked the slope around his head.

"You're taking him so perfectly," Augustus praised, veins standing out on his forearm as he tipped his head back, the V of his Adonis belt straining.

Kharon's eyes flooded with crimson as he engaged his Chthonic powers.

Waves of unimaginable pleasure rolled over me.

His emotions were jumbled, vulgar and erotic—*my woman, knees, dominate, control, fuck, brand, own, claim, cherish.*

Heat pooled between my legs.

I moved my right hand to the base of his hardness, cupping lower gently—Kharon's hips jerked as he let out a guttural groan.

One emotion burned the brightest—*love her.*

I whimpered around his hot hardness as the pleasure increased.

"You're so perfect for us." Augustus stroked faster.

They were both undone before me.

The Patron Saints of Sin.

Kharon released my curls, pulling out of my mouth slowly with a tortured groan.

"Show Augustus what you learned, carissima," he ordered, but his voice was gravelly. It had lost its edge. His cheeks were flushed, eyes glossy.

A heady wave of feminine satisfaction washed over me.

I've undone Kharon.

Augustus pushed his much thicker cock down, the metal jewelry on the tip glistening with precum. "You're doing so amazing, sweetheart."

He stared down at me with pure adoration, which I really appreciated, because I was pretty sure I wasn't actually doing it well.

I parted my lips.

Augustus brushed hair back off my forehead with unbelievable tenderness.

I grabbed his thighs, his skin much warmer than Kharon's, as I wrapped my mouth around his velvety softness, straining to take his width.

The cool metal of his piercing brushed across my tongue.

My lips were on fire.

It felt depraved.

Augustus tipped his head back and swore, hands bunching in my hair as he trembled beneath me, cock throbbing in my mouth. "I'm not going to be able to last," he said with a strangled gasp. "So exquisite, *so* fucking perfect."

I sucked, digging my nails into his thighs, needing to see him unravel. He thrust into my mouth, precum salty, his movement becoming more erratic.

He pulled away with a groan—velvety hardness popping from my lips.

I gasped for air, confused by his sudden lack of presence.

"Touch yourself," Kharon ordered harshly, but the effect was ruined by his obsessed expression.

My fingers went between my aching legs—I rubbed against my soaking, already fluttering clit—white-hot pleasure mounted.

Kharon and Augustus moved closer.

They fondled my breasts, plucking my nipples, nails scraping across my feverish flesh, as they each stroked themselves faster.

I touched myself harder as they lavished me with attention.

Augustus stared down at me, expression soft. "You're doing so beautiful, pleasing your husbands like this. I'm so proud."

Flutters mounted as I reached closer to the fall.

Slapping flesh echoed obscenely under the heated spray.

Kharon made a guttural sound as he swore, teeth bared, jaw tensed. He tipped his head back, stroking himself hard and fast. "I'm going to ruin you," he promised.

Too late.

"You're mine, love," Kharon said with a strangled pant. "Forever."

Waves of pleasure crashed over me, and my back bowed, quivering as my core clenched and released.

Kharon and Augustus stepped closer to my face, groaning in unison, as they came together all over my parted, gasping lips.

Their cum mixed, dripping down my chin, onto my chest.

Aftershocks fluttered through me.

Kharon dragged his thumb through the mixture, pushing it into my mouth. It was salty and sharp against my tongue. I grimaced and spit it out—it tasted genuinely disgusting. *I'm never doing that again.*

Both men laughed.

"Love you." Augustus gathered the cum as it dripped off my chin, dragging the liquid down, across my breasts, massaging it into my skin.

I leaned forward, boneless and spent.

Their thighs were inches from my face—the tiny words tattooed across both their left legs in cursive font became visible.

"Alexis Hert" was written with a Roman numeral—our wedding date.

My gaze shot up to theirs.

I tried to speak, but couldn't.

Augustus lifted me up and cradled me against his chest.

Kharon dried me off with a towel as Augustus held me. He focused on my curls, peppering my face with butterfly kisses as he gently scrunched the water from them. With a determined expression, he wrapped my hair into a bun.

Finally, when Kharon was satisfied that I was dry, Augustus carried me into the room and gently laid me down on the bed.

Kharon brought a wet washcloth between my legs, and he wiped me off tenderly as he whispered words of love. He swiped it over my face and chest, eyes shining with emotions.

When he was done, Augustus spent a while tucking the covers around my shoulders, legs, and feet.

He kept tugging the blanket up higher on my face, and it took me a second to realize what he was doing. *Poco likes to have just his ears out.*

My heart melted in my chest as my scary husbands fussed.

Finally, they both climbed into bed, draping themselves around me like another layer of bedding.

Kharon pressed a tender kiss to my forehead. Augustus feathered a kiss on the side of my neck.

I smiled sleepily as I closed my eyes, feeling warm inside and out.

Why didn't we do this sooner?

I was so content, I'd forgotten to ask when they'd gotten my name permanently placed on their skin.

Sleep pulled me under.

40

The Hunter

Kharon

Eyes fluttering open, intoxicating heat surrounded me.
    I squeezed Alexis against my chest with a satisfied yawn. Sometime in the middle of the night, I'd pulled her from under the covers and draped her on top of me.

She was a delicious weighted blanket.

Divine.

Augustus's bronze thigh was hooked over both of us, pinning us in place. Her name was tattooed across it.

We'd gotten the ink the day after our wedding, the day she'd disappeared.

It was a promise that we'd earn Alexis—our *wife*—back, with bloodshed or tenderness, *whatever* it took. No cost was too high. Not when it came to her.

And now she was lying in my arms, trusting me to hold her while she slept.

I'd thought standing over her all night, watching her breaths rise and fall, was what my soul yearned for.

I was wrong.

This was what I'd been born for—clutching her close, our hearts beating in rhythm, while she snored into my neck.

I smiled into her curls.

Before the competition, I couldn't remember the last time I'd slept, let alone *rested* peacefully for hours on end.

All it had taken was a week of isolation with my wife—the punishment was the cure.

Hands tracing over sleep-heated skin, I mapped the marks that were scattered haphazardly across her back. They covered the front of her torso too.

Her skin was a patchwork of survival—cigarette burns, a dagger wound on her sternum, jagged notches from what looked like the ends of twigs, the indents of perfect edges like she'd been thrown against the corner of a counter.

My lips quivered, falling.

I tucked my face into the crook of her neck, moisture blurring my eyes as my chest heaved raggedly.

Life had not been easy for my wife, yet she'd endured and was still so . . . *good*.

It was no wonder we'd fallen in love with her. Alexis was like no one else on earth. *Angelus Romae.* No creature, Spartan, or human could ever compare to her.

She was divine.

She was my wife.

She was my other soul.

I've found you again.

41
THE ELDEST HEIR

Augustus: SGC Day 10

It was a bright summer's day, the mountain air scented from wildflowers. Poco sat on my shoulder, purring as he gnawed noisily on my crown.

I'd seen the world, but the Dolomites stood apart, surreal in their beauty. *Sacred land.*

The electric dome hummed as it caught the light.

Black scorch marks across the stone were the only signs that hellfire had been burning a day earlier.

In front of me, Alexis leaned into Charlie as they held hands, knuckles white with fear for their friend.

Kharon traced along the necklace he'd gifted her, tattooed thumb stroking down the back of her neck.

Just looking at my wife made my chest ache—she was too good for us—and yet I knew in my bones, there was nothing that would *ever* make me leave her side.

Kharon felt the same.

I twirled one of her curls and she shot me a smile over her shoulder.

My black heart cracked.

I was devastatingly obsessed with my wife.

So obsessed that anxiety gnawed sharply at my gut, because at the edge of the stadium, Zeus looked smug with sparks of electricity leaping off his shoulders.

What the fuck type of game is he playing at?

There was no reason he'd *actually* suspect Achilles and Patro—or *any* of us for that matter—of helping Medusa.

A smattering of applause filled the stadium as Drex walked out onto the sand holding a broadsword.

He looked terrified.

Alexis stood up and clapped, hollering at the top of her lungs. Helen, Charlie, and Agatha joined her as they cheered for the nervous young man.

"Wahoo," Kharon drawled sarcastically.

I kicked him.

He didn't look repentant.

He still hadn't gotten over his jealousy with their friendship (neither had I).

"One round—two labors!" Zeus announced. His famous lightning scepter was noticeably absent. "For the first Olympian to ever participate." There was another smattering of confused applause. Sparta didn't know how to feel.

Drex pulled his shoulders back, sword pointed at the entrance.

The gate lifted.

Two exotic-looking beasts stepped out onto the sand: Chimeras.

The crowd "oohed."

Chimeras were three-headed beasts—they had the body of a lion, the head of a goat protruding from the middle of their backs, and a tail that ended in a snake's head. Rare creatures—and they lived in the wilds of North Africa.

Drex visibly trembled as they prowled toward him.

The Olympians were going easy on him.

This should be quick for him.

Chimeras were twice as small as Nemean lions, and while dangerous, they were only a class five beast because of their shorter stature. They breathed out fire, but only in tiny amounts.

He'd be fine.

Both beasts sprinted across the sand toward Drex. They opened their mouths—flames burst from their maws.

Drex turned and sprinted away from them.

What is he doing? I looked at Kharon with confusion.

Alexis screamed as she covered her mouth, shaking from fear.

Kharon rolled his eyes and lazily stood up. "Just . . . stab them!" he yelled in a bored tone like it was obvious (it was).

Unfortunately, Drex was not the brightest.

Thirty minutes later, the gate opened. "End of the round," Zeus announced with exasperation.

Two very *unstabbed* Chimeras were panting with exhaustion as they chased Drex around the sand. I had to give it to the kid, he had stamina.

For the last half hour, he'd managed to run around and avoid both beasts. However, he had zero killing prowess and was a disappointment in every other way that mattered.

Drex zigged left quickly—and one of the beasts tumbled to the right as they tried to follow.

There was a smattering of laughter in the crowd.

Technically, a round ended after thirty minutes and you could leave the arena, but you'd lose.

No uninjured Chthonic had ever chosen that route.

Because we had pride.

And weren't pathetic.

"RUN—you got this!" Alexis shouted as Drex hauled it toward the open gate.

He definitely does not.

Drex dove out of the stadium, and there was another smatter of applause and laughter. Olympian guards ran out with guns. *Pop. Pop.* Both Chimeras dropped dead, bullets through their eyes.

The crowd clapped as the bodies were dragged away.

Zeus shook his head and jumped from the platform through the force field, landing in the sand.

Guards escorted Drex back out into the arena.

Zeus walked toward the boy with Vulcan metal in his hand.

People shouted that it wasn't necessary as boos echoed all around. Apparently, Sparta felt bad for the Olympian mutt; he didn't deserve to suffer, not like us.

"Two labors lost," Zeus announced with a sigh.

He waited patiently as the boy pulled open the top of his toga.

Zeus stepped back and pointed the circular metal over his exposed chest—his outstretched arm brightened with sparks, metal turning yellow in his fingers—he placed the brands on his skin in quick succession.

Drex screamed in agony.

The crowd winced in sympathy.

Zeus put his hand on the boy's shoulder as he whispered something to him with an encouraging smile, like he was trying to make amends.

Drex sneered back at him, his expression openly hostile.

Maybe we'll make a Chthonic of him after all.

Zeus gestured for Drex to walk forward, then followed behind him out of the stadium.

Everyone stood to leave.

As our section exited, I gave Helen a big hug.

I mouthed silently over her shoulder at Charlie, "You *better* be sleeping on the floor."

He nodded vigorously, looking aghast at the insinuation of impropriety.

Relief coursed through me as I reluctantly released Helen.

I would never admit it aloud, but I was grateful she had Charlie; I saw the way he looked after her. He was a good kid.

The way he grew up was criminal.

Alexis leaned into me as I escorted her to the symposium.

They deserved so much better.

Drex arrived a few minutes after us, looking mostly unharmed. Bandages peeked out from beneath his toga. They'd clearly just given him medical treatment, then released him.

"Drex!" Alexis called when she saw him, releasing my arm and running over to him.

The boy smiled when he saw her, and they fell into conversation at the edge of the room.

Kharon started to stalk after her, but I held him back.

"He's just her friend," I reminded him (and myself) calmly.

"I fucking hate him."

"I know."

That night in bed, the three of us didn't say anything as Kharon and I held Alexis between us.

The unspoken reality hung in the air.

Tomorrow—it was Kharon's turn to fight.

SGC Day 11

It was another bright summer's day in the coliseum.

Thank you, Kronos.

Zeus couldn't use his scepter to threaten Kharon during his fight. A small mercy.

I'd slept soundly, clutching Alexis to my chest. Sometime in the middle of the night, I'd wrestled her out of Kharon's grasp and into mine.

It was the best thing I'd ever done.

Waking up to her sleepy face was like waking up to a brilliant sunset—glorious, *warm*, perfect.

Even now, her golden curls formed a halo around her face as she leaned close to Charlie in the row before me.

Angelus Romae.

I rubbed at my aching chest.

I wanted my arms around her like I wanted to breathe.

My woman.

The keeper of my soul.

The love I felt for her was greedy—a new sort of madness.

I tried to focus on anything but the fierce emotions gripping me.

Achilles shifted with discomfort a few seats away. The upper half of his face was covered in bruises, the skin distended and turning green.

Patro sat ramrod straight next to him, his severed tendon still wrapped in thick bandages. Achilles had a matching one around his ankle.

They'd both been mutilated.

Complicated feelings churned inside my sternum; they weren't my favorite people right now, but they were under my charge. Achilles was a fellow victim of the House of Ares—*House of Horrors*, as we used to call it. They were my responsibility. My half brothers.

Guilt scoured me.

Hermos and Agatha sat further down, also covered in bruises.

I've failed all of them.

Drex made a noise in front of me, elbowing Alexis's side as he tried to get her attention. She kept signing and whispering to Charlie.

Drex nudged her again.

I took a deep breath.

He'd been practically hanging off my wife ever since his round yesterday and was officially getting on my nerves.

Kharon wasn't the only one with a jealousy problem.

Drex's elbow touched the side of her arm, and Alexis turned to him with a beaming smile. They laughed together, sharing an inside joke.

Mental note: break his left elbow.

Alexis turned around and shot me a glare, like she could hear my thoughts.

I smiled back.

She frowned. "*Stop* it," she said as she looked over at Drex.

"Stop what?" I mouthed with feigned confusion.

Alexis rolled her eyes and turned back around to Drex, her features soft and radiant as she talked animatedly, waving her hands.

I sighed heavily. She clearly enjoyed their friendship and would be upset if something bad were to happen to him.

Mental note: make his shattered elbow look like an accident.

Stone vibrated as the crowd began a chant.

Stomp. Clap.

"Hunter!"

Stomp. Clap.

"Hunter!"

Stomp. Clap.

"Hunter!"

Sunlight glinted off the sand, creating a harsh glare.

Kharon sauntered out in the light, Hell and Hound flanking him on either side.

Gasps echoed and the chant paused, then continued.

Sparta was not used to seeing Kharon's hellhounds; Olympians had always called him weak, saying he was too feral to have a protector; but he didn't have just one—he had two, and they were monstrous.

The three of them stalked in tandem, his skeleton tattoos taking on a whole new meaning.

A silver bow flashed where it was slung across his arm. Artemis stiffened in her seat as she realized.

Kharon had chosen her weapon on purpose.

She'd secretly disowned him, called him a disgrace, but the rest of Sparta thought he still represented her House.

Kharon was making a mockery of everything she stood for.

Pride filled me.

As a boy, they'd mutilated his legs and watched him crawl desperately across the sand. Then the Olympians had dragged him back into the arena, branded his chest until he passed out from pain, and left him to crawl out for a second time.

They thought they'd broken him.

But Kharon was now grinning, sauntering without a care in the world, and shoving it back in their faces. Sharp pain streaked up my knee with each of his steps, but he gave nothing away.

The stadium chanted, *"House of Artemis!"* with growing fervor—none of them could even comprehend the hell he'd endured.

If the House of Ares was all about physical torment, the House of Artemis was a study in psychological games.

Scarlet mist expanded around Artemis as Kharon saluted up at her.

He stopped in the middle of the arena, pulled a silver arrow from his back holster, and cocked his bow.

"House of Artemis . . . Hunter . . . House of Artemis . . ." The chant increased in decibel as all of Sparta joined in.

The gate slowly opened.

Squakkkkkkkk.

Leathery black and green scales slithered through the sand.

Someone shrieked.

Cracks echoed around the arena, people disappearing in clouds of smoke, as cowardly Olympians leapt away to safety.

Not again.

Hades fisted his hands with rage and shouted, "What in Kronos is this?" All the leaders stood up. Aphrodite pointed down at Zeus—"EXPLAIN YOURSELF."

Zeus didn't take his eyes off Kharon.

Three Typhons slithered across the sand.

The twenty-foot-long, thick-bellied serpentine beasts had monstrous beaks on their wide humanesque faces. *Clap. Clap. Clap.* Short leathery black wings flapped uselessly as they moved.

Class seven beasts.

Designation: kill on sight.

They lived on abandoned islands in the Adriatic Sea. At night, they infamously slithered into the water, hunting sharks that lived in underwater caves. Highly territorial and dangerous—their saliva *boiled* flesh.

The ultimate monsters of Sparta.

Zeus smiled, electricity zapping across his teeth as he watched them advance on Kharon.

Yes, this was war.

Squakkkkkkkk.

Kharon loosed an arrow—with perfect accuracy, it burrowed deep into one of the Typhon's open beaks.

Green blood sprayed.

The creature gagged as it choked, tail thrashing wildly beneath it. An arrow slammed into one eye, then the other. The beast crashed down onto the sand, twitching as it choked on the weapon.

But the other two Typhons were heading directly for Kharon.

One of the Typhons spit—Kharon and both hellhounds rolled at the same time. They dodged the sizzling pile of goop melting the sand where he'd just stood.

They ran, circling around the remaining two Typhons.

Squakkkkkkkk.

Kharon unleashed another arrow straight into an open beak—a second beast choked, flailing about. Hell and Hound jumped from behind—teeth sinking deep into the creature's serpentine neck as they mauled it.

The last standing Typhon whirled in a circle, its eye remaining on Kharon, who was stalking around it with his bow cocked, waiting.

It didn't squawk.

Time stretched, but the beast never opened its beak wide.

It was smarter than the others—it had *learned*.

Instead, it flung its head to the side, caustic spit shooting from the crack of its beak.

Kharon jumped—the crowd screamed as he narrowly avoided the danger.

Hell and Hound climbed off the second Typhon and crouched low, positioning themselves at the last creature's back. Kharon tensed in front of it.

All three of them were waiting, cornering the giant beast.

Kharon slowly reached back for another arrow.

The Typhon spit again as it exploded forward, and Kharon jumped straight upward to meet it. With a mighty heave, he slammed the arrow down through the top of the beast's skull.

Agonizing pain boiled across my chest, and I saw stars.

Someone gasped nearby.

But I could barely see through a haze of pain and squinted lashes. *Thud.* The beast collapsed to the sand, and Kharon rolled away. His hounds jumped up on the carcass, green blood splattering as they finished it for good.

Everything blurred.

The crowd gasped. I couldn't see why.

I squinted at the sand, focusing through the throbbing agony.

Kharon staggered up to his feet, clutching the side of his pink chest—his toga had burned away, revealing boiling, blistering skin—the saliva dripping from his chest.

Fuck, he needs to get medical attention.

My uninjured chest throbbed in tandem.

We needed medical attention.

The crowd quieted, waiting to see if he'd fall.

Kharon raised his silver bow with his good arm—and pointed it at Artemis.

He took a bow.

Cheers erupted as those who had remained to watch the fight applauded and stomped, loving the theatrics of it all.

I leaned forward and tried not to pass out.

Run and get help, you fucker. Hurry.

Casually, like his skin wasn't melting to the bone, Kharon took his time sauntering out of the arena.

I was going to kill him.

Skin boiling, I staggered to my feet. I needed to make sure he got help.

Movement flashed in my peripheral vision, and I tried not to vomit as I clutched my chest.

Drex and Charlie were motioning frantically as they bent over . . . Alexis?

My wife was slumped back in her seat, clutching at her chest, face pale, mouth open wide as she struggled to breathe.

No.

My world turned upside down.

Everything slowed as I stumble-crawled toward her. Shoving the boys aside, I pulled down her toga, inspecting her sternum for wounds.

There was nothing.

No.

Her eyes were glazed over, face tight with excruciating pain.

"You . . ." My voice sounded garbled, like it had come from someone else, far, far away. "It *can't* be."

I blinked—I was partially lying beside Alexis in a collapsed heap. I didn't remember moving.

Her lashes fluttered, face full of agony.

"You . . . feel it . . . too?"

In slow motion, Alexis nodded, curling in on herself.

"FUCK."

Someone tried to pull me away from her, and I threw a blind punch, agony strumming, hot lava dripping down my front.

"KHARON . . . *HELP!*" I bellowed, trying to get him to understand as she twitched with torture beside me.

Hades smacked me across the face.

I didn't feel a thing.

The pain across my sternum was too great.

His expression was frantic as he pulled me close. "What's happening to her? Explain what's . . ."

His voice warped in and out as I sank toward unconsciousness, then clawed out: *Help Alexis, help Alexis, help Alexis.* The repeating thought was the only thing keeping me awake.

"Augustus, explain what's . . ." Hades shook me back and forth.

Poco climbed up and rubbed at our hearts like he was trying to help.

"*EXPLAIN RIGHT NOW WHY MY DAUGHTER IS IN PAIN!*" Hades bellowed straight into my face, his words piercing through the haze.

"Kharon—" I gasped. "Our bond . . . feel . . . his pain . . . him . . . *help.*"

Hades's eyes widened with panic, and his edges blurred—*Crack*—he leapt away.

He'll fix it.

That was what I needed to be doing, but I could barely move.

I heaved onto my side—Alexis's face hovered near mine.

We rasped together.

Suffering.

Crimson splattered on her forehead as it dripped from my eyes.

"I love you," I mouthed, unable to speak, the edges of my vision turning pitch-black.

She grunted in agony. "Love you . . . too."

Nails digging into stone, I reached for her face.

I couldn't stop, I needed to fix this, I needed to help her.

Alexis was counting on me.

I would save my wife, or I would die trying.

Kronos save us both.

42

The Hunter

Kharon: SGC Day 11

Every inch forward was a million miles.
  Sizzle.
Flesh boiled and bubbled, melting away as sand and stone blurred around me.

Bright sunlight made the anguish grotesque.

There was nowhere to hide.

Heaving through my nose, each step jostled my deteriorating flesh—I bit down on my tongue, tasting copper—Typhon spit was dripping down my chest, dissolving my muscles, eating away at my bones.

"*Hunter . . . Hunter . . . Hunter!*" Sparta chanted for me, the sound warping in my missing ear.

Years ago, I would have killed to be where I was, but now the victory was hollow.

I screamed into my closed mouth, a serene expression still plastered across my face, as I walked unhurriedly toward the open gate—three dead Typhons lay mangled in the arena behind me.

Knees wobbling, pieces of me popped as they boiled and emulsified, dripping.

I smirked up in the direction of the Chthonic section; Artemis and Erebus were watching.

They'd never catch me on my knees again.

Ten feet.

Breathing roughly, I concentrated with everything I had.

Five.

Two.

One.

I lunged out of the arena, up the step into the coliseum, and collapsed.

Crack.

Hades caught me.

Screaming and twitching in pain, I writhed in his arms.

Hades shouted something garbled about Alexis.

A white toga came into view, sparks, a hand reached out. There was a fight. Yelling. A vial was pressed to my lips. Zeus yanked me out of Hades's arms.

Everything went dark.

"Wake up!" Icy water splashed across my face, and I sputtered awake. The first thing I noticed was the scorching agony across my shoulder and chest.

Torchlight illuminated a low ceiling.

I was tied with chains to a chair, seated at a low metal table, in a small . . . crypt?

Stacks of skulls were piled high, lining the walls. The air was chilly and stale. I was somewhere in the labyrinth of chambers under the Dolomites Coliseum.

Zeus sat across from me at the table, his storm-gray eyes narrowed with disgust as he stared at me.

"Where is Medusa?" he asked, tapping a small glass bottle on the metal table. The tin sound echoed harshly in the quiet.

I opened my mouth—agonizing pain exploded in my chest, air whistling through my mouth.

"He needs more salve to speak," Zeus said to someone.

Everything spun.

A guard leaned over me with a jar of paste. Rough hands slapped at my ruined skin—I screamed—air whistled through the open cavity of my ribs.

Darkness dragged me under.

Freezing water drenched my face. "Wake up!"

I sputtered.

The agony was still present, but slightly muted.

Zeus was still sitting across from me at the dingy table. "Can you speak?" he asked, electricity bright across his tongue.

My vision doubled—two Zeuses stared at me expectantly.

"SPEAK!"

"What—"

"Good," Zeus said calmly. He held up a full glass vial. "Like I was saying, *this*—" he swirled green liquid in the torchlight "—is your incentive." The Rod of Asclepius was stamped on the side.

I tipped my head back, heaving.

"Aren't you going to ask what it is?"

I opened my mouth—and threw up all over myself.

"Very well, I'll tell you," Zeus said calmly. "You've already had a tiny sip; it's why you're not in a coma. It's an advanced Olympian healing tonic—*very* expensive, our lab's newest technology . . . Once you drink it, you'll barely feel any pain. It's going to change the world."

My vision tripled.

Three Zeuses stared at me—three glass vials twirled.

"I'll give you the tonic." Zeus spoke slowly. "If you tell me where Medusa is."

I was fucked.

"Don't . . . know." I slumped weakly. It was the truth.

There was a long moment of quiet.

"Liar." Metal clattered against stone as he stood up. "She's *your* sister—it had to be you . . ." He leaned across the table. "Tell me where you stashed THAT MONSTER!"

"I . . . don't . . . know."

My head snapped to the side as Zeus slapped me.

Guards flooded the space, brandishing sparking batons.

Time warped in a blur of pain.

A vial was dangled in front of my face.

Metal creaked.

"I . . . don't . . . know . . . Medusa," someone whispered repeatedly; it might have been me.

More blows fell.

Zeus stood composed in front of me. "I need to know. Is he telling the truth?"

Is who telling the truth?

Patro's face blurred in and out of focus.

"Remember, if you lie to me," Zeus said quietly, "Achilles will be sent to the Underworld."

Patro leaned toward me, his mouth moving. "Do you know where Medusa is?"

Who is he talking to?

"Kharon—answer me!" Patro yelled.

"No."

Patro searched my face, and his shoulders slumped with relief. "He's telling the truth."

Zeus was silent.

Patro asked more questions and someone answered; it might have been me.

Glass pressed against my lips.

Smooth liquid poured down my throat.

A switch flipped—the pain turned off; I felt nothing.

I was sitting chained to a chair with warm blood dripping down my face. My eyes were almost fully swollen shut, and I could only see out of small cracks.

Patro and Zeus were arguing.

"Someone has to know where the *fuck* Medusa is." Zeus gritted his teeth. "The safety of Sparta is at stake."

"I already told you . . . We're not involved," Patro said calmly. "Maybe you should interrogate the Olympians."

Zeus pointed at me. "Get him out of here . . . Now."

A few minutes later, I limped beside Patro, holding on to his shoulder for support. I couldn't feel anything, but my body wasn't cooperating—I was walking through molasses.

"Thank you," I whispered as he led me through the underground tunnels, my voice hoarse from screaming.

Silence stretched.

"I miss . . . our friendship." Patro spoke so quietly I almost missed it.

I leaned against him. "Me too."

"Forgive me," he said, his voice trembling. "She was ours first . . . ours to mentor. We were trying— We *do* care for her . . . We were trying to do what was right for—"

"Stop," I said softly. "Don't."

Patro halted, and I fell against him.

He turned, holding me up, torchlight illuminating his handsome face. "Why?" he asked. "Why can't you let it go and—"

"Because—" I coughed violently. "I . . . *love* her."

Patro's face fell with devastation.

"She cares . . . about you," I whispered. "She'd want me . . . to forgive you." I tried to open my eyes wider, to see him more clearly, but I couldn't. "And I care about you—so much." Tongue heavy and dry, I forced out, "*I care about you. I miss you . . . but I can't do this right now.*"

Patro squeezed me tighter as he held me up, embracing. I rested my head on his shoulder, gasping for air.

Finally, we pulled apart and resumed staggering down the cavernous hall.

Two reluctant brothers, not of blood, but of heart.

What felt like hours later, we made it back to our individually assigned prisons. Guards were waiting for us in front of our doors.

Patro touched his forehead against mine.

We went our separate ways.

Our doors slammed shut.

"Honeys—" I coughed "—I'm home."

I stumbled in the dark, pulling off my ruined clothes. I had a faint memory of an Olympian doctor wrapping bandages around my wounds, giving me a shot, and telling me to sleep it off.

No one answered.

Rubbing at my swollen eyes, it took a second to focus on the bed: Augustus was in the fetal position, his body blocking Alexis's. The air smelled like sweat, like pain.

Shit, he could feel everything.

I gingerly lowered myself onto the edge of the bed. The mattress jostled and Augustus sat up, but Alexis remained sleeping.

"What?" I rasped out, not liking the expression on his face.

"Alexis—" Augustus dragged his hands over his face, twitching with the aftershocks of my pain.

"What?" I repeated, too exhausted to do anything else as I lay beside him.

"She . . . she . . . she . . ." Augustus was unable to finish his sentence as he stared down at her.

"She—what?"

He turned to me. "Alexis can feel our pain."

Static filled my head.

That would mean . . .

No. No. No. No. No.

I'd just been tortured; *she'd* been tortured.

I was free-falling. Plummeting.

"Breathe!" Augustus's voice warped above me as black spots dotted my vision. "Breathe, Kharon!"

There was a commotion as someone fell to the floor; it might have been me.

I blinked.

Augustus heaved me upright.

I blinked again.

Augustus forced my jaw open with his hands.

I inhaled air like a starving man. When I finally stopped hyperventilating, Augustus gently rested me back on the bed.

Alexis sat up, leaning over me—two-colored eyes wide with shock.

"Sorry." My voice cracked, agony pulverizing my soul. "So . . . *sorry*. Why didn't you . . . tell us?"

Soft fingers touched my cheek.

"Because—I didn't want you to worry," Alexis said with heartbreaking sincerity. "I'm strong . . . I don't need you to take care of me—I've been surviving on my own for years."

My vision blurred.

"It's all my fault," I whispered.

"No," Augustus said, his hand resting on the top of my head.

Alexis wiped the moisture off my cheeks, her thumbs shaking. "No, Kharon—we're in this together."

I reached up, my fingers wrapping around a golden curl. "Together . . . forever—promise."

She nodded, a tear spilling down her lashes. "Lacrimosa," she said under her breath.

I smiled. "From Requiem Mass in D Minor."

Her breath caught. "Wait . . . you know—"

"Mozart? Carissima . . . I'm a *pianist*." I coughed. "Of course I do."

Alexis stared down at me like she'd never seen me before. I tried to tell her how perfect she was, but I could no longer find my voice.

"Shhhh." Alexis kissed my forehead. "Sleep . . . heal."

Nodding to let her know I understood, I mouthed, "I love you," but no sounds came out. Defeated, I closed my eyes.

"*Familia*," Augustus whispered. *Family.*

"I love you both so much," Alexis said, then she whispered into my ear, "You're my Piano Concerto No. 20 in D Minor."

Tears leaked down my face.

It was Mozart's most romantic composition.

Turning, I pulled Alexis against my aching body and held on to her as Augustus wrapped around us both.

I could only sleep when she was in my arms.

SGC Day 12

*B*ang. Bang.

"Time to head to the arena," guards shouted.

I peeled open swollen, crusted eyes and looked around. In the middle of the night, I'd once again pulled Alexis across me like a blanket.

Her heartbeat pounded against my chest.

"Where's Augustus?" Alexis shifted as she rolled off me, and I fought the urge to grab her and pull her back.

Wait, why didn't he wake us up?

A muffled voice bellowed, "Three minutes!"

Swearing, Alexis and I dressed quickly.

As the guards led us through the stone labyrinth, I clutched the back of Alexis's neck, stroking her necklace to soothe myself.

When we were led out into the stands, bright sun blinded me.

The air was warm. The scent of grass, fresh flowers, and earth filled my nose.

Alexis didn't move away like she had the last few days. We sat together behind Drex, Charlie, and Helen.

The youngsters recoiled as they saw my face. My bruises must look gruesome.

I gave them a sheepish smile. It was hard to be upset.

Tender emotions washed over me as I inhaled the scent of clean soap, soaking up Alexis's presence. She was holding my hand, touching me, choosing me—she *loved* me.

Nothing else mattered.

The crowd clapped with excitement as Augustus walked onto the sands holding a sword and wearing no armor. In contrast, Poco stood on his shoulder, fluffy gray belly protruding, his teeth bared, wearing a silver chest plate and matching Spartan helmet—he was in full battle regalia.

Static crackled as Zeus announced Augustus had two rounds and six labors.

The stadium hollered with excitement.

Augustus tensed, both hands gripping his sword, a strange expression on his face.

He looked . . . *cold*.

The gate opened—sweat dripped down my spine, memories of Typhons playing—Alexis squeezed my hand, and I focused on her touch.

ROARRRRRR.

Four Minotaurs charged out, already fully shifted into beasts with monstrous snouts, curling horns, and thick hooved legs.

They charged with axes held high in their powerful arms.

Gasps echoed.

It was an *extremely* aggressive first round, and labors usually didn't repeat. Achilles had already faced Minotaurs. This didn't make any sense.

The leaders must have agreed with my assessment, because all of them stood up.

Hades bellowed something at Zeus, but I couldn't hear what, because Alexis's thumb was slowly stroking the top of my hand.

Augustus didn't move; he just stared at the beasts.

Chthonic blood filled his eyes—droplets spilled over like tears.

"KNEEL." His voice, warped and deep, not his own, exploded through the stadium.

Thump.

Thump.

Thump.

Thump.
All four Minotaurs fell to the sand, their hairy bodies limp. Beastly eyes glazed over.

The crowd got to its feet, unable to believe what they were seeing. Everyone leaned forward, jockeying to get a better view.

Augustus took a step toward them. "DIE!" His voice was unforgiving.

Pop—Minotaur eyeballs exploded from their skulls. Brains poured out of their oversized ears.

There was a moment of dead silence, then the stadium erupted. "BEHOLD THE HEIR . . . BEHOLD THE HEIR . . . BEHOLD THE HEIR!" Sparta screamed wildly, losing their minds at the display of sheer power.

Zeus scowled. "*Second round!*" Sparks fell from his lips, his lion growling at his side.

The gate lifted.

More of them?

Two monstrous Minotaurs appeared in the dark—taller than the others, they towered above the sands, both the size of a Cyclops—they were fully shifted.

The axes gripped in their hands were larger than Augustus's body.

Hooves touched onto sand as they stepped forward and—

Augustus gently covered Poco's eyes.

THUD.

Both Minotaurs lay dead.

The crowd gasped again with shock, but this time, they fell silent and stayed that way.

What is he doing?

Augustus always held back the strength of his true power. If the Olympians knew how strong he was, it would put a target on his back.

They would try to constrain him, just like they did Achilles.

He'd just risked *everything*.

Zeus glared down at Augustus from his podium.

The Chthonic leaders clapped respectfully, but their faces were pinched—he'd revealed his hand—he was *supposed* to be the diplomat.

From the nervous murmuring in the coliseum, no one in Sparta would think of him that way again.

Poco let out a mighty screech, the noise echoing as he banged his tiny black hands against his chest plate.

Augustus smiled at his antics.

They made quite the sight—a monster and his dressed-up raccoon.

Augustus stopped and turned to our section of the stands. He shielded his bloody eyes from the sun and put a hand on his heart.

"What . . . is he doing?" Alexis asked.

I swallowed thickly, fingers curling around hers.

"This was—" I struggled around the lump in my throat "—all for you."

"What?"

"Augustus . . . revealed the full extent of his power—to keep you safe. He ended it quickly so the Minotaurs couldn't hurt him, *nor* you . . . It was all so you wouldn't feel his pain."

Alexis looked around the stadium. "But now they're afraid of him." Her voice was small, unsure.

I brought her hand up to my beating, blistered heart.

"He doesn't care about them," I said. "You're all that matters to us."

Gratitude for him swelling, I nodded down at Augustus.

Alexis's fingers trembled in my grip.

Soon . . . it would be her turn to fight.

Lifting her hand up to my mouth, I softly kissed each of her knuckles.

She was going to be okay.

She has to be.

If not, we were going to war.

43

The 12 Labors of Hercules

Alexis: SGC Day 13

Fists banged on the door as Olympian guards shouted something.

My eyes shot open.

Phantom aches coursed along my limbs.

Torchlight burned low, shadows dancing across the blood-streaked empty bed. "Augustus . . . Kharon?" I called out, searching the darkness.

No one answered.

Fluffy Jr. whined as he stumbled to his feet. He was alone on the floor. Poco and the hellhounds were also missing.

They wouldn't abandon me . . . not now. Not right before my labors. Not on the most important day of my life.

"Let's go!" a guard yelled outside.

Something is very wrong.

Heart racing, I stumbled on strangely sore legs into the bathroom and threw icy water onto my face. Monochrome eyes stared back at me, full of panic.

"HURRY UP!"

I hastily braided my hair down my back. Curls escaped around my face, and I patted them down with desperation.

A guard screamed, "One minute—and we're coming in!"

I shoved my feet into my boots, fingers slipping as I tied the laces.

The door creaked as it started to open.

I stood up, ready to go—

My eyes widened and I turned frantically. I grabbed my lucky calculator off the bed and tucked it into my toga pocket as I yelled, "Nyx!"

A sleepy hiss sounded from the pillows. Diving across the bed, I slapped until I felt warm scales.

"*No*—sleeeep," Nyx complained, as I yanked her up and wound her around my neck, heart in my throat at the realization that I'd almost forgotten her.

BANG.

The door slammed open and light streamed in.

A dozen guards waited. Titus and Alessander stood toward the back of the group. They made eye contact and opened their mouths like they were going to say something—whatever they saw on my face made them stop.

"MOVE." An older guard stepped in and pointed a sparking baton out into the hall.

I didn't need to be told twice.

Fluffy Jr. barked as he ran out of the room.

"No, stay back. It's not—" My jaw dropped. "*Jesus Christ.*"

The guards staggered out of his way.

Fluffy Jr. had seemingly undergone another growth spurt. His head was now at my chest, his body monstrously proportioned.

His back was still grossly distended, and he was in *no* shape to fight.

"Move!" A guard shoved me and Fluffy Jr. growled.

Boots pounded against stone, the guards stomping in synchrony in front and behind as they led us through the labyrinth.

Nyx slithered slowly around my shoulders.

We turned right down an unfamiliar cavern—it opened into a room with copper torches hanging from walls that were covered in silver.

"CHOOSE ONE." A guard pointed.

Weapons covered every inch of the walls: swords, axes, knives, whips, throwing stars.

We'd just started training with manual armaments—I wasn't particularly good at any of them.

You can do this, Alexis.

Shouts echoed all around; guards were surrounding me bellowing things; sparking batons pointed; my teeth ached from the proximity to voltage; Fluffy Jr. whined, his wet nose nuzzling at my face.

I hadn't even realized that I'd fallen to my knees.

Stop it. Get control of yourself.

Hyperventilating, I got to my feet. I gathered my courage, even though it felt like fear.

"What's the easiest weapon to use?" I asked Nyx under my breath.

"A spear," she hissed.

I yanked a long titanium pole with an arrow-like end off the wall.

Before I could even process my choice, I was shoved out of the narrow room and down a different labyrinth of paths.

The metal was cool in my hands, barely weighing anything.

The guards marched to a stop in front of me. They parted in unison, revealing a wide gate. Titus stepped forward and turned a lever. "I'm sorry," he said. "For everything."

"Shut up." I tried to ignore him. The gate slowly lifted.

Terror cracked my ribs, one by one, until my chest was concave. *Fuck me.*

It was the worst-case scenario—the day was dark and stormy. Wind whipped and clouds churned across the sky.

Discussion buzzed around the packed stadium.

"GO!" A guard shoved me forward.

I staggered out, Nyx tensed around my shoulders, and Fluffy Jr. raised his head high.

Whispers traveled through the stadium.

"HERCULES—TWELVE LABORS!" Zeus stared down at me from the end of the podium, long white toga whipping. He held his unholy scepter, the golden eagle sparking atop it.

You're in grave danger.

Zeus's lion roared beside him; cheers thundered.

In a trance, I walked until I stood in the center of the arena.

The stadium was staticky and warped on the other side of the force field—neon-green lines shimmered—my skin prickled.

The whispers morphed into a chant that spread until all of Sparta was shouting, *"Angelus Romae . . . Angelus Romae . . . Angelus Romae!"*

I hurtled into the past, the coliseum disappearing.

Augustus carried me against his chest as he walked through a Roman street. Rain splattered across my face and humans chanted, "Angelus Romae," as they reached out and touched my head. Kharon snarled at them, his head bleeding, as he hung on to Augustus. Bound Titans screamed behind us.

Augustus stared down at me—midnight eyes intense as he cradled me.

I blinked.

The present came back into focus.

I was standing in the middle of the Dolomites Coliseum with a spear clutched in my fist. The gate was rising again, and Sparta was screaming for blood.

Out of the dark, multiple shadows moved.

One, two, three, four, five . . .

"Oh, come on."

Eight oversized Nemean lions prowled out onto the hot sands—an entire pride.

The first round was only supposed to be *four*.

The Chthonic section erupted with outrage, but their shouts were drowned out by the growing stomps and chants. "ANGELUS ROMAE!"

Zeus stood at the edge of the podium, watching calmly.

I made the sign of the cross.

A hair-raising growl echoed and my gaze snapped back to the sand.

The Nemean lions were creeping closer, fanning out on both sides in a big circle as they got ready to attack me from all sides.

I gripped my spear with both hands and pointed it forward.

So this is how it ends.

Nyx slithered around my shoulders. "You stab them," she hissed. "I'll bite."

Fluffy Jr. growled back at the beasts, the sound as deep and terrifying as theirs. He stood about a head taller than them.

A Nemean lion tipped back its maw and roared.

Two charged forward; one at my back, and one at my front.

Fluffy Jr. sprinted to meet the one at my back.

Squatting, I raised my weapon.

I fought the urge to run for my life as a lion headed straight toward me—it leapt, flying through the air.

"NOW," Nyx screamed.

Crouching low, I raised the point of my long spear straight up into the air, arms shaking as I held it steady against the resistance.

Blood and guts rained down.

The lion's momentum carried it over my head and the spear split it from neck to navel.

It slumped onto the sand, twitching, gore everywhere. Nyx leapt off my neck—and the lion fell still. It was dead. "*Sorry,*" I whispered down as I clutched my spear until my fingers cramped.

The crowd went wild.

I hope it doesn't have a family who are going to be sad—

YOWL.

I turned—Fluffy Jr. had ripped out the throat of the lion and was standing over its dead carcass, his maw dripping blood. He pranced with glee atop it, pulverizing it to pieces. The hump on his back was also glowing. *Is it . . . moving?*

Another roar echoed.

Scales slithered around my ankle as Nyx returned to my side.

"Two down, six to go," she hissed. "Easy."

As if they heard her, three lions charged forward together. "I call the left one!" Nyx shouted, sounding excited. I turned to the middle one and Fluffy Jr. sprinted at the one to my right.

This time, the lion didn't leap.

It came to a stop in front of my spear and roared.

Internally, I was screaming in horror. Externally, I lunged forward at the beast. The lion stumbled back, fangs flashing.

In my peripheral vision, a lion dropped dead, convulsing. *Nyx.* There was a murmur of confusion from the crowd.

Roars and grunts sounded from across the sand as Fluffy Jr. fought.

Movement flashed and I scurried backward, waving my spear. A buzzing sensation scoured my hands. It was hard to grip my spear.

Oh god. The four remaining lions stalked forward, sensing the weakest prey—*me.* Golden coats gleaming, their maws were open and ready.

Backing away, I kept waving the spear back and forth.

They followed, playing with their kill, waiting for an opening.

This was how I died.

"Your power!" Hades shouted from somewhere nearby, the rest of his message drowned out by the shrieking crowd.

Right.

The power I don't know how to use!

Fuck me.

My palms burned.

The lions were approaching.

A split second of lost focus, and I'd be mauled to death. If I got close enough to bleed on them, I'd already be dead.

Movement flashed in my blind spot.

In slow motion, I turned my head to the side.

A lion was leaping straight toward me, paws and claws distended, jaw open wide—I hadn't seen it coming, there was no time to stab.

I grabbed my spear with two hands and held the bar up defensively, eyes closing.

Hundreds of pounds of beast slammed into my body—something slammed against my skull—I saw stars—teeth snapped at my neck—I held the bar up to its open jaw—teeth clacked around titanium—I barely held it back—drool dripped onto me—claws streaked across my side—I screamed—its breath was hot—teeth snapped closer, my arms giving out.

Weight slammed down and I was crushed into the sand.

Breath knocked from my limbs.

Everything hurt.

I throbbed, an aching carcass of agony.

I'll just rest here.

"I killed it," Nyx hissed from somewhere nearby. "*Move!*"

I shoved against the crushing weight, but it didn't budge. Panic set in. Tears of desperation blurred my vision as I wiggled and pushed. The beast didn't budge an inch.

I sobbed.

Pinned to the sand by a—

The weight lifted off and I gasped, sprawled limply. Everything was blurry, my vision a tiny slit.

I squinted as Fluffy Jr. dropped . . . a lion's leg?

He'd saved me.

It's a miracle.

Nyx hissed from nearby and Fluffy Jr. growled.

Three Nemean lions were still circling us.

Not a miracle yet.

Everything slowed as I lay spread-eagle in the sand—half comatose—my body weak from being crushed. A euphoric sensation washed through me. I was spinning with the earth.

I felt nothing.

"*Alexis . . . I'm . . . injured,*" Nyx hissed weakly from somewhere nearby.

Motion restarted, my hands were buzzing like they were on fire, the burning unimaginable.

Pain throbbed in my side. The stadium was chanting "*Hercules!*"

Nyx and Fluffy Jr. were in danger.

Get up.

They needed me.

Get up now.

Barely able to see, I rolled to my side, desperately searching the sand with my hands.

Something splashed as my fingers dipped into thick, viscous wetness. A metal pole was buried in it.

I squinted down.

I was lying in a puddle of my blood—my palms were coated in it—the tingling intensified.

A lion's growl echoed through the air and my hair stood on end.

Help them.

Fingers slipping, I gripped my spear and staggered to my feet; agony made me weak; bile dripped from my lips as I tried to breathe but heaved.

There was no time left.

Fluffy Jr. was nothing but a flash as he leapt, yowls and screeches erupting as he rolled through the sand. Jaws snapping as he fought a lion.

But I couldn't look over because two lions were crouched low approaching me. They were heading for the kill.

The sky darkened as storm clouds multiplied.

My fingers sizzled. If I didn't know better, I'd think they were on fire.

They weren't.

It was just in my head.

It was *always* just in my brain. I was so tired of the endless mental struggles and thoughts of death.

I was tired of being weak.

Tired of failing.

Tired of being defenseless.

Tired of being attacked.

Tired of fighting.

I widened my legs and pulled my arm back—a lion leapt with a gruesome roar—I threw my spear at it, and it let out a strangled yelp as it crashed down to the earth, skidding past me.

There was no time to dive and grab my weapon—the other lion was already jumping, headed straight for my throat.

God save my soul.

I bowed my head.

The lion slammed against me—stars exploded—pain was everywhere. Yet again, I plunged face-first into darkness. Back to where I belonged.

A gagging, choking noise echoed far away and everything went still.

Time warped strangely.

There was a bright light.

I tried to blink, but my right eye only opened the smallest crack.

I was lying on my side, staring into golden fur, gagging on sand.

Coughing, I spit out the dirty granules as I rolled onto my back.

The lion lay still beside me. It wasn't breathing, which meant it was . . . dead, and I was somehow still alive.

Someone had killed the lion—they'd saved me—they'd slain the beast.

A pleasant tingling sensation tickled my palms, streaming down my hands to my fingers.

The light brightened.

My left hand searched my pocket, and I gasped with relief as my metal calculator seemed to be in one piece. Kharon hadn't been joking about it being bulletproof.

Chuckling, feeling half dead, half alive, I tipped my chin back and looked around for my savior. *Augustus, Kharon, Hades, Persephone?*

The lightness slowly dissipated.

No one else was present.

I frowned.

I was all alone, spread-eagle in the middle of the arena, lying on blood-drenched sand as clouds scudded across the leaden sky.

There were entrails all around—I was surrounded by dead lions.

Fear sank teeth deep into my throat.

Thoughts broken—nothing made sense—I looked down, searching for an answer.

For a reason.

Who saved me?

I tipped my head to the side, sticky curls falling away as I glanced down.

The bronze skin of my arm was unblemished, and it was all the same, my bicep, elbow, forearm, hand, and fingers—I gasped as I turned my right hand over.

Oh, my fucking god.

I sat up and scrambled back, kicking desperately at the sand, but the mirage didn't disappear. The heavy weight in my hand prevailed.

It's not a miracle at all.

Father John would not like this.

No one had appeared; no one had saved me; no one else had slaughtered the beast.

A throbbing sensation pulsed through my swollen eye as I tried to open it wide and see better. I licked my cracked lips and once again turned my hand over.

I was holding an object.

A thick scarlet rod, with a wickedly sharp point and a ball at its wide end.

What the heck?

It didn't look like any weapon I'd ever seen.

It was also made entirely of crimson. I was holding a rod-like object made entirely of scarlet—*my blood*.

Bits of lion fur were stuck to the end, and I slowly looked across the sand. The lion that attacked me had its stomach ripped open. There was foam on its lips.

It was my blood.

My *poison*.

Overwhelmed, I opened my tingling fingers.

Midair, the rod melted—a pool of smoking blood spread across the sand where I'd dropped it.

In slow motion, with prickling fingers, I knelt to the pile of sizzling blood.

My face reflected in it, one eye swollen and black, barely parted, the other an unseeing white.

I didn't recognize myself.

The tingling intensified as my fingers grazed the viscous liquid—blood hardened and reshaped—I grasped the rod.

Once again, one end was sharp, and the other was round. It was heavy and thick in my hand, like a staff that was meant to be held high, not a weapon to be wielded.

What . . . is this?

A pained whine echoed, and Fluffy Jr. stumbled to his feet, staggering toward me—the white fur of his face was stained red. Deep claw marks riddled his body.

I reached for him with my left hand.

There was an explosion of sound, sand vibrated beneath my boots, my left ear rang with awful feedback, and I tripped, disoriented as I looked around for the source.

It took a second to realize that it was coming from the stands.

Sparta was on their feet, cheering.

Their bodies warped beyond the humming electric force field.

"Hercules . . . Hercules . . . Hercules . . . Hercules!"

Zeus was staring down from his podium, sparks leaping around his scepter. His lion was lying on its belly, its head averted from the arena.

Fluffy Jr. collapsed at my feet and my panic increased as I realized why I felt so alone.

"NYX?" I shouted, unable to hear myself over the roaring stadium.

Sand moved near my feet and there was a faint hissing sound.

Cool, bloody scales slithered slowly around my leg.

I bent down. "Are you okay?" I screamed, barely able to hear my own voice.

"Little . . . injured," Nyx hissed weakly. "Sleep . . . need . . . heal." I caught every couple of her words.

Warmth dripped down my leg where she held on for dear life.

I brought my shaking fingers to her scales.

She was bleeding.

Profusely.

I stood up straight, struggling to see through my swollen eyes, barely able to hear because of the ringing in my ears.

Icy terror morphed into something fiery and dangerous.

All of this was Zeus's fault.

Every.

Single.

Part.

I'd never hated, not like this, but now it was boiling me alive.

Eleven-year-old Alexis stood tall in a decrepit trailer and faced down two murderous adults.

I pointed the ball end of the rod up at Zeus.

Twenty-year-old Alexis faced down the murderous leader of Sparta. Humans worshipped him as a god—he was still just a man.

Zeus arched a golden eyebrow as he mimicked my motion, pointing his scepter down at me.

Do it.

Smite me.

Hades bellowed something—his fog filled the stadium—Sparta hovered on the precipice of war.

Mutually assured destruction.

Persephone screamed.

The crowd was wailing, fog multiplying.

Lightning flashed off in the distance.

"*I know what you did!*" I shrieked at the top of my lungs. If I was going to die down here, then he was going to know, and I'd take Sparta down with me.

The human world was already in shambles. Spartans didn't deserve to emerge unscathed.

Zeus's expression was unimpressed.

I kept the rod pointed at him.

Hades thundered something and Zeus turned—he recoiled as he looked around the fog-covered stadium.

Zeus lowered his scepter, pointing it away from me.

Slowly, Hades's inky power also dissipated.

Creatures and Spartans cowered in their seats—war was narrowly avoided.

Zeus turned back to the arena. "SECOND ROUND!"

The gate slowly lifted.

A familiar ungodly screech echoed through the arena.

Murmurs and gasps of shock chorused.

"HOW *DARE* YOU!" Ares's voice boomed.

"They are under INVESTIGATION!" Hades shouted. "WHAT IS THIS?"

Zeus's voice echoed around the stadium. "The federation has ruled this appropriate to test her might—she's defeated them before, she can do it again."

"YOU WANT WAR!" Hades responded.

"NO," Zeus bellowed. "I WANT WHAT IS BEST FOR SPARTA . . . This is on *her* honor—she must prove her might." He waved his scepter. "Don't . . . make me use this."

Absolute power corrupts absolutely. Lord Acton must have been a Spartan with the power of fate foreseeing this very moment.

Turning toward the Chthonic section, I shook my head no, hoping Hades understood the message.

This was my task, *my* revenge.

Fluffy Jr. whined at my feet, and Nyx was still unmoving, wrapped around my leg.

Agony throbbed. My field of vision was rapidly diminishing.

The gate lifted fully.

Acceptance washed over me—I'd found my limit—there were no emotions left to feel.

Screeeeeech.

44

The 12 Labors of Hercules Continues

Alexis

The sound filled the coliseum.

Abject fear rooted me to the spot.

Spartans screamed in terror.

Fluffy Jr. twitched next to me, whimpering as his hump glowed brightly.

Two blurry monsters stomped out of the darkness, objects protruding from their backs.

Titans.

Jagged wings jutted from their backs, and golden tags were threaded through their lips. It was the same two Titans I'd fought in Rome.

They were once again unchained.

Is this why the federation had us tag them? Was this their plan all along?

There was no doubt left in my mind—Zeus was trying to eliminate me.

Everything was fuzzy, colors bleeding together. I gripped my calculator in my pocket and clutched the strange rod in my other hand.

Screeeeeech.

The Titans unhinged their jaws, their eyes locked solely on me.

I stared back, face throbbing in time with my heartbeat.

RIPPPP.

The Titans hadn't moved.

In slow motion, I looked down—the sound had come from Fluffy Jr.

RIPPPPP.

The lump on his back had split down the center. Something was . . . emerging?

The Titans shrieked in unison, leathery wings flapping.

My head shot up.

Sweat dripped down, stinging my swollen eyes. Visibility worsened. For a second, everything went dark. I shook my head to clear my vision.

Patchwork wings spread wide as both Titans leaned forward, ready to attack.

Fluffy Jr. howled as he kicked sand at my feet, another ripping sound echoed, but I didn't have time to look down.

I raised my arm and pointed the sharp end of the bloody rod up at the beasts.

The Titans screeched.

I was already running, sprinting across the sand—rod held high.

Wings flapped and they shot toward me, flashes of black.

Lungs heaving, my side throbbing, I pumped my legs, sand spraying as I sprinted with all my might.

Air whistled.

I dodged swiping talons and swung the heavy rod with both hands like a baseball bat.

White-hot agony scoured my already ruined side as their

talons sliced at me—they screeched in my face—I screamed back. Our pitch was flat. *Mozart would not have loved this.*

Black wings beat loudly as all three of us stumbled—I'd clipped both of them with my swing, and pain was exploding inside my chest as my power activated. My blood was inside them, *devouring.*

The Titans fell to their knees, foam streaming from their lips.

I clutched at my side—sticky blood poured from deep talon grooves that aligned perfectly with lion claw marks, coating my fingers in liquid.

The Titans' gurgles quieted, ligaments snapping as they looked up at me in unison.

Eighteen-year-old Mary Shelley winked at me as she penned Frankenstein.

I backed away.

There was nowhere to run—the steel gate was still lowered. The round wasn't over, and electric lines hummed above—I couldn't leap away.

My wounds throbbed.

I was losing too much blood.

I stumbled across the bloody sand, away from the monsters, and my own failings—toward Fluffy Jr.—grunting through the pain.

The stadium was dead silent.

Dropping my rod—it sizzled into a puddle of blood—I fell to my knees beside Fluffy Jr., twisting so I didn't put pressure on Nyx.

He was still collapsed on his stomach, panting heavily.

Mucus and . . . something pointy was sprawled behind him. Half covered in sand, it was impossible to tell what it was with my limited vision.

I didn't have time left to figure it out.

I clutched at his muzzle and peppered kisses across his face.

"*I love you. I love you, I love you,*" I whispered, the mantra falling from my lips, tears pouring from my eyes.

Titans screeched behind me.

I ran my hand down my leg, across Nyx's blood-crusted scales. Words, whispers, pleas—I wasn't even sure what I was saying.

As a child, I'd always thought I'd die in the cold, alone in Montana, surrounded by monsters of the human variety, starved and weak, all alone.

Instead, I would perish loved by many, and my death would start an apocalyptic war—both thoughts were comforting.

I dipped my fingers into blood, and a rod solidified in my palm. I planted it into the sand and hoisted myself up, leaning against Fluffy Jr.

Better to die fighting monsters, than to live cowering at their feet.

Something soft moved against my side.

Oh my god.

Fluffy Jr. rose to his feet with a loud flapping noise—he towered above me, his head taller than mine. He opened his mouth, and the sound that rumbled out was straight from my memories.

It was the terrifying noise from the back of the menagerie.

Flaps echoed, appendages moved, bright blue feathers shimmered.

Fluffy Jr. bellowed louder—majestic wings protruded from his back.

Mother of God.

Goose bumps exploded across my body.

Augustus had been wrong.

Fluffy Jr. *was* one of the rare creatures who molted, and he'd just grown *wings*—they were stunning shades of sparkly blue, straight from lore.

I *had* in fact bonded with a horse, and it all made sense, he *really* wasn't the brightest.

He was a half-breed—part dog, part Pegasus.

His wingspan was at least thirty feet, bigger than the Titans, his feathers glorious.

Fluffy Jr. tipped his head low, as if he was asking me if I was ready, determination and love strumming through our bond.

His intentions were clear.

He bent his body low onto the sand so I could climb on. Holding my blood rod out so I didn't accidentally cut him, I mounted his back.

I sat at the base of his thick neck, straddling him like a horse.

He rose up to his full height.

Wings flapped downward, air whooshing—we jerkily flew up above the blood-soaked sand.

From my higher vantage point, the world moved in slow motion.

Zeus was standing at the end of his podium, donned in white, holding his scepter—Hades had moved and now stood with Cerberus, blocking Zeus's path, black toga trailing, fog swirling at his feet.

Gods of a golden era—facing off—in these tragic modern times.

Both were frozen, their heads tipped back as they watched me.

"*Behold.*" Hades's voice strummed with pride as he raised his arms wide. "*The* heiress to the illustrious House of Hades!"

Zeus flinched.

Make Sparta fear you, daughter.

Shrieks echoed as both Titans rose from the sand to meet us in the air—their black patchy wings unfurled wide, and they hovered, toes dragging across the sand—Fluffy Jr. barked, a thunderous, booming warning.

Luminous wings beat faster around me.

The crowd gasped.

We rose higher until we hovered just below the dome of the electric grid.

The Titans matched our height, hovering fifty yards away, monsters in the sky.

Power deserves to be seen.

Far, far away, a little girl freed herself from a rope outside a dilapidated trailer. She ran into the woods, climbed under a fence, and collapsed into a field of wildflowers.

I raised the rod up high.

For her.

Pleasant humming buzzed along my palm.

Shakily, I got to my knees.

I planted my feet and slowly stood up in the middle of Fluffy Jr.'s thick back, rocking back and forth to keep my balance, as his wings flapped.

Gasps echoed.

"Angelus Romae!" people called out from every direction.

Screeeeeech.

I pointed the end of my rod at the Titans.

They shot toward me, a blur of black.

Everything slowed as blood lust pounded through me, my senses heightening.

I raised my rod and, once again, swung—one Titan screamed, slashed mid-flight. Agony exploded inside my sternum as it dropped like a rock toward the sand.

The other Titan dodged my swing. It turned around midair and streaked toward me.

I leapt forward.

Legs wide, rod extended.

Suspended over free air, I slammed into the remaining Titan.

Everything blurred.

Talons scoured my side. Shrieks echoed. I stabbed it with my rod.

We careened to the side, its patchwork wings struggling to keep the two of us up as I ripped downward with all my might, dragging my rod through its innards.

Air whistled. The sand approached.

The classic Euclidean problem: What is the closest distance between two points? *A straight line.*

Pressure exploded as we slammed into the sand in a tangled roll.

The world went still.

A loud ringing muffled both of my ears.

Peering groggily through my obstructed eye, everything was fuzzy and out of focus.

I was lying on my side.

Nyx moaned miserably as she shifted around my leg.

A Titan lay limp beside me—a crimson rod was protruding from its open stomach; black blood was everywhere. I was covered in it.

I rolled onto my side, clawing at the sand. I pushed and heaved, fighting gravity.

Thud.

Fluffy Jr. landed beside me.

In a blur of white, he ripped off the Titan's head—bones crunched and snapped—he tossed it in the air and swallowed it whole.

"Good doggie," I whispered, digging my fingers deeper into the sand and grabbing my bloody rod with both hands—I yanked it out of the downed Titan.

Hunched over, gripping my side, I barely stood upright.

Agony was a living, throbbing beast.

The arena was spinning.

Fluffy Jr. tipped his head back and howled. The muffling in my ears split; the loud sound filtered in.

The world snapped back into motion.

I scanned the arena with my sliver of vision. Both Titans lay decapitated, organs strewn across the sand.

Nyx moaned in pain.

Her scales were freezing cold around my leg.

Please God, please heal her.

"You're going to be okay," I whispered, willing it into existence as I gently pulled her off my leg, holding her in one hand, and the rod in the other.

Dark scales shimmered into existence. A long slice mark had split her body almost in two. She was covered in blood.

I gasped and Fluffy Jr. whimpered beside me.

"Love you . . . kid," Nyx hissed weakly.

"No." Tears poured down my face as I bowed my head and prayed, clutching her to me, waiting for someone to save her.

Scales grew colder against my skin.

My fingers tingled.

The pain in my heart was worse than anything I'd ever experienced when I'd activated my powers. I sank to my knees. Sobbing.

I brought my rod next to my heart beside Nyx, bowed my head lower, and prayed harder, cradling them both.

The tingling in my hands intensified—sharp pain skewered my sternum.

A familiar bright light emanated from my fingers, and the scarlet rod also lit up with a golden glow. It warmed beneath my touch, the circular end shining brighter than the sun.

Scales vibrated where they touched the rod.

Snake skin slowly knit itself back together.

Seconds later, Nyx reared her head back, her body fully healed, as tears of relief streamed down my face.

"So warm," Nyx hissed as she slithered out of my grasp and wrapped her scales fully around the rod, shuddering with relief, her eyes closed. "I've seen this before . . . in a dream."

Gray clouds parted as the heavens opened up, golden rays streaming down.

Climbing slowly to my feet, I raised the glowing staff up to the sunlight—Nyx's black scales shimmered against it in stark relief.

Fluffy Jr. stood up to his full height and unfurled his wings.

A gasp tore from my throat.

It was the crude symbol Ceres had shown me in her book on predestination. The one that had disappeared from the page. The line with a circle was the staff, the squiggle a snake, and what I thought were clouds were *wings*.

"*Radius Asclepii!*" someone shouted, awe in their voice.

I choked on a sob.

Everyone knew the story behind the famous Spartan healing symbol.

The wings represented creatures, the snake Chthonics, and the glowing rod Olympians.

Hades was Chthonic. Persephone was the daughter of a dark creature and Demeter.

My heritage was all three.

I raised the Rod of Asclepius up into the light, Fluffy Jr.'s wings raised high on either side.

The ancient symbol of healing—of life and death—was mine to wield.

45
WHO DID THIS TO YOU?

Alexis

Right eye partially shut, my vision was nothing but a sliver—darkness closing all around.

In my hand, the glowing Rod of Asclepius was warm, a myth in the flesh, composed of writhing, poisonous blood. The same blood ran through my veins, dripping from the open wound on my side.

From the solemn heaviness in the air, I wasn't the only one that recognized the global symbol of healing.

Is this real?

Nyx went invisible as she slithered around the staff like she was born to do so; Fluffy Jr.'s wings framed it.

Destiny was a curious thing.

Did I choose them, or did they choose me?

"THIRD ROUND," Zeus's voice was jarring in the deathly quiet.

I tilted my head back, neck swiveling as I struggled to see.

Sparta stared down at me in silence.

"TWO MORE LABORS." Zeus banged his scepter down against stone.

Persephone and Hades were blurry figures standing together. I imagined they were smiling, watching me with loving pride.

Steel lifted.

Fluffy Jr. shook his head, wings raised, as he turned to face the gate.

Right eye throbbing, I raised my staff up higher and waited.

Let them come.

Two shadowy figures stalked out of the dark, heat forming a mirage of waves at their feet.

They headed toward me with their hands in chains.

Lowering my arm, I pointed the sharp end of the rod at the approaching monsters, ready to kill.

With my powers, I was a murderous healer—the duality of a woman.

The monsters approached, wavering in and out of focus, and I squinted, trying to see them better.

A gasp shredded my throat.

No.

Silver cuffs restrained their hands; bright sunlight created a haze around each of them.

Twenty-five-year-old Mary Shelley opened her desk, revealing a beating heart.

Everything blurred.

Augustus and Kharon stalked toward me.

I blinked—their shadows blocked out the punishing sun—they loomed above me, an arm's length away, scowling.

Up close, they were covered in bruises.

Kharon swayed slightly and Augustus stumbled, like they'd been drugged. They righted themselves, clearly fighting off the effects of whatever the Olympians had given them.

They glanced down at the staff in my hands, recognition flickering.

This can't be happening.

A booming vibration rattled as the stadium stomped, a chant starting up, *"Angelus Romae . . . half Olympian, she wields the fated staff . . . Angelus Romae . . . half Olympian, she wields the fated staff."*

Twelve House flags waved in the stands.

Olympians screamed at me to finish the men, as if they'd reclaimed Persephone, as if I was now one of them.

The ancient coliseum spun.

Kharon cleared his throat.

I looked away.

You just have to defeat them and render them unconscious.

I couldn't do it.

Memories played: *We held each other as we slept. Kissing. In the shower. On my knees. Them between my legs while I sat on an altar.* "I love you," they whispered, and I breathed back, "I love you."

"My carus," Augustus said.

Kharon worked his jaw back and forth, his eyes cold as he stared at my injured side.

Voices screamed all around, begging for violence. The greatest trick Spartans ever played was convincing humanity they were civilized.

I missed the nuclear wastelands of Montana.

"Alexis—*look* at us." Augustus's voice was hard as steel.

I couldn't. I was too busy shattering into little pieces.

Augustus's combat boots stepped closer.

I flinched, eyes squeezing shut.

"Wait," Kharon said slowly. "Alexis—do you think . . . we're going to . . . *harm* you right now?"

I took a shaky step back, and Augustus inhaled sharply.

Kharon swore.

Lethal emotions stretched between the three of us.

"*You will face us,*" a smooth masculine voice echoed inside my head.

It had come from within.

I'd officially made the final descent into evil—*possession*—only an exorcism could save me now.

As if in a trance, I looked up.

Blood covered Augustus's face, streaking from both his eyes; Kharon stood unnaturally still, his jaw clenching and releasing.

"Why?" Kharon asked.

"You have to defeat me," I whispered, the rightness of the words settling over me. "I *won't* let you get branded . . . not again. Not for me."

"Did you really think—" Kharon's lashes fanned across eyes so cold, they were more gray than blue "—that I was going to come out here and *fight you* with my bare fucking hands? The woman I love?"

I held his gaze. "Yes. Because I *won't* do that to the men I love."

Augustus stared at me in silence.

"Your pain is mine—you're my fucking heart and soul," Kharon said as he thumped at his chest. "Do you know what that *means*, Alexis? I would sooner die than see you hurt. I've given you *my* ear . . . What more do you want from me? What do you need me to do to prove to you that I'm madly in love with you? Do you want my heart ripped from my—"

"I *have* to be the one to lose!" I cut him off, terror and rage spreading like fire, leaving me desperate.

I spread my arms wide.

"*Defeat* me," I begged, the wound in my side throbbing.

Kharon shook his head as he backed away. Augustus stood still, unmoving in the face of my desperation.

"DO IT!" I screamed.

Neither moved.

"*Please,*" I whispered with a broken rasp.

Darkness closed in as my injured eye filled with blinding tears.

"We're sorry we couldn't be there for you this morning," Augustus spoke slowly. "They must have drugged us at the symposium. When we woke up, you were fighting already—we tried to leap through the electric dome—guards stopped us."

That was why they looked so awful, why I'd woken up with aching limbs.

"We're sorry we failed you," Kharon said with anguish. "This is all our fault."

Tears fell faster and I staggered into one of them. They righted me and I pulled away.

With my right eye swollen, I was fully blind.

I spread my arms wide again. "Just fight me!" I pleaded. "Just get it over with. *Please*. I love you—I *can't* do this."

Calloused fingers gently touched my face, restrained by manacles—I startled, not realizing he'd gotten so close.

"Alexis. Why are you acting like— Your left eye seems fine . . ." Augustus trailed off, air whistling through teeth.

He stilled.

A new sharpness expanded between us.

"No," Augustus said shakily.

"What is it?" Kharon asked, his voice getting louder as he neared.

Augustus didn't speak. His thumb burned where it traced against my skin. The pungent scent of ozone stained the air, as if lightning had struck.

"*It's* on the same side as your . . ." Augustus's voice trailed off.

Ear.

Kharon stepped closer so all three of us stood chest to chest. "What are you talking about? What's going on? Someone *explain*."

My tears stopped falling—a fragment of vision came back—Augustus was staring down at me like he'd seen a ghost.

"She's—" Augustus's breath hitched. "Partially blind."

"What?" Kharon stepped back, shaking his head, cuffs rattling. "No, that . . . that can't . . . *that can't be*. We would have known if—"

"It's true."

My voice sounded far away, like it belonged to someone else.

Neither man moved.

The stadium echoed with murmurs of confusion and shouts for violence.

Kharon lunged forward, his face hovering in front of mine, close enough I could see the silver flecks in his eyes.

"WHY?" he screamed, then his voice dropped to a barely there whisper. "Why . . . didn't you tell us that your left eye was . . . *blind*?"

"Because—" I cleared my throat. "I'm okay."

They looked at me with horror.

"I survived," I said, needing them to *understand*.

The crowd started shouting slurs, turning violent as they demanded the action we weren't giving them.

Kharon pressed his trembling lips to my forehead.

We breathed together, deep shaky inhales, for there were no words left to be said.

Augustus leaned in, resting his arms against mine, a mimicry of a hug, all he could do with his hands bound before him.

"THIRD ROUND!" Zeus's voice boomed, crackling with violence. "FIGHT OR YOU WILL ALL LOSE AND BE BRANDED." He slammed his scepter down on the stone podium, but the sky shone, clear and blue above. The stormy weather had cleared out.

The moment broke.

I pulled back, stumbling away from my husbands.

This was Sparta. We were Chthonics.

There was no choice—we had to fight.

"Defeat me," I said, waving the heavy rod through the air. Nyx was still invisibly wrapped around it. "Just do it. Get it over with. I can't . . ."

"Stab us both," Augustus ordered as he straightened.

"Excuse me?" I shook my head. "That's not—"

Augustus looked down at me with pity. "You *will* defeat us."

Kharon nodded.

There was no softness left in either of them. They'd donned their Spartan exteriors, the armor they wore to survive in this brutal world.

I wasn't looking at my husbands.

The eldest heir to the House of War and the Hunter stood before me, merciless, *unyielding*.

So this was how it was going to go.

Pulling back my shoulders, I straightened to my full height—matching their postures—the heiress to the House of Hades.

"Make me," I said.

Augustus shook his head sadly.

"*I tried to warn you*," resonated loudly inside of my skull.

Kharon bowed to me, like he was saying goodbye. "I love you." He turned to Augustus. "Handle this. Like we agreed."

What is he talking about—

Augustus's eyes glowed as he held my gaze—Kharon dropped to the sand behind him, boneless.

I cried out.

"*He's just unconscious*," the voice said as Augustus took another step closer, scarlet streaking down his face.

"You're . . . inside my head," I said with dawning horror.

"*My powers changed because of our bond.*" Augustus's voice was inside my skull. "*I can now . . . push my thoughts into others.*"

I heaved.

"*Now, wife, end this. Stab me with your weapon.*"

I shook my head. "But . . . but . . . Kharon's scars. He doesn't deserve any more."

Augustus looked down at me calmly.

"*He was never going to let himself win.*" His eyes were pools of crimson-filled darkness. "*Not against you—you know that.*"

"No." I stepped back, tripping over a dead lion, stumbling away from it, I used my staff to catch myself.

He followed.

"No. No. No," I repeated as I kept backing away.

Augustus stalked after me, chasing me across the sand with shackles on his hands.

Step after step.

A predator and his favorite prey.

His voice lingered inside my head like an intrusive caress.

There were no winners here.

I slammed back into stone—I glanced around desperately—Augustus had cornered me.

We were at the very edge of the arena.

Zeus's podium hovered high above us. He stood at the edge, peering down into Hell, watching us.

Nyx slithered off the rod onto my shoulders.

There was nowhere else to run.

Augustus loomed before me, his face stoic.

"*Alexis Hert,*" he commanded inside my mind. "*You will stab me right now.*"

"I can't." I shook my head desperately, needing him to understand. "My blood . . . it could kill you."

He pressed his lips together into a flat line.

"*You won't. You had your chance, and you didn't.*"

"But I could!"

"*But you won't.*"

"You don't know that."

"*I know you love me, and I love you—stab me. Now.*"

"I refuse!" I yelled at the top of my lungs.

"*I'm not asking.*"

There were no traces left of my gentle husband.

The House of Ares—the House of War—was brutal.

"But . . . but . . . but . . ." I racked my brain, searching for a solution, an escape.

Augustus struck, cuff rattling—he grabbed my right hand and wrist, the one that held the rod—he squeezed, his nails digging painfully into my skin.

"No," I whispered.

"*Yes.*"

He slowly rotated my arm until the pointed end of the staff aimed toward him.

Augustus took a step back, still holding my wrist in a punishing grip, the long crimson rod stretched between us, its end wickedly sharp.

"*Alexis Hert,*" whispered through my skull. "*I love you.*"

With un-counterable strength, he yanked my arm forward—straight into his heart.

I screamed as he fell to his knees, skewered on the staff.

Desperately, I yanked out the sharp end, touching it gently over the bleeding wound.

I focused on healing.

On the tingling in my hands.

The pain in my chest.

My fingers lit up with white light, the rod glowing brighter as if set on fire from within.

"*No, my carus.*"

Black eyes flashed as they opened—he smacked the rod away and it slammed against the wall in a sizzling splash of blood.

"No!"

"*The greatest honor I've ever known . . . is being your husband. It's a privilege to be branded for you. Thank you.*"

Lashes closed.

Reeling from blood loss and the shock of it all, I tripped over the sand.

Your hands are glowing—heal him yourself.

I stopped and turned back toward Augustus, pure panic making it hard to think. I didn't know if it would work, but I had to try.

"THE ROUND IS OVER," Zeus announced.

No!

He jumped down through the force field and landed right next to Augustus, holding Vulcan metal.

Too quickly, Zeus ripped Augustus's toga open.

Storm-gray eyes met mine as he plunged the brand down onto his unblemished skin and flesh sizzled.

Pure, unadulterated loathing filled me.

Guards swarmed out, picking up Augustus's limp body, and carrying him away.

I fell to my knees.

Nyx hissed and wrapped around my neck. "Don't look, kid," she whispered.

It was too late for me.

Without preamble, Zeus stalked across the sand. He ripped Kharon's toga open as he grabbed him by his dark hair and lifted his limp body up.

Zeus slammed the brand into his already mangled chest. I clutched my heart.

When Kharon awoke, he'd have another scar.

Fluffy Jr. growled as he stumbled across the sands, turning to stand in front of me, his wings tucked against his back.

Clutching my stomach, I vomited its contents, then I dug my hands into the blood-soaked sand and pushed myself to my feet.

I staggered upright, screaming at the top of my lungs, "I know what you did!"

Zeus stopped walking.

He fisted his hands.

"You're playing a game that you can't win," Zeus said, his back still to me. "If you don't make it to the gate, you lose."

He resumed walking away.

Choking on rage, I took a limping step forward, chasing after him.

One foot at a time.

A strange buzzing echoed.

It was clapping.

A new chant started, voices growing in strength, until Sparta was bellowing at the top of its lungs.

"*A hero is forged—behold, the twelve labors of Hercules . . . A hero is forged—behold, the twelve labors of Hercules . . . A HERO IS FORGED—BEHOLD, THE TWELVE LABORS OF HERCULES.*"

Finally, what felt like hours later, I stepped out of the harsh sun, into the shadowy hall of the coliseum, and collapsed on all fours.

Lying on the stone floor, I unzipped my toga pocket and pushed my hand inside—the graphing calculator was warm to the touch.

The odds were always in my favor.

I wanted to curl into a fetal position and sob for Augustus and Kharon, but I was still alive—I could still do this.

As darkness beckoned, my bloodline chanted my name. Hades and Persephone had made me in their image.

Zeus would learn.

I was the *heiress* to the House of Hades—and hellhounds, not lions, were the top of the food chain.

46
Interrogations

Alexis

Freezing water splashed across my face, and I struggled to breathe as someone pinched my nose. The pressure released. I coughed violently.

The room was dark.

Something cold dug into my skin—I shifted—chains were wrapped around my chest and legs, constraining me to a chair. My hands were at my sides, mostly free.

I was sitting in front of a metal table that was streaked with dried blood.

Skulls were stacked all around.

I'm in a crypt beneath the coliseum.

Marvelous. Not.

Nyx slowly slithered up to my shoulders, her invisible weight comforting. "Are you okay, kid?" she hissed, her tongue flicking against my cheek.

I coughed aggressively. "Hard . . . no." My face and side were still throbbing. "How about you?" I whispered under my breath.

"Your power," Nyx hissed with awe. "It healed me. There's no pain anymore—I feel amazing."

Not relatable.

Wiggling my shoulders back and forth, I dug my hand into the pocket of my toga and clutched my calculator with all my might.

"Alexis Hert," Zeus said from behind me.

I flinched, then sat up as straight as I could. "Call me *Hercules*," I said, cuts on my lips splitting open.

Zeus walked around the table, light crackling across his skin.

He stopped when he stood across from me, hands resting on the metal.

His scepter was gone.

The two of us were alone.

Perfect.

"*What* . . . do you know?" Zeus enunciated each word slowly.

I smiled. "Everything."

Zeus slapped his hands and leaned forward. "You're bluffing." Electricity warmed the stale air.

I held his gaze, face throbbing.

"Vyco," I said.

Zeus narrowed his eyes. "What . . . about him?"

"He was working for you."

"So . . . what?" Zeus asked slowly.

"At the crucible graduation ceremony." I cleared my dry throat, projecting my voice and reciting the facts that we both knew. "Vyco said there was a Titan attack at the House of Zeus during the federation meeting, and that he grabbed a baby and leapt away, there was blood everywhere and he passed out. When he woke up, the baby was gone."

Zeus leaned closer. "And . . . ?"

I inhaled deeply. Everything from this point on was my own speculation.

"He lied."

Zeus laughed, relief on his face. "Is that what this is all about—is *that* the secret you know?" He laughed louder, skulls rattling as his voice rang.

"There was an attack because *you* planned it!" I shouted my suspicions, gasping for air.

Zeus clutched his stomach as he laughed harder.

"*You* sent the Titans to attack the federation meeting. Not Medusa . . . You framed her. She didn't do *anything*. You planned it all so Vyco could KILL ME!"

I struggled against my chains, trying to free my arms so I could show him the scar on my chest. It all made sense.

"Vyco took me and the echidna he'd illegally bonded with—he'd *enslaved*—to Montana!" I yelled, fury mounting, because it was so obvious in retrospect. "But even as a baby I must have fought—he cut me and my blood got into his veins. I incapacitated him before he could finish the job."

Nyx's cool scales slithered around my neck. "Kid—I didn't know . . . you figured it out," she hissed with wonderment. "My oath. I can't hurt him."

"I know," I whispered to Nyx. I'd had my suspicions as soon as Vyco told his story.

Zeus looked amused, his posture relaxed.

He thought it was all genuinely funny.

"Vyco leapt away to get medical help." My dry throat burned as I continued. "He technically wasn't lying when he said he woke up and I was gone—I wasn't there because he'd *already left* . . . He'd left a baby—me—alone to die!"

Zeus's smile widened.

"Both the echidna and I were left in Montana."

He didn't react.

I gritted my teeth. "Tell me I'm wrong—I *fucking* dare you," I goaded him. "You *spineless*, weak, pathetic, powerless coward."

Gray eyes hardened.

"You're correct." Zeus made a mocking face down at me.

"But is that it . . . is *that* your big secret? Is that all you knew? All this time I've been worried, and that was all."

He resumed laughing.

I tipped my chair, trying to break free. "You framed Medusa and tried to have me killed—you *ruined* both our lives."

Dark memories played: a trailer park; foster parents screaming at me; fists being thrown; years of starvation; shivering in the cold as I lay awake terrified of every sound; a woman screaming for help as men assaulted her.

Zeus rolled his eyes. "Grow up. This is Sparta—*no one* cares about little girls."

I tried to kick my feet out, the urge to rip him to shreds burning me alive, but the chains held me tight.

"Well—this has been enlightening." Zeus rapped the table with his knuckles. "Let's move on, shall we?"

He stepped to the side and pulled the lever on the stone wall. A heavy steel door lifted, revealing a handsome male figure.

Vivid green eyes met mine.

Patro was surrounded by Olympian guards with sparking batons.

Zeus pointed at me. "Question her. Now."

Patro didn't move.

"Achilles," Zeus said simply.

A long second passed, and I thought he was going to disobey, but then Patro walked stiffly into the room, the guards moving in tandem around him.

He stopped in front of me.

I opened my mouth—

He gripped my forearm, hard.

Blood filled the whites of his eyes.

"Alexis Hert—Hercules," Zeus's voice boomed, skulls rattling together. "Do you know the whereabouts of Medusa?"

I tipped my head back to Patro, silently pleading with him.

"No."

Electricity sizzled as the silence stretched. Nyx stilled on my shoulders as she waited. The guards shuffled, jostling my chair because there wasn't enough room in the small space.

"Well?" Zeus asked Patro.

"She's telling the truth," Patro said slowly, his voice monotone and expressionless.

Zeus punched the table, and the metal dented. "Alexis Hert—Hercules, did you in *any way* facilitate the escape of Medusa?"

"No."

My bones creaked under Patro's punishing grip, and his eyes widened for a split second.

"She's telling the truth," he said, the corners of his lips curling downward.

Zeus stared at both of us distrustfully. "Are you sure?" He gritted his teeth. "Remember, if you're lying, Achilles *will* be incarcerated."

Patro stared down at me. "I'm sure. She doesn't know anything."

I winced as he clutched me harder.

Thank you, I thought silently, emotions choking me.

"We have the closing symposium to attend to," Zeus said as he fisted his hands like he was trying to get control of himself. "In the meantime, the guards will loosen her tongue—then . . . we'll come back."

It was a threat.

"Let's go," Zeus ordered.

Patro reluctantly released my arm, but he didn't leave my side. He glanced at the guards.

The unthinkable was written all over his face.

He was about to risk everything.

For me.

"I won't repeat myself," Zeus said.

"Go," I whispered.

Patro searched my face, a promise of *we'll talk about this later* in his somber eyes.

He opened his mouth, like he was going to argue.

I shook my head no.

His jaw clicked shut, face twisting with pain.

I smiled sadly as he slowly backed away, out into the corridor.

"Remember—" Zeus looked back at me. "If you attempt to leap away before the interrogation is complete, it's an act of sedition and the federation will find you guilty of conspiring with Medusa."

"So guilty of . . . nothing?" I asked with disgust. "She's innocent. We both know it."

Patro looked deeply unsettled.

"Don't worry," Zeus said, not bothering to deny it. "I'll be back."

The metal door groaned as it lowered, blocking them both.

Crack.

Their feet disappeared as they leapt away to the symposium, smoke billowing into the crypt.

The hatch door slammed against stone.

I was once again sealed in.

But I wasn't alone.

The half dozen guards were still inside—they raised sparking batons. One of them swung. My face exploded with agony.

Apparently, we'd reached the bludgeoning portion of tonight's program.

It was too bad for them.

I'd had enough.

"Kill them," I said.

Nyx hissed. "It will be my utmost *pleasure*." Her scales slid off my neck as she sprang forward.

There was a loud snapping sound, then a grunt. The closest guard dropped like a rock with a bite mark on his neck.

I struggled against my binds. *I'm so fucking tired of being tied up.*

Fingers tingling, I pictured the rod.

Nothing happened.

I needed fresh blood.

The five remaining guards looked at each other with horrified expressions as they waved their batons at an invisible enemy.

A second dropped.

"It's the girl!" Another baton slammed across my face, electricity scorching my skin.

Pain exploded.

I yelled out.

He stumbled back, screaming as Nyx attacked him.

There was a flurry of activity as the remaining guards focused on attacking me. Chains strained as I tried to shift in my chair and duck.

Blows rained down mercilessly. My nose crunched, blood splattering in an arc across the table.

I groaned, bright lights dancing in darkness as I struggled to stay conscious.

There was a flash of black.

Purple eyes.

Opal fangs went for the jugular.

The men screamed, pissing themselves with fear as Nyx became visible, and they understood the full extent of their doom.

"How *dare* you hurt her," Nyx hissed as she reared back.

The last guards shrieked, skulls crunching around them as they clawed at the stone walls.

Nyx struck fast, a blur of death.

Gurgles of pain echoed, raspy final breaths—then silence reigned.

It was a crime scene.

The guards lay still, strewn around crushed skulls and stones, their eyes wide open, full of fear.

Nyx slithered back up around my shoulders, draping across me like a scarf. "I really needed that." She sighed with satisfaction, her tongue flicking against my cheek.

I tipped my head back and gurgled, then leaned down and spit my blood onto my raised tingling palms.

A long glowing rod solidified in my hands.

I pulled my arm back until my hand was at the chain level—the razor-sharp point of the staff sliced through the metal like butter. I made quick work of the rest.

The chair tipped back, banging against a guard and bouncing onto the stone.

I cracked my neck with relief and stretched, wincing as the healing wounds on my side pulled, and my battered face ached unmercifully.

I dropped the rod, blood splattering across the floor in a steaming puddle.

"What's the plan?" Nyx hissed.

"Vengeance."

"I knew I raised you right."

There was no time to waste, so I pictured the symposium.

"Domus."

The world shifted.

A frescoed ceiling stared down at me, music blaring loudly.

I was on my knees, behind a column, in a dark corner of the symposium.

There were bodies everywhere, crushed together jumping with their hands raised. They were barely able to move.

All of Sparta was in attendance.

Music wailed as the three members of a famous rock band danced on a small stage, the lead singer screaming as he jumped around.

It's really happening.

I can do this.

I turned and gasped.

I was kneeling directly in front of two chairs: Augustus and Kharon sat before me, bound to the metal with ropes and gagged. Blood covered their knuckles, and fresh bruises covered their faces. Olympian guards stood behind them.

Their eyes widened.

"What the hell happened to you two?" I shouted over the thumping music.

They both stood up and pulled their arms apart violently, snapping the ropes that bound them, then they ripped their gags out.

"Hey!" a guard shouted as he swung his baton at them.

Kharon moved faster, snapping his head to the side, violently breaking his neck.

Four other guards lunged to intervene—Augustus's eyes filled with blood—all of them dropped to the ground, unmoving.

I blinked, staring down at the carnage. *That was quick.*

Kharon stepped over the bodies, and tattooed fingers cupped my face. "My sweet carissima."

"You can't just do that . . ." I stared down at the fallen Olympians. "They'll imprison you and charge you with—"

Kharon peppered soft kisses across my forehead. "Are you okay? Are these bruises new?" he asked into my curls.

"Angel," Augustus said as he rubbed my back, scanning the room. "Did they hurt you? Patro was going to tell us where you were held . . . We were waiting for him to come back before we acted." He waved dismissively at the prone guards. "I think I saw him over—"

"It's fine," I said quickly.

"Who left these marks on you?" Kharon asked. "Describe them all. Now."

"I handled them," I said with a wink.

Kharon studied me. "Wait . . . did you . . . kill them?"

I nodded.

His blinding smile transformed him from handsome to devastatingly attractive. "Oh, wife, do tell."

Augustus pressed a kiss to my cheek. "I'm so proud of you."

"I helped," Nyx grumbled on my shoulder. "Where's my thank-you?"

The screeching rock music brought me back to reality. I pulled away from them, taking a deep steadying breath.

"I need to do something right now," I said. "But I need you both to promise to *not* interfere . . . no matter what happens."

Augustus nodded curtly. "Whatever you need, my carus."

"No." Kharon raked his hand through his messy hair. "I'm tired of standing by while my fucking wife has to—"

Augustus yanked him back and nodded at me. "Do what you have to do . . . We'll be waiting. I promise . . . we trust you."

Kharon shook his head. "I don't tr—"

Augustus put a hand over his mouth and restrained him. "*We* trust you," he reiterated.

Love strummed through our marriage bond.

The urge to fall into their arms was overwhelming, but this was my plan—I'd done the calculations myself.

Before I lost my courage, I turned and disappeared into the crowd.

"Wow, that was *sexy*," Nyx hissed as she slithered around my shoulders. "I need to find four or five good men like them—only a harem could *handle* all this woman . . . if you know what I mean."

It was a testament to how stressed I was that I didn't react to her perverted ramblings. *Who would ever want that many husbands?* I could barely handle two.

Hunching low, keeping my face concealed, I slunk along the edge of the room.

There.

I saw my target.

Falling to my hands and knees, I crept the remaining distance. Heart pounding erratically, I was so close.

The floor bounced as everyone jumped in unison, fists held high.

I stopped on the edge of the dance floor, behind a vibrating speaker. It was a mess of chords.

Panic filled me.

Unfamiliar with advanced technologies, I'd assumed there would be one plug for the speaker. This was a complicated system, and the music was hurting my head.

I didn't have time to figure it out.

Sitting back on my heels, thoughts racing, I almost missed it.

A piece of tape had squiggly sea symbols written across it.

I'd heard about such a language—it was the writing of sirens. I focused on the letters, hoping it would work.

Slowly, they rearranged themselves.

Just like when I spoke siren, one second it was gibberish, and the next it made complete sense.

"Unplug this orange cord and plug into the USB port below. Love, Lena."

Arrows pointed with the instructions.

Please work.

Holding my breath, I pulled my calculator from my pocket, ripped out the orange cable, shoved the end plug into the port on the side of my calculator, and . . . I nearly passed out with relief. It fit.

The music shut off.

People grumbled and shouted.

The floor stopped vibrating as the jumping stopped.

Fumbling, I pressed buttons on my calculator, until I got to the saved recording logs. I pressed Enter on the last one, heart in my throat, sweat streaking with fear.

My recorded voice filled the room. "Vyco."

The room fell silent.

I stood up, stepping onto the speakers so everyone could see me.

Zeus's voice boomed over the speakers. "What . . . about him?"

"He was working for you."

"So . . . what?"

There was a commotion in the corner of the room as Zeus shoved his way forward, everyone looking around with confusion.

I was ready.

Pushing my right hand onto my reopened wound until my fingers were coated in blood, I held my hand out, and the glowing staff formed.

Nyx hissed as she wrapped herself around it, her invisible body blocked the light, creating a strange dichotomy of color across it.

I held the sharp end forward and guarded the speaker.

People gasped.

Whispers of "Radius Asclepii" spread through the room like wildfire.

Sparta stood transfixed.

My voice played over it, the conversation from our interrogation booming as I accused Vyco of lying.

Zeus laughed over the speaker. "Is that what this is all about—is *that* the secret you know?"

Gasps echoed around the room and people stepped away from Zeus as they sized him up. He stopped trying to push through the crowd, and instead he raised his hand toward me threateningly, as if he was preparing to smite me, but quickly dropped his arm like he'd forgotten he didn't have his scepter.

"She's lying!" Zeus shouted instead. "This is all a ploy."

"What is the meaning of this?" Athena yelled.

"This was the interrogation I just had with Zeus." I swung my rod as guards tried to approach from the side. "I recorded him!" They came to a halt, eyes wide as they stared, transfixed by the glowing staff.

Whispers grew.

On the speaker, Zeus laughed after I accused him of planning the Titan attack.

My voice shrieked over the speaker, full of pain. "*You sent the Titans to attack the federation meeting—not Medusa . . . You framed her—you planned it so Vyco could KILL ME!*"

Slowly, I pulled down the top of my toga, revealing the scar across my chest.

People gasped.

I made eye contact with Augustus. Blood dripped down his cheeks, and his mouth was tight with rage. Next to him, Kharon looked murderous.

My voice grew in strength over the speaker as I laid out Zeus's sick plan.

"HOW DARE YOU!" Hades bellowed from the far side of the room as my voice echoed, too loud in the quiet packed space. He and Persephone were staring at my exposed scar with horror.

The Chthonic leaders were all on their feet around them.

Inky fog was rolling through the room and people were whimpering.

"Shut up!" Poseidon called back. "I want to hear his answer."

Zeus looked around like he was trying to find a way out, but he wasn't sure what to do.

My crackling speaker voice filled the room as I goaded him. "Tell me I'm wrong—I *fucking* dare you. You *spineless*, weak, pathetic, powerless coward."

Zeus's voice echoed. "You're correct. But is that it . . . is *that* your big secret? Is that all you knew? All this time I've been worried, and that was all."

His crackling laughter filled the silent room.

Persephone let out a war cry.

Dionysus and Apollo were shouting something.

More gasps sounded and people whispered as they pushed back, leaving a circle of space around Zeus.

The guards backed away from me, turning to their leader with distrust.

"You almost started another war!" Athena shouted, her face pale with betrayal. "The dishonor."

Ares raised a sword.

My voice cracked over the speaker as I accused Zeus of ruining my life, and across the room, gray eyes narrowed as they met mine—they promised death.

Years ago, I'd seen the same expression on two people's faces as I'd stood in front of Charlie protectively.

Zeus's voice was loud and clear. "Grow up. This is Sparta—*no one* cares about little girls."

All hell broke loose.

Hades roared, dense fog filling the room alongside Artemis's glittering mist.

"Yessss," Nyx hissed with excitement. "Kill the lion!"

Pure terror gripped the symposium as every inch of the room filled with Chthonic power.

Spartans and creatures fell to their knees, pulling at their hair.

Only the Chthonics and Olympian House leaders remained standing, gritting their teeth as they withstood the onslaught.

Augustus and Kharon were shoving people aside as they stalked toward Zeus.

Screams crescendoed.

Fate stood up on a chair, waving a smoking pipe. "The federation has been betrayed—by Zeus!" she announced as the recording clicked off. She winked at me.

I spotted a familiar muzzle. Patro stood next to Achilles in the corner of the room, whispering something in his ear. His hands waved with urgency.

Shit. I knew exactly what he was saying. *I need to stop them.*

"BETRAYER!" Poseidon shouted, pointing at Zeus across the kneeling room.

Kharon and Augustus were nearing the exposed leader.

Zeus shook his head, eyes darting around with shock as the Olympian and Chthonic leaders closed in on him.

"STOP," Hades ordered.

Kharon lunged.

Crack.

Smoke billowed around Kharon.

The space where Zeus had stood was empty. He'd leapt away.

Bodies were prostrated all around.

The leader of the federation had fled.

I did it. I'd calculated the odds correctly—math had yet to fail me.

Fate tipped her head back, the pipe falling from her lips. Her voice deepened, reverberating through the room. "At this century's turn! All of Sparta applauds. The federation falls to the exposer of gods."

Hades's fog receded.

"The prophecy is fulfilled!" someone screamed, and once again, all hell broke loose.

In the yelling chaos, cracks echoing as people leapt away, Lena's pastel eyes met mine.

"Thank you," I shouted.

She smiled, disappearing into the stampede of fleeing bodies.

Sparta had reason to panic.

Just like Rome, the House of Zeus had fallen.

Persephone beamed across the room at me with pride, and next to her, Aphrodite tipped her head to me as she clapped.

My chest prickled.

A *crack* in my peripheral vision brought me back to reality—Patro and Achilles had just leapt away.

Crap.

I jumped off the speaker, Nyx slithered up my arm, and I dropped my rod to the floor as I pushed through the crowd.

"Alexis!" Kharon shouted. People cried out as he violently shoved them aside, trying to reach me.

"Kharon! Augustus!" I fought to get to them.

More screams echoed.

Finally—the three of us collided.

"We need to get to the villa right now. It's urgent—Helen's room!" I said in a rush.

Augustus nodded and grabbed both of us.

The world once again disappeared.

"*Ceres*," I screamed with warning as we landed amongst pink lace. "*Patro knows about you!*"

But the adjoining door was ajar, and voices were shouting in the other room.

We were too late.

47
THE IMPERSONATOR IS REVEALED

ALEXIS

Smoke swirled in sinister tendrils.

Starlight shone through the long windows, framing the towering mountain ranges that hugged the Lake Como banks.

Time slowed as I ran into the adjoining bedroom.

I skidded to a stop, books flying at my feet. Kharon and Augustus bumped against my arms as all three of us took in the scene.

There were strange symbols written with ink across the walls, textbooks were strewn everywhere, pages pulled out, their margins covered in drawings.

A male voice shouted something vulgar.

"This isn't good, kid," Nyx hissed from my shoulders.

I turned toward the noise, the throbbing in my eye and side increasing—three people stood in the corner of the room.

Ceres tucked her left arm against her body, hiding it under the long sleeves of her oversized purple T-shirt.

Her cheeks were flushed with anger.

Patro was snarling in her face, his right arm pinning her against the wall.

They stood toe-to-toe, shouting.

Achilles stood sentinel behind Patro with his arms crossed.

Ceres had recovered to a healthy weight, but Patro still stood a head taller than her, dwarfing her curvy stature.

"Snake scum," Patro snarled down at Ceres, his voice cruel.

There was a blur of purple—a loud crack echoed and we all gasped—she'd punched him in the face.

Patro touched his bloody lip. "Oh, you *bitch*."

Achilles yanked Patro behind him protectively.

"Better a bitch . . . than a coward." Ceres arched her brow, standing on her tiptoes to peer at Patro around Achilles. "You just hide behind him—he's your little guard dog. All you ever do is corner me and accuse me of things you have no idea about. You're all bluster."

At *little*, Achilles stood up straighter. At *dog*, he cracked his knuckles.

Wait, Patro's cornered her before?

"You have no idea how much worse I could be." Patro bared his teeth. "How *dare* you speak to him with such—"

"How dare *you*—" Ceres cut him off "—speak to me like you have some authority over me. You think you can just come in here and accuse me of—"

"I'm not accusing," Patro said. "I know what you are. I've always known you were a dirty fucking liar who needed to be—"

"You play the fool." Ceres pointed at him. "Careful, pre-determination doesn't smile kindly on those who spit in the face of people with the foresight to—"

"I know *all* about your kind," Patro said, and for a second, his face twisted with angst, then he masked it.

Ceres sized Achilles up, like she was debating taking him on, so she could throw another punch at Patro.

Achilles arched an eyebrow, daring her to try it.

"What's going on here?" Augustus's voice cracked like a whip. His voice startled me out of my shock.

"Move away f-from her," I said.

Achilles stepped back—but Patro lunged forward, and my heart stopped in my chest—his fingers tangled in her hair.

He yanked.

Pink tendrils fluttered as Helen's fuchsia wig dropped to the floor.

Long silky black hair tumbled out.

Rattling echoed.

Three pale serpents rose from her head, pink eyes bright in the candlelight—Gorgon snakes.

An ominous hissing sounded, and all the men went still.

The snakes slithered down to her chest, twining around raven hair. She raised her right arm to shield them.

Achilles's eyebrows rose.

"Hello again, my precious darlings," Nyx hissed in greeting.

The other snakes fell silent, turning like they were bashful.

Patro pointed at me. "You idiot! I thought I must have been wrong. There was no way that you *really* did it . . . but you . . . you . . . you freed her." He looked at me with betrayal. "*You're* the reason for the interrogations and—"

"I know you're not speaking to my wife like that," Augustus said quietly.

Kharon glared at Patro. "Apologize—now." He narrowed his eyes, but there was something different in his expression.

Hurt flashed across Patro's face. He'd been blindsided by the truth earlier, yet he'd still lied to Zeus's face for me.

He'd risked everything to help me.

I was in his debt.

"He doesn't need to apologize," I said with a sigh, and my husbands looked at me with confusion.

Patro threw his hands into the air. "Obviously—you freed MEDUSA! What were you thinking? She's a criminal!"

Medusa shook her head infinitesimally, as she silently begged me not to reveal her secrets.

I narrowed my eyes. *"They need to know what you went through."*

She shook her head harder. *"Please don't."*

Patro turned on her, radiating his signature haughty arrogance. "Why are you looking at her like that?" He spit at her feet. "Traitor."

Medusa's snakes rattled, rearing up from her head.

Kharon yanked me protectively behind him.

Smoke rose around Achilles's muzzle as he stepped up beside Patro, ready to attack.

"STOP IT!" I screamed. "You heard Zeus—she was framed, she's innocent."

Patro chuckled darkly. "*She's* Medusa." He said her name like it was the highest damnation. "A fucking abomination."

Medusa stepped up to Patro, poking his chest. "That's rich coming from the son of Aphrodite."

Patro reared back. "What's . . . that supposed to mean?"

"Oh—I think you know." Medusa bared her teeth. "Your House is known for its seduction and deceit."

Achilles glanced between them, then turned to me. "How could you?" he signed. "You put all of us at risk. You endangered Patro."

Hot coals burned my insides.

"What the fuck are you saying to my wife?" Kharon asked.

I signed back jerkily. "If you saw what I did, what they *did* to her, you would have done the same."

"Never." He slashed his hand violently.

"That's because all you care about in life is Patro," I said as I signed. "To hell w-with everyone else. Right?"

"Correct," he signed, nodding. "No one cares about her."

"I care," I whispered, my throat sore from yelling, from screaming at Titans, from fighting with Zeus.

Dizziness hit me and the floor seesawed.

Kharon grabbed my shoulders, steadying me. "I care," I repeated numbly.

Augustus rubbed my back soothingly. "How . . . did this even happen?" There was no condemnation in his tone. He seemed genuinely curious.

My legs gave out and Kharon caught me.

Achilles and Patro stood together, the former glaring at me, the latter still toe-to-toe with Medusa.

Gorgon snakes rattled.

Everyone wanted answers.

I took a deep steadying breath. "My last leap during the initiation hunt—I tried to get to Hades at Crete. But I was injured and . . . something went wrong. I ended up in . . . the Underworld."

48

MEDUSA

Alexis: May, One Month Earlier

I swiveled my head, vision blurring.

Before me, a tunnel forked.

One side led to a light; it looked like an exit. The other was dark—a woman's screams echoed down it.

"We need to get out of here—run, Alexis. Now," Nyx hissed as she slithered down my legs onto the floor.

With a deep steadying breath, I made my choice.

Stumbling forward, I half ran, half limped through the humid rocky corridor. Blood gushed from the bullet wound in my leg.

I ran toward the woman's wails.

"Do you hear that?" I whispered. "Or am I imagining—"

"I hear it," Nyx said.

Fear wrapped its fingers around my heart.

The floor was slanting downward, torches spaced out further, darkness rising. Pain throbbed through my calf, my knee, and my head.

I grabbed at the wall, leaving a trail of blood across the stone that had strange skeleton symbols drawn on it.

"Do you know . . . where we are?" I asked, unsure if I wanted to know the answer.

Fangs clicked together. "Prison."

"What kind of—"

"The Underworld," Nyx hissed.

I tripped.

A woman screamed at the top of her lungs.

Men laughed.

"We should help her," I whispered, not sure what I was even saying.

Scales coiled around my leg. "Hug the wall."

I followed Nyx's instructions, my bloody nails dragging along rock for support.

The cries were getting louder.

There was a dull light ahead, a break in the shadows where the stones opened up—steel prison bars were halfway up, like a gate had been raised.

I peered around the rocks.

A woman was strapped in chains to a titanium table. She wore a blue hospital gown. A metal box sat over her forehead and hair—a clear mask with a tube covered her mouth, attached to a strange beeping machine.

Green letters flashed across it: *Age stasis: twenty-one years old.*

The woman opened her mouth and screamed into the device, eyes squeezed shut, the rest of her body unmoving.

Two men stood at her midsection.

I swallowed bile.

They both had blond hair and short beards. Green fish were embroidered on their guard uniforms—*the House of Hermes.*

"Are you sure she can't feel anything?" one man asked as he grinned. "She sure screams like she can."

The other shrugged as he reached for her chest. "Who cares? The CTE has already begun."

Nyx coiled tighter around my leg, her fangs clicking together.

The woman whimpered and the men laughed.

I'd seen enough.

"Kill them," I said, but Nyx was already gone.

There was a clattering as one of the guards stumbled back, gripping at his neck.

The other brandished a Spartan gun and swung it.

He turned around wildly.

I took the opening.

Running forward, I drove my shoulder into his midsection. We slammed to the rock floor and the gun clattered free, but neither of us went for it.

Clawing at his face, he grunted as he used his larger frame to pin me to the ground.

It was too late for him.

My sternum was already exploding with pain—there'd been blood on my hands. *Die. Die. Die.*

He convulsed on top of me, foam dripping from his lips. He mouthed words as he choked, silently begging for my help.

I shoved him off me and climbed to my feet.

The guard pleaded for help, his twitches slowing.

I stood over him and watched.

A tumultuous nothingness welled inside my sternum.

He took his last breath and a dark satisfaction filled me, one I didn't even know I was capable of.

"They're dead," Nyx hissed, her scales sliding along my leg.

The room was splattered with blood.

A soft feminine wail filled the room, a hopeless fractured sound.

"I'm not leaving her here." I felt like my head was underwater as I bent down and pulled the keys out of the guard's pocket.

Nyx hissed, "Kid . . . there will be consequences."

A strange feeling gripped me—*fuck the consequences.*

"I don't care," I said, because I didn't.

"Then I support you," Nyx said confidently. "Move quickly."

The guard's key unlocked the woman's chains, and they fell free. Cautiously I removed the last constraint—the metal box at her head.

Rattles echoed.

Three pale snakes slithered out.

I stared at them.

A part of me had known exactly who she was.

There was only one infamous Spartan so powerful, she was incarcerated using Olympian age-control technologies. Excess measures were taken to keep her from maturing. To keep her from breaking out of the Underworld.

Medusa.

A violent criminal.

A traitor.

Synonymous with evil.

But the guards had been violating her, and my gut was telling me that she was just a victim of circumstances. I was too exhausted to question it.

Hades said I needed to claim my destiny.

Well, I was making my choice.

"*Hello*," Nyx hissed as she became visible, hovering in front of Medusa's snakes.

They rattled and hid under long tresses of black hair, shaking with fear.

I grabbed the tube of the mask, and yanked it off her face.

The machine beeped, its green lights flickering off. The screen went blank, and the whirring sound stopped as it powered down.

Medusa took a deep breath, her chest rising.

Long dark lashes fluttered open, pastel lavender eyes met mine, and her mouth opened—she slumped back, unconscious.

Before I could talk myself out of it, I put my arm under her shoulders and hauled her off the table.

Grunting, I staggered, carrying her out of the cell, down the stone hall.

She was just skin and bones in my arms, but my legs still wobbled. I could barely support myself.

"Follow me," Nyx hissed as she led the way through the infamous prison.

We turned a corner, and strange beasts flung themselves at titanium bars, roaring at us.

I barely heard them.

Each step sent agony shooting through my bullet wound; I dragged us both forward.

Clawed hands stuck out between the bars. Gruesome fangs flashed as creatures bellowed.

We were causing a commotion.

Crack.

Smoke filled the hall.

"Who's down here?" a male voice echoed, bouncing off the rocks. He sounded furious.

Mentally screaming, I looked around hopelessly.

There were prisoners reaching on either side.

Nowhere to go.

Nowhere to hide.

A spiky silver crown, glinting with rubies, came into view.

"Daughter—*what* . . . are you doing?" Hades stepped out of the shadows, eyes widening as he looked from me to the woman hanging limp with her arm draped across my shoulders. "Is that—"

"Medusa." I nodded jerkily, struggling to keep my balance.

The name hung explosively in the air.

We both waited for the detonation.

Hades tilted his head to the side, as if sizing up something he'd never seen before.

"She's the property of the federation," he said slowly. "She's held in their section of the prison. I have no jurisdiction over her. There's nothing I can do to—"

"I don't expect you to help." I cut him off, arm straining as I held her up. "This is all me. I'm *making* a choice."

I stared down at the floor, waiting for his censure.

The shouts.

The fists.

"I'll let you in on a little secret," Hades said quietly as he raised his hand toward me. "The House of Hades is known as the House of Death because when we feel passionately about something . . . we wage war. *Always.*"

Nyx slithered up my leg.

It took me a second, then I realized he was reaching his hand out for me to take.

"Welcome to the family, daughter." Hades's voice brimmed with pride.

I grabbed his outstretched hand.

"Domus," he said as the Underworld disappeared and we leapt to Crete.

The roaring villa fireplace burned bright on the far wall, and the sparkling night sea glittered with moonlight behind the couch.

Charlie and Persephone greeted us with expressions of shock. They immediately started tending to my wounds, as Hades laid Medusa down on the plush couch.

"I'll cover for you," Hades said. "We'll take you back to the training center and I'll say I found you here."

"What about . . . Medusa?" Persephone stared down at her with a tender sadness. "I remember when she was just a little girl."

"The federation will search here first." Hades's eyebrows lowered with worry. "We'll need to find a place to hide her that they won't expect. The safe houses will all be searched."

"I'll figure it out," I said quickly. "Just give me a little time to come up with a plan. Please—I'll come back for her as soon as I can."

Persephone, Hades, and Charlie all stared at me. Concern was written across their faces.

"I'll h-handle it," I whispered. "Please, trust me."

The moment stretched.

Persephone nodded first. "Okay—I'll prepare a room for her. And if the federation comes before you do . . ." She smirked and pet the dragon on her shoulder. "The island will attack them. Violently."

My mother was beyond ferocious.

Even now, there was a strange energy rising from the floorboards, as if the island was sentient and welcoming me back.

"Be safe, daughter." Persephone smiled at me, and I leaned forward, gratitude filling my heart as I hugged her tightly.

She smelled like lilacs and something fruity, *pomegranates.*

"Thank you," I whispered into her curls.

She squeezed me three times, in quick succession. "Anything for you, my sweet Alexis."

When I pulled away, Charlie was waiting for his hug.

I embraced him.

Hades cleared his throat, his eyes full of moisture. "We have to go."

With one last look at the sleeping woman on the couch, we leapt away. This time straight into the Chthonic medical center. Jars of body parts lined the walls.

Hades spoke in a hushed tone to the doctors, and I made myself useful by flopping onto a medical gurney and passing out.

Time spiraled after that.

I chose my mentors as my hunting partners.

The next day, I woke up in the villa.

It was the middle of the night, but I couldn't sleep because I needed to find a solution to the problem I'd just created.

A woman's wails echoed—and for a second, it sounded like Medusa—in a blind panic I followed the sound.

I stopped when I realized the woman in the dungeon was Ceres, the traitor who'd worked with Theros during the crucible.

As I stood in the damp dungeon, an idea struck.

A horrible, *brilliant*, awful idea.

"Did you . . . help Theros kill all those children?" I asked softly.

Ceres went still, eyes widening.

"Did you help Theros?" I repeated. "Yes or no?"

She didn't answer, her silence a damning omission.

Gathering my courage, I sliced my forearm open on a jagged stone, grabbed Ceres's chin roughly, and dripped blood onto one of the open wounds on her face.

Pain exploded in my heart and my fingers tingled with the strange pain.

"Did you assist Theros in killing all those children of the House of Zeus?" I asked.

She grunted in pain, twitching as my blood poisoned her.

"ANSWER ME!"

"It was my pleasure," Ceres spat as she writhed in pain. "They deserved to die the—"

Sharp pain flared in my sternum, and I let the rage free.

She gurgled, unable to speak as foam dripped from her lips.

Seconds later, Ceres lay limp.

I backed away.

It was all over in seconds.

"Fantastic work, kid," Nyx hissed on my shoulders.

I waited to feel . . . *anything*. This time, there was no satisfaction, only emptiness.

Regret welled up.

I shoved it back down—I couldn't afford distractions—I needed to stay out of my head. I was making choices.

Turning, pulling at my hair, my thoughts raced.

The dungeon was shadowy and ominous, magnifying the feelings of doom.

Tingling fingers pressed over my chest as I tried to physically slow the racing beat of my heart.

"Breathe," Nyx coached as I gasped in the dark.

"Alexis?" Helen whispered.

Jumping, I screamed.

Helen was kneeling on the stairway in a sparkly nightgown, holding a bedazzled Spartan gun.

"Do you need help? I woke up when you left and was worried. I saw you . . ." She looked from Ceres to me, mouth opening in shock.

I tried to tell her to go back to sleep, but all that came out was a pained sound.

"Let me help," Helen said.

I pressed blood-streaked fingers to my mouth.

"Uh," I whispered hoarsely. "I n-need t-to—" I took a deep inhale and tried again. "I need to remove the cuffs . . . and dispose of a body. I've done something—*big*. Bigger than this." I gestured at Ceres. "If you don't want to know, I totally unders—"

"Tell me. I want to help. You saved me from Theros . . . I'm forever in your debt." Helen pulled up her nightgown, revealing matching pink shorts. She tucked her gun in her waistband.

A few minutes later, Helen finished picking the locks on the manacles.

Ceres's body crumpled to the floor.

"Now what?" Helen asked.

"Now I'll dispose of the body and get Medusa," I whispered. "We have to make it look like we broke her out of the dungeon."

Helen nodded. "I'll get a wig and dirt to conceal Medusa's face."

"Will that be enough?" Copper flooded my mouth as I bit down on my cheek. "She's so much shorter and her eyes are a different color. The men will notice that—"

"Men *never* notice." Helen smiled sadly. "Trust me."

We hugged each other.

Reluctantly, I stepped back and hauled up Ceres.

"Domus."

Just like that, I was back in the House of Hades palace at Crete.

Medusa was sitting next to Persephone in front of the fireplace. Classical music was playing. They dropped their books and jumped to their feet.

My arms gave out—Ceres dropped to the floor with a thud.

Medusa's eyebrows rose.

"I n-need to get rid of a body," I said, feeling faint.

Persephone walked toward me.

I flinched.

"I'll handle it, daughter," she said gently, her amber eyes bright with power. "Don't worry. You came to the right place."

A long heartbeat passed.

Persephone opened her arms.

I collapsed against her, tears streaking down my face, as she rubbed my back soothingly.

That night I returned to the villa with Medusa disguised as Ceres.

The deception was complete.

49

FEDERATION MEETING

MEDUSA: TWO WEEKS LATER

The leader of the House of Athena raised her hand. She stood behind the speaker platform at the bottom of the packed amphitheater.

Her long brown hair glinted with decorative gold foil that matched her heavy laurel crown. As she moved, her white toga shimmered with layers of silk.

Athena cleared her throat. "I will be acting as the interim federation speaker because of these . . . *extenuating* circumstances."

A hush descended.

House leaders, generals, and distinguished creatures all gave her their attention.

No one knew how to react to the fact that their illustrious Olympian leader had admitted to attempting to murder a child (outside of the crucible—the distinction was key) and then had disappeared after being publicly humiliated.

On the far side of the amphitheater, the Spartans wearing lion crests all ducked their heads with shame.

The House of Zeus had fallen.

It was a glorious time to be alive.

"It is noon on the dot. This federation meeting is now called into session." Athena pointed up at the gold clock on the wall behind her.

I rubbed my eyes, but the clock stayed the same.

Oh no.

Not again.

The big hand was on the two, the small hand was on the twenty, and the second hand hovered right above it. It said it was two twenty-two.

Fumbling hastily, I pulled my small notebook out of my pocket and scribbled—*Athena announced it's twelve, but the clock behind her says 222. Third time this week seeing that number.*

Alexis glanced over at my book, and I quickly closed it.

When you saw things that other people didn't, you learned the value of discretion.

Athena launched into a speech about taxes and human resources, and as she spoke, a small glowing dot materialized in the air above her head, so tiny, I could barely make it out.

Act natural, keep it together.

Discreetly I looked behind me—oh, wonderful—all around the room, dots of light were flickering into existence above people's heads.

No one else could see them.

Alexis looked over at me again, her two-colored eyes narrowed, and I opened my mouth to reassure her everything was fine (it wasn't), but my jaw clicked shut—a strange glow also emanated above her curls.

She gently touched my arms, pushing me back.

I hadn't realized I was leaning toward her, trying to get a better look at the hovering light up close.

"Are you okay?" Alexis asked with concern.

No.

Three simple words.

As a previously incarcerated individual who'd been labeled clinically insane by Olympian doctors as a child, there was only one right answer.

"Oh yeah, I'm doing fine," I said as Athena continued monologuing about taxes and protected zones. "One could even say I'm *really* great right now. Fabulous. I've been doing a lot of research and reading. It's been very informative. Did you know the great Cyclopes rebellion of . . ."

I trailed off as Alexis grimaced.

Right.

Rambling makes people uncomfortable.

Act normal.

The problem with being a Gorgon, a Chthonic, an opinionated woman with the power of Fate, and a bookworm was that it unsettled people.

I was too passionate.

Too strange.

My existence was a walking red flag.

"I think I saw a fly," I finished lamely. "Above your head. Pesky little buggers. *Very* annoying." I waved my hand and pretended to crush a nonexistent animal.

Alexis didn't seem convinced.

"Now to our next manner of business," Athena announced. "The reason we're *all* here today."

Alexis reached out her hand and I quickly took it, wrapping my fingers around hers and shuffling closer. If she was alarmed by my proximity, she didn't show it.

Physical touch had always been my love language.

Murmurs echoed all around as Spartans whispered to each other.

"Snake scum," someone spat in the row behind me.

I didn't turn around.

Athena unrolled a scroll. "In the case of the federation versus Medusa—in light of new evidence, acting in my power as interim speaker to rule from the podium . . ."

The clock behind her was frozen at two twenty-two and the small glow on top of her head was growing stronger.

Everything was narrowing to this singular moment.

Alexis gripped me harder.

"Medusa is . . ." Athena's mouth moved with painful slowness. "Pardoned of all alleged crimes."

Holy Kronos.

Sharp and heady relief filled me. I fought the urge to pass out.

I was free.

After everything, I was really—

"On one condition," Athena said sharply.

I stiffened.

It didn't take the mystical power of Fate to know this wasn't headed in a good direction (heavy on the mystical because I had zero clue how to understand my powers, let alone *wield* them).

A rattling filled the air as my hair shifted—my snake darlings trembled—I shivered as the vibration traveled across my scalp and down my spine.

Alexis squeezed my hand with both of hers and my bones creaked. I tried not to show the pain on my face.

My creature heritage overpowered my Spartan genes: my stature was short and curvy, my bones weaker than other full-blooded Spartans. I wasn't built for war. I was built to read.

Athena smiled. "For the safety of Sparta, the federation requires Medusa to attend ROU, Rhodes Olympian University, and obtain a mastery in Fate studies."

The murmurs increased.

Wait.

That's it?

My snakes relaxed.

It was perfect, since I had no money to my name and was homeless as of next week.

Disowned by the House of Artemis since birth—Gorgon

traits were not acceptable, one snake would have been ignorable, three were unconscionable—I technically had no inheritance and nowhere to go. For the same reason I was rejected by Artemis, I had too much Spartan blood to be accepted into Gorgon culture.

Alexis acted like it was fine, but I knew the truth—I wasn't welcome at the villa. Patro was vocal with his hatred.

This was my chance to make a plan.

"Could be way worse," I said to Alexis. "I've always wanted to get a higher education, but as a Chthonic creature, there are limited options. This is *really* good. I can figure out everything I've been—"

"No," Hades said calmly a few seats down.

Uh, what?

A fresh wave of murmuring filled the federation.

"It will not be safe for her, surrounded by Olympians," Hades said louder. "Especially with . . . everything that's happened."

My spirits fell.

I'd somehow forgotten that I was Olympian enemy number one, and synonymous with the downfall of the great House of Zeus.

Years in prison really did numbers on a person's reputation.

Maybe I'll win them over with my natural charm?

Oh wait—I have none.

When I'd been put under an age stasis at twenty-one, I was known as the "talkative bookworm who sees things and everyone mostly ignores." I woke up in a world where *The Falcon Chronicles* labeled me a "violent, powerful, dishonorable snake-scum traitor in league with Titans."

It would have been iconic, if I wasn't too busy having panic attacks as memories of the guards rose up and—

Don't think about them.

Don't think about what they did to you.

During my lovely (hellacious) imprisonment, Gorgon relations had deteriorated, Titans had somehow mutated with wings, and war was brewing.

I leaned against Alexis, feeling unmoored. A calming, competent energy wafted off her, and, in her presence, it felt as if everything would work out. She respected me, listened to me, believed me. She valued what I could do.

Unlike the Olympians who framed me and the guards who—

Don't you dare think about it.

Alexis squeezed my hand like she could feel my spiraling thoughts.

She was my only tether to safety.

She stood between the panic attacks, the deep abyss of pain that I held in pieces around my heart, and the dark thoughts.

Alexis Hert was my hero.

"What do you propose?" Athena raised her brow as she stared at Hades. Ares and Artemis both leaned forward and murmured something in his ears.

I froze as the latter glared over at me.

Mommy? I chuckled to myself, then stopped because it wasn't helping my "crazy" reputation. Artemis disowned me as soon as I popped out with snakes, so I'd never really known the woman.

From the glares she was sending my way, I was lucky for it.

Hades nodded at them, then turned back to Athena. "The Chthonic leaders," he said with an air of authority, "will allow her to attend with the stipulation that two bodyguards are allowed to attend with her. They will board with her and stay by her side twenty-four seven for protection."

Bodyguards?

Shivers trailed down my spine as memories strangled me.

There was *nothing* good about a guard.

Athena pursed her lips like she was considering it. She

looked up at the rows of the amphitheater. "Does anyone have an objection to this proposal?"

Murmurs increased, more taunts of "snake scum" were shouted (unoriginal), but no one raised their hand.

Most likely because all the Chthonic leaders had turned around and were glaring up at the rest of the federation with expressions that promised war.

Since the peace between Olympians and Chthonics was *extremely* strained after Zeus's revelation (I could already smell the trench foot and hear the battle chants), they probably weren't bluffing.

Athena looked back to Hades. "Who do you recommend?" she asked.

Hades slowly smirked. "The Crimson Duo."

There was a long moment—then loud conversation erupted.

Alexis blanched beside me.

"Who's that?" I asked, as someone shouted something from the back row.

I wasn't up-to-date with the modern Spartan lingo because of my violent imprisonment. The age stasis ensured I wasn't conscious for the incarceration—and was physically only twenty-one—which was why my powers were still weak in their development.

Somehow, even though my body had been in stasis, my mind remembered . . . *everything.*

There was also the horrible throbbing pain in my left arm that I refused to show anyone.

Don't think about it.

"The Crimson D-Duo is . . ." Alexis trailed off like she was afraid to say it.

There was a commotion to my left. "No," Patro said a few seats down. "We refuse to—"

What is he talking about?

He was silenced by a hand over his mouth—*DEATH* was tattooed across the restraining knuckles.

There were dangerous men, and then there were *violent* men. The distinction was crucial.

Achilles and Patro were the latter.

I'd never met anyone so volatile in Sparta, dark creature or Chthonic.

There was something *especially* unhinged about this new generation.

Patro had cornered me about a dozen times in the villa. Whenever people weren't looking, he'd trap me against a wall and tell me he knew I was playing a game.

Now, he glared over at me.

Emerald eyes met mine, pure hate blazing in their depths.

Fear wrapped around my throat as I realized just what was happening here.

Oh . . . my . . . Kronos.

"*They're* the Crimson Duo?" I said to Alexis. "Why are they called that? Is it because Achilles's eyes are red or is it something to do with blood? Maybe a play on—"

"Yes, you will!" Aphrodite shouted as she pointed at her son. "You *will* obey orders."

Patro nodded curtly.

Please, Kronos, no.

This can't be.

They're going to hurt me just like the—

"Perfect," Athena said. "That matter is handled—Medusa will enroll at ROU with Patro and Achilles as her bodyguards this September. I'm sure they can obtain a mastery in . . ." Her eyes narrowed as she sized up the two dangerous Chthonic men. "War studies."

Patro rolled his eyes.

"Alexis would also like to attend," I blurted.

Alexis dropped my hand, and I was too panicked to give her an apologetic smile.

Kharon and Augustus leaned forward beside her, both of them hitting me with a death glare.

I felt nothing.

Survive.

You need to survive.

Patro and Achilles are going to hurt you and—

"It's an Olympian university. Chthonics are historically not allowed to enroll!" a Spartan in a small laurel crown shouted from a few rows back.

"Yeah!" more Olympians chorused back.

Jeers echoed.

Kharon's expression twisted as he sized me up, sadness in his blue eyes. He'd been acting strange ever since last week when Alexis had revealed how she'd freed me.

Alexis said it was because he was my brother, but I didn't understand. Spartans rarely formed familial attachments—our culture was all about power and competition.

"What are you doing?" Alexis whispered out the side of her mouth.

They're going to hurt me.

"Education is good," I said quickly. "You've said it was always your dream to go to a Spartan university. Now you can get your mastery in mathematics. We can be together."

We can be safe.

She blinked as she stared at me like she was in shock.

"Alexis—is this true?" Hades asked, his voice rising above the clamor. I clutched her hand tightly.

Alexis closed her eyes for a few seconds, but when she opened them, her expression was determined. "Yes—I would like to attend," she said, giving me a small smile.

Warmth exploded in my chest, and the strange light above her head flared brighter.

Kharon made a choking sound.

I threw my arms around her. "Thank you," I repeated into her curly hair. Alexis hugged me tightly.

Safe.

You're going to be safe.

It's all going to work out and you can—

"It is decided," Athena said. "The Crimson Duo will room with Medusa. She will not leave your side. You will shadow her and protect her."

Patro leveled me with a glare—slowly he dragged his pointer finger across the front of his throat, handsome face contorting with malice.

"Moving on to our next order of business," Athena said calmly, unaware that she'd just sentenced me to death. "The federation is still investigating leads as to why the Titans are mutating. So far, our efforts have found nothing."

"You'll regret this," Patro mouthed silently.

I made a face back.

I already did.

50
CORRUPTION

ALEXIS

As I leapt away from the federation meeting, waves of relief washed over me.

Candlelight cast ambient shadows along the villa's decorative amphoras and olive trees.

I'd chosen this exact hall because I liked the marble sculpture in the corner—a naked man leaned against a wooden club, covered in a lion skin. His eyes were downcast, conveying exhaustion, and behind his back, he held two golden apples.

I met the man's weary gaze with my own.

He's tired, but he's still standing.

The last few weeks had been a blur of worrying over Medusa. I hadn't had much time to focus on anything or anyone else.

She was finally free.

We did it.

I was so grateful for how it all played out, I could curl into a fetal position and never move again.

Outside the hall windows, Lake Como reflected the Milky Way. I'd heard a ridiculous rumor that before the apocalypse, humans had lost the stars. A world without them was unfathomable.

Tonight, the lawn was serene under moonlight, and the electric fence had been taken down—the threat level was once again low.

When I left hours ago, Nyx and Fluffy Jr. had decided to stay back with Helen and Drex in her room. My throat felt bare without scales around it.

Crack.

Two shadows stretched across the marble at the end of the hall.

I'd just been with them, but we'd been surrounded by people; this was different.

We were alone.

"My sweet honey—I'm home," Kharon rasped in a mocking, singsong voice. Augustus stood beside him, eyes sparkling.

Of all the places in the villa they could have leapt to.

They'd come straight to me.

It reminded me of the nightmares that I was having again—ever since the SGC, the grim reaper stood above me at night, watching me sleep.

Dress shoes echoed across the marble as they headed toward me.

Kharon sauntered; Augustus walked with clipped precision.

The real headline of *The Falcon Chronicles* should have read: "Two Deviant Chthonic Royals Seduce Unsuspecting Prudish Woman."

I could have told them *all* about it.

Spiky ruby crowns sparkled.

Kharon wore a tattered black cloak, Augustus an air of heavy responsibility.

Both looked divine in white button-down shirts, sleeves rolled up to their elbows. Leg holsters stretched across their thighs, loaded with weapons.

Augustus's tie was loose, like he'd been pulling at it, a sliver of his bronze chest visible.

Red was splattered across Kharon's shirt.

"Hello, husbands."

My voice was hoarse from disuse, because in my stress, I hadn't spoken much lately. Medusa did all the talking.

"Wife." Augustus's lips twitched like he was trying not to smile.

"Carissima." Kharon arched a dark brow, his face chiseled marble, blue veins almost glowing beneath his skin. "I believe we made a promise to you before your labors. Are you . . . *ready* to collect your reward?"

I gathered my courage.

"Yes."

Kharon blinked, his composure slipping. "Are you . . . sure?" His voice deepened.

I nodded.

They both sauntered closer, stopping inside my personal space.

"I might just *devour* you yet." Kharon's breath tickled the shell of my right ear.

Augustus held my gaze, then dragged his eyes down to my lips. "*Pardon our insatiability,*" his voice rang indecently through my skull. "*My carus.*"

Augustus didn't speak aloud, just stared at my lips as I gasped at the intimacy of having him inside my mind.

Kharon reached up with black painted nails—he gripped the back of my neck—nails digging into my skin.

A gothic romantic melody played inside my head.

Reaching out, I ran my hands down their silk-covered chests.

A flush stained the top of Kharon's sharp cheekbones; Augustus clenched his jaw.

Individually they were intense.

Together, they were as complex as the elliptical curves and modular forms of Fermat's last theorem, the hardest math problem ever solved.

My hands traveled lower, fingers dancing over their straining zippers—I squeezed.

"Careful, darling." Kharon dug his nails into my sensitive skin in warning, his expression feral.

Augustus's hand shot out in a blur. He grabbed my forearm as it flexed, squeezing him harder.

They'd fallen straight into my trap.

I smiled. "Domus."

Crack.

Smoke rose around us—we were once again standing in the empty, dark dining room—the blinds were drawn, and a fire burned low in the hearth.

We were back at the scene of the crime.

I'd meant to leap us to the bedroom, but something inside me must have wanted differently.

"You . . . just . . ." Kharon trailed off as he gaped at me, like he genuinely couldn't believe my audacity.

Augustus wet his lower lip.

Laughter bubbled up my throat as I pulled my hands away from them.

Kharon looked incredulous as he found his voice. "Don't tell me you just leapt with *two* people a dangerously short distance—*after* you just leapt back from the federation meeting."

I rolled my eyes; we were all fine.

"Okay, I *won't* tell you," I said.

Kharon looked around at his surroundings. Awareness lighting in his eyes, he tipped his head back and chuckled, a deep throaty sound.

Augustus joined him, his dimple flashing.

"Do you trust me, carissima?" Kharon's amused voice dropped an octave, dark lashes fanning.

I stared at the scar on the side of his head. "Yes."

Kharon brushed a curl off my neck. "You *really* shouldn't, darling." He gently took my crown off and placed it on the table.

Augustus glanced between us with hooded eyes.

Beethoven tipped his head back at his piano. Partially deaf, he felt the vibrations in his soul.

So did I.

Kharon walked over to the table and yanked a chair out—Augustus did the same next to him.

They turned the chairs, so they were facing each other, about an arm's distance apart.

My face flamed as I remembered what Kharon had said weeks ago.

Then . . . Augustus and I would sit down in two chairs across from each other—we'd pass you back and forth, fucking you on our laps, for hours.

Suddenly, I couldn't breathe.

They sauntered toward me.

Kharon grabbed the back of my neck, his fingers tangling in my hair—he yanked me flush against him, his mouth claiming mine with a desperate groan.

I kissed back just as hard.

Augustus moved behind me, his nails biting my skin as he grabbed the back of my dress toga with both hands.

Rippppp.

The silk material fluttered to my feet, cool air blowing against my exposed body.

I was naked beneath it.

Augustus grabbed my ass, kneading both globes with his strong fingers, nails pricking as he kissed down my spine.

"*So gorgeous . . . so perfect . . . so divine,*" purred deep inside my mind, in rhythm with every brush of his lips.

The taste of a rainstorm on my tongue, I grabbed at Kharon's short silky hair, deepening our kiss.

His crown fell to the floor with a metallic ring. No one moved to get it.

Kharon tipped my head back, tongue plunging with more

fervor down my throat. His hands cupped my breasts, thumbs teasing across my nipples until they were hard, every brush sending pleasure to my core.

They were *everywhere*.

Mouths and hands devoured me—a total corruption.

I grabbed at Kharon's shirt, tugging, needing to explore his skin, but the stupid buttons wouldn't budge.

Kharon yanked back from me. I stumbled, but Augustus held my hips, steadying me as he continued kissing down my spine like a man possessed.

Kharon grabbed both sides of his shirt and yanked it apart.

Diamond buttons flew off, rolling all around the room, and he threw the ruined cloth to the floor, flexing as he fucked me with his eyes.

Thick brands covered his chest—the pale skin was a network of fresh pink scars and old white lines—the newest of all sat smack-dab in the middle and he rubbed his hand over it, face full of pride.

I'd never seen anything more beautiful in my life.

I reached for him, while Augustus dragged his nails down my spine, and followed it with his tongue.

Kharon shook his head no.

Stepping back until his legs knocked against the chair he'd positioned earlier, he settled into it, legs spreading wide, his branded chest drenched in firelight.

Tattooed fingers flexed as he slowly unzipped the fly of his pants, and Kharon palmed his hard, pale shaft. Blue veins wrapped around it, the tip glistening pink in the moonlight.

"Come—sit, wife," Kharon ordered wickedly. "*Now*."

Augustus's hands trailed up to my neck in a gentle caress.

Chills followed his path.

"*Go to him*," Augustus's voice scratched deliciously through my mind.

Entranced by them, I walked toward Kharon.

Augustus went with me, kissing the back of my neck with each step.

The devil spread his legs wider in the chair, lips swollen.

Weapons holsters stretched across his thighs, splattered with blood.

"I love you both so much," I said abruptly, suddenly needing to say it.

Augustus chuckled as he kissed the back of my shoulder, then bit down lightly, and lapped at the mark.

"We know, carissima. . ." Kharon's eyes were bright in the dark. "Because we feel it too."

I stopped in front of him, and Augustus halted with me—his fingers trailed across my rib cage, lingering on my scar—he cupped my breasts, holding them with his calloused palms, so they were raised to Kharon's face.

"Lean forward," Kharon ordered, his voice hoarse.

Augustus pressed a leg between my thighs and spread them wide. His stomach clenched against my back, buttons digging into my spine, as he pushed me forward with his weight toward Kharon.

I grabbed the arms of Kharon's chair to steady myself.

Kharon smirked, my chest even with his face.

He opened his mouth and stuck out his glistening tongue.

Augustus palmed my breasts harder, dragging my swollen nipples across Kharon's unmoving tongue, as he pushed his thigh up harder between my legs. The hilts of his daggers pressed against my core.

I gasped with pleasure.

"*I can feel your cunt dripping through my pants, sweetheart,*" Augustus whispered inside my mind. "*Good girl.*"

My arms trembled where I leaned against the chair.

Kharon closed his mouth around my nipple and sucked.

I whimpered.

"Kneel on my lap," Kharon ordered, a wet pop echoing as he released me. "*Carissima.*"

Augustus picked me up, spreading me out across Kharon's lap, *a sacrificial offering*. The silky ridge of his cock nestled against my heat and we both gasped.

Augustus stepped back, the other chair creaking as he sat in it.

Kharon's long fingers wrapped around my face. He dragged me down and kissed me hard as I gripped onto his wide shoulders, the warm skin bunching and flexing.

Kharon released my face and reached down between our naked bodies.

He fisted his cock, tattooed tendons in his pale forearm flexing, as he positioned it at my entrance.

My thighs quivered.

"Are you ready, carissima?" Kharon asked breathlessly. "I know it's your first time—breathe with me, stay relaxed."

I nodded, unable to speak.

His hips flexed, his blunt tip slipping inside of me.

Kharon moved his fingers up, stroking through my curls, rubbing at my clit. His other hand gripped my hip and pushed me downward a little.

He stopped. "Are you okay?"

"Yes," I gasped at the overwhelming fullness. It had an edge of pain, but was nothing I couldn't handle.

He thrust a little deeper, then paused again. "Still, okay?" His eyes searched mine, glazed with lust and feelings.

"Yes—more."

I gripped his shoulders for dear life as he slowly slipped deeper. Finally, he seated himself fully, throbbing inside of me.

"*Good girl,*" Augustus praised in my mind. "*You're doing such an amazing job.*"

I looked back over my shoulder, whimpering at the hardness stretching me indecently, holding me in place.

Augustus was sitting naked in his chair, pierced cock fisted in his hand as he stroked himself, watching as Kharon fucked me.

His crown was askew on the top of his head—a Machiavellian glint was in his eyes; a single brand covered his unblemished bronze skin, it sat on the edge of his left pectoral muscle, directly over his heart.

Despotic, hungry, disturbingly competent.

The stretching pain took on a warm, pleasurable edge.

Flutters traveled through my core as I turned back, trembling on Kharon's lap, his weapons digging harder into my thighs, as I sat spread across him.

He still wasn't moving, waiting for me to adjust.

"*Fuck*," he swore. "You're so unreal—I'm not going to be able to last long."

"Please." I didn't even know what I was asking for.

Kharon leaned his head down and licked at my nipples as he rubbed my clit.

He stayed motionless.

"Kharon," I begged, tugging at his silky hair.

He made a depraved hungry sound around my nipple, eyes meeting mine, and he thrust shallowly—we both moaned.

Tingling spread as I spasmed around his long cock.

Sucking on my breast, holding my gaze, Kharon thrust up and down below me. Stretching me unbelievably wide, his little movements were sublime.

Kharon touched my clit possessively, rubbing through my wetness, and I clawed at his shoulders, head tipping back.

"*Look at me* while I fuck you," Kharon demanded roughly as he thrust harder, filling me deep, the burn exquisite.

I looked down at the man nicknamed SEX, fully appreciating his talents.

Blood filled the whites of his eyes.

His pleasure and emotions slammed into me in a tidal wave as he engaged his powers: *I love her. Mine. My heart. Mine. Consume.*

Cherish. Dominate. My love. Soulmate. Own her. My woman. Tie her up. Mine. Ravage. Love her.

Kharon jerked his hips harshly, slamming deeper, and I cried out with ecstasy—waves of pleasure crashing over me as I clenched his cock. The shock waves were endless.

Swearing, Kharon held my hips with both hands as he tipped his head back, hot wetness pulsing inside me as we came together.

Seconds passed as we both sat connected, chests heaving.

I leaned forward to rest against him.

"Not yet, carissima," Kharon whispered huskily. He grabbed my hips and slowly lifted me off his lap.

My knees shook as I got to my feet.

Kharon gently pushed me toward Augustus. "Now . . ." he whispered, pressing a kiss to my cheek. "You fuck him."

The man in question, *the* eldest heir to the House of War, was waiting in his seat, legs spread obscenely wide. His bronze skin shone in the firelight, thick cock maroon and weeping; metal glinted on the tip.

His crown was even more askew, eyes hooded.

Pleasure still fluttering through me in aftershocks, on shaky knees I started to crawl onto Augustus's lap.

"Not like that, my carus—turn around."

Augustus's nails bit into my hips as he turned me, so I was facing Kharon. Gripping me from behind, he moved forward to the edge of his seat.

"Open your legs," Kharon ordered.

I obeyed, flushing as I was exposed.

Kharon palmed his soft cock. It was already hardening again in his hand. *Is that normal?*

Augustus gently pulled me toward him, and I gripped the chair arms for purchase, as he hovered me over his lap, and positioned his cold metal head at my entrance.

"Sit back down on me."

Face flushing with heat, I lowered myself onto his dick. The stretch was unholy.

"I can see my cum dripping from you, princess," Kharon said hoarsely as he watched us with hooded eyes, stroking faster.

"Does it hurt?"

I shook my head.

Augustus thrust his hips up forcefully, sheathing himself fully inside of me so I was sitting on his lap, my back to his chest.

I bit down on my lip, overwhelmed. He was everywhere. I was fully exposed, cool air pebbling my skin.

Augustus kissed my shoulders tenderly, cupping my breasts.

Kharon stroked himself faster, skin slapping wetly.

"Are you doing okay, my sweet carus?"

"Yes," I whispered.

His metal piercing was cool inside of me and my stomach clenched at the new sensation.

"You did such a good job—you're so beautiful, sweetheart. Your cunt feels so good squeezing around my cock."

Gasping, still holding on to the chair arms, I looked over my shoulder at him.

Heated lips claimed mine—Augustus pulled my thighs wide apart and flexed inside of me. I moaned into his open mouth, and he bit down on my bottom lip.

I was displayed before Kharon, impossible pleasure once again mounting as Augustus kissed me, exploring my stomach and chest.

He flexed his hips up with a hard thrust, fingers moving lower and parting my curls as he pressed against my clit, his piercing dragging pleasurably deep inside.

It was too much.

I screamed into Augustus's mouth as I clenched around him, my thighs shaking.

"I love you so much, my carus."

Augustus swore, sucking on my tongue as he pulsed and flexed, coming with me.

Warm spurts spilled out seemingly endlessly, wetness dripping down my thighs and onto the chair beneath us.

I tipped my head back, melting against him, boneless.

Thumbs traced under my eyes, wiping tears away.

I hadn't realized I was crying.

Kharon wrapped his soft cloak around my shoulders and lifted me off Augustus, cradling me against his chest. I rested my head against his new scar, his heart beating beneath my ear.

My eyes closed.

"You did so beautifully," whispered through my mind.

Half-conscious, I barely noticed as Kharon laid me down on silk sheets, and a wet cloth was dragged between my thighs, cleaning me with tender carefulness.

The comforter was pulled up over my shoulders. Augustus tucked it under my legs and arms, fussing until only my ears were exposed.

I drifted to sleep with a grin.

The darkness shifted—I dreamed of the grim reaper hovering inches away from my face, watching.

My lashes fluttered open, heart thudding with fear.

I was lying in a velvet-draped four-poster bed, and the bedroom was dark. Augustus lay pressed against my side, his bronze thigh draped across my body as he hugged me tightly.

I turned my head—and gasped.

A pale blue gaze shone in the dark.

Kharon stood next to the bed, leaning over me. His face was predatory, eyes narrowed with a single-minded intensity. He didn't move; he just watched me like a man possessed.

My personal grim reaper.

He leaned closer so our noses touched. "You're *ours*, Alexis Hert," he whispered in a gravelly voice. "Ours to watch, to protect . . . to devour."

I brushed an inky lock of hair off his forehead.

"Calm down, *Karen*."

He stilled—I arched my eyebrow at him—his posture relaxed, and he sighed like he was resigned to my audacity.

"You're *my* angel," he said vindictively, like he needed to make a point. "Rome can't have you." His voice deepened with unhealthy possessiveness. "I won't allow it. Do you understand what I'm—"

I pulled Kharon down, cutting his tirade off—he melted into my arms with his face burrowed against my throat. He inhaled deeply.

Augustus shifted in his sleep, draping his powerful thigh across both of us, pinning us to the mattress.

"Go to sleep," I whispered as I ran my fingers through Kharon's short, silky hair.

"*You* go to sleep," he grumbled under his breath.

Augustus shifted, his arm joining his leg as he squeezed us tightly.

They were obsessive, villainous men.

I've never felt so safe.

They were my husbands, and I wouldn't have it any other way.

51
The Sins of the Father

Alexis: The Next Day

Morning rays sparkled across masculine black silk sheets. I was lying draped across Kharon like a blanket; he was snoring beneath me.

Augustus stretched under the covers, his eyes meeting mine. *"Morning, love."*

He crawled on top of me, and Nyx hissed sleepily from somewhere under the pillows—she said something about smothering all of us and "killing the ugly cow with wings."

As if summoned, Fluffy Jr. rolled across the floor in his sleep, his hooves kicking out wildly—a dresser crashed to the floor—he snored with pieces of wood covering him (he wasn't the brightest).

Kharon yawned sleepily, looking adorably disheveled as he sat up. He shook his head as he took in my sleeping (passed out?) protector, then he turned with a devilish smirk, and shifted so I was pressed between him and Augustus.

In unison, they kissed down the sides of my neck.

A few hours later, the three of us stumbled into the bathroom, drunk on each other and satiated. Kharon and Augustus had shared lessons on debauchery all morning. They were *very* hands-on teachers, and I was a quick study.

Now Kharon whispered sinful things while bathing me in a gold tub; Augustus washed my hair tenderly, his voice echoing words of praise straight into my mind.

I lounged deeper into the bubbles. Both Nyx and Fluffy Jr. were still sleeping, and I'd discovered over the last weeks that when our lives were not actively threatened, they were *extremely* lazy (relatable).

"Alexis." Kharon's voice had a strange tenor. His thumb brushed gently under my left eye, and there was a long pause like he was gathering his courage. Finally, he asked, "How did it happen with your eye . . . and ear?"

Augustus's fingers stilled against my scalp.

They both waited.

Sighing, I sank deeper into the suds.

The warmth of the present was a comforting blanket that muffled the cold pain of the past.

There's nothing they can do now anyway. It's just a story. It has no power over me.

"There was a storm . . . and my foster parents threatened to kill Charlie," I whispered into the quiet bathroom. "I threw a toaster at them." I chuckled to myself at the idiotic bravery of my childhood self.

I told a tale of fists, starvation, a dead body, the police, secret poisonous blood, staring at my face in the mirror, and the trailer being towed away while we watched.

When I finished my story, a cathartic peace washed over me. It sounded fictional and it felt that way too. It happened to a different version of me, so many years ago.

That scared young girl was gone.

I scooped up some bubbles and blew them across the bathroom. They popped in the light.

Silence stretched.

Augustus made a strange noise.

A washcloth splattered suds across the floor as Kharon dropped it.

I turned to look at them.

A single bloody tear streaked down Augustus's face, and Kharon's jaw was clenched so tightly his face was turning purple.

"It's over now," I said calmly, raising up my hands. "It's okay—it's in the past. I'm not what they made me . . . *I* made me."

The truth of it settled into my chest.

I smiled with relief.

"No," Kharon said vehemently, his voice echoing like a gunshot.

Augustus shook his head.

"No," Kharon repeated.

"*No, it's not*," echoed through my mind.

"It's fine." I reached for them.

Augustus grabbed my wrist and turned it over, he unhooked the golden cuff I always wore, and it clattered to the marble floor.

"And . . . this?" Augustus asked aloud as he traced his thumb gently over the layers of old scars. They crisscrossed with new ones.

I stared at the ruined skin, feeling numb.

"My foster father tied me up with a rope as a child." My voice was neutral. I shrugged casually. "I was young and desperate, and I fractured my wrists against a rock pulling myself free."

Augustus released my arm.

"I should have just dislocated my thumbs, but I was so young and hungry, it . . ."

I trailed off as Augustus and Kharon both stood, stepped out of the tub, and left the bathroom. Buckles clicked as they dressed quickly.

"Uh—what are you doing?" I stumbled out of the tub and picked up a robe, pulling it on.

A safety clicked.

Kharon palmed two guns.

Augustus sheathed a wickedly sharp hunting knife into a holster in his sweatpants.

They nodded at each other and left the room.

For a second, I blinked in disbelief, then I sprinted after them. "Wait!"

A few minutes later I stumbled to the bottom of the stairs and gasped with my hands on my knees; cardio had never been my strong suit, and they moved ridiculously fast. "What are we doing in this stupid dungeon?"

"Vengeance." Kharon's voice warped with rage.

It took a second for my eyes to adjust to the dark light.

Chains clanked.

Augustus and Kharon were standing in front of a dirt-covered prisoner.

Déjà vu.

I had to stop coming down here; nothing good ever came of it.

Instead of explaining why they'd lost their minds, Augustus calmly cracked his knuckles and threw a punch at the prisoner's face.

Bones cracked.

Blood splattered.

A man moaned.

Lunging, I grabbed Augustus's arm as he pulled it back.

"Seriously what the hell is wrong with . . ."

I trailed off as I took in the prisoner's features.

"Alex." Foster Father coughed violently, showing off a familiar row of rotting teeth. "Tell these . . . men to . . . let me go."

The world stopped spinning.

"It's y-y-you."

He nodded his head eagerly.

A cold Montana wind slammed against me as I crouched in the corner of a trailer.

Foster Mother screamed.

Charlie whimpered.

I'd lied to myself; I was still a child, hiding from the man who wouldn't stop hurting me.

I turned to my husbands.

"We did some digging." Kharon's eyes glittered with wrath. "We were waiting for the right time to tell you. We figured we'd decide what to do with him when—"

"He's *not* yours to handle," I cut him off.

"We know." Augustus ground his teeth together. "That's why we haven't touched him. He's a gift."

"For you," Kharon said, guns creaking in his hands as he squeezed them tightly. "It's your vengeance to take." His eye twitched. "Or not."

Augustus took a step back, and yanked Kharon with him. "He's all yours—it's your decision—we support you, no matter what."

Kharon made a sound of disagreement.

"*Either* way," Augustus said, but his expression didn't match his words.

"Please, Alex," Foster Father begged.

I flinched before I could stop myself.

"Please," he repeated. "You were *never* violent. You were always a good, God-fearing kid. Father John loved you. You always wanted to help people. You don't want to harm me. You don't want to—"

I dug my nails into my hand, blood pooling.

The Rod of Asclepius formed in my hand.

Foster Father gasped with awe as it glowed brightly. "You were always such a gentle soul," he said. "So pious. So good."

"Haven't you heard?" I asked softly.

He smiled at me like we were old friends. "Heard . . . what?"

I turned the staff.

Brightness filled the space between us.

I shoved the sharp edge into his sternum—the light went out.

The dungeon was dark.

"It was me. *I* killed her," I said coldly. "I murdered your wife on that winter's day."

He screamed, foam dripping from his lips, eyes widening with abject terror.

I yanked the rod from his chest and dropped it.

Blood sizzled in a steaming puddle.

He choked and twitched; chains clinked as he struggled, his face contorting with betrayal.

I turned my back to him, because he was no threat to me.

Kharon slung his arm around my shoulders, and Augustus draped his arm around us both.

We walked away.

Foster Father gasped loudly. "Alex . . . you'll . . . regret . . . this."

"No," I said, not looking back. "I really won't."

52

The Lover

Patro: One Day Later

"Is something going on in there?" Augustus shouted from the hall as he knocked. "What's that noise?"

Shit.

Achilles wrenched the door open, blocking the empty room with his body.

"We're fucking," I said as I joined him. "Sorry—we got a little *carried* away."

Together, we didn't let them see inside.

Poco sat perched on top of Alexis's head, gnawing on her curls, and her oversized protector was prancing down the hall with the potted end of a decorative olive tree sticking out of its mouth (I had no words). Augustus and Kharon were draped around her, their arms strewn across her shoulders possessively.

I scoffed. *They're so whipped, it's embarrassing.* I would never be so obsessed with a woman.

Alexis was my mentee, and sure, I'd thought we could be more. I'd wanted to give us a chance, so I'd done the unthinkable—I'd *tried*. But she'd made it clear whose side she was on.

My chest tightened.

I hated how betrayed I felt.

Alexis smiled at me, her cheeks flushed with satisfaction, two different-colored eyes bright and unguarded for the first time since I'd met her. Poco hissed.

I wasn't so selfish that I couldn't admit to myself that the three of them suited each other.

At first, they'd been a fucking disaster. They were all so similar, different shades of stoic suffering that was beyond exasperating.

But now, they'd found their wedded bliss.

Stomach heavy with dread, I tried to ignore what that meant for Achilles and me. We'd still have to get married to a stranger who'd try to ruin us with their petty jealousies. *They'll try to take Achilles away from you.*

No one would ever marry someone for immortality and be happy playing second fiddle to me, but that was the only option we had left.

Bile filled my throat at the mere thought.

I'd pitch myself off this villa's roof before I loved anyone *half* as much as I loved Achilles.

He felt the same.

It was why I'd tried so hard to make something happen with Alexis. That, and she wasn't as annoying as most people. A part of me still genuinely considered her a friend. Not that I'd admit it aloud.

Augustus narrowed his eyes. "Interesting—*keep* it down."

"Of course, brother," I said smoothly.

He raised his eyebrows at me. We'd never had a particularly close relationship, but I respected his ability to stay calm in the face of Sparta's perpetual bullshit.

Achilles slammed the door shut in their faces.

Poco screeched belligerently.

Their footsteps receded.

Achilles turned to me and adjusted the obscene bulge in his cargo pants.

No one has ever been as handsome.

He studied my face with intensity. Ever since I'd been interrogated during the SGC, he'd been struggling with possessiveness and separation anxiety.

We were already unhealthily codependent on each other, but it had somehow gotten worse.

He's so perfect.

I reached for Achilles's muzzled face, and he tilted his head, leaning into my reverent touch.

Going up on tiptoes, I pressed a kiss to the hollow on the front of his neck, warm, heated skin tensing beneath my touch.

He gripped my hips, pushing himself flush against me. I groaned, licking at him.

Smoke from his muzzle wrapped around us.

He smelled like carnal sex, fire, and everything I'd ever wanted.

He's a dream come true.

"Can you maybe wait to do that? Also is there a reason you've cornered me *again*? Or do you just want me to watch?" a throaty feminine voice asked with annoyance. "I don't think I'm into that. Also, are you prone to outbursts and random acts of violence? If so, I think you have a diagnosable condition called—"

I wrenched away from Achilles, his intoxicating taste still tingling on my tongue.

I'd gotten distracted from what we were doing in here—getting answers.

"Do you ever shut the fuck up?" I asked, with genuine confusion, because from what I'd seen, she didn't. *Ever.*

Medusa scoffed.

I enjoyed silence, *preferred* it, and she rambled constantly.

She was the opposite of Achilles in every way.

"*No.*" Medusa clutched her left arm, eyes narrowing as her

long black hair shifted, three monstrous snakes rattling. "I will *not* be quiet just because you can't stand the fact that you've been threatening an innocent woman for weeks like a cowardly—"

I laughed. "Oh please—you forget who you're talking to. I *read* people, that's my power, and I know for a fact that you're still hiding things. Drop your innocent act."

Medusa stomped toward the door.

I blocked her.

"*Move* out of my way," she demanded. "I'm done with this crap. Corner me again, and I'll bite you."

Her snakes rose up around her head, rattling louder.

A lesser man would have been cowed by her display of power—one Gorgon snake was intimidating, three was a hideous show of might. Achilles and I both studied them with open curiosity.

We'd always been intrigued by dangerous things.

Medusa shifted.

I stepped with her.

Smirking, I glared down my nose at her.

She was *no* match for me.

I would discover what she was hiding and prove to the world that she couldn't be trusted.

"I said *move!*" Medusa shoved at my chest, and I laughed at how weak she was.

Her nails dug into my chest.

My skin prickled where she touched me, heat flushing across my sternum—*with disgust*—and I wrenched away from her.

"Never lay your hands on me again, *snake scum*," I warned.

She threw a punch, and I caught her hand, twisting her wrist painfully. Her bones creaked, embarrassingly fragile in my hand. She was all soft curves and long, jet-black hair. There was nothing Spartan about her. Kronos, most *humans* were built stronger.

I'd never met anyone so useless in my life.

Someone really should protect her. I shook my head, refusing to acknowledge the ridiculous thought.

"How about *you* just stay away from me." Medusa glared, snakes rising higher, and all of them focused on me as she tried to tug her arm out of my grip. She failed.

Heinous memories clawed at my spine.

I held on to her wrist tightly.

"You're nothing but a pathetic mutt. Stop crying. You won't survive Sparta," my Gorgon tutor snarled.

Hands flashed in front of my face, drawing me back to the present.

"I'm here—they *can't* hurt you," Achilles signed.

I nodded, feeling faint.

"Stop following me around," Medusa said haughtily, but for some reason I couldn't make myself release her.

"I can't," I whispered, still feeling out of sorts from the memories. "Since we're your new bodyguards." I forced my lips up into a cruel smile, even though I wanted to fall to my knees and scream. "You're the reason we were tortured."

She was found innocent, and it's a good thing the Olympians never got to her, because she wouldn't be able to withstand torture.

Medusa kicked my shin.

I looked down incredulously.

If I hadn't seen her move, I wouldn't have known she'd just tried to attack.

Someone really needs to teach her self-defense.

She wasn't my problem.

She kind of is.

I shook my head at the ridiculous thought, taking a jerky step back, dragging her with me.

The back of my right leg tweaked at the movement because my severed tendon still hadn't healed fully. The Olympians had poured a strange poison on the open wound so many times that I was worried it might never heal.

I didn't care.

The *real* problem was, Achilles thought it was all *his* fault, and he was coddling me endlessly these days, acting like I was made of glass.

Medusa narrowed her eyes. "Release me!"

I twisted her wrist, making sure not to actually cause harm.

There was something immensely satisfying about toying with her.

Achilles shifted closer. "Don't hurt her," he signed, mirroring my thoughts.

"*Obviously*," I drawled, voice dripping with sarcasm.

Achilles glanced down at where I was touching her, then back to my face, a question in his eyes.

He didn't understand why I was acting this way.

Neither do I.

"Get over yourself," Medusa said. "It's not me you're angry at—it's the Olympians. You're just another prideful narcissist from the House of Aphrodite—I can see through your self-absorbed despondent act. You'll *never* be anything . . . but the man who lived in Achilles's shadow."

I dropped her arm.

My fingers *burned* where they'd touched her—they felt cold when someone lied, and warmed at the truth—vision blurring, I gasped for air.

"*You're nothing but a weak mutt.*"

Tortured screams from my past rang in my ears.

It took every ounce of control I possessed to harden my features and don my mask of cruel indifference.

"You know *nothing*," I said quietly.

Medusa gripped her arm tighter, and for a second she looked small and lost, but then her eyes flashed, snakes rattling, as she also donned a blank expression.

"Just leave me alone," she spat.

I can't.

This time, my smile wasn't faked. "Didn't you just hear the announcement?" I taunted, raising my eyebrows. "We're your new bodyguards—we're going to be spending a *lot* of time together."

Achilles stepped up next to me, his arm wrapping around my shoulders, fingers caressing my bicep.

I melted against him.

Medusa frowned, her ruby lips curling down, creating a pouty effect, and I stared at them, unable to look away.

Achilles traced his fingers up and down my arm in a soothing pattern.

Medusa looked between the two of us, curiosity flashing in her strange lavender eyes.

"We're going to be sharing a room," I said with dangerous softness. "There's going to be *so* many nights just the three of us. *Alone.*"

Her lips parted on a gasp.

Pure masculine satisfaction squeezed my gut.

For the first time, she had nothing to say.

Yep, I just found a new hobby.

I caressed Achilles's chest, enjoying how he flexed and pulled me tighter to his side, his bulge unmistakable.

A blush stained the top of Medusa's cheeks, as she still struggled to speak.

Achilles flexed his hips, his hardness pressing against me.

Medusa bit down on her lower lip—hard—then she covered her mouth. Suddenly, she pushed past us, running out of the room, and as the door slammed shut behind her, the most inane urge gripped me—*chase after her.*

My breathing was too loud in the silence.

Achilles turned to me.

He exploded, movements jerky with need—blood rushed

south as he grabbed me by the arms and pushed me back until I was pinned against the wall. His fingers trailed across my abs, then lower. He unzipped my cargo pants, freeing my aching shaft.

Ever since the SGC it had been like this between us—frantic and rushed.

I pulled out his man bun and tangled my fingers in his silky hair.

He palmed me roughly, stroking hard, just the way I liked.

I tugged on his hair.

"I love you so much," I said as I traced my hands over his face, then lowered them and reached for his zipper. I pulled out his hard, tattooed cock. It pulsed in my hand, unbelievably thick. Precum beaded the ruddy head.

His hips jerked, smoke pouring from his muzzle, as he fisted both of us.

I looked down—and spit.

Then once again buried my hands in his hair, holding on for dear life as he stroked us both faster. Slippery sounds echoed, mixing with my grunts of pleasure. He didn't stop until our cum covered his hands, dripping onto the floor.

Heaving after a powerful orgasm, I buried my head in the divot between his neck and collarbone, my favorite part of his body. I kissed his skin, his sweat an aphrodisiac on my tongue as I licked and suckled.

With his muzzle, it was the closest we could ever come to a kiss.

53

The Dragon

Achilles

I held on to Patro's bicep, my fingers shaking. He was my heart and soul. *My everything.*

The urge to chain him to my side was overwhelming. Ever since they'd severed his tendon, I'd been plagued by the need to massacre every Olympian on earth.

Dostoevsky must have seen inside my soul when he wrote, "no animal could ever be so cruel as a man, so artfully, so artistically cruel."

There was no mercy left inside me.

"I adore you," Patro whispered against my neck.

I shuddered.

Start a war for him.

Do it.

Patro kissed down to my collarbone. "I love you so much."

I just need to get this muzzle off.

Then I'll kill them all.

"I love you more than anything in the world," Patro said with reverence.

The Olympians were smart to muzzle me. Most of the time I was a calm, collected man, but then there were the other times, the moments when I *snapped*, and lost all pretenses of civility. I was close to the latter.

Patro sighed heavily.

Pulling away from him, loathing every inch that separated us, I signed, "Don't worry."

"About what?" Patro's shockingly green eyes were glazed with pleasure.

"Medusa," I signed, bracing myself for his rage.

Patro's lips curled into a sinful smile.

Pheromones and something new, a forbidden *dark* urge, lingered in the air between us.

"Oh, *I'm* not worried," Patro said, his tone wicked. "But Medusa should be."

If I was a good man, I would have told him to leave her alone. I didn't.

My own curiosity was piqued by the infamous Gorgon.

Everyone assumed that I was the only dangerous one in the relationship, but when Patro set his sights on someone, when he was *truly* intrigued, no force on earth could stop him from getting what he wanted.

Toxic anticipation filled my chest.

We were already assigned as Medusa's bodyguards, and we were going to be spending a lot of time together in the future.

She can't escape us.

Leather creaked as I tried to smile.

Fate's Full Unseen Prophecy

The lost one shall change what is before
Chained to death's soldiers, becoming evermore
Her healing light shall mend the injured four
Drex, Lucia, Kharon, and the Serpent of Lore

The chained one shall reveal the evil underscore
Guarded by Crimson men, seeing afore
Their love shall change the tides of war

The monstrous one shall mend and restore
For the lost one hears his beastly roar

★ ★ ★ ★ ★

For an exclusive bonus chapter from
Bonds of Hercules, join Jasmine's newsletter at
blog.jasminemasbooks.com

ACKNOWLEDGMENTS

Thank you to my mother, who for months on end read this book as I wrote it. Your constant insistence that I "add more spice and stop being a weird prude" was truly invaluable. This book is as much my work as it is yours. There's no one else in the world I'd want to call over fifty times a day to discuss a story.

Thank you to my team of beta readers, who read *multiple* versions of this book. This story would be nothing without your detailed feedback and requests. Special thanks to Jamie for aggressively demanding more Patro and Achilles. You were so real for that.

Thank you to everyone at Canary Street Press for all your support. Special thanks to my editor, Cat Clyne, for helping to polish the plot, and for making sure Kharon kept his unhinged edge. I'm immensely grateful that you understood the vibe.

Thank you to my agent, Kimberly Whalen, for believing in me and bringing this series to over twenty different countries. I don't know what I'd do without you.

Thank you to my brother, Cameron; my sister-in-law, Kait; my Aunt Allie; my bestie, Caitlan; and Grandpa Jim for telling literally *everyone* you know to read my books (even though I repeatedly tell you to stop doing that).

Finally, thank you to my husband, Evan, and my cat, Boo-Boo. Neither of you helped with the book at all, but I'm so glad we're all alive at the same time.